THE KAZOLA CHRONICLES

THREE

TETHERED BY FATE

KATHRYN MARIE

TETHERED BY FATE

For information contact:

Kathryn Namenyi

55 Spencer St

PO Box 342

Lynn, MA 01905

authorkathrynmarie.com

Cover design by Saint Jupiter

Map Design by Vanessa Garland

Developmental Edits by Cassidy Clarke

Copy Edits and Proofread by Karen Sanders Editing

ISBN: 9781734832372

First Edition: June 2024

10 9 8 7 6 5 4 3 2 1

Author Note

Thank you so much for picking up my book! Before you begin, I just wanted to make you aware of a few things. This book contains scenes and talk of PTSD, depression, anxiety, panic attacks, sexual assault/rape, suicide, grief, kidnapping, physical and mental torture, starvation, strained family relationships, grooming, spousal loss, war, fantasy world fighting and battles, death, and mild language. This book will also contain on page sex scenes.

Dedication

To all those in high school who thought I was a dork for reading fantasy books all the time.

Jokes on you, because now I'm a dork who reads and writes those fantasy books.

PS: Just because I was reading, doesn't mean I couldn't hear you gossiping about your friends. Don't worry, all of your secrets are still safe with me.

THE ISLE OF AZVULA
XOBLAR
ROTHERLLI
BELDWAR
DALCHUS
FOLANOCH
TERLANTRIK
OCHRAT
CAELFALL
LUSPAN
RYSTIN
ORILON
CRELANTI
ILFRA
KILERTHE
ADRO
SEATHRA
EROSTE
ARKALEY
VAPALLES
ACCRITON
RAVAGHT

GLOSSARY

Amalgam Blade-(uh-mal-gm blayd) The primary weapon of the Onyx Guard

Blackthorn-(blak-thorn) An illegal drug primarily used by Shrivikas

Blood Consort-(bluhd kan-sort) A person meant to assist a Shrivika or an Ibridowyn to properly feed and stay strong

Faction-(fak-shn) A military unit in the Onyx Guard

Fuiliwood-(fwee-lee-wood) The strongest tree in Kazola

Futeacha-(foo-teh-chaa) Old Kazalonian swear; means tainted blood

Hierarchy-(hai-ur-aar-kee) The Leadership team of an Onyx Guard Faction

High Faction-(hai Fak-shn) The ruling government of the Isle of Kazola

Ibridowyn-(ih-brih-doh-when) Genetically modified soldier created from either a Varg Anwyn or a Shrivika

Iona Silver-(ai-ow-nuh sil-vr) The purest silver in Kazola

Kazola-(ka-zoh-la) Means Peace-Bearer in the language of the God and Goddess

Keturi-(kah-tur-ee) The top four leaders of an Onyx Guard Faction

Lectracycle-(lec-tra sai-kl) Primary form of transportation for the Onyx Guard

Ogdala Dagger-(ahg-dah-la da-gr) The ceremonial dagger of the Onyx Guard

Onyx Guard-(aa-nuhks gaard) Special ops section of the military, made up exclusively of Ibridowyns

Shrivika-(shriv-ick-ah) Vampire, child of the God Firenielle

Tsio a Chisain-(si-o ah chee-sahn) Old Kazalonian for Protect the Peace

Varg Anwyn-(varg awn-win) Wolf shifter, child of the Goddess Lunestia

Wolfsbane-(wulfs-bayn) An illegal drug primarily used by Varg Anwyns

Faction outline

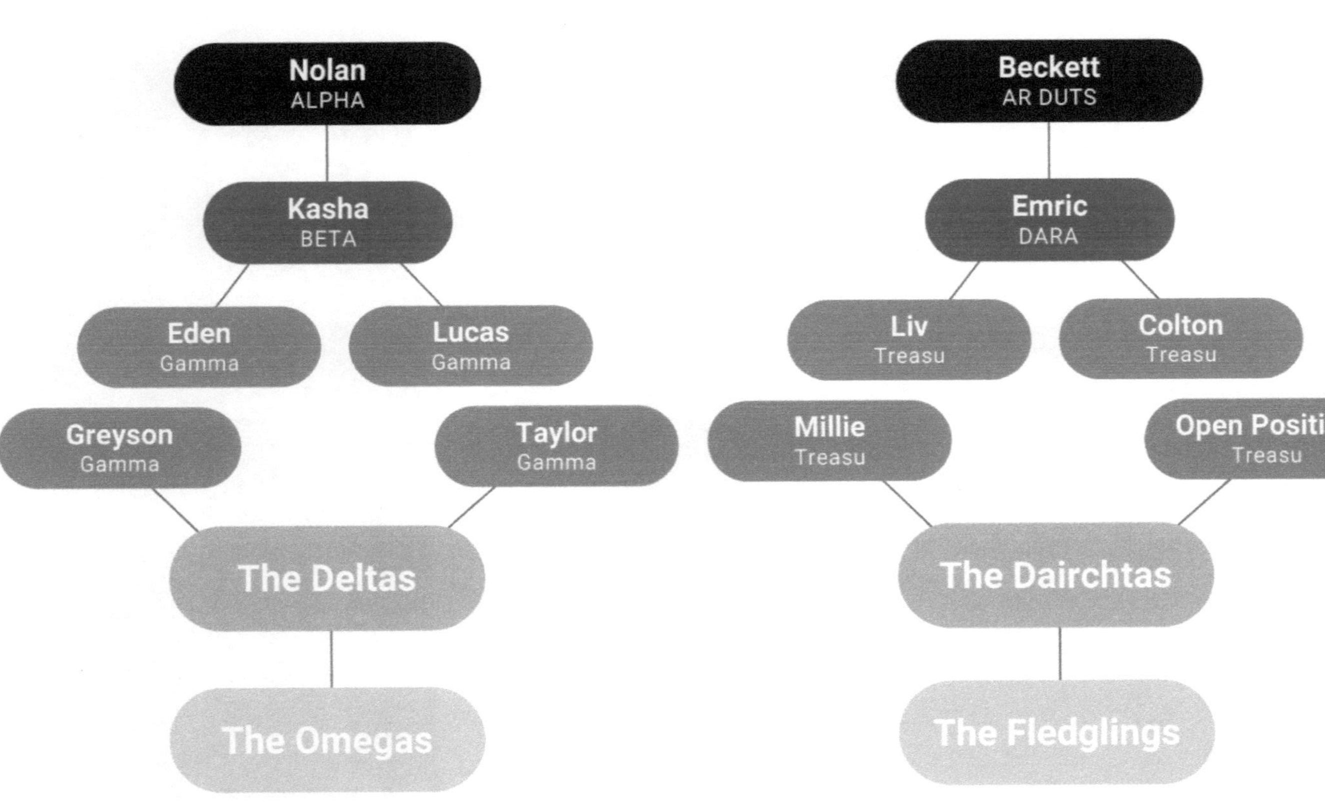

CHAPTER I

Kasha

I knew life was never easy. I knew some things were just too good to be true.

But was it really so much to ask that when I was saved from the psychotic cult leader I could have a bit of time to breathe again?

Apparently, it was.

The bright sunlight that woke me the next morning contrasted with the harsh chill of winter. A light frost coated every bit of the forest floor, including the tips of my fur that had been coated in sweat and dirt.

I barely remembered transforming into my wolf form or the hours' worth of running that I did when the moon still hung high in the starlit sky. My mind had still been reeling from the realization that my thoughts were no longer safe, that my mind was no longer my own.

Or maybe it was, but the sound of his voice penetrating my safe place made terror thrum through my veins, setting my skin on fire. Could he get in whenever he wanted? Was I no longer able to control who could and could not come within?

As always with Elliot, there were too many questions and not enough answers.

By the placement of the sun, it was already mid-morning, my body having collapsed when the bright rays started to peek through the horizon. It was barely enough sleep, but at least I had gotten some after tiring myself out.

Standing up from my makeshift sleeping tree, my muscles groaned under the deep stretch I pushed my wolf form into to help wake myself up to start the day.

I had to head back; Nolan was probably going out of his mind without me near him. But I couldn't stay contained, not after spending so much time in captivity last month. When Elliot had left my mind, I needed freedom, air, and speed. I needed the reminder that I had made it through so many horrible things and was still alive.

I had survived so much, so I should be able to survive this too. Right?

And Nolan, the incredible paramour that he was, had let me leave and didn't follow. As always, he knew what I needed and respected that. But now it was time for me to do the same for him. To show him I was still alive and hold his hand. I knew he was trying to hide it, but since I returned, touching me and keeping me close helped to keep him calm.

I couldn't fault him for that. After what happened to Cleo and almost losing me last month, I was happy to let him be nearby. His scent and his calming presence gave me peace as well, especially when I was healing from my ordeal.

I trotted along the path that led back to the open Compound that my Faction in the Onyx Guard occupied. Even with four legs, I had obviously overdone it last night, all of them tight and tired from so much running.

It didn't matter, though. I had needed to force myself into sleep, and overdoing the running was a way into it.

I broke through the last of the trees, the circle of buildings coming into view. Some of our Fledglings and Omegas were already awake and heading into early morning workouts and training, their gazes tracking me as I made my way past the barracks and to the row of townhouses my Hierarchy resided in. When I made it to the last one, the Alpha's house, I made quick work of transitioning back into my human form and, as quickly as possible, shoving the door open and entering the heated house.

As a Varg Anwyn, I was fairly used to others in my Faction seeing me naked after a transition into wolf form. It was the biting cold that made me rush inside.

"Nolan?" I called out, closing the door. My skin was still covered in dirt and sweat, but I shivered now the protective fur that had kept me from getting frostbite all night had vanished.

He appeared almost instantly at the top of the stairs, my gaze locking with the forest-green eyes I had come to love over our time together. I watched as he descended, his muscles tight as he forced himself not to jump down to me and instead walk at a decent pace. When he was semi-close, I yanked him down the rest of the way, crushing him against me.

"You're shivering, sweetheart," he whispered into my matted hair, his arms tightening around me. My chilled skin tried to leech the warmth he exuded.

"It's winter out there," I mumbled, rubbing my cheek against his chest.

"Kasha, what…" He took a deep breath. "What happened last night?"

I pulled back, dragging him into the common area to grab the mist gray fleece blanket he always kept draped over the couch. I wrapped myself in it, relishing the warmth it provided before turning back to him, his rigid self still standing by the door.

"It's Elliot."

His jaw ticked. "What about him?"

"He's…" *How do I even explain this?* "He…."

My mind jumbled, the terror, shock, and horror that had consumed me last night flooding back. It hit me like a punch to the solar plexus, stealing my breath and making my legs shake uncontrollably. It ruined me, draining every bit of strength I had left until I was nothing but a tangled web of emotions I could no longer understand.

It was too much. My legs crumbled beneath me, forcing me to kneel, tears falling freely as I pulled the blanket around me tighter.

Why? Why, why, why, why, why?

The word kept repeating itself over and over, racing faster and faster as darker thoughts crept in. Was I even safe? Could he hear every thought or just the communications I sent him? And how had he reached me? He was being detained in the Capital, close to a hundred miles away. No Brido, even those with the same blood running through their veins, had ever been recorded to mentally communicate at such a distance.

So, how had he found me? How had he breached the mental door we all had in place, no one allowed in without expressed permission? He had broken through it as if it was nothing, and never had I felt more vulnerable. I knew how to protect my body, but my mind? That was a new torture even I was unsure I could handle.

The reddish-black tattoo he had forced into my skin only two weeks ago must have something to do with it. But what?

Too much. Too much. Too much!

I rocked back and forth, trying to compose myself to string at least a few words together to explain.

"Kasha…" Nolan whispered, joining me on the ground but not touching. He sat in front of me, shoulders hunched so he didn't tower. "You don't have to tell me."

No, I didn't have to. I could have kept it a secret like I might have in the past. But that was before. When I was repressed and scared and angry at all that had happened. My anxious, traumatized mind trying to protect me from those who could hurt me, telling me no one was worth trusting with these pieces of myself anymore.

But slowly over the last few months, Nolan had shown me that frame of mind wasn't helping but hurting. It isolated me, kept me alone. It may have protected me from feeling hurt again, but it also kept me from feeling the good emotions. Joy. Freedom. Love.

And the love. It was worth the sometimes torturous emotions that still raced through me at a moment's notice. That love was safety and trust. It was compassion and understanding. It was peace.

And with the horrible shaking and the over-anxious thoughts running through my mind trying to figure out exactly what all this meant, I knew I couldn't do this alone. I needed the one I trusted the most, and there he was in front of me.

Using one hand to keep the blanket secured around me, I reached the other out to him, lacing our fingers together. With tears still streaming down my face, I told him the newest complication I was about to blow our lives up with.

CHAPTER 2

Nolan

I knew she could probably hear me pacing back and forth in our bedroom as she showered off her night in the woods, but I couldn't seem to stop.

She had been in there for about ten minutes already, which gave me about fifteen to continue to freak the fuck out before I had to put on a brave face and be the partner she needed. It felt near impossible, but I would do it.

I hadn't been able to go back to sleep once she had run out of our house and into the dead of night. She had screamed at me not to follow as she fled down the stairs, and I had respected her request, even if my wolf itched within me, begging me to find her.

The time without her near me, without her safe in our house, had been torturous. My skin had itched and tingled, my body on the precipice of shifting multiple times, and I had shredded many pillows in my fits to calm myself and stay in human form.

My mind had concocted too many ideas of what had happened.

Was it a nightmare about her time in captivity? Was she struggling to connect with her wolf again? Was she safe alone?

Hours upon hours of trying to occupy myself. Cleaning the house, reorganizing my spice cabinet, and even going as far as to start emptying space in my closet and hanging some of her clothes up. Yet, with each project I started, I would abandon it when a thought of what horrible thing could be happening to her popped into my head, making my rage simmer back to the surface. That made the cycle of the entire night and morning continue until she returned to me.

When she had finally stumbled through our door, naked, covered in sweat and dirt, with twigs and leaves in her hair, my heart had jumped into my throat. Cooling calm rushed through my veins knowing that she was still here and alive and safe.

Then, I had seen the terror in her gaze and the pain she was desperate to conceal from me, making all that worry sink into my heart even deeper. My stomach clenched at the sight of her hurt in some way.

It took every bit of my self-control to move at a normal pace, to walk down to her, listen, and be the calming partner I knew she needed.

Then she opened up and talked.

With tears streaming down her face and confused pain within her gaze, she had told me every single fact. Nothing about how she was feeling, nothing about what she was thinking about. By the time she was done talking, the tears had dried up, her back had straightened out, and that brave, impassive face was secured on her features. A soldier through and through.

Somehow, that cold look that had glazed over her eyes scared me almost as much as the disgusting invasion Elliot had done from too far away. Almost.

How could he do this to her?

It was all I could think about, the question rolling repeatedly in my mind as I continued to pace. After everything she had gone through, survived and fought for, this was the last thing she deserved. What she deserved was peace and a moment of calm. To relax and smile and maybe even find the time to play her piano or read a damn book like she loved to do.

What she did not deserve was to live in constant fear that the man who had kidnapped her and tortured her for a month could pop into her head whenever he fucking felt like it.

My footsteps faltered, my fingers grasping the footboard of our bed and curling in, breaths labored and tense as I forced them in and out.

Kasha had been through so much. I had been through so much. We were healing together. We thought we had found ourselves in a place to just be, to explore and decide what we wanted.

Yet, that had all been blown apart since this horrid megalomaniac was trying to take her away from me. Again.

A growl ripped from my throat at that thought, my wolf stirring and waking within me, making my skin burn and my eyes glow gold. He had been on edge for far too long. I had hoped that once we found Kasha, he would calm down, knowing she was near, but it only seemed to get worse.

Protect. Save. Defend. Protect. Save. Defend.

It was all he wanted to do. He had to keep her in sight or else he stirred and pushed against me. She didn't need me constantly trying to protect her; it was actually the last thing she needed. She hated being coddled, and she hated being seen as weak. I would continue to support her, to be by her side and fight with her, but not for her. I was exhausting myself by battling against the instincts. I had to hope he would tire out soon and realize she was going to be okay.

Although, with the newest development, I had little hope that would happen.

As my thoughts continued to spiral within my frenzied mind, she emerged from the washroom. Her medium-length golden brown hair was still wet, the tips soaking into the black cotton tunic she wore with one of her many pairs of black training pants and boots. I couldn't read her expression, her gaze vacant, lips in a straight line.

It was that neutral, blank expression that broke my heart the most. At least when it was twisted with anger or crumpled with sadness, I knew what she was feeling. I could help or fight with her through it, but not this time.

I approached her, flexing my fingers a few times before I reached her. "Are you feeling better, sweetheart?"

She looked up at me, a short smile pushing against her lips, yet it didn't match that vacant expression. "Much. I hate feeling all dirty, even in wolf form."

She breezed past me like it was any other morning, my stomach falling as she went to the bedside table where her hairbrush lay. I was stuck in place, staring at her, the rapid shift in my emotions making me dizzy.

"Do you want to talk more? About how all of this is making you…"

"No." She shook her head, quickly braiding the wet strands of her hair back from her face, the plait hanging down her back. "I can't talk anymore. I can't keep going over and over it in my mind. I need answers, so I'm going to work to find them. There has to be something in the cases and evidence still piled into our offices."

I walked over to sit next to her, reaching up to brush my fingers against her cheek, a shiver running through her. "Are you sure? Maybe you should get some more rest. You're still technically healing," I said hesitantly, even though logically I knew it was a waste of time.

"It won't help." She reached out to clasp our hands together, her trembling fingers still freezing, even though she had soaked in warm water for the past half an hour. "Sitting in the stillness… it will make it all worse. I need to work, be productive. I need…"

"I know." I leaned forward, placing a kiss on her temple, her shaking diminishing a bit under the gentle touch. I knew her well enough to know that facts and investigating helped her find mental peace, so I couldn't fault her for wanting to get right to work and research what was happening to her.

"Do you need any help?" I offered, squeezing her hand in mine.

She shook her head, leaning forward to press a gentle kiss to my cheek. "I think I'd rather work alone this morning, but I'll let you know if I need company later."

I nodded, solemnly resigned. "All right. Just let me know."

She stood up, taking steps towards the bedroom door. "I love you, sweetness." She gave me one more smile before disappearing through the door, her footsteps echoing down the stairs and out the front door.

I slumped forward, my head falling into my hands, hot tears streaming silently down my face. Powerlessness sank into my heart and weighed it down to ache in my chest, everything within me heavy.

I couldn't even begin to imagine what she was going through. Even worse, I had absolutely no idea how to help her.

CHAPTER 3

Kasha

I went to work like I said I was going to. I hadn't stopped for hours.

Nolan had stopped in after hour three, trying to bring me food. The beautifully prepared veggie burger and hand-cut fries should have made my very empty stomach gurgle with happiness. Instead, it turned my gut even further, the earthy yet salty scents making me nauseous. I took a few bites, though, to placate him, trying my best to show him I was going to be all right and that the research was helping.

Even though I was far from fine.

My mind was spinning and hadn't stopped since the night before. It was going through every possibility, every outlandish idea I could come up with for how this vile man was now in my head.

I knew he was an Ibridowyn and could mentally communicate with me due to that fact. However, no one should have been able to get into my mind without permission. I had always been able to keep my mental doors secured and locked, only letting those in when I wanted.

Yet, he had waltzed in like it was nothing, waking me up when he was close to a hundred miles away from me in a high-security prison. It was something that never should have been possible, and I knew there was a chance he could do it again.

I knew deep in my gut that he would do it again.

A shiver forced its way up my spine, my stomach threatening to force up the meager bites of food, churning and making me dizzy.

I stayed firmly planted in my seat, piles of boxes and case files crowded closely around me in the conference room I had shut myself in, a sign taped to the door not to disturb me unless absolutely necessary.

I didn't want anyone to witness this. I didn't want anyone to see that all the progress I had made, the hope I was starting to build back up, the confidence, was slowly crumbling. It was fragile and brittle. It made my insides like glass, the turmoil rolling inside of me pressing tiny fissures into every inch within, my body aching at the heaviness of it all.

I was weak. I was no longer the strong woman I thought I was becoming again.

I slammed my hand on the desk, trying my hardest to force those intrusive, dark thoughts away. So reminiscent of my weeks leading up to my life attempt. So similar to the words I had bleakly spoken out loud to the psycho-physician who had treated me in the clinic during my three-month stay.

Was I becoming that version of me once again? Had Elliot's

invasion of my mind brought me right back to that place?

"No, no, no, no…" I shook my head, whispering the words to myself in the dim, empty space. I was not that woman anymore. I had grown. I had learned how to control my darkened thoughts and crippling anxiety. I knew what I needed to do to bring myself back to focus.

Facts were what I needed. Facts, evidence, and truths were what kept me sane.

I was in there for far too long, pulling out as many case files as I could and looking through all the autopsy reports. Any sign of body tampering with tattoos. I needed to know what he had done to me. I needed to know how this branding he had laced into my skin made it so he could talk in my head whenever he wanted.

Answers. I needed answers.

My fingers were numbing with each page I turned. The stack of files with mentions of a brownish-red tattoo on the skin was not as substantial as I wanted it to be, but it was there.

I was combing through, wanting as many as I could find before putting them together and going through to find similarities to my own. I knew this had to be a part of it. I had sat through plenty of tattoo appointments, and no ink outside of the traditional black was considered safe to use. Even if artists were trying to find new ways to incorporate lasting color, nothing had been approved.

This meant Elliot had mixed something within this, likely some kind of Alchemist compound he had created to do something to me. To link us as he had said in my mind only a few hours ago.

I raked my fingers down my face, my insides trembling once

again. Last night. It had only been last night.

What has he done to me? I screamed. I couldn't stop myself, shrieking into the room. I picked up the empty cup of coffee I had finished hours ago and hurled it across the room, the ceramic blue shattering on impact and raining down the beige wall.

Footsteps pounded down the hall, my sign ignored as the door flung open. I had expected it to be Nolan, but Beckett and Liv stood at the door.

"What happened?" Beckett's bright blue eyes seemed alert, his white-blonde hair falling into his face like it did a little too often for a physician turned military man.

"Sorry." I forced myself back into the chair below me, pulling my shaking fingers into my lap and twisting my hands together. "It… um… slipped."

They looked at me skeptically at my weak excuse.

Liv didn't say a word as she left for only a moment and came back with a dustpan and broom, sweeping up the sharp pieces and throwing them away in the trash can in the corner.

"Where is Nolan?" I asked, my eyes darting around the room to look at anyone but them.

"He had a class to teach," Liv said, placing the broom in the corner near the door. She turned back to me, her dark brown skin lightly blushing with reddened cheeks and concern deep in her chocolate brown eyes. "He tried to pass it off to someone else, but we convinced him it would be good to focus on something else for a while."

Translation: He had been obsessing while I was locked in here and they sent him away to cool down.

Guilt swirled in my gut. I told him all the facts about what was happening but not how it made me feel. I should have told him the truth, but to talk about the dirty, sticky feelings swirling within me felt impossible.

"What have you been doing in here all day?" Beckett asked as casually as possible, coming to look down at the case files I had organized in my own chaotic manner. Liv joined him, my eyes finally wandering up to look at the two of them.

Two people I had always trusted since the day I met them on my transfer to Seathra.

The two people I had gone to on that last fateful night, when my body had been invaded by someone I trusted. It had been their house I sought refuge in. It was them I felt safest to speak my truth to first.

Liv had held my hand, stroking my hair as Beckett's gentle, warm hands examined me and patched up my body. They had taken care of me so well, making sure the last shred of trust I had in others didn't disappear entirely.

So why, when I had once again been violated by someone made of pure evil, did my mouth clamp shut? Why did the idea of talking to them seem impossible?

Liv approached me, looking at the case files. "Did you have a new idea on how to figure some things out about his followers?"

I shrugged, my throat clogged. I couldn't seem to force words through my lips.

Which, of course, they both noticed.

"Kasha…" Liv tried to lay her hand on my shoulder, but I jolted away from her touch as if burned.

Her face did not change, the look of peace still settled on her round face, but her eyes gave her away, glancing over to her husband. I knew I would never be able to hide things from them. They knew every tic, every micromovement my anxiety played within me. They knew my fake smiles and real ones. They knew when my voice pitched a bit too high to be real.

They knew me because they were my family, and they had spent months protecting me from not only others but myself.

So, I wasn't even a little bit surprised when they both slid into chairs across from me, refusing to leave.

A part of me was expecting them to get answers, to want me to talk to them. Instead, Beckett pulled the closest stack of papers towards him and asked, "What are we looking for?"

They asked for no details about why I was acting like my old, wounded self. They didn't seem even remotely interested in prying into me. Instead, they looked at me as their colleague and friend. They looked at me with professional interest, with a hint of support within those all-knowing gazes.

They looked at me and waited for what I was ready for.

Damn, did they know me well. After everything, I shouldn't have been surprised, but the sparking within my chest proved I still was.

I found my words again, explaining my research within the autopsy reports. I didn't go into detail about why I was looking, but they knew about the tattoo on my arm.

We fell into silence as they started on their stacks, my stomach nervous for the first five minutes before it finally dissipated into comfort.

At some point, Liv's gaze caught my own before she hesitantly reached out again. This time, I didn't flinch away when her hand covered mine.

"We're here for you, Kas." She squeezed my cold fingers. "All of us are. When you're ready to talk, just… we're all here for you."

I didn't say anything back but nodded before returning to my work.

I knew they always would be. My mind tried to convince me to open up. It was my weary, battered soul that was slower to realize.

And I wasn't sure exactly when it would be ready to let them in again.

CHAPTER 4

Kasha

It was my fourth night spent in the woods, my legs burning with each push of my run in wolf form. The night air was still a bit chilled, although as each day passed, winter disappeared a bit more into spring.

Sleep was still impossible. Running and moving and exhausting myself was the only thing I could even consider doing to force my body into it. I could have taken a drug to knock me out, but I had refused sleeping drafts ever since they used to drug me during my clinic stay.

The movement helped to clear my mind a bit, but still not enough for the constant barrage of thoughts popping into my head, forcing me to obsess over the how and why of Elliot's new form of torture. He hadn't even talked to me since that fateful night, yet I had not known a moment of peace since.

It was only about two hours in when the pounding of paws followed me through a stretch of trees. My steps faltered, but I quickly recovered, keeping my pace as I ran away. Yet, when the wind shifted, that citrus-spiced scent I knew so well wafted around me.

Nolan.

I kept going, the brush of someone asking for permission into my mind causing a jolt of fear to spike in my veins. I shook it off, reminding myself that Elliot didn't need to knock. He didn't need permission.

It was Nolan. Nolan was safe.

Yet I was unsure if my mind was, not with Elliot potentially lurking about. He was here to talk to me, and I wasn't ready to let someone in my mind again, which meant I had to stop running.

I couldn't avoid him any longer, and the settling of my heart made me realize I didn't want to. He was my partner, my paramour, and shutting him out… it was hurting me even more. I didn't like the ache that had formed in my chest over the days as I pretended to get better around him. It had been easy to fall back into the habits formed over the past year, but no longer with him.

For him, I would push myself to limits I usually skirted around.

I stopped in a more open area within the woods, counting down the seconds until he caught up to me. His pace slowed, his midnight black wolf standing a few inches above my own. His deep gold eyes looked down at me, understanding yet questioning in his gaze.

My shift was quick, bringing me back into my human form to kneel naked on the ground, my hands gripping my knees. Nolan shifted too, sitting in front of me in a mirrored position.

"I don't like waking up without you in bed," he said gently. No accusations, just a calm, honest statement.

"I couldn't sleep." I rubbed my palms against my chilled thighs, smearing dirt across my pale skin.

"I figured." He tilted his head. "How are you feeling?"

I tried to form ideas of how to explain what was knotting deeper and deeper into my gut, but my lips stayed sealed, a pathetic shrug pushing at my shoulders in answer.

"That's it?" he questioned.

"I don't know what to say," I whispered.

"Anything. Say anything about what's going on, how it's affecting you."

"I told you all about what happened." I stood, still needing the movement to keep my mind from spiraling downward.

"You told me the facts." He stood as well, although at a distance, leaning against a nearby tree. "Like the soldier and investigator you are. But I am not just your Alpha, Kasha, I'm your paramour. I love you."

"I love you too," I said, looking over at him, my stomach twisting.

His lips turned up into a soft smile. "I know, sweetheart. But you're starting to close me out again, trying to pretend. I knew you needed space, but no longer can I let you get lost within yourself. I won't watch you slip away back to a place I know you fought so hard to escape."

His unabridged thoughts shocked me, my body stilling to stare at him. I was used to people letting me stew in my own emotions, getting lost within the drowning of them. Not with Nolan, though. He knew when to give me space, but he also knew when to call me out.

I took a few deep breaths before walking over to him. His arms that were crossed against his chest fell to his sides, his back still against the tree, stance open, ready for whatever I needed from him. Finally, I reached him, our bodies not touching but close enough that his warmth and scent brushed against me, reminding me he was here.

With an unsteady deep breath and a prayer to the Goddess, I took a moment to compose my jumbled thoughts before looking up at him.

"He's in my head." The words came out in a whisper, my throat clogged.

His fingers twitched on his legs, but he didn't reach out to me. "I know, sweetheart."

I bit my lip, my chest burning. "I…" I shook my head, trying my best. "I'm so scared. Why can't he just leave me alone?"

He didn't have an answer, and truthfully, I didn't want him to give me one. He looked down at me, concern on his face and understanding in his gaze. It broke something within me, my chest fracturing, my heart aching.

"First, it was my body, sullied by Logan." My legs were trembling, my arms reaching out to steady myself and catching Nolan's biceps. His hands reached out to grab my waist. "Then my pride and honor were stripped by my father and the High Faction. And now? Now my mind has been violated, the one place I thought was safe to escape to! To be a place for me. No matter how dark, twisted, and depressing it got, it was mine! And now he's taken that too."

It was so much, the pressure building within me intense, but with each admitted word spoken into the light, it lessened a bit more, so I kept going.

"Why, when I think I finally found myself in a safe place, is it ripped away from me?" I dropped my forehead against his chest, my breaths labored as I tried to get my voice back through the dripping tears.

Everything I had allowed to build inside me for the past five days was erupting from within, desperate to escape, to for once be heard and seen for what it was.

"And then, when I realize how deep the fear goes, I get so angry!" My fingers curled into a fist, shaking as it pressed against his sweaty chest. "Angry at everyone who chose to hurt me. Angry at those terrible people who follow Elliot and were complacent in all of this. Angry at Lunestia for thinking I could handle this, after everything!"

The beat of his heart pressed against my forehead, his breath even as it brushed along the top of my head. He stood there, listening to me, supporting me, and gently rubbing his hands up and down my upper arms in a soothing gesture.

"Why me?" The final sob warbled through my throat, making the words quake.

His arms finally moved to encircle me, pulling me closer into his warm embrace. "I wish I could give you an answer. I wish I could take it all away, but that isn't the case."

I sniffed, moving my hands awkwardly between us so I could wipe away the tears. "I wish you could too."

"But you're not alone. You never were before meeting me, but especially now. And I know in here..." He tapped his finger gently against my temple, "...you know that. Yet, in here..." He pressed his hands between my breasts, my heart beating rapidly against his palm, "...you still need reminding. So, if I have to, I will spend every day reminding you that you have me by your side." He shifted us a bit, our bodies entwined. "I will make sure you never forget it. I am here for you, always."

My heart bloomed with heat, silent now-happy tears leaking from my eyes and down my cheeks. My insides trembled at his beautiful words, his honesty sinking in and marking my soul in a way I never expected. I did the only thing I could think of, pushing up onto my tiptoes and pressing our lips together.

When I thought no one would be able to make it through those walls I so easily constructed, once again, he proved me wrong. He was willing to hunt me down and support me through these terrible times. He let me fight for myself, while also being the greatest support when I faltered. He called me out and kept me accountable.

He was my partner. My paramour. My love.

And I needed him. I needed to know that I was not alone.

"Show me," I mumbled against his lips, pushing up on my tiptoes, one leg going to wrap awkwardly around his waist. He caught me, grasping behind my thighs and lifting me so I could wrap my legs around his hips, my soul settling at our closeness. "Show me I'm not alone, please, Nolan."

This was reminiscent of that moment in my bedroom, when I had tried to kiss him to forget about the pain. Then, he had said no, realizing I was doing it for all the wrong reasons. This, however, was very different. I needed a reminder of who he was to me. I needed to remember that through it all, the darkness and struggles, I had found a wisp of light in the love that had bloomed between us.

Something that had brought me joy and happiness. A place for me to feel safe. Here, in his arms, with our bodies and lives joining together, I was safe.

And I was desperate to be reminded of that, to feel him consume me. To have even a few moments where it was just him and me, no fear or worry that Elliot or others would find me and take something else from me. I needed it. I needed him.

One hand reached out to cup my cheek, his appraising gaze looking me over for any signs that this was a bad idea. I had no clue what he saw, but understanding soon bloomed in his gaze, no words spoken or necessary as he leaned forward to kiss me hard. He poured everything into it, my hungry, desperate self taking every bit, kissing him back with as much fervor.

He turned us around, pressing me gently against the tree before angling his hips to thrust himself within me, our bodies connecting in that way that utterly destroyed and completed me at the same time.

"Goddess, Nolan." The words slipped out of me, my mind focusing on the man in front of me, the one who had snuck into my life and heart so unexpectedly. The idea of living without him felt nearly impossible.

"You are not alone." He rocked into me again and again, the pleasure he knew how to thrum within me so well gaining a steady build within my lower belly. "You will never be alone again. So please, sweetheart, let me help you. Come home and let us figure out a way to fix this together."

I rocked my hips, a moan escaping me at the brush of my clit against his pelvic bone. "Yes," I said breathlessly. "Yes. Take me home, Nolan."

A growl escaped him, his lips pressing kisses along my jaw and throat, my pleasure building higher and higher with each thrust. My head fell back, our moans echoing against the trees as I allowed myself to be lost to him, my thoughts silent and focused only on him, us.

And as our movements became frenzied, our joined climaxes consuming us together, I felt a shred of peace for the first time in too many nights.

CHAPTER 5

Kasha

Sleeping in a bed and not on the scratchy, dirt-coated ground really helped.

My body was still buzzing with anxious energy when I woke up, but at least the past few nights, I was able to get a few more hours in. Nolan's warm hands stroked my hair or back each time I jolted awake from a nightmare, soothing the terrified edges and bringing me back to center enough to drift back off to sleep.

It wasn't a perfect night's sleep, but it was better than running until I passed out. Progress, I suppose.

Still, the morning was hard, the coffee I had brewed not strong enough to take away the ache of exhaustion laced in my bones. So, I tried my best to get myself to focus on something else and asked Nolan to teach me how to make breakfast.

He seemed very enthusiastic when I first asked. After we started and I almost cut my finger off while slicing apples, grabbed baking soda instead of powder, forcing us to restart the pancake batter, and overheated the stove, I think he was starting to regret trusting me in his kitchen.

He kept a calm face, even when I forgot to grease his favorite skillet and almost scraped the bottom trying to get my first pancake out of it.

"I love you so much…" His words were hesitant.

I couldn't help it. I smiled up at him, lightness filling my chest. "But?"

"But…" He took the spatula from my hand. "…How have you survived so long with terrible cooking skills?"

"I found enough people to take pity on me and make me food," I admitted. "I tried to learn so many times. So many people were convinced they could teach me. It never worked."

He tilted his head to me. "Never thought to warn me?"

"I figured like all the others, you deserved to experience my helplessness firsthand." I gave a little laugh, which made his smile beam at me, even with the charred scent of overcooked pancake wafting in the room.

"Well, I guess there is only one way forward." He stood next to me, showing me how to portion out the batter into the well-buttered pan. We kept going, and I even managed to successfully flip a pancake without half of it flopping onto the side. Progress.

It was all feeling normal and nice. Domestic and lovely.

"Hello, Rogthna.*"* The words were so simple, so smoothly whispered into the depths of my mind. Yet, they incited so much terror within me that I dropped to the floor, almost flinging the still-hot skillet off the open-flame stove.

"Kasha!" Nolan lunged in time to catch it so it didn't fall right onto my head. I didn't care, though. I couldn't because the voice was back.

His voice was back.

"I thought I would give you a few days before reaching out again." He kept talking. I hated every bit of it.

"Go away," I whispered, pulling my knees up to my chest, curling within as if trying to contain whatever was happening to me as best I could.

"Not this time." I swear, I could almost picture him shaking his head from wherever he was. *"You need to get used to the connection."*

I squeezed my eyes shut. *"No."*

"You need to understand why it is even here."

"It's here because you branded me," I shot back, trying to calm myself. I knew I shouldn't engage, but the conflicting emotions warring within my heart and mind were impossible to ignore. *"Leave me alone!"*

I didn't realize at first that I had not only said that within my mind but screamed it out loud.

"Kasha." The voice seemed so far away, but it wasn't in my mind, it was in front of me, in my space. "Kasha, open your eyes."

I let them flutter open to see Nolan crouched in front of me, concern and fear creasing his handsome face, and love filling his gaze.

I looked down at my knees. I didn't deserve to look at him. I didn't deserve to have him. I was tainted and broken. He deserved to love someone so much better than me.

I shook my head again, but this time at my own terrible thoughts of myself and not Elliot's invasion.

"Look at me, sweetheart." Nolan reached forward, and for

once, I didn't flinch away as he grasped my face between his hands. "Look at me and listen to my voice. Listen to what I'm saying."

"I could answer your questions for you," Elliot said as if completely unaware of what was happening in front of me. Maybe he was. Maybe he couldn't hear my thoughts like I worried about before. Just talk, like any normal Ibridowyn mental link.

I was shaking, tears slipping down my heat-flushed cheek, but I kept looking in front of me, focused on those stunning green eyes of Nolan's.

"Is he talking to you?" he asked calmly, no judgment on his face. Although, by the slight shaking of his fingers against my cheeks, he wasn't as calm on the inside as he was trying to pretend on the outside. I nodded, whimpering a bit at the admission. "I don't care what he's saying or what he's trying to tell you. Listen to me instead."

"I know you have many. It's who you are." Two conversations, one within my mind and one right in front of me, warring for attention. A throb behind my eyes formed, a groan escaping my lips.

"He isn't here. It's just you and me. Us, in our kitchen, in our home." His fingers firmed a bit on my cheek, pressing to remind me who was with me. "We're cooking terrible pancakes to have for breakfast before we go to work together."

Home. This was… home?

Yes, this was home. This place and this man in front of me was home.

"Nolan…" My voice cracked.

"Yes, it's me. I'm here with you, not him." He shuffled a few inches closer, his knees brushing against my calves. "What do you smell?"

"What?" I shook my head, his hands moving with me.

"Remind yourself where you are and ignore him."

"I know you want to know," Elliot crooned inside my mind.

"Burnt bits," was all I could say, but it was something. "And cinnamon."

"Yeah, the burned remains of our dearly departed breakfast." He smiled at me.

I pulled in another deep breath. "No, the cinnamon is you."

That made him smile even brighter. "I'm right here. Not him."

I nodded, still hearing the echoes of Elliot whispering into my mind, but I refused to listen and focus. I kept talking to the man in front of me.

"Thank you for finding me. I'm not sure I ever said that." I wasn't really sure what I was saying; I was just trying to talk. "Thank you for still letting me flip the pancakes even when one fell on the stove."

"How is someone who is so coordinated at fighting so terrible at flipping a pancake a few inches?"

"Rogthn—" I forced it away. I kept it out.

"It's a special talent, I guess." I reached up, pressing my hands on top of his.

"Goodbye." The one word I let slip past my block-out of him before silence settled back in my mind.

Finally, after a few more breaths, I let my muscles relax. "He's gone."

Nolan let his hands slip enough so I could uncurl from within myself and into his welcoming embrace. "What can I do?" he whispered, stroking the ends of my ponytail.

I had been searching for answers that were taking too long to find. I needed someone to tell me something. I needed a shred of hope.

So, I thought of the one person close by who might have even a shred of knowledge, who had worked with Elliot unknowingly to prepare people for experiments. Who had seen the vile things Elliot was willing to do for his disgusting curiosity and needs.

I gripped tightly onto Nolan's black shirt before saying, "I need to talk to Vanessa."

***

Vanessa arrived quicker than I expected, Nolan right behind her. I saw a peek of her guards right outside the door to the house before he shut it. Before he left, he had helped me to my seat, pouring me an extra tall glass of water and placing a slice of buttered toast in front of me instead of the heavy pancakes we had planned to eat. I had drunk most of the water and nibbled on the toast while I waited, but I pushed it away when Vanessa arrived.

"Kasha." She approached me hesitantly, taking in my tear-stained cheeks and disheveled outfit and hair from my freak out on the floor. "What's wrong?"

I grasped her hands, tugging her to sit next to me. Her face wrinkled in concern. "If you know anything, please, Vanessa, tell me."

"What's going on, Kasha?" She gripped my hands.

"He's in my head." The tears started to flow again, my heart rattling and aching. "Why is he in my head? How did he do it?"

"In your…" She looked at me with confusion before a spark of angry light flicked into her gaze. "Elliot is in your mind?"

I nodded my head quickly. "Yes. He found a way in even when he's so far away. Do you know what this is? Did he ever do this to any of your patients when you were with them?"

Guilt flashed across her face, her throat quivering. "I've never heard of anything like this. He never told me about it."

"But the experiments you saw…" Nolan said from behind us.

"I was never involved, and I ran away before I could learn more. I'm so sorry."

"Vanessa, please!" I begged. "I need something, anything! You are the closest thing I have to finding an answer. You don't know anything?"

"I don't…" She looked over her shoulder at Nolan. He narrowed his eyes on her. "I don't know what this is."

"But?" he prompted, realizing as I had that she was hiding something.

"You could ask someone else."

I froze, pulling my hands from hers. "I am not going to see him."

"No!" She shook her head emphatically. "I would never suggest that."

I tilted my head, starting to realize the lines of thought she was considering.

"James?" My voice was weak, but I forced that name through.

She bit her lip, gnawing on it before letting out a breath. "He was always close to Elliot and escorted him to the labs. He would most likely know."

I had spent a lot of time with James during my captivity. My annoyed, hulking shadow. "I… I don't know…"

"You don't have to, Kasha," Vanessa said. "It was only a thought, but you don't have to unless your mind and heart are ready to see him again."

She was right, I didn't have to.

But if I wanted answers, did I have any other choice?

CHAPTER 6

Kasha

It was another two days before I finally decided what to do. Before I realized it was time to stop hiding from those who cared about me. I had called the meeting early, the sun only just risen as Nolan and I walked into the office building and up to the top floor.

The conference room was stuffed with all my Hierarchy teammates as I walked in, Caleb and Ollie joining as well. They had both gone back to their Compound the day after the last meeting with the High Faction, but when I had called them yesterday morning to come back, they had dropped everything to be here.

Both of them.

"Kasha." Ollie was the first to approach me, wrapping me in a tight, warm hug. I stiffened before reminding myself that Ollie was safe and relaxed into the hug. Caleb hovered behind him, still seeming a bit unsure, but he gave me a timid smile as I peeked over Ollie's shoulder.

A few more seconds passed before pulling away, Nolan leading me to a chair. He winked at me, my hammering heart settling a bit. I didn't want to be passed around in a parade of hugs, and I had a feeling he knew that. My stomach flipped again.

Nolan took his place next to me, Beckett to his left, and Emric on the other side of him. The rest of our Gammas and Treasus took their seats, my brothers choosing to stand. Warmth captured my knee, Nolan's hand tightly gripping it under the table in silent reassurance.

"There's…" I shook my head, collecting my thoughts. "There's something I need to tell you all."

So many ways I could tell them, and yet words seemed unapproachable as I looked around at the group of people who had been there for me. Their gazes were heavy, my palms beginning to sweat and my pulse pounding against my throat. They all looked so concerned, waiting silently for me to continue.

Yet, my voice was still lost within me. Would they consider me tainted? Unable to do my job or be an effective Beta to our team? Would this be the final thing that would make them decide I was officially a lost cause or too much to handle?

The tainted thoughts made my stomach roll with nausea, forcing me to lean over and calm myself. I knew logically that none of those thoughts would ever come true. These people had stood by me through my lowest, darkest times. They would never abandon me as I tried my hardest to keep myself from falling back into that place. They would do whatever it took to help and support me.

I knew that was the truth, even if it took a few extra seconds for my anxiety to catch up.

I looked over at Nolan, who gave me an encouraging nod, reminding me silently that I could do this. That I was strong enough to let them in again.

"I don't know how exactly, but Elliot was able to communicate mentally with me the other night." My gaze lowered to the table, unable to look at any of them. "I couldn't block him out."

Liv's voice strained around her words. "You mean... he can just... talk to you?"

I gnawed at my bottom lip. "Seems like it."

"Little Shadow..." Ollie's words were barely above a whisper, slipping out on his breath. Caleb stood rigidly next to him, his pallor a bit green-tinted.

"I don't know the extent of it or if there is more he has yet to show me." My arm shook as I rolled up my left sleeve, revealing the rust-colored tattoo on my forearm. "But I think we all know this has to do with it."

The branding of Elliot's crest was still fresh, the last of the scabbing still clinging to the healing skin. I had been keeping it hidden under thick sweaters, trying my best to block it out and pretend it wasn't there. However, I knew that was no longer an option. No matter how much I wished I could continue to play make-believe, I knew I couldn't any longer.

Elliot probably wouldn't let me even if I tried.

I looked around, wondering and questioning on everyone's faces.

"Ask me," I whispered, slowly rolling my sleeve back down with numb fingers.

"Ask you what?" Beckett said.

"The many questions I know you're all filtering through." I took a shaky breath. We were all investigators. When faced with a problem or a mystery, we couldn't help but think up questions. "I don't know if I can answer all of them, but it might help."

Everyone gazed around at each other, before finally, Emric was the first to lean forward, his usual calm, level-headed presence settling into the air around him.

"If he can talk to you, can you talk back?"

My voice warbled a bit. "Yes."

"Does that mean you can reach out to him as well?" Lucas was the next to speak up, the usually rough temperament of his voice smoothed out a bit.

A chill swept through my veins at his perfectly reasonable question. "I—I don't know. I hav—haven't tried to."

"And we don't expect you to." The usually hard-looking twin gave me that kind smile he only reserved for his closest friends. "I just thought I would ask."

I nodded, giving him a reassuring smile that it was okay, even though that question was one I had been actively trying to ignore over the past few days. It was horrifying enough to know that he could get into my head, but the idea that I could force myself into his mind on a whim disgusted me even deeper.

That was a violation I wouldn't wish on anyone, even him.

"How…" Eden shook her head, leaning back in her chair, Grayson's arm casually draped over the back of it.

"What?" I furrowed my brow.

"How did he sound?"

My stomach dropped, the answer easy. "Strong. Fearless." The words tasted like ash on my tongue, but I continued, "He wasn't acting like he had given up. He sounded confident, like we were all acting exactly how he wanted us to." I shook my head. "He said… he said we would be together again soon."

Nolan's grip on my leg tightened, his face creasing with anxiety, green eyes glistening under the harsh light. I wondered if my own terrified thoughts echoed his, knowing Elliot seemed so confident that our time together was not over. Terror coursed through me, raging within, and I had to force myself to focus on the heat of his hand bleeding through my pants. It reminded me it was not Elliot and his people near me but Nolan and the rest of my family. They were here, not him.

I was safe.

I was safe.

"But he's imprisoned," Beckett said, his white-blonde hair still a bed-head mess. "He can't get to you anymore."

"Apparently, even incarceration can't bring him down." I slumped back in my chair, my hand sliding over to release Nolan's grip on my knee and lace our hands together.

Silence filled the air, all of us trying to process yet another unexpected twist of what our lives had become. We may have been soldiers, but even this was beyond the training we had spent years learning or the experiences that had shaped us.

"What does this mean?" Taylor asked, breaking the silence.

"It means Elliot's plan is far from over." A wayward tear finally escaped, slipping down my heated cheek.

We had no answers, no direction or idea of what to do next. The only thing we knew for sure was that war was coming. Even with Elliot behind bars, we would need to fight for our freedom.

"Do you have a plan?" Greyson asked.

"No." I shook my head, wishing I did. "But I do have someone I need to visit. Maybe then I can get some answers and a plan will reveal itself."

That perked them all up, so I told them the very risky and terrifying idea that I knew I needed to follow through on. My final hope for getting answers, even though it meant I had to go to one of the last places I ever wanted to visit.

CHAPTER 7

Kasha

I wasn't even a little surprised when Ollie and Caleb ushered me into my office once the meeting concluded. Nolan left us for a few minutes, having told me he would be in his own office if I needed him.

I collapsed into my chair, limbs heavy, gaze unable to focus properly as my brothers fell into the chairs across from me. My mind and body were equally exhausted after filling in the team about my plan to go and visit James. It was a plan I wished I didn't have to think about, a risk I didn't want to have to take for my own sanity, but I was running out of options.

Going through those case files was coming up with nothing. I had found victims with a similar reddish-brown tattoo, but the autopsy didn't reveal anything new. I didn't even know if the experiment had been a failure or if these people had been killed because it was successful. Too many questions, and I was desperate for answers.

So desperate that my fear was worth facing just for the clarity it might bring my mind and heart.

"Are you all right, Little Shadow?" Ollie pushed a cup of water toward me. It wouldn't relieve the pounding behind my eyes, but it would help as I had only had coffee today.

"I just…" My thoughts were too chaotic, too fear-filled that I wasn't alone, my mind not properly protected. When I tried to focus on facts and theories, ways to help myself, only one thought kept popping into my mind.

You are not alone. You are not alone. You. Are. Not. Alone.

It went around in my head in a loop, a constant reminder that my mind was no longer my own until I could figure out how to expel him from it.

"We should push with the High Faction to execute Elliot," Caleb rumbled, his arms crossed tightly against his chest. "Logic serves that it would keep him from your mind if he wasn't alive anymore."

"We can't." I shook my head, taking a few big sips from the cool glass of water. "They've already announced that they plan to keep him alive for interrogations about the extent of his people and army. If we start pushing, they'll want to know why."

I left the rest unspoken. They had betrayed my trust one too many times over the past year. If I were a good soldier, I would report this right away. But through their own neglect, they had pushed me to silently rebel, to keep this secret until I was ready to tell them. Until it was absolutely necessary, the need to protect Kazola superseded my lack of trust in those I was supposed to take orders from.

"Besides, we don't know the extent of the experiment," Ollie chimed in. "For all we know, his death could harm Kasha even further. Knowing him, it's not as simple as killing him to make it stop."

"Especially since he's a Brido," I whispered, remembering the bloody moment I had discovered that little tidbit. "He won't be easily killed."

That silenced us all, my stomach lurching once again at the knowledge that Elliot had turned himself into an Ibridowyn. He had already been too strong when we thought he was a Shrivika, a species created by Firenelle, the God of Blood and Truth. Those who could learn all about a person through drinking their blood, using it for truth-seeking as well as sustenance to survive. They were as strong as us Varg Anwyns, the wolf shifter children of Lunestia, the Goddess of Moon and Hunt. Along with the many humans, we all lived peacefully on the Isle of Kazola.

It was disgusting to know he had stolen a vile of the genetic serum that transformed a Varg Anwyn or Shrivika into an Ibridowyn soldier. Taken it after being fired as a State Alchemist decades ago for crossing ethical lines and experimenting on people. Not only did it strengthen his typical Shrivika abilities, it also fortified his physical attributes so much that he was almost invincible like us Onyx Guard members. I had seen firsthand how he used that to manipulate his people, to make them believe the god Firenelle had blessed him with protection to never die.

It was all just overly complicated. Like everything was when it came to Elliot.

"Are you sure going to see one of them is the best idea?" Ollie asked me gently. Caleb sat on the edge of his seat, waiting for my answer as well.

"I want to go. I plan to call in the favor this afternoon and get the meeting." I let out a stuttering breath. Admitting that released a bit of the pressure building in my throat. It was a hard thing to admit, to not let the fear and anxiety over seeing James get to me and convince me that this wasn't worth it. Seeing him would only make it worse, and I needed to protect myself.

But I couldn't revert to old habits. That if I avoided a problem, it would go away. That wasn't going to work this time. With Elliot able to invade my mind, he would make sure I would never forget that I was slowly falling into the places he wanted me to be. I had to push against the fear.

"Why?" Caleb asked, leaning forward to rest his elbows on his knees, an inquisitive look on his sharp-featured face.

"We need answers." I swallowed, looking between my two older brothers. "I need answers. I need to know why and how the fuck this is happening to me. I need to be able to go to sleep without the constant fear that his voice is going to wake me up. I need to know if this is it or if something worse will happen. I just…" I shook my head, willing myself not to break down again. "I need answers."

Ollie's usually relaxed, smirking face creased. "But Kasha…"

"Listen to her, Ollie." Caleb cut him off. "Let her tell us her reasons."

I looked up at him, worry still creasing his face, but openness and understanding shone in his silver gaze.

We had been through too much, our splintered sibling bond only in the beginning stages of repair. He had caused so much hurt, pain, and isolation for me and Ollie over the past year by deciding to take the side of my rapist, his best friend, when I had accused him of sexual assault and taken him to trial. He had publicly spoken out against me and severed any trust I had had in him.

But when he had told us the truth, that Father had groomed him to follow orders and be the perfect little soldier for him, it at least started to make sense. Then, Caleb had chosen to use his position as Logan's best friend to go undercover and catch him with the *Marc Gealach,* the crest of our Goddess Lunestia, shown on those she deemed a criminal during a special moon phase. It was created for her Varg Anwyn children to hunt and catch those who would harm the people of Kazola.

Caleb had caught him with the Mark as I had expected. And even though Logan and his deplorable Uncle Cole had gotten away, they were branded as criminals and on the run. They were wanted men, and they could only run from us—from me—for so long.

I gave a genuine, appreciative smile at his words of support, my chest warming. Although I didn't trust him completely yet, I did a little bit more each day.

"I can't keep my thoughts straight." I turned back to Ollie, my gaze flicking between them again. "I'm terrified he'll hear something he shouldn't or plant something I don't want there because I have no idea how this works. I can't trust my own mind. Do you know how that feels?"

I could sense it already settling into my mind. The fear. The paranoia. Even if he wasn't in my mind at this very moment, he could be whenever he wanted. I had few defenses to keep him out and no idea if my ignoring him a few days ago with Nolan had forced him away or if he had grown bored and left on his own.

I needed protection, from myself and him, and the only way to get it was with answers.

***

After we talked for a bit longer, they sat with me as I called Evette, one of the few Delegates on the High Faction I trusted. She was one of the few who had voted for me during my case against Logan and had reached out to let me know I had allies on the High Faction. It was why I felt comfortable asking her for a no questions asked favor to set up a visit with James. She had nodded and said I should be at the prison in Ilfra in two days.

I wasn't sure if I would be able to sit still or make my racing, terrified thoughts stop and my pulse slow, but I would try my best. I needed rest so I could properly prepare my heart and mind to see one of my captors again.

We emerged from the office building around noon, the sun shining high in the clear blue sky as we walked out. Ollie was heading back to his Compound in Vapalles, the territory south of Seathra, and Caleb would be heading back to Ilfra, our Capital territory directly north.

"Little Lea!" Ollie called out, waving and looking towards the entrance to the forest where my childhood best friend, Lea, emerged from.

She was dressed down, barefoot, and in a pair of loose black linen pants and a long-sleeved cream shirt, both of which were covered in dirt. Her golden-brown skin was sweaty and her cheeks red, her curly hair tied back from her face.

"Just come back from a run?" I asked as she approached us.

"Yeah, needed to get some energy out," she said when she reached us, standing a few feet away. A Varg Anwyn like the three of us, she must have used some of the paths to run in her wolf form.

I reached out, hugging her. I hated that she was stuck here with us. Unlike most who lived on this Compound, Lea was not a member of the Guard but a blacksmith who ran a thriving forge in Seathra's capital city of Eroste. However, when Elliot's people started to cause more public unrest, it led to them attacking government contractors and their businesses. Since Lea was our Compound's contracted blacksmith for all our weapons, she was considered a target, which led me to use my place as Beta to give her a safe haven, which she equally appreciated and hated.

She hugged me right back. "Plus, I wanted to check on you."

I pulled away, letting her warmth soothe me. "Thanks."

She turned to my brothers, her gaze catching on Caleb and cooling a bit. He stiffened under her intense, appraising gaze. "It's good to see you again, Adalaide."

She quirked her eyebrow at him. "Not sure if I feel the same, Caleb."

She knew everything, having lived with me for the past six months in a townhouse in the city and more recently coming to visit me every day as I recovered from my injuries in captivity. She had always been an amazing listener and gave an incredible perspective of my family drama, having known both of my brothers for most of her life.

She had been there with me through all the pain Caleb had caused. Just like Ollie and me, it would take a bit more time for all three of us to trust him completely again. Still, hope was back, and I tried my best to focus on that.

"What about me, Little Lea?" Ollie said before coming right up next to her and slinging his arm around her shoulder. "You're always happy to see me, aren't you?"

I rolled my eyes at his typical teasing with her. Her gaze glinted with mischief as she looked up at him, shrugging as if his presence didn't faze her.

"I suppose you can stay." She turned back to me, Ollie's arm still around her. "Are you hungry? Want to have lunch?"

I smiled, my gurgling stomach giving me away. "Sure."

"Would you two like to join us?" she asked, her gaze fixed on my eldest brother.

Caleb's shoulders relaxed a bit, and he let out a deep breath. "I would love to."

"Are you cooking?" Ollie asked.

"Of course."

His infectious smile bloomed even brighter. "Then count me in."

CHAPTER 8

Kasha

My heart was ready to burst out of my chest as I paced in front of the prison two days later.

The high-security Phyros Prison sat ten miles northwest of Kazola's Capital City of Ilfra, the watch tower spires rising so high they were visible once you broke free of the city and into the gravel roads. Constructed of black stone and gray cement, nothing about this place was welcoming. It was cold, defensive, sending a chill up my spine as the officers at the gate checked my and Nolan's credentials and Evette's approval letter that said I was allowed to visit to question one of their prisoners.

They nodded us forward, but my feet seemed stuck in place as I stared up at the imposing structure, the cold, unyielding walls unwelcoming.

"I can't do this," I whispered, shoving my papers back into the bag slung over my shoulder.

"Yes, you can." Nolan stood strong behind me, his hands resting on my shoulder to squeeze them. "You don't have to if you don't want to, but that's not for lack of strength and ability to walk through that door."

Terror clawed up my throat, trying its best to smother me. I had spent the past few days convincing myself that this was the right, smart decision to discover answers surrounding what was happening to me and my unsafe mind. Yet, now that I was here, only steps away from facing someone I never wanted to see again, I wasn't as sure of my strength; not after everything they had all done to me.

"What if they escape?" The words were barely audible, lost within the breeze that blew around us, but Nolan caught them, slowly turning me around to face him.

"They aren't getting out, sweetheart." He hunched over a bit, forcing my gaze to snag on his. "They cannot escape or get to you. The interrogation room is secure, and you've beaten him before."

This was the third most secure prison on the Isle. The second was located in Rystin, and the first wasn't even on the Isle proper at all. It was constructed on a small island, more like a glorified rock, twenty-five miles off the northern coasts.

I reached up to clutch his forearms, his grip tightening around the shoulder bracers that were secured to my armor. "I wish you could come in with me." I could use his strength, his constant presence, but the favor I had called in could only go so far. Evette could only approve me to go in since they limited the number of visitors in the prison daily for security reasons.

"I'll be right here the entire time, waiting to take you home when you're done."

I nodded, taking a shaky breath. We had left early in the morning to arrive here by noon and planned to leave when I was finished if we could. I had no desire to see the High Faction. I wasn't sure I would be able to face them while keeping this secret. Besides, all I wanted was to be in my bed with Nolan tonight, in the home the two of us had started to build. I needed that consistency.

I pushed up onto my tiptoes, moving my hands to grab his face and kiss him. He kissed me right back, sharing his warmth, love, and protection with me. A throat cleared behind us, reminding me we were not alone. A prison guard still stood there, waiting for me to come inside.

Nolan gave me one last smile, gently brushing the backs of his fingers across my cheeks before stepping away. I steeled my spine and turned around, nodding to the guard to lead the way. He nodded back and moved forward.

And I took my first step into the bleak building to face one of my fears.

★★★

Four guards in brown leather armor led me down a low-lit hall. The black stone walls created a narrow path, closing in on me with each step, and I struggled to pull in deep breaths. My captors were being held here. Not just Elliot, but the guards who had followed me around and kept me in line. I knew I would see them again, there was no avoiding it, but I hadn't thought it would be so soon. I hadn't thought it would be to ask about what was happening to me. What he had done to me.

But with each day that passed, my freedom slowly slipped back into their grip and I would do anything in my power to cut that tie before it was too late.

"Are you coming to visit me, Rogthna?"

My bones chilled and my steps faltered. How… how did he know I was here? No one would have told them, would they?

No, this wasn't happening. This wasn't happening.

"Ho—how?" was all I could say back, my hand reaching out to steady myself. The rough stone was sharp against my palm.

"Beta Mallanis?" The guard in front of me asked, but I shook my head, staring down at my boots, trying to think of anything. Nolan, my friends, my books, a piano melody. Anything to force him out.

I can do this.

I wasn't here for him. He was locked away in an isolated cell in the depths of this place. Evette had all but confirmed it when I asked for permission to visit James. He had strict guard rotations and schedules. He was never removed from his cell and was isolated from anyone who wasn't a guard. No one could see him without permission from all members of the High Faction signing off on it.

He wasn't going to get me. He couldn't, not anymore. I was safe.

But he was in the building. We were occupying the same space once again.

I can do this. I can do this. I can do this.

"I'll always know where you are, Kasha. We are bound."

"Get out!" I screamed back at him, clawing my fingers against the wall as I struggled to pull in air.

"Beta Mallanis, are you okay?" The young guard's voice sounded scared, his face paling.

"Not until you find me again and release me," he whispered, that smooth voice raking over me, scratching at my mind to let him in. *"Not until we fulfill our destiny."*

"I will never release you," I said. *"You will never get to me."*

He chuckled in my head. *"If you say so."*

"I'm not here to see you."

"I see," he said, disappointment lacing the words. *"Tell James I said hello, then."*

"Screw you," I snarled, trying and failing to push him out, to force him back behind the walls of my mind. *"Leave me alone and get out of my head."*

"Have a nice chat, Rogthna. I hope you find it useful." I could hear the smile in his voice before he disappeared, my shaking fingers slowing to a gentle tremble.

I took in a few more deep breaths before straightening, looking at the timid guard who no longer looked able to do his job. Instead of succumbing to the fear that raced through me, I forced it to be a reminder of why I was even doing this. Why I had even stepped into the same building as him. He could come into my mind, unbidden. He could talk to me no matter where I was.

Although, as we began moving forward again, my legs tingling, I couldn't help but wonder if there were limits to his being in my mind. He wasn't aware until the end of the conversation that I wasn't here for him. So, maybe he could only talk but not hear my thoughts. Maybe he didn't have as much control as I worried.

Maybe.

Hopefully, James was willing to talk today.

***

The interrogation room was much smaller than the ones I was used to. Most likely an old cell that was repurposed, with two chairs and a thin wooden table that shook with any little impact, the legs no better than toothpicks. James had already been escorted into the space, his hulking body chained to the chair bolted into the stone floor, wrists and ankles cuffed to the legs, and his torso wrapped in thick iron links circling around the back. He sat farthest into the room, leaving my chair near the entrance.

They were taking no chances.

I kept my shoulders pulled back, my chin high and my face calm. I strode into the room, taking the seat opposite him, and refused to think about the days he kept watch on me. Of him being compliant in the torture Elliot put me through. Of him dragging me away, half-starved and going feral, before locking me into my room for Goddess knew how long.

No. If I thought about that, I would crumble.

These people had taken much from me, but I would not give them my fear.

I held on to the one not-so-bad memory of James. He had fed

me before the experiment, giving me enough strength to pull myself back from the brink of mentally breaking when this bond was originally formed. I knew he had done it for Vanessa, his estranged wife, but still. It was something. It was a speck of good within his tainted, twisted heart.

"Hello, James." I looked him over, the gray linen prison outfit barely fitting his ogrish form. His face was smeared with dirt, making the jagged scar on his face even more prominent. His black hair had been shaved completely off, not helping to soften his sharp features.

"Hello, Kasha," he said, his body twisting a bit in the chains, failing to get comfortable.

I could start with pleasantries and small talk, but there was no time and no patience left within me. I wanted answers.

"What did he do to me?"

He cocked his eyebrow. "Excuse me?"

I kept the growl crawling up my throat contained as I rolled up my left sleeve, revealing the now-healed tattoo. "What did he do to me?"

"I am no Alchemist," he stated simply.

"But you were close to him. You were his right-hand man, his head of security. I have a strong suspicion you knew what he was doing to me that day." I forced myself to stay leaned back against my chair.

"How do you know?"

"You fed me when you didn't need to." I looked him right in the eye, his gaze flaring with memory. "You believed this inking would make me lose my sanity if I was too malnourished. Stands to reason you knew enough about it to give me some answers."

"Where is my wife?" he asked abruptly.

My fingers numbed. "Excuse me?"

"If you want answers about that tattoo, then I deserve something in return." I wasn't shocked by any of this, but it still chilled me to the bone, his desperation to know even a little about her. "We're all hopelessly waiting for answers in this room, so why shouldn't we all benefit from this little meeting?"

"It's classified." I gritted my teeth. "I will not betray her when she doesn't want to be found by you."

"She is my wife!"

"And you were her husband and let her down!" That made me lean forward, my eyes flashing gold, his own flashing red in response to the challenge. "You put her in danger. Do not expect me to hand over that information when she hasn't consented to it."

His nose scrunched upwards. "I love her to this day."

"If you love her, that means you should also respect her." I glared at him. "Prove you do by letting her stay hidden."

He snarled at me, his fangs peeking out, but the chains kept him right in place. Minutes passed before he calmed down, his eyes shifting back to their typical hazel.

"Then answer me this. What did you tell her about me upon your return home?"

I tilted my head. What was he getting at? Maybe he wanted to feel better about himself or was concerned that I told her horrid things. Maybe he wanted to know if there was still hope that she could still love him.

"The truth," I stated simply. "Which included the fact that you most likely saved my life at the very end. That in your own twisted way, you kept me safe while I was in Folanoch."

He stared at me, emotions flitting through his gaze and wrinkling his face as he processed my words. His head hung before he lifted his chin back up, taking in a deep breath before speaking again.

"I will give you answers," he stated, hope flaring in my chest prematurely. "If you do something for me first."

The hope smothered before it could even bloom, my stomach aching. "What's that?"

"You're right, I should respect the fact that she hasn't consented to me knowing where she is." He tilted his head, a smirk tilting on his lips. "So, get it."

My stomach dropped. "Excuse me?"

"Get her permission to tell me where she is," he clarified. "Then, when you come back here and reveal the location, I'll know you got it. Only then will I give you guidance on what happened during the procedure."

I wanted to kick him and scream in his face. I wanted to punch him and watch him bleed. Somehow, by the grace of the Goddess, I kept myself in my chair, the raging heat of anger boiling within, but that was where I kept it. My fingers gripped the edges of my chair, threatening to snap it into kindling.

"How did she ever love you?" I shook my head. I had peeked at soft-hearted moments within James over our weeks together. It made me wonder if it had been that James Vanessa fell so deeply in love with. But that James wasn't here. In his place was the soldier who had stood next to a madman genius for decades.

"Desperation is known for making people a bit manic." His gaze trailed me, hardening back to the guard I remembered him to be. "I hope to see you again soon, Kasha."

I stood, my insides quaking. I was desperate for answers like him, but was I willing to stoop so low for them? Was I willing to put another in danger?

CHAPTER 9

Kasha

As planned, we drove straight back to Seathra after stopping for a quick lunch at a small tavern on the way. By the time we got home, I had just enough energy to let Nolan feed me before I collapsed into bed, not needing a long run to push me into sleep this time.

When I woke up, tucked into the warmth of Nolan's arms, James's words were the first to flood back to me, hitting me hard in the chest and almost stealing my breath away. I had snuggled closer to Nolan, pulling in deep breaths clouded in his scent to help calm my racing heart and try to make sense of the many thoughts surrounding his demand.

Should I even consider asking her? Was it the right thing to do? A dark part of me, one that was fueled by desperation, wondered if I could use her guilt over our shared past to get her to agree. I was *that* desperate for answers.

Vanessa had betrayed me deeply. She had spent weeks with me as my psycho-physician, helping me overcome some of the hardest hurdles of my mental healing, organically getting me to open up and release some of the pent-up pain and anger I had been repressing. Yet, when her safety had been threatened, the life she had been running from finally catching up to her, she had chosen to hand over my medical records for Elliot to look at. That was how he knew about Logan and all my issues with my family and the High Faction.

It was a betrayal that had cut into my soul and threatened to undo a bit of the trust I had started to rebuild.

Even with all of that, could I ask someone to step into their dark past so I could keep escaping my own?

In my gut, it didn't seem fair.

Of course, I didn't even have time to consider going over to visit her that morning, as all Keturis across Kazola had been called into an emergency meeting with the High Faction. That was how I found myself in our conference room, dressed in my formal Onyx Guard uniform and sitting to Nolan's right, with Beckett and Emric on his other side, the four of us making up the highest-ranking members of our Faction.

Thank Goddess we had decided to come home. I would have hated to do this meeting in the Chateau, the gilded place where the High Faction sat in session and lived for most of the year. I wasn't ready to face them in person again. Particularly, my father.

"Ready?" Beckett asked all of us, his gaze lingering on me for a second longer. We nodded before he leaned forward and pressed the on button, activating the large Comms unit that projected against the wall farthest from us. Soon, the screen lit up with the High Faction taking a large portion of the center screen, small boxes of the other Factions surrounding them. We were one of the last to arrive at the meeting.

When the last one joined, Mitchell stood from his High Tribune seat in the center of the Human branch, staring right into the screen to address all of us.

"As you all know, we recently captured Elliot and many of the leaders in a raid led by the Seathra and Luspan Factions in a joint effort." He nodded as if in recognition of our teams, even though it was directed at the entire group. "With this arrest, we had hoped that the recent upsurge in criminal activity that we highly suspect to be linked to the cult following of Elliot would diminish and eventually die out with the loss of their leader.

"However, reports of continued unrest and attacks on local businesses with government contracts have not only continued but increased, along with a recent influx of missing person reports starting to flood the garrisons."

He paused, all four of us gazing around at each other, unrest settling in my stomach. What did that mean?

"Because of this, we are deploying measures to all Onyx Guard Factions to help us better understand the brewing threat that seems to be increasing at a rapid rate."

"*Did you have a nice visit with James,* Rogthna?" That smooth voice spoke in my mind.

My spine stiffened at the instant invasion, his voice scraping along my mind. I couldn't move, breathing almost impossible. If I moved, if I let out a puff of air, I might break down and I couldn't do that. Not here. Not in the middle of this meeting.

Ignore him. Force him out. Make him leave. Pay attention to the meeting.

Easier said than done. My hands fisted on the table as I used every bit of willpower to ignore Elliot and keep listening to Mitchell babble on the screen. "You will send your teams out to major cities and heavily populated areas of your territory," he said. "Then, you will have them gather up the different missing person cases that have been reported in the last two years and try your best to determine if they are missing due to joining Elliot, being taken by Elliot, or unrelated."

"Only two years?" Beckett asked, pressing on the talk button out of turn, Mitchell's frowning face letting us know he did not appreciate the interruption.

"To start, yes…"

"Did you get the answers you were hoping to?"

Ignore. He's not here. Focus on the job.

"The point of this is to get an understanding of the numbers, see if we can begin tallying up how many we may potentially be fighting against…"

"Come now. I know you can hear me," he teased, my stomach rolling. *"Might as well let me know."*

Ignore. Ignore. Ignore.

A light tap within my mind caused a bit of a distraction, a familiar one, making me look at Nolan next to me. His body was still angled towards the camera, but his eyes were looking over at me. "Is he there?"

I nodded, keeping myself staring at the screen, although Mitchell's words were harder to make out as my focus continued to split.

"I think it's good you went to see him." Elliot was having a conversation for one in my head at this point, my stomach threatening to empty the meager contents of my breakfast onto the table in front of me. My insides sank, everything within me failing to get him out from where he did not belong.

"Let me in," Nolan mumbled to me, but I shook my head. "Please, Kasha. Maybe if I talk to you in there, it will be easier to ignore him."

"Or worse." My head was going light, my vision blurring along the edges. "He could hear you."

"We don't know that."

I shook my head again, nudging Nolan's leg with my foot to get him to focus back on the meeting. We needed to know these things, and if Elliot was going to keep distracting me, then I had to rely on the other three to catch me up after the call hung up.

"Did he ask about that traitor wife of his?" My breath hitched at his words, although I shouldn't have been shocked that he had an idea of what James would ask me for. *"I would be interested to know more about her as well if we're being honest."*

"Leave her out of this," I defended. Vanessa and I might have a complicated history, but that didn't stop the instinct to protect her from someone who had caused her pain, who had forced her to leave a life behind for one on the run, constantly fearing for her life.

"Ah, there you are." He laughed. *"It's good to hear your voice."*

I clamped down on the words within me once again, instinctually biting my tongue too tightly, refusing to let him have any more.

"I hope you have a wonderful rest of your day," he said abruptly, as if making me crack under his pressure was enough for him. *"Until next time."*

And with that, his presence in my mind disappeared.

I slumped my shoulders a bit, Nolan's foot now tapping my own to remind me he was there. I looked at him, shaking my head to let him know Elliot was gone. But for how long, I didn't know.

I was getting better at ignoring him and letting him talk himself out until he left. Yet, he knew how to push my buttons and get me to crack and talk back to him. Was this only the beginning of what this tattoo linked between us? What else was he planning to do with this chain now created between us?

How long would my strength hold out before I gave in?

My heart splintered at that last question, threatening tears to spill down my cheeks. I could do this. I could make it through this meeting, and I would because I would not give the High Faction another reason to doubt me.

Somehow, with the ghost of Elliot's presence still lingering in my mind and forcing a chill to settle deep into my bones, I found myself looking to where my father sat in the High Tribune chair of the Varg Anwyn branch of the High Faction. The man who had caused me so much pain, who had put our family's position and legacy above the safety and health of his children. A man who had chosen the side of my rapist if it meant saving face. The man who had forced me into hospitalization and made his youngest son tell me. Who had groomed his oldest son to be a mindless soldier and follow every one of his orders.

A man who didn't see a family but pieces to be used at his whims.

And yet, even with that, my gut twisted into painful knots knowing I was keeping this secret from him and the rest of the High Faction I had sworn to report to.

Once again, I was the disappointment he was so convinced I was.

CHAPTER 10

Nolan

Kasha hadn't spoken since we started this meeting.

After we hung up with the High Faction, she said she needed time alone and bolted from the room as we gathered up the rest of the Hierarchy to start the brainstorming we were expected to do.

She had come back once everyone was assembled, a tired smile on her face that she was attempting to hide. We all acted as though we didn't notice, even though my gut churned, my impulse telling me to reach out and help her.

But I couldn't. This battle was within her own mind. It was hers to fight.

He had been talking to her again. He had been in her head while in front of the High Faction. She had been strong through it all, she had kept her composure, but at what cost? She looked like she was about to fall out of her chair, her eyes glazed over and her frown lines deep.

Desperately, I wanted to reach out, to soothe her in ways I

had in the past when in crowds. With soft words spoken into her mind, just for her. But she wouldn't let me in, and my heart cracked each time she shut me out.

Logically, I knew why she was doing it. Safety precautions, as we didn't know how he was doing this or what she could do to combat it. But to be shut out when she needed to not feel alone the most was excruciating on my soul. It twisted it into knots, made that whispering, second-guessing voice begin to talk in the back of my mind. Trying to remind me that I hadn't kept her safe the last time she faced this man, so what made me believe I could help her stay safe now?

Was I worthy of being her partner?

Yes. I had to keep reminding myself. Yes, I was worthy of her. My partner, my paramour, my equal.

I could not let the bad thoughts win. I wouldn't let them at a time when she needed me the most.

"I think we need more than five people on that base." Lucas tapped his fingers against the table, helping to bring my attention back to the conversation at hand. "The towns and cities around that area are so spread out; traveling is going to be terrible. If we assign more, then they can go out in smaller groups to cover more territory."

"I agree, but ten is too much for one," Beckett said, pointing at our roster of names currently in our Faction. Deltas and Derchtas would primarily be sent out, but Omegas, Fledglings, and Gammas would also be going. The Keturi would be staying on Compound for the most part, to facilitate the different groups, collect their data, and then prepare it to be sent to the High

Faction as soon as possible.

"Seven then," Lucas countered as if he was haggling at a shop.

As Beckett went on, discussing with Lucas the pros and cons of sending five soldiers to the far west base of Seathra instead of seven, I looked at the woman I had fallen in love with. Helplessness settled in my veins, weighing down my chest with a pain I was not unused to. Yet, it didn't make it hurt any less.

I wanted to help her, to protect her, be there for her. I wanted to do…something.

Anything.

Yet, there I sat, listening to my teammates talk, all while she sat idly by. If he wasn't torturing her whenever he wanted, she would be at the forefront of this planning. She would want to be the first to know all the numbers, to calculate, and begin strategizing on how to fight them. But she wasn't and watching her barely be able to follow along broke a bit of my heart with each minute that passed.

And still, I could not come up with a way to help her.

I shook my head, taking a deep breath and turning back to the team. "In the end, we must get people out to all the bases, and we don't have enough people to spare the extra soldiers, even if it is the biggest base."

"You're right" Beckett nodded. "But I suggest we plan to have the team we send to the base that is south of that one head on up to assist if they finish early."

"That should work." Liv drew on the large map of Seathra that we had tacked onto one of the walls. She was creating borders for each team to oversee research in, to see if we could figure out a basic idea of Elliot's numbers. Something my gut was telling me wouldn't be the easiest to nail down.

"I think it's time we take a break," I suggested.

Half of Seathra was assigned, and it wasn't just Kasha who looked exhausted. We were all carrying a burden we weren't entirely prepared for. The burden of war loomed over us like a dark cloud, and we had no idea how much time we had to reconcile that fact in our hearts and minds before it was upon us.

We needed to prepare, both logistically and personally.

Everyone nodded in agreement, people pushing up out of their chairs and opening the conference room door to escape somewhere else for a bit. I leaned over, grasping Kasha's hand and tugging slightly to get her attention. "Come to my office with me?"

She nodded silently. Her frown didn't waver, but she allowed me to lead her out of the room, her fingers tightening around mine as we walked down the hall and to my office.

When I closed the door and turned around, she wrapped herself in my arms, my heart settling at her closeness and the delicious scent of vanilla musk. I pulled her up against me, settling my back against the door and letting her be, allowing her to leech anything she needed from me: comfort, warmth, strength. If I had it to give, I would have gladly passed it on.

Her body started to shake in my arms, my heart clenching as I looked down to see the tears streaming down her face. I gently leaned her head back, rubbing my thumb along her warm cheek to wipe them away.

"How can I help?" I whispered, silently pleading that she give me some kind of direction.

"I need my mind back," she finally spoke, the words quiet, almost broken, shattering me. "Can you give that to me? Can you make him go away?"

"I wish." I leaned forward, kissing her temple. "But we will get you the answers. One way or another."

"How can I ask that of her, Nolan?" She rested her chin on my chest to look up at me.

I took a deep breath. "You wouldn't be doing anything to her, because you would never betray her like that. Even if it's tempting to do so." The sag of her shoulders told me I had guessed correctly. "If someone was requesting knowledge about you, wouldn't you want to be told about it?"

She gnawed at her bottom lip, briefly contemplating. "Yes, because after everything I've been through, I deserve to know when people think they have the right to information about me."

"Do you think she deserves that same courtesy?" I reasoned. "I get the mindset that even asking her would be selfish, but telling her what was said about her is something she has a right to know about."

She let out a loud groan, gently banging her forehead against me. "Why does life have to be so Goddess-damn complicated?"

I pulled her close against me again, praying that the answer to that question would magically appear in my mind. Yet, everything stayed blank.

What if that isn't enough to help her?

CHAPTER II

Kasha

After a much-needed nap, some lunch, and far too long pondering what I should do, I made my way to the townhouse, where guards stood watch over Vanessa.

My stomach still churned with a bit of unease, wondering if talking to her was the right thing to do. If my actions were selfish or not.

But she had a right to hear what was being said and discussed about her. So, I went to the house she was being held at. I didn't even knock, walking right past the guard on duty. She was in the kitchen, a soft smile on her lips as she noticed me enter.

"Hello, Kasha." She was still wearing the gray linen pants and shirt set that all prisoners were issued, but at least she was showered and clean. Her cheeks had filled out again from eating. "They told me you were on your way. Would you like some tea?"

She had settled into the one-bedroom house well. She had been moved when I had been in Folanoch, a courtesy after trying her best to help the Faction find me. So, besides a guard keeping watch, she was confined to the home.

"Sure." I sat down at the table, clutching the mug she sat down in front of me before taking the seat opposite.

"So, to what do I owe the visit?"

"I took your advice."

She stopped her mug a few inches from her lips, looking over it at me. "Oh?"

"I went to visit James."

She sat up a bit taller. "And? Did he tell you anything?"

"No." I shook my head solemnly, wishing I had a better response. "Instead, he tried to bargain with me for information. About you."

She froze before looking down to place the mug back on the table. "What…What did he ask for?"

"He asked me where you were." I bit my lip, my fingers numbing a bit. "When I told him I wouldn't tell him your whereabouts without your expressed permission, he told me to get it, and then he would give me answers."

Hurt flashed through her gaze. "I see."

"I didn't tell him." I squeezed the cup tighter in my grip, still filled to the brim with mint tea. "And this isn't me coming here to ask."

"It's the least I owe you after everything I've done."

"Even so." I shook my head, looking up at her. "I would never ask it of you. To risk your safety after everything James and Elliot put you through. I wouldn't feel right about it."

"I don't even know why he wants to know." She rubbed the bridge of her nose gently. "If Elliot had a say, I'm sure he wishes

James thought of me as dead."

"I remember talking to him about you in Folanoch." The memory of that fight where he opened up about her and told me about their past was still fresh in my mind. "I think a part of him still wishes for you to come home one day. To him."

She dropped her chin to her chest, running her fingers through her long, wavy brown hair that framed her round face. I didn't think I'd ever seen her hair so wildly free before. "That is not my home anymore."

"I know." Even though Vanessa had once been a part of Elliot's cult, she had escaped. Although it didn't condone her allowing Elliot to read my patient file and get his hands on my history he had no right to, I couldn't fault her for self-preservation. I could never trust her as a medical professional again, but I was inching towards forgiveness.

In times of brewing war, things were put into perspective. Holding grudges against those who had admitted their wrongs and working towards betterment and forgiveness was a weight that was not worth holding onto. Which was what was helping me on my journey to forgiveness for Vanessa and Caleb.

It brought a lightness to my chest. To my soul. And to my wolf. A bright spot in a sea of turmoil that had become my life.

"I ran away from him just as much as I ran away from Elliot's cult, even if I still loved him at the time." I didn't miss the intentional use of the past tense in her words. "He can't know where I am. I…"

"I know." I nodded. "I won't tell him."

"Kasha, I want to help you. I really do. I—I—"

The fear in Vanessa's eyes was excruciating, her trauma and past swirling within them. She had told me everything she had been through. How Elliot made it seem like she was helping people through their addictions and trauma, when in reality, he was using her medical professional opinions to see if her patients were strong enough to undergo his disgusting Alchemist experiments. How she had fled and been on the run ever since. How, when Elliot found her, he threatened her, unless she let him finish reading my medical file.

Even with the sting of her betrayal still pinching at me, my heart twinged.

"Vanessa…" But my words cut off. Something slithered up my spine, like a warning. It was one I would get if I felt like I was being watched in public, but we were alone.

I wanted to throw up, knowing I was recognizing his intrusion, marking it as familiar to me. Even worse, he didn't speak or interact. He didn't say anything. Yet, with my spine tingling and my mind almost heavier, occupied in some twisted way, I knew I wasn't alone.

He was there, waiting.

A new tactic perhaps? A way to slowly go insane?

I waited, Vanessa looking over at me with a concerned look, but I said nothing to her, just stared ahead. My hands slid to rest on the table, bracing myself for what was to come.

Time went by, yet no words entered my mind. No comments or attempts to talk. Just a presence, unwelcome and uninvited.

"Leave me alone!" I screamed into my mind. He had already intruded that morning. What did he want now?

No response came, only that lurking, slithering caress raking over every inch of me. It began in my mind and slowly branched out to cover every inch of my skin and bones. Again and again and again.

"Go away. You aren't welcome here." No response. *"Get out."* Nothing.

I dropped my head into my hands, staring down at the table, my fingers curled into my hair to scratch at my scalp. "I …it needs to stop! Stop, stop, stop!"

I screamed the words into the room and within my mind, trying to get his horrible presence out, to make the invasion stop. I rocked back and forth, my breathing ragged, my insides curling in on themselves. Everything was wrong, gross, and tainted.

Could I survive this?

"Kasha." Vanessa's voice was soothing in my ear, but she didn't touch me. "You need to breathe."

"I-I-I—" Words were never easy for me in the height of a panic attack. Where was Nolan? I needed Nolan. He helped me through these so well.

"You can do this. Nolan is a wonderful partner, but you can do this on your own. You have before and you can again." I didn't even realize I'd said it out loud. "Now breathe in, count to five, and then breathe out. Make each inhale and exhale as slow as possible."

My mind fogged, spiraling into a darkness I had come to know so well, where I tried to destroy myself from within. But I focused on her instructions, pulling in my first breath, shaking and unstable. I kept it slow, counted to five, and released.

I did it again. And again. And again…

Finally, I pulled a stronger breath, my shaking insides slowly calming, my mind pushing out of the desperate spiral.

The ghost of Elliot's presence finally released me, disappearing from within like smoke on the wind.

He was gone. For now.

I completed five more cycles before looking back up at her, her tightened expression full of concern. "Thank you."

"That was all you." She patted my shoulder, the first contact. "Was he talking to you?"

I shook my head. "But I know he was there, lurking. To remind me he can come and go as he pleases." I gagged, clutching my chest and dry heaving a few times. Luckily, I kept my food down somehow. "Why is he doing this?"

Vanessa pulled her chair up next to me, angling herself so I could see her face directly. "I don't know. I wish I did so I could give you answers."

Exhaustion began to settle in my bones, my vision blurring a bit. I leaned back in my chair. "It's fine, Vanessa. I'll figure out another way forward."

"You might not have time." She rubbed her hand over her face. "Not when I know we can get the answers from James sooner."

I sat up, my heart skipping a beat at what she was leading to. "I can't let you do that."

"No. I still don't want you to tell James where I'm staying. I can't let him know that." She reached down to clasp my hand, squeezing it tight. "But maybe he'll answer your questions if I'm the one who's asking them."

CHAPTER 12

Kasha

"You don't have to do this," I said to Vanessa for probably the two dozenth time since we arrived at the prison four days later.

It had been difficult to get the first favor from Evette. It was near impossible to not only get another approval letter for a visit to James but for her to secretly sign off on letting me bring Vanessa. It took a lot of convincing, and ultimately, I had to agree to go straight to her after this meeting and discuss the reason I had been asking for them at all.

The request made me doubt, my voice lost, until she promised to keep what I told her a secret from everyone else until I was ready to let answers out. I had still been reluctant, but Evette had reached out a hand to me when I was scared I had no allies on the High Faction. She made sure to fight for me when I needed it, and I had to trust that she would hold true to the promise.

So, I had agreed, and Nolan and I had a meeting set up with her that afternoon.

I tried not to think about it, focusing on the reason I was back in the morbid prison.

Vanessa and I stood outside the same interrogation room I had met him in before. We had given her a change of clothes so she wasn't in a prison uniform herself, not wanting to give any clues to James about her typical whereabouts. We had pieced together an outfit from mine, Liv, and Eden's closets, her evergreen knit sweater, black pants, and leather booties understated and comfortable. She had brushed her hair and made a simple braided crown along the top of her head, letting the rest fall freely down her shoulders. She looked almost like herself again, from when I first met her at the clinic.

She stopped to turn to me. "You deserve answers and I know I can get them for you. This was a long time coming. I'd rather it be with armed guards and him chained up than outside these walls."

"I don't feel right about this," I admitted. "You've been running from him for so long. You shouldn't have to see him so I can get answers."

"Answers to a problem that I was a factor in creating." She looked at me, fierce determination in her gaze. "Did you ever consider that Elliot might not be after you if he hadn't gotten his hands on the medical files I let him look at? It was in there he confirmed certain suspicions of you."

I had thought of that, but I pressed my lips together, refusing to speak it out loud.

That was answer enough for her as she continued, "I've been running from my past for too long, and after everything I did to protect myself, let me make amends to you. Let me apologize through my actions and not just my words."

That softened my heart, a tense smile pushing at my lips. I needed her help. She needed to find a way to eradicate the guilt that must still have been eating her up over what she did so long ago. Maybe not just to me, but to the other patients Elliot had her work on. Perhaps, through helping me, she felt like she was apologizing to those lives tortured or lost.

"Okay." I nodded. "But let me go in first, check to make sure he is in a decent state of mind. If he's agitated in any way, it might not be the best idea to bring you in there."

"All right."

I patted her shoulder, steeling my mind and heart again before pushing my way inside. The room was set up exactly like before, two chairs in a claustrophobic room, a table, and a chained-up James.

"Did you bring me the answer I asked for?" He didn't even wait for me to sit down.

"Hello to you too." I stayed by the door, my arms crossed against my chest.

"You wouldn't come here for just anything, Kasha." His voice was even and calm, posture as relaxed as it could be within the lengths of chains keeping him contained. "I'm assuming you got what I asked for."

"I can't answer that question and I won't tell you where she's been staying." I knocked on the door, signaling to let her in. "But I brought the next best thing."

When Vanessa stepped over the threshold, James tried to stand up abruptly, but the chains kept him secured to the chair, the rattling echoing loudly off the stone walls. His face paled, eyes unblinking as he stared up at her. The door closed, the air thick with tension as Vanessa stood there, staring at the man she once called her husband.

"Hayden." His eyes lit up at the sight of her, my memory reminding me that Hayden was Vanessa's given name before she changed it after leaving Elliot's cult.

"Hello, James." She nodded, somehow keeping her composure as she moved to sit in the chair across from him. I took up a place standing next to her.

"Where are you staying? Are you all right? Are they keeping you safe?"

She frowned, her brow furrowing. "I won't tell you anything except that I'm safe."

"Good." He sighed. "I'm glad you found a place to hide for now."

I gulped, staying silent as I promised to for the start of the conversation, but my insides tightened a bit at the last two words he spoke.

She shook her head, biting her lip. "Tell us what Elliot is doing to Kasha. Tell us about the experiment."

"You grew your hair out." He ignored her question, still roaming his gaze over her to take in every inch of the wife he hadn't seen for many years.

Vanessa reached up to stroke the ends of her rib-length hair, her cheeks pink. "I prefer it this way."

"It looks beautiful on you."

"Thank you." The words were barely above a whisper, a stunned expression on her face as she stared at him for a few silent moments. After a minute, she shook her head, breaking the trance he had on her, and stiffened her spine. "I came here to get the answers you were denying Kasha."

"Technically, she didn't hold up her end of the bargain." He looked at me.

"I'd hope seeing me would be better than just knowing where I was living." Vanessa leaned forward, staring her ex in the eye. "I'm here, proving to you that I am alive and well. I'm safe. Now, allow her to start feeling the same and answer her questions as best you can."

He gave her a soft smile, awe in his gaze. "You were always the best physician, Hayden. It was one of the things I loved most about you, how well you took care of your patients."

Her fists balled on her lap. "James, please."

He sat up a bit straighter in his chains, the pensive look on his face making his jaw tic, the scar across his face going taut. At least two minutes passed. My breath caught in my throat as I waited in soul-churning agony for him to say something, anything.

For him to help me just as he had once before because of her. Because I was her patient.

"I wasn't lying last time you were here when I said I was no Alchemist." He slumped into the chains. "I don't know the particulars, but Elliot came up with this bond as a way to replace a matrimony oath for our future king and queen. He said it was even stronger than one of love and a piece of paper. This tied the king and queen together, blending their abilities so their strengths and weaknesses could balance as one. A true united leadership for the people."

"Is that why he can get into my head so easily?" My voice shook over those words.

He nodded. "Yes. Part of the bond breaks all barriers before the Varg Anwyn queen and her Shrivika king. It showed ultimate trust between the two leaders to set an example to Kazola that through that trust you would bring the Isle and its people into a golden era."

"All barriers?"

"The mind link was the first step," he explained. "The first snapping into place. He said there were three links in total, but he only ever spoke of the mind link since it was to be the first. I don't know the others. He used to talk about how it had to be accepted on both sides of the bond. It could not be forced."

"I did not accept him into my mind," I growled at him, heat rising in my chest.

"My only guess is that you were weakened from blood lust and he was able to sneak his way in." He looked me up and down. "Now that you are back to full strength, he will not be able to get away with that again."

"Can I block him out?" Ignoring him made him eventually leave, but I didn't elaborate or tell him how I couldn't trust my own mind. It seemed there could come a day when I couldn't trust other parts of myself either.

I could lose myself completely if I wasn't careful.

"I don't know, but if there is, it might be difficult to construct," he said. "The point was to break barriers, not remake them. If you want him to stay out of your mind, then you'll have to come to an agreement with him."

"That's not an answer, James," Vanessa chided.

"That's the best I have, Hayden." He looked at her with that forlorn gaze. "If you want him to stay out of your mind, then you'll have to talk to him."

"Like I trust him," I mumbled.

He turned back to me, eyes softening. "That's all I know about it. When it came to his experiments, he kept them close, rarely even letting other alchemists around to assist him. He would talk about the basics to me, but more as a friend discussing work woes than a detailed briefing."

I knew that was the truth, and I didn't expect him to know the science behind it all. Still, the only man who did was one I refused to see. At least I had a better understanding of what was happening to me. That knowledge, at least, was a start.

I nodded to Vanessa, who stood, both of us turning our back on him and walking away without another word. There was no more for me to give, nothing else to say, and it seemed Vanessa felt the same. I raised my hand to knock on the steel door to signal that we were ready to leave, but James's voice from behind made my fist pause an inch away.

"He wrote everything down in journals. They would have been in one of his offices in Folanoch, either in the house or the labs. The details of how the bond was formed and what it entails would be in there."

"Why are you telling me this?" I asked.

"I still believe you are to be my queen, Kasha," he said, truth in every word. "Even so, you deserve to understand what is happening to you, so you can make the right decision. Find the journals and give them to a trusted Alchemist. Have them decipher what Elliot came up with. Only you can decide if you are ready to accept your fate from the Goddess or not."

I looked over my shoulder at him, giving him a nod of thanks before pounding my fist against the door. Vanessa stood next to me, the tremble of her hands knocking against my own. I looked over, the conflicted look on her face palpable with confusion and fear.

The guard opened the door, but before we could leave, James called out, "I love you, Hayden. I never stopped."

Vanessa paused, not turning back to look at him before running out the door and down the hall.

CHAPTER 13

Kasha

W e stopped by the cells at the Château first, my heart lurching a bit knowing this was the only place we would be allowed to let Vanessa stay overnight while here. I asked her many times if she would be all right. Her distant nods that she would be were a bit concerning, but the pensive look creasing her face showed me she needed alone time. So, Nolan and I went right to the meeting we had promised to attend once we were done with James.

Evette's apartment had become a bit of a comforting place for me, from the black stone fireplace that glowed with flames to the abundance of soft seating and oversized décor pillows everywhere. Even the little chirps of her pet lovebird, Mango, while he perched on her shoulder added to the soothing nature of this place.

Evette herself lounged on the long, velvet teal couch that was the statement piece of the room. She looked comfortable, even dressed as if ready for the council chamber in high-waisted magenta pants and a deep navy-blue blouse, paired with a pair of nude heels. The whole outfit brought out the cool undertones of her deep umber skin. A smile graced her lips as she saw me, her warm brown eyes welcoming. She stood from where she sat on her couch. Kyler, my old Alpha and current High Faction Delegate stood as well from his place across from her, having come even at the last-minute request I had sent ahead to Evette to invite him.

She approached right away, coming to shake my hand and then Nolan's. "I hope your elusive visits to the prison have been educational."

I quirked a smile, loving her typical straight-talking nature. "Yes, I think it was."

Kyler stood a bit hesitant a step behind, worry creasing his brow. I took the step toward him this time, knowing he needed a bit of reassurance that I was no longer angry with him over my court case. He had proven to be on my side, and there were far worse people who sat on the High Faction for me to worry about.

"Good to see you again, Ky." I reached out to hug him gently, which he happily accepted. When we pulled away, he shook Nolan's hand.

"You as well. Both of you." His pitch-black hair was pulled back into a smooth ponytail that flowed down his back. He was dressed in a pair of black slacks and a dark plum-purple button-up shirt, which complimented his copper-toned skin. A simpler version of what had become his style choices since joining the High Faction. "Please sit."

Nolan and I followed his gesturing to one of the cream velvet loveseats. Once we were settled, Kyler sat next to Evette, who was on the matching couch across from us.

"So," Evette said, leaning over to rest her elbow on the arm of the couch. "A deal is a deal."

I sighed, my hands reaching down to grip my knees, Nolan's arm slung over my shoulders in support. "Yes, it is."

"Why did you need to see James, Kasha?" Evette's tone was gentle, not demanding, yet a shiver still ran up my spine, fear pulsing in my veins at telling my story again.

Letting more people in. Letting more people learn the truth.

I looked at Nolan. His encouraging smile and the warmth of his hand squeezing my shoulder gave me the stability to turn back towards the High Faction Delegates and tell them everything.

"So." My voice was horse and shaking by the time I was done, exhaustion settling in my bones from partially reliving it all. "Can I have the journals?"

My heart dropped when neither of them spoke right away, their glances moving to look at each other. Evette worried her lower lip between her teeth.

"What is it?" Nolan asked, sitting up straighter. "You have the journals, right?"

Kyler nodded. "Yes. They were collected during the sweep of the town. We have them stored in the vaults here."

The vaults were below the High Faction's Council Chamber, almost impossible to penetrate, and held only the most dangerous evidence that had been collected since Kazola's beginning. I swallowed a lump in my throat, my heart pounding. They weren't taking any chances with Elliot's fanatic ideas. They would rather store them in a dark, pit-like vault than let an Alchemist get their hands on them to study.

"The vault," I echoed as if trying to believe the words myself.

Kyler nodded grimly. "Which means…" He cut himself off, shaking his head in sorrow.

"It means that we cannot give you approval to take them. Not us two alone." Evette leaned forward, even Mango looking somber with the melancholy aura that now penetrated the room.

I swiped my fingers through my hair, gripping gently at the roots as I processed this. It was a part of the law that the only way to get something from the vault was to petition the High Faction to release it into your custody. My heart sank even deeper, my body instinctively leaning closer to Nolan.

"We will happily fight for you to get them if you want to present your need to the rest of the High Faction," Evette explained. "But if you want them, you will have to tell them and call a vote."

I let out a deep groan, shaking my head as I looked at the ground to think. I had hoped I could easily grab the journals and leave, but even I knew that was wishful thinking.

I needed those journals. I needed to not wonder if my mind was a safe place.

But did that need supersede my desire for privacy? Would I be strong enough to speak this story again, in front of all those who had once called me a liar and voted against me?

"We can find another way," Nolan whispered. "If you aren't ready to tell them, maybe we can…"

"There is no other way. I don't have the time to find one. This already took far longer than I wanted it to." I shook my head, knowing my words were true, even if I wanted to believe in Nolan's hope of finding a different path. "If there is time for an emergency hearing in your schedule, then I would like to petition the High Faction. Tonight."

Evette and Kyler each gave me a grave nod before Evette stood and walked out of the room, mumbling that she was going to find her assistant to run immediately to add my petition hearing to the agenda for the evening session and fight for it no matter what.

My lip quivered as the truth settled in my veins, my head falling to lean on Nolan's shoulder. He was quiet next to me, but firm, allowing me to lose myself in my thoughts. I was running out of options, and I was barely holding onto my sanity each day. I needed to get my hands on those journals no matter what. Even if what I had agreed to made me want to vomit.

I had agreed to tell the rest of the High Faction.

I had agreed to tell my father.

CHAPTER 14

Kasha

"We call for a vote," Imogene, the High Tribune of the Shrivika branch stated, her gaze heavy on me.

That caused a hush to settle over the room, gazes removed from me, allowing me to finally take a breath from where I stood on the raised platform I had presented my case from. Nolan stood next to me, although he was but a silent companion, standing tall and proud, allowing me to tell my story in my own time.

It had been even more painful than I had expected. The weight of their stares, the judgment that settled around me, the questions they had berated me with before I had even finished talking. Why hadn't I told them sooner? What was he saying to me? What was the point of it?

Every single one had twisted my insides tighter and tighter, forcing me to talk through the turmoil that raged within my soul. Speaking to them about something that was cutting so deeply, that was once again making me feel violated and terrified, felt like betraying myself and all the progress I had made over the weeks.

The vote was quick and ruthless. It was in less than a minute that I got my answer, yet it felt like an eternity as I held my breath and watched the hands rise to approve the journals being turned over to me.

I finally let it go when the majority agreed. Even my father.

They even voted to let me oversee who would be the Alchemist to research the journals. Although they stipulated that I was only allowed to give the Alchemist the journals that pertained to the tattoo and none of the others. The rest would need to be returned to the vault once we found the correct ones.

I had agreed, not willing to rock the boat when I was finally getting somewhere.

After a few other details were finalized, and they let me know the journals would be released the next morning, they dismissed the meeting. They filed out first, Nolan and I standing at attention as we waited for everyone to leave before we filed out as well. I stepped out of the Chamber, my shoulders dropping. The soldiers on duty closed the imposing, heavy doors behind us.

Caleb stood quickly, dressed in his formal uniform, even though he wasn't permitted to come into the room like Nolan had been. "How did it go?"

"They'll be giving me the journals." The words were good ones, even if my exhausted tone made it seem like I was unhappy with the outcome. I began to walk away, my steps slow. "Let's go, I'm hungry." Both men followed me, Nolan starting to wonder out loud where we should go and eat when steps pounded behind us.

"Excuse me, Beta Mallanis?" A voice called to me from down

the hall.

We stopped, waiting for the willowy man to catch up, his breathing a bit heavy once he got there. "Yes?" I asked.

"High Tribune Mallanis would like a private word with you."

My veins ran cold. "I'll pass, thank you."

He gulped audibly before saying, "It was not a request but an order."

I gritted my teeth, fists forming at my side. Ordering me? *Ordering me?* Like I was nothing more than a soldier who barely knew him. Although, I suppose, that was where our relationship had evolved to.

With tension laced in every bone in my body, I half said, half growled, "Bring us to him."

"Oh… he said only…"

"Nope. It's all three of us or none of us." I walked on, figuring he was back in his office. The aide scurried to catch up, Nolan and Caleb right behind him.

If Father wanted to see me, then fine. If he was going to order me, then I would follow like the well-trained Guard member I was.

Didn't mean I was going into the lion's den alone.

★★★

Father was not happy to see Nolan and Caleb with me, but he didn't comment. He sat behind his desk, the high-back black leather chair almost dwarfing him with its ostentatious look. He raised his fingers, curling them back in summons for me to come closer, as if I were a dog waiting for its master's orders.

I tried my best not to growl at the demeaning gesture as I stepped forward, Nolan and Caleb staying at attention by the door.

He appraised me silently, probably to draw out my anxiety and fear; the things I had a deep feeling he liked to instill in everyone, including his children.

Finally, he said, "Haven't you brought enough attention to our family, Kasha? You had to make this whole war about you as well?"

My eyes widened at his words, my chest shaking. "Excuse me?" I bit out, somehow able to get the words out as my wolf shifted within me, already sensing a threat rising in the room.

"That whole speech, trying to get our sympathy for something you could have stopped." He shook his head. "You're lucky the rest of the High Faction feels guilty over what happened with the Logan case, or those journals would be staying locked in the vault like they should be."

Was he really saying all of this? Blaming me for the kidnapping, torture, and experiments that were performed on me? For the fact that a psychopath now spoke in my mind? That he was torturing me?

Every time I thought we had reached the bottom of what lengths my father was willing to go, he did something to prove he was far from as good as I once believed.

"You voted yes," I argued, my fingers twisting together behind my back.

"Yes, for how would it look if I didn't allow my daughter to learn what was happening to her?" His face was so cold and passive. "Do you even know who you plan to hand them over to?"

I let out a shaky breath. "I was planning on telling Nana Aggie." She was the only one I trusted with this, and with her family all being heavily involved with the government, she kept all of her necessary credentials and security clearances up to date even though she didn't actively research or work for a lab.

Father leaned back in his chair, nodding slowly. "Yes, that will work. We will bring Mother here…"

"No," I stopped him abruptly. "We will be going to her."

"I would prefer it if she came here."

"Yes, I got that." I snorted, shaking my head. I was done with propriety. We were not in the Council Chamber or in front of other members of the High Faction. He was no longer talking to a Beta of the Onyx Guard but his daughter. "However, the High Faction agreed to let me take the journals back to Seathra and deal with them there. That is where we will be going. That is how this will be handled."

Father let out a haughty laugh. "So determined, I see? And tell me, daughter, where has that determination gotten you over the last year?"

I swallowed, the brunt of his words hitting me square in the chest, dark, evil memories trying their best to play through my mind and torture me once again. Logan's teeth sinking into my neck. Father coming to tell me the High Faction's ruling. My blood coating my bed as it seeped from my gaping neck wound.

The burning of a tattoo puncturing my skin. Elliot's melodic laughter seeping into my mind.

It engulfed me and ruined me, it forced me to look away from the man in front of me, the shame making my gaze fall to the floor. My insides twisted, my mind and heart trying desperately to find the strength I had worked so hard to regain. I had survived all of that. I had made it through.

So why was this what made it all fade away as if it never existed?

He stood slowly, fingertips resting gently on the top of his desk. "You will do as I say. You will stay here for the duration of your research, you will call Aggie to help here, and you will be staying with me in my apartment."

"Why would you even want that?" My words were soft but weary, thoroughly confused over this behavior. He had been doing everything to keep himself as removed from my 'drama' as possible. He avoided me and only seemed to care when it was convenient for him or when he thought people were watching and judging him. To want me to stay here, when the High Faction deemed it unnecessary was off.

"Because I am done letting you wander around this country with such lack of control." He shook his head. "I taught you better than that. I taught you to take pride in your family name. Now, you continue to ruin it and I must put a stop to it. You wanted my attention, fine. Now, you have it. Now, you get to relearn everything you seemed to have forgotten about family loyalty and all that is expected of us as legacies in the Guard and the High Faction."

Each word sliced through me, depleting me and any strength I had gained to talk against him. Instead, I regressed, back to a time when I always listened to him. When I was in my early teens and desperate for his approval. When I wanted to make him proud as my older brothers had. When he had complimented me for my shooting skills and how proactive I was for learning to train with a bow and arrow before I was even in the Guard.

A time when he was my father and not my High Faction leader.

I was small and meek, each word he spoke slicing into my chest, cutting deeper and deeper until I would eventually bleed out and give him everything he desired. Until I was nothing but a hollow, mindless follower with her father's approval.

My insides shook as he continued to rant, "You're going to prove that you can be the good soldier I raised you to be…"

"Leave her alone!" The voice boomed from behind me, powerful and demanding. Yet, it didn't come from Nolan like I would have expected it to.

It came from Caleb.

Father's gaze darkened. "Excuse me, son?"

"I said to leave her alone." He lowered his tone, menacing and deep as he strode to stand beside me, and my spine straightened.

"You are out of line, Alpha." My father's words were low, his lethal gaze trained directly onto his oldest son.

"Am I?" Caleb mocked shock, placing his hand over his heart. "Or are you just stunned to see me speak words against you?"

"Caleb…" I whispered, reaching out to pull him back.

Caleb smirked at Father, whose face was twisted in confusion. "I must say, seeing that baffled look on your face is much more satisfying than even I expected it to be."

I knew my mouth was gaping, Caleb's words of defense and defiance settling over me, shocking me and shaking me to my very core. He had been trying to prove to me that I could trust him. Slowly, I had been seeing him in that brotherly way again, the stain of his betrayal slowly washing away. I knew he would stand beside me, especially while navigating the minefields that had become my life.

But what I hadn't expected was for him to outright defy my father, to speak against him. To defend me to him.

"You are the most loyal of my children." Father studied his oldest child. "Stop trying to make it up to your sister and follow the orders I gave you all those months ago. You stand by me on these matters, not them."

"Loyalty and trust are not easily obtained between two people, and they shouldn't be easily broken if a solid foundation is built," Caleb said, my gaze wholly trained on him, unable to look away as I watched him gain more and more confidence in his words with each spoken. "It is not built on fear and lies and manipulation. It is not maintained by ideas brainwashed into a child's head until it is all he can think about. And it is certainly not upheld when an older brother has to sit by and watch the sister he has loved his whole life be torn down again and again and again by a man who was supposed to love her unconditionally."

"These are not your words." Father shook his head, disbelief creasing his usually stoic face. "They are hers or Oliver's."

"Oh, no. See, Ollie and Kasha had all but given up on me." Caleb stalked forward. "These words are the ones I've been repeating in my head over and over for weeks now, ever since realizing how horrible you truly are. I wondered if I would ever get to say them to you. If I would ever find the courage to let you know how I feel about you. So, I suppose I should thank you for giving me the perfect opportunity to do just that."

Father balked at him, eyes wide and mouth gaping. My chest swirled with something akin to glee, all of my attention transfixed on the two men who had been with me since the beginning of my life. I couldn't say I ever expected this to happen, but I was thanking the Goddess I was there to witness it.

"My sister has been given permission to do whatever she wants with those journals. The High Faction, which includes you, gave her that freedom." He took a step back, coming to stand next to me once again. "It is her right to learn what is happening to herself as she sees fit, not you. So, kindly shut the fuck up and let her do that."

I couldn't help it. I laughed like a deranged lunatic, the boisterous sound echoing off the walls and ceiling. My chest burned at the inability to pull in a proper lungful of air, my head shaking. Caleb looked over to me, smirking at my reaction, while Father sighed as if not surprised at my outburst.

But I couldn't help myself. Even before his betrayal, Caleb never spoke to Father this way. To witness this showed that Caleb really was coming out of his daze. He was starting to become the man the Goddess always intended him to be.

He was becoming himself, and I was all of a sudden very eager to learn exactly who that was.

Once my laughter calmed down, Caleb's words helped to remind me who I was, even in front of our father. I straightened, looking up and forcing myself to keep my father's gaze. "Now, if there is nothing else you need, *High Tribune*, we all need rest before we collect the journals and head back to Seathra. We will see you later."

I didn't allow my father to say another word as I yanked Caleb away from him, spun on my heels, and walked out with my brother and paramour in tow.

I almost collapsed when we exited his office, but Nolan's arm was there to catch me, wrapping around my waist to keep me steady. I looked up to him. "Thank you."

"Of course, sweetheart." He smiled gently.

"Ugh, this day keeps getting worse and worse." I scrubbed my hands down my face, not even caring if it smudged the cosmetics I had lightly applied before the meeting.

"You need food and rest," Nolan encouraged.

"She needs to punch our father in the face," Caleb grumbled, which made me chuckle. "Seemed to make you feel better when you punched me last time you were here." He shrugged nonchalantly, although a dark look cast over his face for a second before disappearing with the memory of that day when everything changed for him. When truths were set free.

"He may be on to something." Nolan chuckled, and I lightly smacked him on the chest with the back of my hand. "What? You started liking me a lot more after you got a few punches in as well."

I dropped my head to my chest, shaking it a few times. "Even if that was an option, I'm too tired to throw a decent punch."

"We can go back to our room…" Nolan's voice trailed off,

already knowing what I was going to say.

"I don't want to stay here tonight." My mind was too exhausted, my body too weighed down with the events of the day. I needed to be somewhere the expectations of everything I was about to do didn't weigh on my shoulders. Where I didn't feel watched and judged. Which certainly did not describe the Chateau. "Let's get a room at an inn or something in the city."

It wasn't ideal, but we didn't have many other options.

"Or," Caleb cleared his throat, "you can come stay with me for the night."

CHAPTER 15

Kasha

Sleeping was far too difficult. Yet, for the first time, it was not because of my fear of Elliot.

Paranoia was still there, and I refused to let anyone else in until an Alchemist gave me straight answers about it all. Yet, it was a step forward, which alone gave me an extra sliver of calm after a few too many weeks of chaos.

But I still couldn't sleep, my insides trembling and my hands and feet numb. Every bone in my body felt weighed down with exhaustion, begging for rest, but my mind would not stop running a mile a minute, thinking about everything, sometimes so fast I was barely able to contemplate the random thoughts that passed through. It made my skin sensitive, having to push Nolan to the other side of the bed and the covers off me.

It was like coming off an adrenaline rush after a battle, which I suppose was exactly what happened in my father's office. A battle that was a long time coming, yet completely unexpected at the same time.

Being in Caleb's space, trying to sleep in the guest room of his penthouse on his Compound, was not making it any easier. I had no idea how I went from hating him only a few months ago to lying in his residence feeling…safe. Protected.

It was confusing and made my heart twist. It was a good thing, a soothing thing, yet…

After too many hours of tossing and turning, trying to get myself to calm, I gave up. Quietly getting out of bed, I pulled one of Nolan's sweaters over my head to cover my sleep shirt and shorts. I yanked on a pair of socks before tiptoeing to the door, closing it as quietly as possible behind me to not wake Nolan.

I trudged into the darkened common area, clicking on a single lamp to illuminate the space. I poked around his kitchen cabinets, which he had rearranged since the last time I set foot inside his penthouse, until I finally came upon a glass. Pouring myself some water, I downed half of it while leaning against the counter, taking a shaky breath after swallowing.

I looked around at the open concept space, the oversized kitchen with black stone countertops and slate gray cabinets. It overlooked the living room with its navy-blue couches and cream-white accent chairs that surrounded a glass-top table and mist-gray stone fireplace.

I always thought this place was very Caleb: simple, clean, and efficient.

Although, after watching him with Father today, it made me wonder if this space was really Caleb or someone else. Was it Father? Or what Caleb designed with Father's expectations in mind?

Making up with Caleb was a rush of relief and created anxious curiosity all in one.

"Are you all right?" The voice came from behind me, making me jolt and spill a splash of water onto my sweater.

Clutching a hand to my heart, I turned to see Caleb standing in the threshold to his bedroom in black flannel sleep pants and a white cotton shirt. A concerned look creased along his chiseled features, his dirty blond hair bed ruffled and half falling in his eyes.

I gave him a tentative smile. "Couldn't sleep, but I'm fine."

"That doesn't sound fine." He shuffled closer, the oversized island between us.

I shrugged, a pang aching in my chest. "For me, it's normal. After…everything, I don't always sleep through the night."

And it was, even before my time with Elliot. It all started after the rape, when I was terrified to fall asleep in my townhouse on the Seathra Compound, knowing that the man who had attacked me slept only a few houses away. Didn't matter that I had added multiple locks to my door, even my bedroom, or kept my daggers next to me. I couldn't sleep, but I also refused to leave the house. Then the clinic stay was just as bad, although since I was surrounded by physicians, they drugged me enough to get me to sleep until morning. Now, with Elliot's voice in my head and trying to combat it all while preparing for war… no wonder sleep was impossible.

Guilt flashed across his face. "Oh, I guess that makes sense."

Awkwardness settled in the air, our gazes flicking around the room at anything but each other. I honestly had no idea what to say in this in-between place with him. When we had a topic or a focus or other people around, it wasn't as bad. Yet, in the middle of the night, when it was just him and I, it was like our shared past hovered around us waiting to remind me of all the bad we had been put through, the hurt and pain.

It clogged my throat a bit, choking me, keeping me from reaching out with something, anything to say.

"You didn't always sleep well after Mama died either," Caleb stated, so evenly my gaze lifted to look at him. "I remember when I came to visit for a few days after her Last Rites. I caught you trying to sneak out of the house."

I let out a breathy laugh at the memory, the words helping to clear a bit of my mind and voice. I hadn't slept the best after her death, the Last Rites the first I had ever had to participate in not the easiest to deal with. Father never noticed when I snuck out and wandered the streets of Ilfra. Half the time, he wasn't even home that late, choosing to stay at the Chateau and work all hours of the night.

But Caleb had, intercepting me outside my window with his arms crossed and a disapproving look on his face at his baby sister's antics.

"You didn't stop me, though," I whispered.

He shook his head. "I went with you instead."

"Every night until you had to go back to your Faction." My chest swelled at the memory, even more coming back from our times growing up.

Caleb teaching me to swim in the pond behind our old house in Seathra.

The three of us going shopping for birthday presents for Mama and Papa.

Him patching up my scratches after I fell from a tree when Lea and I were playing in the woods, and then taking me back out there to teach me how to properly climb.

Him being there, a prideful smile on his face when I was sworn into the Onyx Guard. He gave me the biggest hug before I was sent off to my assigned territory for Omega training.

He had always been there. Even through his pain, he had made sure to be there for me.

He was a good brother until he wasn't. Yet he was trying to be a good brother once again. Even better, he was trying to be himself, and my heart knew that was what mattered the most.

"Thank you." I took a step forward, placing my half-full glass on the countertop before moving around the island halfway.

He cracked an amused smile. "Well, I knew you were gonna try again the next night, so I figured at least you could have someone armed with you just in case."

"No, not that." I creased my forehead. "For standing up for me today. With Father."

A startled look flashed across his face, stunning him momentarily. "Oh."

I smiled. "I am eternally grateful that I was able to witness you telling our father to fuck off for the first time. Ollie is going to be extremely jealous when I tell him."

He sighed, coming around the island to stand in front of me. "You shouldn't have to thank me for that, Kasha. It should never have to be something that surprises you so much that you thank me."

"I'm not doing it out of surprise, I'm doing it out of relief." I didn't have a better word for it, but that lightness that settled in my chest at witnessing what he did today, at knowing Caleb was speaking out for not only me but himself, spoke volumes.

His head dropped, chin to chest, shaking back and forth a bit. "I hate that it's gotten to this point. I hate that even now, while I try to fix things with you and stand up for myself with Father, I feel like it will never be enough. I can't help but wonder if I'm just delaying the inevitable."

"And what's that?"

He looked up at me, his eyes glassy. "That I am going to become him. That no matter how hard I try to find myself, to change, he's too ingrained in who I am to expel entirely."

The terror in his words was potent, a fear he probably hadn't known to exist until the truth of it all came out over the past few months. But with reality settling in, I wondered how much it plagued him at night or during the day. Was he second-guessing every decision he was making, both personally and professionally? Did he constantly wonder if those around him were judging him or lying to him? Was he worrying at every moment if he was the problem?

For the first time since we chose to work towards repair, I related to Caleb. I understood his struggles, and all I wanted to do was alleviate the burden as best I could because never would I want him to go through what I did.

"There is a big difference between you and Father, Caleb, and today was the perfect example of that." Warmth bloomed within me as my words flowed freely. "You are rectifying your mistakes and trying your best to be better. Father is continuing on the same path, refusing to see anything else no matter who it hurts."

"I guess," he said, looking and sounding completely unconvinced.

"Today, I saw the man you're supposed to be, not the man Father tried to create." I took a step forward, grabbing his hand in mine, and his body tensed. "Keep exploring that. Find what makes you happy. Don't worry about Father or me or Ollie. Find yourself above all else."

He reached his hand up, squeezing my shoulder tightly. "Thank you, little sister, for not giving up on me."

"Thank you, biggest brother, for saving yourself before it was too late."

I reached out, hugging him tightly, his arms coming around my shoulders to hold me close. With so much going on around me, to have this moment with my biggest brother healed something within me, soothed and repaired it in a way I worried would never happen.

We had been through so much that I wouldn't have been surprised if it was an impossible break to fix. Yet, we were there, in the darkness of midnight and the moon reflecting through the windows, finding our way back to a good place.

The craziness of my life was far from fixed, but at least I had something to look forward to. Because my brother was finally free, and I couldn't wait to be with him while he discovered exactly who he was meant to be.

CHAPTER 16

Kasha

We returned to Seathra the next day, driving as hard and fast as possible to make it home by early afternoon. The journals arrived later that day in a well-guarded transport cart. Once we had gone to retrieve them from the Chateau, we realized there were many more than expected. Well over five dozen. Luckily, we were able to find someone willing to start driving immediately to make it to our Compound.

The conference room table was now littered with them. Nolan, Eden, Greyson, and I began the search for the right ones. Elliot took very detailed notes about every experiment he had ever created. And as an Alchemist obsessed with trying to make everything better and improved, he had many, many notes.

At that point, we weren't able to understand what most of the words or experiments meant. So, we had come up with a list of keywords to work off of to at least help narrow down which journals we would need to set aside. Words like bond, tattoo, ink, blood, Ibridowyn, or even prophecy. However, two hours into looking through them, we had come up with nothing.

I threw my third journal onto the no pile, grumbling under my breath as I pulled the next one on top of the stack. Crumpling a bit into my chair, I tried my best not to let the doubts take over my mind. I tried not to let myself fall into wondering if this was just a wild goose chase.

"Some of this stuff is insane," Eden mumbled.

"You actually understand it?" Nolan peeked over the journal he was working through.

She shrugged. "A little. At least, some of the stuff I've come across about wolfsbane. Looks like he was trying to find different uses for it, or even try to make it less addictive."

I raised my eyebrow at that. "Seriously?"

She nodded. "Blackthorne too. Don't get me wrong, I don't understand the how, but I learned enough about the drugs growing up to understand the basic make-up and chemistry. He… wanted to find a way to harness them for better use, I think. His experiments, though, seemed… well, brutal doesn't even begin to cover it if I'm reading it correctly."

"Goddess," I muttered, shaking the memories of my time in that hallway out of my mind.

I had to find the answers. I needed to get rid of the worry clenching at my insides. I needed to take another step forward until I was free of this man, getting him out of my life and mind for good.

Another hour passed before Eden's stomach started to growl, Greyson trying to conceal a burst of laughter. "Shut up," she mumbled to him, shoving him lightly on the shoulder.

"Make me," he challenged, a whisper of a smile on his face.

"Why don't the two of you go and eat?" Nolan suggested.

"Don't have to tell me twice." Eden shrugged, marking her place in the journal she was working on before standing up and stretching her arms over her head. "Coming?" she asked Greyson.

"Yeah." He stood as well, shrugging a jacket over his black sleeveless shirt. "Want us to bring you both back something? We were planning to make shrimp scampi tonight."

"Not hungry," I mumbled, even though my stomach ached and it was becoming increasingly difficult to keep my eyes focused on the words.

Eden gave me a questioning look, studying me. "I'll bring back something just in case for both of you."

"Thanks," Nolan said, smiling at his two Gammas as they headed for the door.

When Eden and Greyson left, Nolan turned our chairs, yanking mine closer to him. It startled me a bit, my hands instinctively going to the arms to hold myself steady before he stopped me, my legs now settled between his.

I quirked an eyebrow at him. "Can I help you, Alpha?"

"Say it."

I swallowed, biting the inside of my cheek. "Say what?"

"Whatever it is that's buzzing about inside your head." He tapped my temple with his finger. "Because I can see it written all over your face."

My heart lurched, my hand reaching up to gently graze his cheek. "You know me too well."

"I know." He kissed the tip of my nose. "So?"

"What if this is all for nothing?" I whispered the horrible concern into existence. "What if he didn't write anything down about what he did to me?"

He tilted his head at me, appraising me before saying, "What if?"

My brain stalled, shocked by his words. "Excuse me?"

"Well, what if that's the case?" He gave me an encouraging smile. "Think through the train of thought. Don't block it out this time."

I squirmed a bit in my chair, a wave of dizziness spinning my mind. "I—I don't know if I want to."

"I know it's uncomfortable, but try," he encouraged. "Think of it as a case theory we're working through. If this was a question you needed to analyze, where would you start?"

I sat up a bit straighter, rubbing my hands up and down my thighs, my fingertips a bit numb as I tried to think through the question. I contemplated before saying, "If we go through the journals and find nothing, then I am back to square one."

He tilted his head. "Are you?"

"Hm." I thought of his words, thinking back to that first time Elliot spoke to me. "I suppose not. James gave me some answers and I'm getting better at making him leave eventually."

Nolan smiled at me. "Yes, you are. So, what will you do if we don't find anything here?"

It was hard to focus through the cloudiness in my brain, but I forced myself to think on the question. "We could also send out letters to other Factions and see if they found any other hidden towns during their High Faction sweeps to find out more about

Elliot's military numbers. Maybe something came up and another lab was found."

He nodded. "That's certainly an option."

"We could also talk to some of the other Alchemists we found in the lab in Folanoch," I said, able to start seeing different paths forward a bit more clearly now. "James said he mostly worked alone, but maybe they know where other facilities are that we could find more journals in."

"Good." He reached out, squeezing my knee. "But remember, Kasha, that is the worst-case scenario, not the current reality. We've barely made it through a quarter of the journals we have here. If life was easy, we would have picked up the first journal to find the answer, but we know that's never the case. It's going to take time."

"You're right." I nodded slowly, letting those words settle in me.

It wasn't the answer I wanted to happen, but it was an answer at least. It gave me an idea of what to prepare myself for if it came to pass, and it helped settle a bit of the disorder that had been swirling in my chest since I cracked open the first journal. Letting my shoulders sag a bit, I moved forward, wordlessly and awkwardly climbing to settle myself in Nolan's lap.

I needed his warmth, his closeness, and he didn't object at all, my legs slung over one of the arms of his chair while he cradled me in his arms. I rested my cheek against his chest, taking in a deep, soothing breath of citrus spice. It made the dizziness dissipate a bit, the shaking of my fingertips settling.

"How did you know that would help?" I curled up closer to his chest.

"My psycho-physician did that for me whenever I voiced a question that scared me." He drew circles on my back, resting his cheek on the top of my head. "It's not fun, I know, but thinking through all of the possible answers would help me breathe a bit easier. It made me feel prepared to figure out a way forward if any of them came true."

"What kind of questions did you worry over?" I asked curiously, needing a bit of a distraction before I decided it was time to go back to work.

His arms tightened around me. "What would happen if we never got Cleo's killer? What would everyone think of me knowing I was unable to protect her? What if I was incapable of falling in love again?"

The questions he asked broke my heart, making me burrow closer into his embrace. He was such a light-filled person, it seemed almost unbelievable that he would have ever worried over those thoughts. But I knew how easy it could be to hide the pain, and I knew he was probably even better at it than most.

"At least I was able to disprove one of those wrong." He tilted my chin up to look at him, love and devotion shining in his bright green eyes.

"Thank you for trusting me with your heart." I placed my palm over his chest, feeling the steady beat underneath.

"Thank you for giving me a safe space to heal the rest of it." He closed the distance between us, pressing our lips together. It soothed the last of the nervous thoughts that had been circulating within me for hours. It refilled me with encouragement and love, giving me yet another reminder of how lucky I was to have found a man like him.

The Goddess had truly blessed me, and I was thankful every day.

Eventually, we pulled away, pressing our foreheads together, our breaths mingling. He brought me back to center, gave me peace even when I wondered if it was impossible.

He was my forever and I his, the truth of those words settling deep in my heart and soul and warming me from the inside.

"So, what do you want to do?" he whispered, the breath breezing across my cheek, making me shiver.

I took a deep breath, pecking his lips one last time before removing myself from his lap and settling back in my chair, pulling my abandoned journal back to me. "We keep looking until there are no journals left."

CHAPTER 17

Kasha

We didn't find any answers that day. Or the next.

By the third day, we were halfway through them. We had been stopping and taking breaks as we continued to get information from our Faction members who were out in the field collecting the numbers the High Faction requested. The due date for them was looming, and we were finishing up the reports and everything.

Even with my little side project that I wanted to dedicate all of my time to, I wasn't one to neglect my duties as the Beta of this Faction. I was still a leader and would act accordingly. It also helped that this endeavor was more research into Elliot and his cult.

On the third day, mid-afternoon, I sat in my office, Lucas and Taylor with me sorting through the journals we had left.

Still, nothing.

I threw my twelfth journal on the floor and picked up a black leather-bound one from the stack of unread, refilling my coffee before cracking open the spine and beginning to scan through the words again. They were starting to blur together.

The three of us sat in silence, the lack of talking or jabbing a bit unsettling since I was in the same room as my two Gammas. The flipping of paper and the occasional scratching of a stilo were the only things to break it as they continued to stare at their own books, reading with almost identical perplexed, scrunched-up faces. They looked a bit more alike when they did that.

Could I chalk it up to being focused? I suppose. But I had never seen them sit this well-behaved in the many years we had known each other. Honestly, it was a bit unsettling to not watch the twins poking and picking on each other or making a competition over who could find the first journal with the key words. That was who they were, as brothers and around me, so this silence felt...off.

"So, are you two going to tell me what's on your mind, or do I need to beat it out of you?" I peeked up from my journal, both men sitting rigid in their seats.

"Uh…." Taylor said, mouth gaping. "Excuse me?"

"You're overthinking something and trying to keep it from me." I shrugged, leaning back in my seat. "I would rather you tell me."

"We aren't overthinking," Lucas tried to deny.

I looked back up, shooting them a look that screamed I didn't believe one word he spoke. "I know from personal experience when someone is overthinking." I could be crowned the queen of overthinking on my best days, let alone my worst. Especially recently.

Taylor shook his head. "It's nothing, we just…" He turned to his twin, silently begging him to say the words he either couldn't come up with or couldn't say himself.

Lucas sighed, putting his journal down. "The rest of the Hierarchy got to talking while you and Nolan were away."

My insides twisted, my throat closing. "Oh?"

"Not necessarily about you but how we've treated you over the past year," he clarified. "With you coming back to work so soon after your kidnapping, we felt the group of us really needed to talk about how we could be better at supporting you."

I was shocked by their words, my jaw hanging open as I processed it. All of them were closer to me than just my co-workers or even friends. They had become my family over the years, creating a safe space for me to grow as a Varg Anwyn and a leader in the Onyx Guard. I wasn't sure I would be the Beta I was without them.

"Why are you all questioning this?" I finally asked. "You've always been there for me."

"But…" Taylor leaned forward in his chair. "Were we supporting you in the ways you needed, or the ways we thought you needed?"

Ah, now I was seeing what they were getting at. This past year specifically.

I looked at them both. "You supported me the way you thought was best."

"And we watched you struggle for a long time," he said. "We thought we were creating a safe space for you, so you could heal and not worry about daily stresses or other things we noticed had triggered you. We thought we were protecting you."

"But when Nolan came in, he wasn't afraid to push you," Lucas continued. "And that's when you started to speak up again and take back who you were. We watched your confidence and strength slowly build back up. Like you needed that extra push to get past the fear and discover it all once again."

My shoulders deflated. I had noticed that, and I'd guessed that part of it was because Nolan hadn't known me before the rape and life attempt. He knew who I was after and hadn't been afraid to push when I was holding back, comfort me when I felt weak, or let me take the lead when it was time to discover things on my own.

It had been the final step I needed.

"Sometimes, I hated you all treating me like I was fragile," I admitted. "It made me feel weaker than ever when those who knew me the best were worried I would break."

"That was never our intention," Lucas said, sadness filling his bright blue gaze.

"I know it wasn't, that's why I never brought it up." I shook my head at that. One lesson I learned over the weeks was to not keep the emotions bottled up; it tended to lead to some rough times. "But when Nolan was so open with pushing me, with not being afraid to call me out or get me to open up when I desperately needed it, yeah, it did help."

"All of us would like to have that back with you," Taylor continued. "Just…don't be afraid to tell us what you need."

I bit my lip, trying to hide my smile. When I looked back on the past year, I couldn't begrudge them for treating me a bit softer, even if in the lower moments I disliked them for it. They had watched me go through agony and I might have done the same if I had watched one of my close friends go through everything I had. I would have wanted to wrap them in a warm blanket and let me take care of them because that was what we always used to do for each other. Still, it hadn't been helpful in this instance.

But the fact that they realized that too and they wanted to change, to adjust and help in the way that was best for me, made my heart warm.

"Here is what I need from you all." I cleared my throat. "Don't treat me as broken. Sure, watch out for triggers, and if I start to panic help me through. But when I am holding back or letting my trauma get the best of me, then push or let me take the lead."

"We get it, and we can tell everyone else." He nodded.

"And you can always ask Nolan what he does to help." I shrugged. "I highly doubt he's going to be upset to hear you all want to learn how to help me with my coping techniques. He's more the expert on how to support me."

They both smiled at that, Taylor's a bit goofy as he said, "Aww, how cute."

I glared at him. "Shut up, Taylor."

"You're in love. How can it not be cute?" He laughed before puckering his lips and making over-exaggerated kissing noises. Even Lucas was annoyed as he shoved his brother's shoulder.

I rolled my eyes; this was the dynamic I was used to. "Anything else you two are hiding from me?"

"Just one thing." Lucas picked up his discarded journal, standing up and slapping it onto the middle of my desk. "Found the first reference."

Taylor groaned, leaning back in his chair and shaking his head as if we had all silently agreed to play 'the who finds it first' game. Yet it stirred reality back to me, hitting me square in the chest.

We had found the first journal, which meant there were answers hidden within them.

One step closer to the truth.

CHAPTER 18

Kasha

The peace of riding on my lectracycle with not one but both of my brothers and my paramour riding beside me was much more settling than I ever expected it to be. It almost felt like coming home.

After we had discovered three more journals with the keywords we had picked out, we headed to our next stop: Nana Aggie's.

We didn't know who else would be out there or who would report to the High Faction first and myself second. Figuring this out was important to the battle against Elliot and his coup, but I was the one who was directly affected by it. I was the one who had her body defiled and her choice taken away. Again. I was the one who was slowly being taken over by another person, not the High Faction. They had given me the right to choose who went through the journals and how I wanted to proceed with finding a solution. So, that was exactly what I would do.

I needed the answers first. I needed to process them, and then I would pass them on to the rest of my team and the High Faction. This time, I was choosing myself instead of the oaths I had taken. A part of me felt a little guilty about it, my resolve threatening to crack, but I knew this was how I had to do it. For me and no one else.

Plus, it was a bonus that Aggie had worked with Elliot when he was also a State Alchemist. It had only been a year, but he had made enough of an impression that Aggie was able to recount details about him decades later.

We broke through town lines, navigated the streets of Accriton, and made it to Nana's front drive in record time. We parked our cycles in a line, my brothers coming up to stand on either side of me, Nolan's arm already tightly slung over my shoulder.

"You ready?" Caleb asked.

I tightened my hands around the straps of my backpack that was holding the journals. "Now or never."

We took a collective deep breath before letting ourselves in the front door. Aggie was waiting for us at the entrance.

"My grandbabies!" she boomed, a giant smile on her face as she wrapped us all into a giant bear hug, nudging Nolan out of the way to get all three of us. I was squished right in the middle.

"Suffocating in here!" I jokingly said, my voice muffled by the mixture of limbs holding onto me.

"Moonlight." My brothers pulled away so she could look at me properly, her warm hands coming up to cup my face. "How are you healing, my darling?"

"On track according to Beckett. I didn't have the opportunity to even try and rush back to work until cleared with Nolan taking care of me." I took a step back, nudging him playfully in the ribs with my elbow. He laughed, stepping forward and offering his hand to Nana.

"Absolutely not." She reached up, pulling him into a hug as well. "For the person who saved my granddaughter, we do a lot more than shake hands."

He melted into her embrace, even though she was a few inches shorter than him. "It was worth it, ma'am."

"No ma'am here either." She pulled away, swatting his arm. "Only Aggie."

"Thank you, Aggie." He smiled that wicked grin before stepping back to sling his arm back around my shoulder. "Unfortunately, there is no keeping her in bed any longer."

"I was cleared for field work again." I gave a tight smile. I left out the detail that I had been cleared for weeks now.

Fear and sadness passed briefly through her gaze before she forced it away and back to joy. "Good." She kissed my forehead gently before pulling back. "Now I have all of you here, let's get to work."

We went right into our usual tasks like the old habits they were, Ollie helping Nana with the last of the cooking, Nolan joining them, and Caleb making coffee and tea for everyone while I set the table. Within twenty minutes, we were seated around the large round table in the bright, plant-filled dining room, the array of sweet and savory dishes scattered around utterly tempting.

"Was Nana Aggie nice to you in the kitchen?" I asked between bites of the mushroom and gruyere quiche. "Or did she try and kick you out multiple times?"

"You make me sound like a control freak in there." Nana raised her eyebrow at me, a teasing smile on her lips.

"You only let Ollie in there," Caleb pointed out. "Kasha and I have been permanently banned."

"Because you're both hopeless." Ollie laughed.

"Sweetheart." Nolan patted my shoulder. "I love you dearly, but even you told me that."

"Yes, but I'm allowed to say it about myself, my brother isn't!" I threw a half-eaten piece of bacon across the table at him, which instead of hitting him in the face, he caught between his teeth.

Nolan laughed at the spectacle. "Either way, Aggie was very nice once I showed her how quickly I could dice an onion."

"He's quite useful, I will say that." She tipped her glass to him.

"Maybe next time I'm here you'll be able to teach me some of your secret recipes?" he asked in that charming way of his.

"That is an earned privilege. These recipes are for family eyes only. Will I be calling you that one day soon?" She winked at him, and my cheeks burned even brighter. I had to force myself not to slide down my seat and hide under the table.

Nolan's cheeks pinked deeply, but he laughed off her words. "If I have a say in it, yes, I hope so. Although maybe we get through some of our current work problems before that."

"Yes, I suppose that's fair." She sighed dramatically before turning back to me. "How is everything with your investigations? Hopefully coming along the way it's supposed to."

We weren't allowed to tell her anything in detail about the potential war, as the High Faction deemed it highly classified.

Still, she knew enough about what had been happening over the weeks to know it was big.

"As good as it can be," I responded. This was the perfect opening to talk about why we really came here. "Nana?"

"Yes, darling?" She looked up, putting her fork down. She must have known I needed her attention with that grandmother's intuition of hers.

"There was something I wanted to ask you. A favor."

"And what's that?"

I reached down to the bag beside me, hands shaking as I pulled out the stack of journals and placed them on a cleared spot on the table. "These are some of Elliot's journals. Mason's, I mean."

"Really?" Aggie looked at me, her hands twitching on the table.

"We've bookmarked some pages, and we were wondering if you could read through them and research a bit into what they mean." That got her attention, getting her to finally grab the journals and pull them closer. "We think the experiment has something to do with his long-term plans for Kazola."

Nana read through one of the bookmarked pages, her face turning grim. "Moonlight, why do you need to know the details about this?"

My stomach sank. "Told you keeping it a secret wouldn't work," Ollie mumbled next to me, making Nana's eyebrows raise at us in question.

"Shut up," I grumbled back. "If I told you it was classified, would you believe me?"

"Not now," she said tersely, nodding to her middle grandchild. The three men looked at me again, a combination of concern and helplessness settling in. We needed her help, and I knew she wouldn't let this go, especially since I could tell she already understood the basics of the notes written down. She must have guessed it had to do with me.

My breath shuddered a bit, my stomach clenching. I wished I could keep it a secret, but the point of going to Aggie was because I trusted her. Relenting to her request, I rolled up the sleeve of my hunter-green shirt and rested my arm on the table. On full view for all to see was the thorn and vine tattoo, complete with Elliot's initials in the center. I hated it more and more every time I looked at it, tears misting across my gaze. I had to force myself not to gag.

Aggie did a good job of keeping the horror in her expression to a minimum, but she shooed Ollie out of his seat so she could take it instead, gently grabbing my arm to look at it. "The ink has been infused with an unknown compound," she mumbled, her nose almost grazing my arm as she took a closer look.

"Yes, we gathered that already."

"Have any symptoms been emerging?" she asked. "Or side effects?"

Nolan grabbed my other free hand, giving me a bit of strength as I went over everything with Aggie. From my foggy memories of the actual tattooing to Elliot breaking my mental shields and everything James said to me when we met the other day. She listened intently, even sending Caleb upstairs to her office to fetch a stilo and notebook so she could take some notes.

After I finished, and her stilo slowed down against the off-white paper, she looked up at me, a pensive look on her face.

"I can do it."

I sighed in relief. "Thank you, Nana."

"But… you must make me one promise, and then I am happy to do as much research as possible to find out what this son of a bitch did to my sweet Moonlight."

"What's that?

"No secrets when it comes to what's happening to you." She wrote down a few more things before placing her notebooks and stilo on top of the stack of journals.

I pulled my arm back, hastily pulling my sleeve back down to hide the tattoo once again. "Of course, Nana."

"I'm serious." She narrowed her gaze at me. "I am not your nana right now, I am an Alchemist working with you. I cannot help you properly if you don't give me every symptom and detail that could impact my research."

She was very serious, a side of her I rarely saw. "I've told you everything I am legally allowed to say, and I promise to continue to tell you anything new that is discovered."

She nodded, accepting my answer. "Very well, Moonlight. Let us discover exactly what he's intended for you."

CHAPTER 19

Kasha

Waiting for Aggie to get back to me with answers was becoming torturous.

She sent me letters by Falcon Mail every day, although most said that she was still researching and didn't feel comfortable saying anything until she understood the full scope of it. She said to be patient and not overthink it.

Like that was possible for me.

I tried plenty to keep myself busy, and by the fifth day of waiting, I was thoroughly distracted with the rest of the Hierarchy as we put together the final report due in three days. More than half of our sent-out teams had arrived back to Compound, and those who hadn't were finishing up in the last towns.

The numbers were not good.

Based on our team's research and educated guesses, we had close to one and a half thousand unaccounted-for people that could be related to Elliot in some way. Just our territory. It could be so much worse in the others.

And this was an educated guess. It could be a lot worse than we ever expected.

I tapped my stilo against the conference room table as I double-checked one of the reports. Not only were these statistics making me sick to my stomach, my mind couldn't help but worry over the fact that Elliot hadn't talked to me in days, his presence gone. I would have hoped it would put me at ease, but no. I was too on alert now, waiting for it to happen.

At least when he was talking to me, I knew what his motives were in a way. The silence… the silence was terrifying me to the core in a steady constant I hated carrying around.

So, I worked, and I prayed and hoped Aggie would have an answer for me soon.

A ringing pulled all of our attention, each of us going for our Comms until the ringing one was found.

"Thank God you answered, Beckett." It was Ryder, one of our Derchtas who had been sent to the northern area of Seathra for his population research. The urgency in his voice got all of our attention, all of us sitting up a bit straighter and leaning towards where Beckett sat at the head of the table.

"What happened?"

"A fire has broken out in a small town about an hour west of our assigned area." He was frantic and out of breath, but he kept going. "We're here now, but the fire… it's destroying everything. We're evacuating everyone and trying to get it under control, but we need help."

"We're on our way." He got the coordinates to the exact town before hanging up, all of us rushing out of the room to call any available Faction members.

My gut swirled with unease. This wasn't a normal fire. Of that, I was sure.

★★★

Two more calls had come in from other areas about fires breaking out in small, rural towns in Seathra. It forced us to split up. Taylor, Lucas, and I took a team of ten other Faction members to a call that was south of us, closer to Vapalles.

We parked our cycles a mile away because it was the safest option. Running the rest, we were instantly hit by the billowing black smoke that enveloped the whole town already. I choked on it, covering my mouth and nose with the crook of my elbow, and searched for the local officers. It took time, but I caught sight of their carts, leading my team over.

"Who's in charge?" I asked, my voice muffled.

"Me!" a tall, lithe woman outfitted in brown leather armor said, approaching me. She had her nose and mouth covered with a cloth, and plastic goggles on her eyes which were shifted to red, marking her a Shrivika. "I'm Captain Laura Riggens. Beta Mallanis, correct?"

"Yes." I nodded, coughing again over the words. Her team crowded around my group, handing all of us protective gear, which we eagerly took and applied. Now, we were finally able to see and breathe a bit clearer. "We're here to help, so tell us where to go."

Sometimes, leading was about knowing when to take a step back. She and her team were already in the trenches of fighting this fire. She would know best, and she did, seizing control of the extra bodies and assigning us to different areas and teams.

I entered right into the thick of it, running through the pyre that had become the town, the blazing heat causing sweat to pool under my armor and drench my face. I could barely see. Breathing was painful even with the mask covering my face, but I pushed through.

Taylor and I headed west, almost immediately catching the howling sounds of someone trapped, screaming in desperation for help. We finally tracked it to a storefront. I couldn't tell what was sold there, all of the signs and what was once an impressive window display smothered in bright orange flames.

"Help! Please!" Someone was banging against what I believed to be the door, but a mountain of debris was piled in front of it. "We can't get out!"

I looked up, pointing. "It looks like part of the roof already fell."

"That's what's trapping the door shut." Taylor followed my train of thought.

"Don't worry! We're digging you out!" I screamed in response, crouching down to begin pulling away the three long support beams that had somehow crashed in front of the only exit. We worked in tandem, pulling them together and throwing them off to the side where they couldn't trap anyone else.

"Stand back!" I screamed, waiting only a few seconds before kicking the door down. A young female probably in her twenties screeched at the splintering wood flying across the room from the impact. Taylor and I entered, finding her crouched down, folding herself around another young girl who couldn't have been more than ten.

I coughed at the plume of smoke that clogged the space, suffocating almost all of the air. It burned, my hair sticking tightly to my face, but I moved forward, closer to the two women. "We'll get you out of here."

"She twisted her ankle!" the younger girl said, her green eyes reflecting terror and the flames slowly starting to encroach around us. "She can't walk!"

"It's okay, sweetie," I soothed the young girl, wiping a few stray tears from her bright red cheeks. "My friend Taylor here is going to carry her, and I'll carry you so we can run faster, okay?"

She sniffed, wiping her arm under her running nose. "Okay."

"Thank you," the young woman sobbed, arms opening to allow Taylor to pick her up and cradle her. She secured her hands around her neck, and he took off running as I grabbed the younger girl and followed quickly behind.

"Watch out!" the little girl screamed as the first chunks of the ceiling began to crumble rapidly.

I dashed out of the way and through the door just in time, tucking her face into my neck to protect her as best I could. And then, I ran for my life to safety.

My lungs burned with each pumping step I took, extra pressure building on them from the smoke I had certainly inhaled in the building, even with protective gear. The little hairs on my arms were singed from the falling roof, and it wasn't until I was halfway to a safety point that I noticed the sting on my cheek, wetness seeping down it. A piece of the burning roof must have nicked me as I dashed us out of there.

I had to keep reminding myself with each step that I was needed and I could not die in the flames. The smoke clouding my lungs would eventually dissipate, and any burns that were marring my skin would heal.

I could not die in this wreckage, but many others could.

I had to help them. I had to save them.

***

Three people had died as I tried to save them, but at least I had been able to get their bodies out of the flames and to a safe area. At least their families would have peace of mind knowing where they were and they could find closure during any burial rites.

But it hadn't been enough. People died here today.

Even worse, after spending hours in the flames, watching them slowly recede and die down, witnessing the destruction this caused made a dreadful, evil theory form in my mind. We all knew these were not an accident, not with so many popping up in Seathra.

This was planned. This was Elliot, I knew it.

The final check in our area had been cleared, and I stumbled out and hobbled into a safe zone. I tried my best to sniff out my Gammas, Taylor and I eventually separating, but the smoke still coating the air made it extremely difficult. After searching for twenty minutes, I came across them both guzzling down water at a parked cart.

They both looked like they had bathed in the ashes of the fire. I probably did as well.

Lucas offered me a cup of water. My parched, scratchy throat was soothed by the cool liquid. I refilled and chugged another one before turning to them. "Are you two all right?"

"We're alive," Lucas said, wiping his brow with the back of his hand, which honestly did nothing to clear up the soot and sweat all over him.

"Check in with Beckett and Nolan and get a status update from them. Then go and find the rest of our teammates and get them to Riggens to assign them duties," I told Lucas, who was already pulling his Comms unit out. I turned to his brother. "You start helping the local garrison complete the headcount. We need to know how many people are missing."

"Missing? Not dead?" Taylor looked at me, a stony expression instead of his typical easygoing one.

"I have a theory, but I have to do my own check-in first." I nodded. "Meet me back at Riggens' command post when you're done. I'm going to help her there once I finish my call."

They both nodded, running off to their assignments. I watched them disappear back into the smoke, my nerves fried and chest aching. I shook my head a few times to clear it before walking a distance away, finding a local rest stop building not far from the town line. It was crowded with people trying to find shelter as they waited for answers, but I found myself in a quiet corner in the back.

I yanked my Comms unit from my pocket, my fingers shaking

as I scrolled through the contacts to the name I was looking for. I knew when I had left the Compound that something about this was off, but after fighting the fire, seeing the wreckage, and hearing the reports of more popping up, I needed to check in with other territories. Luckily, I had good connections.

"Not a good time, Kasha!" Ollie yelled through the Comms, the inky black soot smeared across his face along with the yells and banging of commotion behind him already giving me the answers I expected.

"Are you dealing with fires too?" I leaned against the wall, crouching over as I attempted to get some semi-clean air into my lungs.

That stopped him, his eyes wide. "You too?"

"We got one under control, but another five have been re-ported," Riggens had told me during one of my check-ins with her. Since we were now under control, she was starting to send a team over to the closest one to assist. "How many are you dealing with?"

"We're up to seven, but I haven't been able to check in for a while." The screen rattled before the handlebars of his lectracycle appeared at the bottom of the screen. "I was able to ride over to another one to assist."

"I'm patching in Caleb." I was trembling, panic rising within and threatening to take over me. This was wrong, all wrong. No one was attacking, no enemy troops and that made a theory that was brewing inside my mind a real possibility. A terrifying, horrible possibility but I needed to find patterns before I spoke it out loud to them.

Caleb answered on the second ring, his face covered by the protective gear I had hanging around my neck. "What do you two—"

"Fires!" we both yelled at him before he could get another word out.

"Futecha," Caleb swore. "Hold on!" The screen went blurry, rustling and wind whipping around before he stopped, the lack of smoke signaling he had moved to a safer area. He removed his gear, the area around his eyes the only thing not covered in black soot. "We've been fighting them for hours now. As one is put out, we get reports of more popping up."

"Have they all been small, rural towns? Miles away from a city?" My fingers clenched around my Comms.

"Yes," they both confirmed.

"How did you know?" Caleb questioned.

My stomach sank. "It's the same here and I have a feeling this is planned."

"Obviously," Caleb said. "Three territories all with fires popping up? It's probably all over the country. But why attack the small towns and not the cities?"

"Because I don't think they are attacks, I think they're escapes." My breath was growing shallower, my cheeks numbing. I didn't want my theory to be true, and there was still a chance it wasn't without the final numbers, but so far, everything was adding up. "I think the fires are a way to cover up people running away to join Elliot's cause."

"What?" Ollie asked, leaning his arms on his bike.

"Think about it, people going missing in a city is common.

Sure, it terrifies the family, but all the other citizens in that area barely pay attention. His people from the larger areas can disappear without a trace." I rocked back and forth, trying to dispel a bit of the adrenaline coursing through me. "But these small towns? Everyone knows everyone, and if someone went missing it would be felt across the community."

"But if they were to be presumed dead in a fire..." Ollie continued for me.

"Where evidence and bodies are destroyed..." Caleb said.

"They can slip away without a trace." I shook my head, my heart breaking at all those people who would mourn a lost love one only to find out they may have just run away. "With everything happening at once, creating chaos, it makes it even easier for them to disappear as troops are being spread thin to contain the fires."

"Goddess, save us all," Caleb muttered under his breath. "What do you think this means?"

Dread pooled in my stomach, my body chilling even with the remnants of the fire still warming the air around me. "It means he's collecting his troops. It means war is closer than we think."

CHAPTER 20

Nolan

The knocking on my door pulled my attention from the pile of incident reports that needed to be filled out about the many fires we assisted in putting out the previous day. I looked up, Kasha peeking in before I could even say come in.

My heart flipped a bit. "Hi, sweetheart."

"Hello, sweetness." She walked over to me, pulled out my chair, with me still in it, and plopped herself right down in my lap, curling up like a kitten.

I didn't hesitate to wrap my arms around her, pulling her close to my chest. "Everything all right?"

What a dumb question. We were in the middle of a war led by a man who was torturing her from within her own mind. We had spent most of the previous day fighting fires that said man's followers had orchestrated all over the Isle. Then, exhausted and dirty, we had to sit in a three-hour-long meeting with the High Faction and other Faction Keturis to debrief about the situation.

Nothing was all right. It wasn't going to be even close to all right for a very long time.

Still, I had to ask.

"Tired. Annoyed. Stressed." Her words vibrated against my throat, her lips gently grazing over it. "I just got off the Comms with Imogene and Mitchell."

I tilted my chin down, kissing her forehead. "How did it go?"

She sank deeper into my arms, my own squeezing her tighter. "They listened, and they said after preliminary investigations and as casualty numbers start coming in from the different garrisons, they believe I am on to something."

I shook my head, letting out a deep breath to calm my racing pulse. It shook most of us to the core when she had explained her theory last night.

A group of people believed Elliot to be their savior, yet completely disregarded the bloodshed and pain he has put countless others through. It was disgusting and strengthened my resolve that I would one day see this man suffer for every person he had ever hurt. For taking Cleo, for torturing Kasha and the hundreds of others that I never met personally but knew he had harmed.

He deserved to feel their pain ten times over, and I would make sure it happened one day.

I tried my best not to think about the fact that he was in jail. That technically, he had been caught and that pain could be dealt with immediately but hadn't been. I had to ignore that because if I didn't, the boiling fury that was growing in the pit of my stomach could one day overflow. I could end up doing something I would regret, that could cause more harm than good.

I turned back to Kasha, seeking the warmth of her in my arms, reminding me why I kept fighting and working towards the end goal of Elliot gone from this world. For her. For us. For the life I realized I wanted with her.

"I'm scared," she whispered, the words almost inaudible.

My stomach flipped, my arms tightening around her. "I know. I am too," I whispered back. "You should try… relaxing."

She snorted. "What is that?"

"It's this amazing thing where you do something enjoyable to help release all of those gross, negative feelings. Does wonders for the mood."

"Oh, yeah, I've heard of that." She laughed before looking up at me, her gaze tired. "I don't know what I need right now, honestly."

I brushed my fingers against her cheek. "What usually helps?"

She pondered for a moment before looking back up at me, a glimmer of light in her silver-blue eyes. "Come with me?"

I nodded, lacing my fingers with hers as she pulled me from the chair and led me out of the office and across the way. We ended up at the guest house Lea was staying in. She waved to us quickly as she left for a run before Kasha yanked me up the stairs and to the room where half of her stuff was still being kept. We really had to find time to get it moved over to my house; there was no need for it to be here anymore.

She let go of my hand as we walked through. I closed the door, and when I turned back around, she was seated on her piano bench, pushing up the hard black cover to reveal the row of keys underneath. She laced her fingers together, stretching and flexing them, preparing.

"Are you going to play for me, sweetheart?" I couldn't help the broad smile that grew on my lips.

She looked over her shoulder, her honey-brown hair spilling out of the loose ponytail it was pulled back in, her own smile a bit brighter than before. "I still can't believe you haven't heard me play."

"There's been enough going on." I leaned against the wall.

She nodded before turning back to the piano, fingers gently resting on the white keys before they started to move. The light, melodic sounds echoed off the walls of the bedroom. It was a lively song, celebratory almost. It rang out, the ups and downs of the notes weaving together in a way that made me feel… hopeful, alive. The tempo picked up after the first thirty seconds, making it hard for me not to tap my foot along with the beat. It filled my heart, warming my chest as I gazed on.

I watched her get lost within herself and the music, her fingers roaming over the keys. She didn't even need to look at a sheet of music or the piano, her head tilted back, eyes closed as if in prayer. Maybe this was how she spoke to the Goddess, through the passion of her music, the melody conveying to Lunestia what she was going through and how she needed her.

Or maybe it was a way for her to try to inject a bit of happiness into herself when life was trying to get her down. Maybe it was the notes and melodies and ups and downs of the music that helped keep her hope beating within. It was through this music, this upbeat, lively song that she could remind herself what she was fighting for and who she was. She was strong, determined, and stunning.

Well, at least, that was what the song reminded me of, so I hoped it reminded her as well.

I listened with rapt attention, noticing every movement and sway of her body to the beat. As her fingers sped up and the final crescendo began to build, I noticed a tear slip down my cheek, the wetness startling me. I was no stranger to letting myself feel a bit more while listening to music, but when it was her playing, when I got to witness her in such a comfortable uninhibited place, it felt like a blessing.

I knew this was something she didn't allow everyone to witness, and I felt incredibly honored that she trusted me enough to be there.

The final notes rang out, her fingers slowing before coming to a full stop. She turned to look at me, her face already more relaxed, her smile less forced. "So? What did you think?"

I wiped a tear away, walking over to stand next to her. "That was stunning."

She looked up to me, her own eyes glassy. "Thanks. I wrote it a few years ago."

"You wrote that?" My mouth gaped. "Do you write all of your music?"

She giggled at my fish-out-of-water expression. "Not much, but some. It was a gift for Ollie on his thirtieth birthday. I wanted to write a part for him as well, but I knew it would be futile."

I took a step back. "I'm sorry… Ollie plays?"

"Not an instrument, but he sings." Her shoulders slumped. "Well, he used to. I haven't heard him since Mama passed. She's the one who taught us."

I nodded, my heart aching in understanding of letting go of things when they were connected to someone you'd loved and lost. Probably why I never knew he had a musical bone in his body.

"It must be really important to you then," I whispered.

"It is, but it's not just because of Mama." Her fingers still grazed over the keys, feather-light touches running over them. "It's an escape in a way, to get lost within the music. To allow myself to not care about my life, or my worries, or my fears. It's one of the rare moments of freedom I can find for myself. Even when I barely have time to sit down and play."

I reached out, squeezing her shoulder gently. "That sounds wonderful."

"Do you want to try?" she asked me, looking up with those stunning blue-silver eyes.

I tilted my head. "What do you mean?"

She stood up, patting the bench. "Sit here."

I gave her a sideways glance before settling on the bench. I expected her to sit next to me on the two-person seat, but instead, she settled herself in my lap, her back pressed against my front. I was able to rest my chin on her shoulder to peek at the piano in front of us. "What are you doing?"

"You'll see." She grabbed my arms from her thighs, placing them on the keys before slipping her hands under mine so they rested on top. "Ready?"

I nodded before her hands started to move, my fingers going along with her on the musical journey she was building. This song was different. Not as upbeat, and certainly not something you would be dancing to at a party like the last one. Yet it was one still full of hope, solemn, darker notes mixed in with a weaving of lighter ones whispering in the background. As the song continued, the darker notes started to fade into the background as the happier ones became stronger.

It was a delicious juxtaposition, reminding me, and probably all who had heard it, that there was darkness and light, happiness and sadness, within us. It was up to us to decide which we wanted to give focus and power to.

As our fingers continued to move, to create something so powerful, my heart picked up, my stomach flipping and my soul soothing. I could see why this was such a beloved thing for her. I now understood how she so easily found herself lost within. Creating like this, blending all the good and bad into something that released emotions or brought happiness and joy was easily intoxicating.

And it was even better that it was her showing me this. It made me feel even closer to her, our souls inching together. As our fingers flew over the last few notes, I buried my face in her hair, pulling a deep sniff of her incredible tonka scent. This woman... I knew it before, and I knew it even stronger now.

I wanted to spend the rest of my life with her.

When she finished, she turned around, adjusting so she was straddling me, a knee on either side of my hips, her arms snaking around my neck to anchor us together. I had no words to describe what I was thinking and feeling, so instead, I leaned forward, capturing her lips with mine and devouring her. She groaned into it, her body melting against my own, my arms snaking around her waist to keep her steady and pulling her closer. It brought me to life, fluttering beats pulsing low in my stomach, a stirring of desire growing rapidly.

She gave my bottom lip a few teasing nips before pulling away. "I love you so much, Nolan."

I reached up to push a fallen piece of hair behind her ear, allowing my thumb to gently brush against her pulse. "I love you too, Kasha."

"You have no idea how incredibly happy you make me." She kissed my warming cheeks before trailing downward along my jaw and throat, her voice rumbling. I groaned, my fingertips digging harder into her hips, my cock stiffening at her gentle rock against it.

"Kasha…" I moaned, my head falling to the side to give her better access.

She continued to explore my skin with her lips, whispering, "You make me feel so safe and protected but never stifled. You are so much more than I ever expected to earn."

"That's not true, sweetheart." My heart lurched that she had once believed that, probably still did a little. She deserved the world, one that I would happily give her wrapped in a bright bow if I could.

She looked down, bashful. "You're mine, right?"

"Always," I said with all the confidence I had. "Are you mine as well?"

"Let me show you how much." She gave me a mischievous grin before slipping from my lap and pushing the bench away from the piano before kneeling before me, her fingertips grazing the hard length of my cock swollen within my pants.

"Kasha, you don't…" I shuddered under her touch, the teasing stroke of her fingertips making my brain stop working for a few seconds.

"I know." She gazed up at me through her long lashes, a faked innocent look teasing me. "But I want to. Let me show you how much I love you. Let me savor every bit of you."

I groaned, unable to say no to her pleas. She grinned up at me knowingly, unlacing my pants and pulling me out. She didn't even hesitate, her hand gripping the base tightly while her tongue reached out to lick across the tip, my stomach clenching instantly.

"Oh, Goddess." The words slipped out and she smiled up at me before leaning forward to wrap her rosy lips around the head and sucking like her life depended on it.

"*Futecha*," I hissed. "Shit, Kasha." I really didn't know what words I was saying as she took me deeper, swallowing me down before slowly pulling back up to repeat again and again.

I knew she was talented with many things, but damn, her lips were absolutely sinful. My head fell back, my hand reaching out to cradle the back of her head so she wouldn't accidentally bang it on the piano as she bobbed up and down on my length. My head was swimming in bliss as she sucked, licked, and grazed her teeth along me, determination in all of her movements.

She was building me up quickly, my spine tingling, stomach tightening, hips unable to control themselves as they slowly thrust off the bench and into her mouth. Instead of freezing at my sudden movement, she groaned around me, taking every inch I gave her.

So, so close to giving her everything…

"Stop," I growled, gently yanking back her head, her mouth pulling off my dick with a pop. She looked up at me, her head tilting in confusion. I shook my head, gently helping her up before my fingers began tearing at her clothes, pulling off her shirt and breastband in one swoop. "I want to finish inside you."

She grinned down at me, helping to unlace her pants and shove them away, and yanking my shirt over my head. Her fingers trailed my chest, tracing my tattoos with light, barely-there touches, my skin goose-pebbling underneath. I snarled playfully before grabbing her behind the thighs, her shrieks of delight adorable as I carried her over to the bed and threw her down. The mattress underneath her bounced a bit.

I didn't wait before pouncing, sprawling on top of her and pulling her thighs apart so I could settle between. I moved my length through her wet lips a few strokes before thrusting inside, her body bowing off the bed, a joint groan of pleasure tumbling from our lips.

"Goddess, you feel so perfect." I thrust within her, holding her hip with one hand so I could push as deep inside as possible, the other arm resting by her head so I could lean down and kiss along her jawline.

Her pussy fluttered around me, her walls gripping my cock and making my head spin with the perfect tight hold she had on me. My heart swelled with warmth deep in my chest, aching for me to give her as much pleasure as she was eliciting within me.

I craved to watch her come undone underneath me with me

buried deep within her. I wanted to remind her, with every movement of our bodies together joining as one, that there was no going back. Our futures were intertwined, our paths no longer separate but forging together as one. No longer could I be satisfied without her.

She was addictive. She was perfect. She was *mine.*

"Nolan," She spoke my name like a plea on her lips. "Don't stop, harder."

I gave her exactly what she needed, my hips pistoning forward, my grip tightening on her hips to the point of almost bruising. "Like that, sweetheart? Are you sure you can take it?" I couldn't help but tease.

"Yes, yes, yes." Sweat began to bead along her forehead, her cheeks and breasts flushed, hair now free from the tie and sprawling out on the pillow below her. She looked incredible when she came undone for me. "More." She yanked at my hair to pull my head up, locking our lips and tangling our tongues together.

I gave her exactly what she asked for, my hips speeding up to give her all the pleasure I could. She finally broke our kiss, my lips trailing to lick downward to the juncture of her throat, the salty taste of her sweat on my tongue making me dizzy.

"Bite me," she pleaded, her head thrown back, her pussy clenching around me. She was so close. It was the perfect time for me to clamp down, the sweet taste of her blood blooming on my tongue as I gripped her with my teeth.

It was the last thing she needed to shatter, her scream echoing off the walls. Mixed with the pulsing of her pussy around my cock, she pulled my own orgasm with her. I released her throat, moaning my release and she leaned up to grab my throat with her teeth, my orgasm stretching out even longer with the puncture of her bite. Thank the Goddess for those contraceptive elixirs we both took each month. Or else, I would have never known the utter bliss that was coming inside of her.

My hips slowed as my orgasm abated, both of our breaths heavy and labored. Blood trickled down her throat, and I leaned down to lap it up with my tongue, her body shivering under me, her fingernails scraping down my back. When it was clean enough for my liking, the crescent shape already beginning to clot, she moved us so we were on our sides and reached up to lick my wound clean.

We lay there for a while, her eyes beginning to droop. I pulled a blanket over our naked, tangled bodies and curled around her, holding her safely in my arms.

CHAPTER 21

Kasha

I should have considered myself lucky that it only took Aggie about two weeks to finish combing through the journals, but it felt like years passed with each day.

Work had been doing an all right job distracting me, Nolan and my team trying their best to give me tasks and things to do. Still, when I least expected it, sharpening blades with the twins, watching Nolan cook dinner, or even training some of the younger members with Liv and Eden, a reminder would pop into my head. Bone-chilling fear coursed through me at the memories of what it was like to have him in my mind.

Then I would ask myself too many questions. Why had he been so quiet? Did he know I had the journals? Was he waiting for me? Was he going silent to try and bring even more paranoia back? Were the High Faction doing something to him that was weakening his ability to reach me?

Every single time I would come up with plausible answers, yet every single one of them made me want to throw up.

I tried my best to shake off the finger-numbing nerves as I let myself into her house, deciding to go alone this time instead of taking Nolan or my brothers with me. Something about finally getting some answers… I needed to process it alone with Nana. I needed to be able to ask any questions or voice anything without them.

There were times when I needed their strength, but I knew in this one, I needed to rely on my own at first.

"Thanks for coming, sweetie," Nana greeted me from the dining room.

She walked over and placed two glasses of tea down on the dining table before gripping me into a hug. I clung to her like a young girl refusing to let go of Grandma, relishing the safety her hugs had always brought. I knew she was the right person to turn these over too. She was knowledgeable and I trusted her. But she also knew me well, and she would tell me everything I needed to know and deliver it to me in a way I would understand.

After a few more minutes in her protective embrace, I pulled away, straightening myself and bracing for everything she was about to tell me.

"Sit." She pointed to one chair, moving around to the other side. "I made some mint ice tea for us to share."

"Thank you, Nana." I took the cool glass, trying my best not to blurt out anything rude, as my grandmother would never let me get away with it, even in my anxious state for answers. Finally, she settled across from me. "So?"

"All right." She pulled out one of the journals, opening to a page she had bookmarked. I even noticed her handwriting now in places on the pages. "What I think he was doing was trying to see if he could find ways to manipulate the Bridos to potentially be even stronger."

My brows crinkled. "What?"

"I know that sounds odd since you're already fortified beings, but this is more focused on the connection between only two Bridos, not a whole Faction worth." She turned the journal to me, pointing to a mark. "You were correct. It was in the mark he put on you."

"So, it's not normal ink then?" I looked up at her, the worried look creasing her face making my stomach roll. "Nana, what is in my arm?"

She breathed out a deep breath. "It's ink but combined with a mixture of your blood and his. He stabilized it with a few compounds that would mean nothing to you, but basically, it combined your Brido genetics into one. Then, when he injected you with it via the tattoo, it tethered the two of you together. It strengthened the bond Bridos already have with each other and created a private channel between the two of you."

I tried with all my strength not to vomit on the table. "I have Elliot's *blood* tattooed on me?" It was even worse than I thought.

"Mixed with your own, yes." She nodded grimly.

"Oh, Goddess." I shook my head, the whirling making the room spin a bit. "So, it really is a one-way connection?"

"No." She shook her head vehemently. "The only way to make this work is to create an even playing field with the bond. For the connection to be forged, you both need to be marked. Did you see something like this on him?"

I thought back to that night. I was so delirious from hunger everything would come back in fuzzy clips of memories. However… "He had a bandage on his arm when he got me tattooed. Does it have to be done at the same time?"

Nana shrugged. "Based on the notes, no, I don't think so. As long as it's done from the same batch of ink and blood. Although, my educated opinion is it has to be done within a certain timeframe, to make sure the mixture is properly stabilized. But I suppose he could have been marked earlier in the day and then gone to have you… tattooed."

I reached out to clutch her hand, needing the steadying presence. It was unfathomable to believe this was something he had been working on for most likely years, if not decades. How many of the victims that had been found over the years had been dedicated to this project? He had believed and preached that a king and queen would one day rule Kazola, and that there needed to be a bond other than marriage since it would be a Varg and a Shriv on the thrones. In a twisted, dark way, this made… sense?

Goddess, I hated with every fiber of my being even admitting that, but it did.

It forged them together in a way that couldn't be undone, at least not easily. It would show Kazola that their rulers had pledged to each other in a way that they could respect and rule together.

It was diabolical and madness but genius nonetheless.

Again, my stomach threatened to revolt with that terrible thought.

I looked back up at Nana, my gaze clouded with darkness. "What is it?"

"There's more, Moonlight," Nana whispered, her voice shaking.

Oh, Goddess. How could this get any worse?

"Tell me," I whisper as if we need to keep it a secret, even though we were completely alone.

"The mind talking you mentioned, it's only the beginning." She pointed out a list at the bottom of the page, bullet points marking different things. "It seems that being able to forge the mental connection is the first and easiest path for two bonded Bridos to complete. Most likely because it's an ability you already have. This is just stronger and allows each person to enter the other's mind without warning or permission."

"So, it is just talking? He can't hear all my thoughts?" My heart somersaulted, waiting anxiously for the answer to the one question that had plagued me.

She gave me a soft smile, reading my worries. "No, darling. It's just a communication path that the door can't be closed to. No mind infiltration at all. He can't just be listening in without you knowing he's present."

"Good." I let out a deep sigh I had probably been holding in since the night he first spoke to me. "So…what else?" I swallowed, dreading what she was about to say.

"Your mind link was the first step, but if you slowly start letting him in, accepting the bond in different ways, it leads to other links." She gnawed at her lower lip before continuing. "If you let him link to your senses, he'll be able to feel physical aspects for you as well."

I physically recoiled at her words, my back thumping against my chair. "Come again?"

"Let me rephrase." She shook her head, staring up at the ceiling briefly before returning her gaze to me. "He will be able to overtake certain senses. He could hear what you're hearing, see what you see, and so on. It would allow him to be in the moment with you, without being in the same physical space."

"Is that it?"

"That seems to be the second link to forge," she explained. "You would then move on to the third. The heart link, which links your emotions. He'd be able to feel what you're feeling, know your heartbeats, and even be able to tell if you're alive or dead. Based on my understanding, the full bond would be complete after that."

I scraped my hands down my face, my cheeks numb. "This sounds like something from one of my fantasy books."

It was the first thing that came to mind as Aggie described it. I had read books before about deity-blessed mates that were destined to be together. Usually, they had some kind of special bond similar to this one. However, this was completely manufactured. We didn't even have Goddess-blessed mating bonds. Although Varg Anwyns called their life partners Mates and had Mating Ceremonies, we all had a choice on who we called that. Lunestia had nothing to do with it.

This was a bastardized version of a fantasy book gone wrong. This was utter bullshit.

My right hand went to my left forearm, beginning to scratch at the tattoo that was under my shirt. Why me?

"I do have some… well, I wouldn't say good news, but better."

I tried to keep my eyes open, exhaustion settling in, my vision hazy as I looked at her. "Tell me."

"He cannot force you to link with him, even with the path started with the tattoo," she said. "You have complete control over if you want to forge the other two bonds."

"But he was able to take my mind link," I pointed out, not understanding completely.

"You were in a weakened state and probably didn't realize you had forged it." She sighed. "I know it isn't what you want to hear, but you're healed and stronger now, so the rest is up to you."

"Can he… control me with all of this?" My gut twisted painfully. "You said he'd be able to feel what I'm feeling and channel all my senses. Does that mean he can control them too?"

"Not based on these notes. He would only be able to experience them with you." She tapped a finger to her chin. "And don't forget, Kasha, this isn't just about him controlling you. This bond is two ways, which means that if he can do it to you, you can do it to him."

My head was spinning with all this new information. I tried to focus on that knowledge, reminding myself this was power in its own way. Yet, it didn't stop the slithering taint of being violated yet again—or at least the looming threat of it—sinking deeper into me.

He was trying to take pieces of me. Every piece if he had his way.

He had taken advantage of me and countless people over the years. It was time to bring his reign of fear to an end.

Emotions clogged my throat, my voice cracking as I asked, "Is there anything else I should know?"

"He did make an odd note, wondering if the bond would be passed down the generations or if they would need to be reforged, but he hasn't been able to test that," she said.

I nodded, mind spinning. I remembered him telling me in Folanoch his plan for each of us to take a consort to carry on our family lines, our individual children taking one of the thrones after we were done. Looked like he was already trying to plan how this bond would continue through them. Even thinking about my hypothetical children having to go through this made tears spill from my eyes.

No one else would ever have this forced on them. I would make sure of that.

"I hate that all of this makes sense," I mumbled almost in a daze, the shock getting to me. "James said this bond is to be forged between the future King and Queen of Kazola to replace a matrimony bond. Elliot wants to know if our bloodlines are now forged or if the heirs would have to directly link with each other as well."

"Spoken like an Alchemist." Nana gave me a weary smile.

"No, that was the Guard member in me." I forced myself to smile back for a second before my concerned frown settled back on my lips. "Does it say anything about how to break the bond? Is there even a way?"

She sighed, biting her bottom lip before gently shaking her head. "I'm sorry, Kasha, no. And with the bonds, I'd be hesitant to kill him."

"What? Why?" That was going to be my next question.

"Even with only one link in place, this bond is a strong connection." She squeezed my hand tighter. "I fear that you would not be able to survive his death. If you didn't die as well, I worry that your mind and or body would not come out of it unharmed."

My stomach dropped at her words, my head dropping to the table and my tears falling in earnest. Nana didn't hesitate, pushing out of her chair and coming to stand beside me. I wrapped my arms around her middle, her own coming to wrap around my shoulders and gently guiding my cheek to rest against her belly.

Safely in her motherly embrace, I let myself break once again. I wailed and let the pain flow free from within me, the terror and anger bubbling up to infect me from the inside out. Whatever this was couldn't be broken, or he was so paranoid he hadn't written it down so no one but him would know.

I was stuck with his words in my mind and the presence of this bond looming over me like a specter haunting my every move.

I was stuck in the in-between, and I was terrified that one day, I would not come back from it. One day, I would be so exhausted of fighting it that I would eventually give in, a shell of who I was.

"Ple—please, Nana. I can't live like this anymore," I blubbered, my words broken up by my heaving chest. "I need to make it stop! Now. Right now!"

I shook in her tight embrace, her hand gently smoothing my hair back. "Shh, Moonlight. It's going to be all right. Even if the journals don't have answers, we can find some."

"Ho—how can you say that?" A fresh wave of tears dripped down my cheeks, my chest burning. "There is no cure!"

"Look at me, Kasha." Nana moved to kneel in front of me,

taking my face firmly between her hands. "I am going to find the answers. We're going to get emergency approval from the High Faction to let me and a select team of other Alchemists dedicate all of our time researching this."

"Bu-but you're retired." I sobbed, my clouded, foggy brain unable to completely understand what she was saying.

"Screw retirement. This is more important." She wiped away some of my tears with her thumb. "I kept my credentials and security clearances up to date, and it will not be hard to prove to the High Faction that this is a necessary project that must be fixed immediately. This is a weapon that, once we figure out the cure, should be destroyed forever."

"Nana…" was all I was able to get out, my heart swelling at her determination.

"You are stronger than this man. I know you are." She leaned forward to kiss my forehead. "And I am going to try my best to find the secret weapon that will bring his whole plan down."

Although it was the best news I had heard in a long time, it didn't stop the tears from falling harder, words no longer possible as I fell back into her embrace.

CHAPTER 22

Kasha

The approval from the High Faction had come quicker than expected, only a week after Aggie had told me about all that was happening to me.

I supposed I wasn't that surprised. She had made a passionate case and used their own guilt against them along with their drive to discover as many of Elliot's secrets as possible. This link he had formed between us was becoming one of the biggest.

Aggie had collected a team of trustworthy Alchemists to join her in the research. Some from her own time as a State Alchemist and others recommended by past colleagues. Their well-packed carts full of their belongings and necessary equipment made their way up to the clinically white laboratory building that Aggie had personally requested she be allowed to research in.

My stomach churned at the sight of it, even without being in the hallways. My hand instinctively went to the Amalgam blade strapped to my thigh, gripping the hilt tightly.

"You didn't have to come with us, little shadow," Ollie whispered to me, his kind face creased with concern. "You didn't have to come back here."

My gaze looked around the eerily quiet town center where I stood with my brothers. No people milling about with creepy smiles on their faces pretending everything was perfect. No talks of the God-blessed man they followed. No guards following me around or dragging me back to the mansion.

I wasn't sure which Folanoch was worse; the one full of people who didn't seem to understand what they were doing there, or this ghost town that held the bitter, terrifying memories of a time I wished to forget.

"Nana is here for me." I squared my shoulders, trying my best to hide the deep-seated ache that was buried in my chest. "The least I can do is make sure she has everything she needs before she starts."

Caleb and Ollie shot each other wary glances but didn't say anything. I wrapped my arms around my middle, wishing I had Nolan here, to bury myself against his side, my heart aching for him. Unfortunately, the High Faction had forced him to stay behind, claiming that only one Keturi member could be gone from Faction territory at a time.

He had tried to fight it, of course. So had I. I didn't like being here without him. He had fought so hard to get me back from this prison. To be here without him made me feel vulnerable again, even without an enemy anywhere near us.

Yet I had gone anyway. I needed to go. Not just to assist Aggie but for myself. The past few weeks had been torturous, and a small part of me wanted to prove that this place hadn't taken everything from me. That I was strong enough to rise above it and heal from it.

The only way I was able to get my very irate paramour to calm down was to play a loophole in their orders and call my brothers to accompany me. Some of the High Faction had grumbled at that request but knew they couldn't say no since they both led different Factions.

"The two of you go with Aggie and the others to start unloading and setting up." I walked over to my lectracycle, mounting it and revving the engine.

Caleb tilted his head at me. "Where are you going?"

"Gotta go check on something," I said ominously. "I'll meet you all up there in an hour."

They nodded their understanding before I lurched forward and headed up towards the imposing brick building that had been my forced home for the month I'd spent here.

***

I was a bit of a masochist for wanting to come here, especially alone. Yet so much of my visits to Folanoch were spent in this room, delirious and starving.

The investigation team had stripped away any important evidence during their weeks of searching and breaking down the town. Yet, the overall layout of the room was the same. The bed with its brightly colored quilt, the chair in front of the long-since dead fire, and the books that had been brought to me, which were strewn on the side table.

Even the chair they had strapped me down to for the tattoo experiment was still here. No wonder it had felt familiar even in my haze of blood lust; it was exactly like the long, reclined leather chairs I had sat in for hours at a time when Lucas would tattoo me.

So much had been taken from me in this room. So much torture, both inflicted by Elliot and of my own bloodlust-rattled hallucinations had occurred here. Forever shaping me, forever changing me. I entered this town one person and left a completely different one.

That was the thing about traumatic moments in a lifetime. Even if you were able to move past it, to cope with the triggers and pain, you were never the same. You could never go back to who you had been.

I had learned that during my recovery from Logan's attack. I had been slowly accepting it and making peace with it. I was having to do it all over again, discovering what changes this trauma had caused me and how it would shape me.

Who would I ultimately become because of this place? Because of these people?

I shook my head, letting out a shuddering, aching breath. This wasn't the place to dwell on that, it was a place for me to prove that I could step within these walls and not break.

They had tried to break me here. They had tried to ruin me. Yet I had survived. I had made it to the end.

I was still fighting, and that was something they couldn't take away from me.

I looked around the room one last time. I took in every inch and memorized it before turning my back and walking out the door, closing it tightly behind me.

I didn't plan to enter it ever again.

I wandered the halls, past Elliot's office, and down the stairs to the second level. I hadn't spent much time searching this house, particularly because I had been locked in my room or followed by guards at all times. I had a feeling they wouldn't have taken well to me poking around in other people's rooms.

I came across a few that looked like they had once been occupied, maybe by some of Elliot's guards. When I came to the final one at the end of the hallway, my skin instantly prickled, my fingers grazing the hilt of my weapon as I slowly, cautiously pressed the door open.

I held my breath as I looked around, finally letting it free when I realized no one was here. I knew no one would have been able to hide anymore, not after reclaiming the area. Still, something about this room put me on edge, even though it was another generically bland bedroom with a blue quilt-covered bed, a gray stone fireplace, and a rosewood armoire in the corner.

I took a few cautious steps in, looking around for any reason this place might feel wrong. I peered into the washroom to see nothing useful, then peeked under the bed as well to find it empty. My skin itched, my mind pushing me to keep searching.

I followed the instinct, the soft voice of my wolf egging me on. She was trying to show me something, something I would have missed if I had run away in fear and listened to my churning stomach, going to find my brothers.

Find it. Discover it. Learn.

Then, when I opened the armoire, my stomach instantly dropped, the neat row of perfectly tailored feminine clothing lined up by type and color giving away whose room this was. Ari's.

The prissy bitch who was obsessed with Elliot and hated me. Who helped hold me captive and told me I was lucky to have Elliot's attention and obsession. Who seemed jealous that he wanted me to be his queen when she didn't even qualify as she was a Shrivika.

And that bitch had gotten away in the end.

Technically, it could have been anyone's room, but I recognized a few of the outfits I had seen her strutting around in while I was here. I pushed the clothing around, looking for anything. My skin went clammy knowing she was out there somewhere, lurking, waiting, and plotting.

She was out there, doing something I could not guess at. All I did know was that she was following orders from Elliot, one of the few hazy memories I had from my time here in Folanoch before my paramour and team saved me.

I had to figure out what she was doing. I needed to find her.

My heart leapt when I pushed the last of the clothing aside, revealing a stack of folders haphazardly strewn across the floor. I grabbed them quickly, but my hope was soon thwarted when I noticed they were all empty. I still looked at them, noticing the broken seam at the bottom of each and the remnants of labels that had once adorned the front. So, they had been used at one point, but whatever had been kept in them was now gone.

I looked at them, opening each and wondering if it had been the evidence-collecting team that had removed everything. That didn't make any sense. They would have taken all of the folders and not tampered with anything. The only reason for these to still be here was if they had deemed them unnecessary and left them behind. Or maybe they had cut corners by the time they got to this room while searching, although I really hoped that wasn't it or I would have to report them.

Something fluttered from the final folder, falling to my feet. I dropped the folders back into the armoire before bending to pick it up. My brows creased as I looked at the crumpled piece of parchment.

The edges were jagged, indicating that this tear wasn't purposefully done but ripped, maybe during a struggle. There wasn't much on it, only a partial note that didn't make much sense:

'Purchased No's: Nine'

What does this mean? I stared at the words. Whatever had been in these folders had been important to Ari, so much so that she kept them close in her own room. She had fled with them instead of a majority of her personal belongings when she had been sent away. These were most likely part of her orders from Elliot.

But what were they?

"Are you asking me, Rogthna, or yourself?" His words popped into my head, making me stumble back. My eyes darted around the room, looking for escape, or even for him. It didn't matter that I knew he wasn't here. I needed to be sure. I needed to know that I was still alone, safe from him.

Although, with this link, I would never be safe from him, not until Aggie found a way to break it. A hope I was clutching onto for dear life so I could make it through the next few weeks.

"Go away," I gritted out to him, pressing my back against the

nearest wall to steady my shaking legs.

"But you reached out to me." His words sounded so innocent, so confused at my demand. So very un–Elliot-like.

My heart stilled at his words. *"No, I didn't."* I refused to believe it, my head shaking back and forth, even though he couldn't see it. I would never reach out to him. I would never want him in my mind. I would never let myself.

And although he seemed to have no qualms about invading my mind, my stomach churned at the mere idea of me invading his without permission. Never. I would never, ever do that.

His humorous chuckle said otherwise. *"Oh, Rogthna, you most certainly did."*

CHAPTER 23

Nolan

I should not be here. I did not belong here.

I belonged with Kasha, next to her during a time I knew was probably eating her up. She needed me and I needed her. Being apart for more than a day was difficult, my insides squirming and my pulse beating a bit too rapidly with each day that passed.

I tried to calm the stirring of my protective wolf deep in my chest, reining him in and forcing him to heel to my needs. However, that was increasingly difficult seeing as my 'needs' were not my own by the orders of the High Faction.

Which was why I was currently stuck in our conference room, my fists white-knuckled in my lap as I sat with the rest of my Hierarchy team listening to the High Faction prattle on with updates from the fires and the final numbers that were expected on Elliot's side of things.

"Stop scowling," Eden's voice whispered in my mind, my Gamma peeking over at me with a wry grin. *"We may be a small square on that screen, but everyone can see you look miserable being here."*

"That's because I am," I grumbled back. Still, I tried to soften my jaw, the ache releasing a bit.

She raised one eyebrow at me. *"Hide it better."*

"I'm trying."

"Yeah, well, you're failing."

I gave her a flat stare, but I didn't have a witty response to shoot back because I knew she was correct. Hiding it was impossible because my anger was but a mask for what I was really feeling: fear.

When she had sped away with Ollie beside her to meet Caleb and the Alchemist caravan to escort them to Folanoch, my stomach had pooled with it. That was two days ago, and now it was festering within me, poisoning me, reminding me of that disgusting, horrid time when she had been taken. When I hadn't protected her. When she had been tortured, starved, and experimented on.

My stomach lurched at the memories assaulting me once again, Eden's gaze turning from teasing to concerned in an instant. *"Nolan?"*

"I'm fine." I shook off her concern, but her gaze hardened.

"She's with her brothers. They will keep her safe." She nodded back to the screen. *"See? They aren't here either."*

I took her advice and looked back to the screen, searching out Vapalles and Crelanti's Factions. Just as she said, both had their Alphas missing, the stoic Caleb and the charismatic Oliver. They weren't there because they were with their sister. They were keeping her safe and making sure she wasn't alone when she needed someone.

She's safe.

I released a tension-filled breath, once, twice, three times before my mind cleared enough, my heartbeat settling to a more normal pace.

"Thank you," I said to Eden, loosening my fingers to rest gently on my knees. *"Now pay attention. Even if we both hate it, they are telling us something important."*

I tried my best to follow my own advice and focus, the numbers Imogene was rattling off to us concerning at best, devastating at worst. We were guessing, but based on the research all our teams did and the post-investigation after the fires, at least a third of the population was gone.

We still technically held the majority, however, that was against the full population, not our military numbers between the Onyx Guard and the general military. Even if we did the math to take down some of the suspected Elliot numbers, it was becoming too much of an even playing field, and by the worried, tired looks on all of the High Faction faces, they knew that too.

"We need ways to get more of the general population to join in the fight," Imogene announced. "With the success of collecting the data and numbers, we now ask all of the Factions to work diligently to come up with ways for us to bolster our fighting numbers. We need to be able to outnumber those who fight for Elliot. So, for the next few weeks, your mission is to present us with ideas of how to convince the general public to sign up to join the military. To note, they would be joining the main military forces. As of today, all recruitment to the Onyx Guard has been put on hold."

Tension filled the room, but none of us were surprised. Between the genetic modification process we all went through and the rigorous training that was necessary to make it past Omega and Fledgling training, it was too much work that would most likely not aid in the ways we needed. Our energies and resources were best focused elsewhere.

"If they are only joining the main military forces, why are you asking your special forces team to brainstorm and not the leadership in their teams?" a member of the Luspan Faction asked. A good question.

Imogene's brow twitched before she re-smoothed out her professionally cool demeanor. "They are currently working on ways to expedite the training for the new recruits. Reformulating their typical procedures so we can move new soldiers into action quicker than what we currently have."

"We need the numbers," Anton, Kasha's father, added from his side of the room. "Those numbers are what will turn the tides of this battle we are being forced to fight."

I squeezed my hand under the table again, a burning ache swirling in my chest. But this time, it was not because of Kasha's absence but because of the High Faction's request. Sure, bigger numbers in a war was an advantage. Getting more soldiers to join the cause was a good thing and would certainly help. However, even if our technical numbers were higher, that didn't always guarantee a win.

And with a mastermind like Elliot, who used strategy and science hand in hand, we knew we were in for battles that were more than sword-to-sword fighting. There would be dirty, impressive moves. There would be ways to take down groups that we didn't know about.

There would be bloodshed, and with the disappearance of so many people, my churning gut knew it was fast approaching. War was coming.

And no one, not even the High Faction, had the confidence to say they believed we could win.

In war, there were no guarantees. We would fight, but would we win?

CHAPTER 24

Kasha

Traveling home was a relief and an anxious burden all in one.

Folanoch was far behind me, helping to settle my mind a bit with each mile that spread between us. Yet, with the long drive alone on my lectracycle, it gave my mind time to wander, to think about all that happened while back in that terrible place.

I had reached out to him. I had cut it off when I realized he was telling the truth, but it didn't make it go away. I had reached out to him.

How had I gotten to the point where I had reached out to him?

I kept trying to tell myself it was a moment of weakness, my curiosity getting the best of me along with my weakened understanding of the connection he had forced on me. I needed to be more vigilant about keeping my thoughts from wandering. I had to be more self-aware and on guard. I couldn't let anyone in and I couldn't let my mind even attempt to branch out to others.

Stay alert and focused. That was how I could stop myself from unknowingly putting myself in that horrible man's mind.

My stomach twisted, bile rising in my throat. I forced myself to take a few breaths, to calm my racing pulse down. Spinning this over and over in my mind just put me in danger while I raced down the road towards my Compound. I had to figure out a way to meditate or calm my mind down. I had to…

The shrill chime of my Comms unit brought me back to focus, forcing me to pull over onto the side of the road and fish it out of the front pocket of my backpack before answering. Immediately, the faces of my two Gammas filled my screen.

I leaned forward on the handlebars of my cycle to prop the unit closer to my face. "Can I help you, boys?"

"Maybe we can mutually help each other," Taylor teased. "How close are you to Seathra's border?"

"Less than an hour before I cross. Why?" I tilted my head, taking the time to reach back and grab my water canteen to quench my parched throat.

"We got a call from the garrison in the west that there have been reports of suspicious activity in one of the abandoned and destroyed towns." Lucas's sharp jaw was tight as he explained. "Since it was the site of one of Elliot's people, they are requesting a team of Guard members to go and check it out, see if someone from Elliot's crew is scoping it out or back for something."

I rubbed at the bridge of my nose. "What are they up to now?"

"We have no idea, and honestly, it could just be some kids playing around in the rubble and getting up to trouble, but the local team didn't want to take any chances, so they called us in to check it out," Taylor explained. "We thought you might need the distraction and would want to meet up there."

"Who's going?" I asked.

"If you join, the three of us. If you can't, we'll rope someone else as backup." Lucas shrugged. "It's not a big deal if you can't…"

"Send me the coordinates," I said. "If there is even a chance that this is Elliot's people, I want to be there."

I wasn't going to sit by and let them desecrate a town they had already destroyed.

***

I beat them to our rendezvous point a mile west of the suspected town by mere minutes. When they pulled up next to me, we didn't even exchange pleasantries before kicking our cycles back into gear and racing towards the town, parking them along the edges of the ruined town lines.

Every building within the town had collapsed into ruins due to the fires, roofs caved in, and walls half burned away to reveal the charred remains of whatever had resided there. Although there was no more smoke polluting the air, the heavy scent of burnt charcoal surrounded us, soot littering every surface and speckled within the dirt of the roads.

"Let's head towards the city center," I said, pulling out one of my Amalgam Blades, Taylor and Lucas following suit. We walked deeper into the depths of the destroyed town, taking our time to look around. We wanted to miss nothing, to make sure that when we reported back, it was with the knowledge that we had searched every inch thoroughly. We took our time, stepping closer and closer to the target of the city center.

The crunching of sand beneath someone's boots. The quick, sharp inhale of a surprised breath.

The three of us whirled around, coming face to face with whoever was tormenting this town. My eyes widened at the sight of three people, two women and a man, dressed head to toe in navy blue leather armor. A color that was not issued by any High Faction-run military unit of Kazola.

Elliot's people.

They looked identical in the well-polished outfit, a sword strapped to each of their backs, a mask made of rubber hanging from their belts next to a metal cylinder that clinked against it at any small movement they made.

The three of us took defensive positions, raising our weapons slightly.

"I will give you one chance to explain what you are doing here," I said, gaze darting between all three of them, who glanced only at one another.

They didn't answer, of course. Instead, they took off running in three separate directions.

"Split and capture!" I ordered before going right, following the blonde woman who was running as if her life depended on it.

I had no idea where we were going. She weaved us through the ruined streets, an obstacle course that made me extremely happy for the years of training as I dodged, rolled under, and jumped over the different pieces of debris blocking a clear path. It was making it difficult to gain momentum and close the distance between us, but slowly, I was eating it up step by step. She never looked over her shoulder, never faltered as she forced me to chase, lungs burning, legs aching, but I didn't slow, determination racing through my veins.

Finally, she skittered to a stop, forced to by the collapsed building now blocking her path to freedom. She whirled on me, eyes blazing gold and hand raised with the black cylinder now unhooked from her belt, a swirled pin poking out from the top. It made me stop dead in my tracks, recognizing it as some kind of bomb. It wasn't a typical weapon in the Onyx Guard, but not uncommon.

I had seen enough of them to know that the one this young Varg Anwyn woman held was not issued by our military. It was not the right size, shape, or coloring to be one of ours. Which meant she held something created by an Alchemist on Elliot's side, if not Elliot himself.

Anything could be trapped within, waiting to be unleashed on me.

My blood ran cold, preparing for a fight, yet the blonde stood there, staring. Her feet were planted wide and her arm raised in a threatening way as if she would be ready to throw the weapon, but she stood as still as a statue.

My stomach rolled, but we couldn't keep staring at each other. So, I took a tentative step forward, every instinct I had honed over the years on high alert.

"You're trapped," I said through a stuttering breath, my two Amalgam blades pointed at her. "Now drop the canister slowly and drop to your knees."

She did no such thing, yet made no move to attack, her bright blue eyes staring widely at me as if in shock. As if she didn't hold what was obviously some kind of unknown weapon gripped between her fingers.

"Disarm and drop to your knees!" I demanded again, adding a bit of a growl to my voice to hopefully shock the young Varg into action.

Instead, she shook her head slowly, her lower lip quivering. "It wasn't supposed to be you. We were told you weren't even in Seathra."

"What are you talking about?" I took another step forward, my grip tightening on my blades.

"They said it wouldn't be you who would investigate. They said it would be okay to use the others, but not you. Not our..." She shook her head, her legs starting to shake, forcing her to lean against the half-demolished wall that stood behind her.

"But why..." My words drifted off as my mind clicked into place what she was telling me.

A trap. This was a trap.

My heart hammered against my chest, my mind running a million miles a minute. The calls had been faked, a way to draw out members of the Guard to an abandoned place. A way to get us here specifically...

The canister she held in a death grip, the group of them forcing us to split up, isolate us.

They wanted to experiment on us. They wanted to see if they could hurt us.

I had no way of being sure, no way of confirming until I

could get her into an interrogation room and talking. But I knew Elliot, his ways and ethics when it came to experimenting. Ethics he would pass on to the other Alchemists who were under his command.

We were going to war, and Elliot knew that the Ibridowyn would be his biggest threat on the battlefield. There was only one weapon that could kill us, a rare blade. If I were someone trying to lead a revolution, I would dedicate a lot of time trying to create a new weapon to take down those who would be the hardest to kill.

My throat closed up a bit. Whatever was in that canister was intended to harm the Bridos. Whether to kill them or torture them I didn't know, but I wasn't ready to find out.

I had to find Lucas and Taylor. We had to flee and get as far away as possible.

But I had to disarm her first. I had to make sure that the bomb didn't go off.

I knew I was about to hate every word I needed to speak, but I had to find the boys. I had to make sure the twins were safe. So, with a deep breath, I said, "You believe me to be your queen?"

She nodded emphatically. "That is what they tell us. That you will stand alongside Elliot and save us all."

It took a lot of effort not to roll my eyes at the ridiculous notion. "Then, you know as well as I that you can't hurt me. So, gently put the canister down." I lifted the tip of my blade slightly, pointing to her still-raised hand. "Do as I say or Elliot and his leaders will not be happy with you."

She whimpered but slowly crouched down, gingerly placing

the weapon on the ground.

I nodded. "Good. Now step away." She did. She didn't even move as I took three wide steps forward and slammed the hilt of my blade against her temple, forcing her to crumble to the ground. I didn't have much time, pulling out a pair of cuffs and hooking her to a broken sewer pipe that was attached to the wall.

And then, I ran for my life.

CHAPTER 25

Kasha

I followed the scents of my Gammas, who were still difficult to track in the rubble and scorched remains of the town, but I used every bit of focus I had to follow them, catching Taylor's first. I forced my leg to run harder, faster, even contemplating shifting but knew it wasn't worth the lost time. I had to get to him and then we could find Lucas and…

I crashed into someone, their strong arms grasping me by the waist to keep me upright. I looked up into the hard, terrified gaze of Lucas, alarm written over every inch of his face.

"It's a trap." I huffed out. "We have to find…"

Before I could get the final word out, an explosion echoed across the rubble, followed by a plume of greenish-black smoke rising to the left of us, at least four blocks away. My heart dropped at the sight, knowing that whatever was now contaminating the air had been secured in the canister I had disarmed from the one I gave chase to. The final one was able to get the pin free.

The experiment had begun, and Taylor was its first victim.

"Taylor!" Lucas screamed, pushing past me, sprinting right towards the danger. I didn't hesitate to follow quickly on his heels, twisting and turning through the ruined streets to get to my Gamma. To get him to safety however possible.

After what felt like too many minutes, we made it to the street where the cloud was thickest, the entry within its inky depths only about twenty feet away before it would consume us as well. But it was close enough to hear the howling shrieks that came from within, echoing off every surface to torture me, to make my insides quiver and my heart shatter within my chest.

"Make it stop!" Taylor wailed from inside the dark cloud, his words punctured with ear-splitting screams of pain. "Please, Goddess, make it stop!"

Lucas started to dash forward, desperation written over every feature to get to his twin and save him. But somehow, I was able to hold on to a last shred of sanity, grabbing him around the waist and using every bit of strength to stop him.

"Let me go!" he growled over his shoulder, trying to use his strength to drag me with him.

"No!" I ordered, lacing my voice with the authority I had over him but rarely used. "The smoke is poisoned. If we go in there, we are going to get hurt as well."

"I don't care." I could feel every muscle of his shaking, the bones beneath my hands starting to crack, his wolf desperate to escape.

I used my body weight to shove us to the right, slamming both of us into a wall. "Control yourself, Gamma!" I yelled. "If we are hurt, then there is no escaping. We need to stay safe so we can get Taylor home so we can heal him. Think!"

"Please, Beta," he whispered, begging in his words. "Let me save him."

"We will." I squeezed him, his body still shaking, but it seemed his wolf was no longer trying to shift. "I promise, we will save him."

I dragged him back, my last shred of self-preservation keeping me from running within myself as Taylor's screams grew louder, lancing me with white-hot pain through my heart and soul. They were sounds I would never be able to expel from my memory, and I knew that they would haunt my dreams for the rest of my life. Still, I stayed planted in the safety of the clean air, trying to will the smoke to clear.

Over the years, I had seen Taylor get beaten up, stabbed, and shot at with an arrow. He was an amazing Gamma, but he had been reckless in his Delta days, running head-first into danger whenever he had the chance. He had never allowed himself to scream in such wailing, painful ways. He had never begged. Which meant it was no person causing him such pain but the deep plumes of greenish-black smoke that still surrounded him.

Physical pain clawed up my throat, the ache of my chest squeezing tighter and tighter with each second that passed and I couldn't run inside. I couldn't get to him. Whatever was occurring, it was because of the smoke. It was poisoning him, and Lucas and I needed to stay away so we could bring Taylor to safety. If only there was a way to enter it, we could drag him out…

"I have an idea." I pulled Lucas a few more steps away, or tried to.

"No!" Lucas tried to wrench free, but somehow, I was able to keep my grip tight.

"Go find the one you put down!" I screamed in his face, shaking him to get his attention. "Mine had a rubber face mask attached to their belt. It must be what protects them from the smoke. Get it and we can try going in."

Realization sparked in his gaze and he took off running, my lungs burning with each pumping step I took toward where I had knocked out and tied up the young Varg. I skittered to a stop in front of her in the dank alley and took a second to lean down and rip the black rubber mask from her belt and sprint back to where Taylor was. Lucas arrived back at the same time. The two of us secured the masks over our faces, the length of clear spanning across where my eyes were so I could see. Without hesitation, and Lucas by my side, we plunged into the dark smoke.

Even with the mask. it was barely tolerable, but it kept us from breathing in the toxic fumes. It also cut us off from being able to attempt to scent him out through the fog. Instead, we had to follow his wailing screams, my pulse picking up as it got closer until we were right in front of him, and I couldn't stop the gasp from escaping my lips.

Even through the thick fog, I could make out Taylor's contorting, writhing figure on the ground. Blood dribbled from his nose, bruising starting to bloom across his cheeks instead of his usual blush. Sickly green vomit was spewed to one side of him, some of it still coated along his lips and dripping onto his black chest plate. And yet, his screaming didn't subside. It increased with each second he inhaled whatever was around us.

"Taylor!" Lucas screamed, lunging to help his brother up from the ground, allowing me to pull myself from my shock and drop to my knees to help grasp Taylor's left arm and sling it over my shoulder. Lucas did the same with his right, and we hoisted him up, trying our best to lean his weight on us so we could get him out.

"It burns! Get it off me. It burns!" His screeching words echoed all around us.

"We've got you, Taylor. We've got you." I tried to soothe him, my back aching under the weight of him. He was taller than both Lucas and me, making it awkward when we started to pull him forward.

"You're going to be all right, brother. It's all going to be all right," Lucas affirmed as we dragged him the last few feet until we cleared the smoke, not caring that whoever had detonated the bomb got away.

Lucas kept whispering calming words to his brother, promising that we were on our way to get him help, and that the physicians would make him all better. I wanted badly to grip onto his words, but even I wasn't that naïve.

Whatever was in that bomb was meant to harm an Ibridowyn.

For all we knew, from Taylor's first inhale of the poison, we were already too late.

CHAPTER 26

Kasha

Getting back to the Compound was difficult and a bit of a fever dream.

We had to stop at the closest town first, Taylor screaming and raging every time someone tried to touch him. At least, in between vomiting and scratching at his skin like he was trying to peel it off. They had been able to drug him, forcing him into a medically induced coma. It was enough so we could move him.

Lucas only wanted him stabilized, so we could get a transport cart as quickly as possible and transfer him back home where Beckett could begin treating him. Lucas had refused to leave his side. We called up some of the Deltas and Derchtas to drive out and pick up our cycles, so the two of us could sit in the cart with Taylor, a physician assistant traveling with us so she could administer the doses of knock-out drugs he needed.

We had been only a few miles away from the Compound when the first seizure struck him, his screams rising back up in earnest as his body lost complete control of itself.

I had seen many terrifying things in my life. Yet, to watch Taylor, a person who had known me for over ten years and had fought beside me throughout our entire time in the Guard succumbed to such pain would change me forever.

And it made my rage and hate towards Elliot's people grow even more.

We had been home for almost half a day, night had fallen, and the entirety of the Hierarchy along with some of the younger members milled in and out of the infirmary to check on him. Beckett hadn't left his side, running test after test that he had access to here. It was limited, but enough that he sat down beside us at Taylor's bedside well past ten at night, ready to start explaining things to Lucas and me.

I had sent Nolan and Emric home for the night. There was no need to crowd the room while Beckett tried to work. Plus, Lucas was hanging on by a thread, and I knew the more people around him, the more agitated he would become. It was best to keep it limited to the three of us.

"Tell us," Lucas croaked from Taylor's left, sitting in a chair and gripping his brother's hand. He hadn't let go unless Beckett requested it to run another test. I sat to the right, my weary and exhausted mind unable to do anything except stare at the prone form of my Gamma.

"Whatever he inhaled is attacking his nervous system," Beckett explained. "It's making his healing abilities work overtime. The moment it tries to heal one part that's being attacked, another pops up somewhere else."

"So? It means he is healing right?" Lucas looked up, gripping his brother's limp hand even tighter.

A grave expression paled across Beckett's face. "Not fast enough. And since we have no idea what was in that poison, I can't give him any kind of medicine or antidote without risking adverse reactions to it."

"Did you try to identify it?" I asked.

Beckett nodded. "I ran a blood test, but I don't have the proper tech to be able to do an extensive one. We can send a sample out to the local clinic and see if anything pops up on their test, but I've never seen anything attack a person like this, particularly a Brido. Any poison would be out of our systems by now. But this is obviously lingering."

The machines next to him began beeping at a rapid pace in time for Taylor to begin seizing again, his choked, rushed breathing and uncontrollable shaking forcing all of us into action.

Instinctually, I placed my hands on his shoulders, trying to steady him while Beckett rushed to get a drug that would help it stop and Lucas turned him onto his side so he hopefully wouldn't choke. My touch seemed to agitate him, his screams intensifying, even in the deep slumber he was still drugged into.

"That's another part of it," Beckett explained, racing to Lucas's side and plunging the tip of a needle into Taylor's neck, pressing a clear liquid into his bloodstream. "He's sensitive to all touch. Whenever he is remotely conscious, it causes him pain."

"Goddess above," I whispered as the drug began to work, Taylor letting out ragged, shuddering breaths as he stilled, finding his way back into the deep slumber. "What did Elliot give him?"

I shook my head, looking over to Lucas who was still staring at his brother, every inch of his vibrating with anger. "I don't know, but I intend to find out."

He kissed his brother's forehead before charging out the door.

***

I ran after him, not saying a word and not even attempting to stop him. I knew exactly where he was heading and I was ready to assist him in any way he needed.

We grabbed the keys from the guards on duty outside the cells, neither of them even speaking as we walked right past and towards the two occupied cells somewhere in the middle of the row. Lucas was quick and efficient, shoving the key within the first door and yanking it open, the young blonde woman I had apprehended lying on the cot within.

We had been able to capture two of the three we had found there. The one who had successfully attacked Taylor had escaped in the chaos. We hadn't even seen her in the smoke, too focused on getting Taylor out of there.

But we had two of them, and if they had been ready to throw those matching bombs, then they must have some idea of what was intended for the experiment. Even if they weren't the Alchemists who created it, no self-respecting scientist would send out someone to test a theory without prior knowledge. It allowed them to know what to look for and the details that would be best reported back to the experimenting team.

Although, since they were Elliot's Alchemists, self-respect was probably low on their list of priorities.

I stayed by the door, leaning on the threshold as Lucas stalked towards the girl frozen in fear, watching his every move.

"What did you do to our partner?" His words were low, the tension building in his body making his well-defined arms bulge even bigger. The close shave of his head and the tattoos peeking out along his throat added to the menacing quality he sometimes put out when he wanted to.

She shook her head quickly. "I do not know."

He ate up the rest of the distance, standing at the edge of the cot, but he didn't lay hands on her. "Then why were you there?"

"I was commanded to."

He narrowed his eyes. "Under whose command?"

"I… um… just the… I can't…" Her words continued to babble, no actual sentence leaving her lips.

Lucas's patience was already thin when we entered the cell, and her lack of answers was irritating him even further. He slammed his hand onto the metal frame at the end of the cot, making it rattle and clang against the stone wall behind it.

Spooked, she screamed at the loud noise. "Please…"

"This is me going easy on you," Lucas growled. "If you want me to stop then give me answers or risk making it even worse for you."

"Oh, Goddess." She began crying, whispered prayers starting to babble away quietly.

Interesting. She was not who I expected to be sent into the field. Why were they risking someone so under-trained and timid to be chosen for the experiments testing?

Either way, Lucas's fear-inducing questioning wasn't going to get us far. It was going to make her pass out eventually as she wasn't taking any full breaths through her tears and prayers.

Sometimes, a gentler hand was needed in these situations. It was all about the person.

I shook my head, walking forward and tugging Lucas back. "Let me try."

His jaw clenched, staring down at me for a few seconds before nodding once and walking back to take up my position in the doorway. I turned back to the cowering girl, tickling along the back of my neck alerting me to the presence of the second rebel in the cell next to hers. He was watching, his gaze tracking me as I approached his partner, but I refused to give him my attention, keeping it wholly fixed on the person in front of me.

I crouched, lowering myself so I was shorter than her as she sat on the bed. I wanted to give her a false sense of security, to make her feel bigger to calm the jittering nerves that were written all over her closed-off posture and tapping fingers.

"What's your name?"

She bit her lower lip, sniffling a few times before saying, "Sage."

"Do you know where you are, Sage?" She nodded, wiping away her stray tears. "Do you know why we brought you here?"

"Because we hurt your friend and you want answers. Because the High Faction thinks I'm a criminal." Her lower lip trembled. "Because that's what was expected of you."

All of those were true, I supposed, in their own right. I had appealed to her on the battlefield successfully, using the power

I loathed but had over her. She was green when it came to interrogations and fieldwork, but I saw the loyalty reflected in her gaze when she had the opportunity to attack me. She had believed her words.

And I knew I could use them again now to get any answers she had hidden away in her mind without hurting her too much.

I peered over my shoulder at Lucas, my insides clenching before turning back and saying, "You dropped the canister for me because you believe me to be your Queen. So, can you explain to me why you were all out there? Can you tell me what is happening to my friend?"

"Don't say anything," the man from the cell next to her growled, his rich blackberry scent thickening with that metallic undertone of the Shrivika.

"But she is our Queen," Sage said, confusion reflecting in her hazel gaze. "All of the leadership says so. All of them talk about what it will be like when she joins us."

"Not yet." He scowled at me, inching closer to the bars that separated their cells. We had purposefully put them next to each other, hoping the guards would catch them talking to each other or riling them up as we interrogated. "Not while she still wears the enemies' armor with pride."

"What a loyal soldier," I said, mocking him to get his anger rising slowly. "Does Elliot know about you?"

"We aren't soldiers," Sage whispered, squirming and tugging at the tight fitting of her navy blue under armor that she still wore. The protective plates had been removed when they were thrown within the cells.

"No?" It made complete sense, though.

"No, we're the brains behind them," the man said, finally coming out of the shadows enough to show his young face. He was probably around the same age as Sage. His ginger hair was shaved close on the sides and slicked back on the top, matching the smattering of freckles that stretched across his cheeks and pointed nose.

"So, you're Alchemists, then?" I tilted my head at him. They seemed very young, still within their university age if I had to guess.

His face pressed closer to the bars. "Alchemist Apprentices."

"Ah, that makes sense." I nodded. "No full-fledged Alchemist would be out in the field or risk their lives like that. Only makes sense to send an apprentice to do the dirty work."

"We were the most logical choice," he argued. "If we die or get caught, the experiment and the knowledge of it will not be at risk. Those who created this need to stay safe so they can continue to work on the weapons we need to win our country back."

"He's right." Sage shook even harder, but her gaze was fixed on her partner, who smiled encouragingly at her. "They needed us. It was our duty to the cause."

"Sage," I pulled her attention away from her companion, my legs starting to cramp in the crouched position, but I didn't move, keeping my shoulders relaxed. "What was in the canister?"

"I really don't know." She shook her head. "This was a top-secret project. No apprentices were allowed in the labs while they worked on it."

"Then tell me what the end goal was." I changed the direction of my questions. "Based on the trap, you wanted guard members. What did the Alchemists want you to report back on? How it hurt us? If it killed us? Anything that was a symptom?"

"They wanted to know how you would react to it," she said. "They wanted to know if it would be a good weapon when we start to fight our way to freedom."

"Sage!" the Shriv yelled, banging his hands against the bars. "Shut up!"

"What am I telling them that they probably don't already suspect, Dawson?" She threw her hands up. "I'm just confirming it. It's not like we can point them in the direction of a cure or anything."

His face scrunched up in defeat, knowing her words were true.

I looked at her. "So, the goal is to use them on the battlefield?"

She nodded. "It's some kind of chemical bomb. It's meant to hit large units of soldiers and incapacitate them fast and painfully."

"Any kind of soldier?"

"I suppose, since we were instructed to wear protective gear so as to not ingest it ourselves once deployed." Her brows furrowed in confusion. "Although, we were required to test it on Onyx Guard members, but they didn't elaborate why."

So, the Alchemists knew of the Bridos but not their apprentices. Elliot and his higher echelon of leaders were keeping that as secretive as possible.

"And if you two are down here all growling and angry, it must mean it was successful." His grin grew, eyes gleaming with excitement. "Your precious teammate is dying and there is nothing you can do to stop it."

A howl echoed in the tight quarters before the slamming of the second door screeched open and Lucas threw himself at the young Shriv. I didn't run to stop him or even attempt to command him. I wanted to see him hurt too. I wanted to see Lucas make him bleed.

The punching of Lucas's fist against bone cracked through the air, wet coughs puncturing between each hit he dove out. I could make out through the bars my Gamma straddling the vicious Alchemist in training, going straight for the face with blow after blow.

I turned to Sage, horror on her sweet-looking face as she stared at the two brawling men. "See, Sage? That's the difference between my people and yours."

She turned back to me, her legs starting to shake. I leaned forward, whispering, "When it comes down to it, your people run and save themselves. Mine will do anything to protect those they love."

CHAPTER 27

Kasha

I only let Lucas get a few more hits in before I dragged him out of there and secured Sage and Dawson in their cells. We went straight back to the infirmary to Taylor's bedside, although before we left, I instructed the guards on duty to get one of Beckett's field medics over to tend to Dawson's injuries.

We spent the rest of the night there, alternating between sleeping on one of the empty cots in the infirmary and keeping watch over Taylor to make sure nothing happened throughout the late hours.

It was during one of my watchful shifts, Lucas tossing and turning a few beds away, that I finally let the tears slip from my eyes. I desperately wanted to reach out to Taylor, even in slumber, and hold his hand, squeeze it tight so he knew he wasn't alone. But knowing that touch was causing him pain, I refrained. Even if in his sleep he wouldn't feel it, I didn't want to risk causing him any more harm. Not when I so desperately wanted to help.

His inky black hair was free from its tether, the shoulder-length curls splayed out across the stark white pillow. The bruising he had started to develop within the poisoned cloud only got worse, now spreading across half of his body. Every once in a while, his face would contort a bit in pain, as if the poison was reaching and torturing him.

My sweet, kind-hearted Gamma. My partner through many years in the guard. My constant companion. He should be awake, smiling and telling us we were making too much of a fuss around him. He should be picking fun at me and his brother for how seriously we were taking this. He should be awake. He should be here.

I rested my elbows on the edge of his bed, dropping my face into my hands to muffle my weeping. "Please protect him. Please don't take him from me."

***

It took hours, but Greyson had successfully set up the large Comms unit in the infirmary. We all knew Lucas would never leave his brother's side, nor did any of us want Beckett to be far away in case he took a turn for the worst. When it was set, all of us crowded around the desk that Beckett had set up at the end of the row of beds, the screen set up in front of it. No one sat. We stood as a team, together.

While Beckett, Lucas, and I stayed vigilant by Taylor's bedside, Nolan and Emric had been working with the rest of the team to get in contact with the High Faction and give them a brief update on what had happened. They had called an immediate meeting for the next day.

For once, the conversation wasn't around me and I wasn't expected to talk. Beckett and Lucas chose to lead the conversation about what happened. They launched into it when the High Faction lit up the screen, going into the details of the attack and all that Taylor had been through since. I peeked over to his bed, which we thankfully kept off-screen, not wanting to put him on display. He was calm, lying completely prone.

And yet, even when he seemed in the least amount of pain, my heart still ached knowing that wasn't where he should be.

"We do what needs to be done," Father said after Beckett and Lucas concluded, looking out to the rest of the High Faction. "Whatever Elliot has created is hurting our most powerful military force. We must figure out what it is and an antidote as soon as possible. Let's get a group of Alchemists assembled and send them over to Seathra to start researching."

"On Taylor?" I couldn't help but ask, Nolan stiffening beside me.

Father's glare towards the camera sliced me even from miles away. "Yes, Beta. We need to know what is happening to him and the only way to do that is to study him. That way, maybe they can come up with an antidote. Not only to save your Gamma but the rest of the Onyx Guard when they ultimately face this weapon on the battlefield."

"He is too unstable to move," Beckett chimed in. "They will have to come here and work on the Compound."

"There is an Alchemist lab in Eroste. They can commute back

and forth," Terrence said from his place at the Shrivika table. "But it would probably be best to keep Taylor there. We do not want to risk anything with unnecessary transport."

Nods and mumbles of agreement rang through their chamber, no one disputing. I let out a shaky breath. None of us wanted to have Taylor moved since we wouldn't be able to follow if he was forced to.

"We will also need to dispatch an interrogation team, a specialized one, to the prison," Evette suggested. "See if Elliot or any of the people will talk. There is no way this is something they came up with overnight. One of the prisoners should know something."

"He won't tell us anything. He is too good." Father looked directly into the camera, staring us down with an intense gaze that said everything about what he was suggesting. "But he may answer to someone."

Although it was through a digital connection and no one could know who he was intending to stare at, we all knew. My back stiffened, Nolan's hand on my shoulder gripping tighter and everyone else around me crowding a bit closer as if creating a shield to protect me from my own father.

"What are you suggesting, Alton?" Imogene all but growled across the room. "Don't play coy."

"We have someone on our side who has his ear. Who has a direct connection to him." His gaze never left the screen, my insides and knees quaking under the intense scrutiny. "He will answer Kasha. Especially since it is someone she cares for."

"No!" I all but shouted, yet it was drowned out by the rest of my team screaming the same word. That helped warm my veins a bit, my grip on reality tightening.

"You'd be willing to sacrifice your own daughter's well-being for this?" Mitchell looked wide-eyed at my father.

"My daughter took oaths to protect this country at all costs. This is a way to do so." He shook his head, his frown deepening. "She could get us an answer quicker than our Alchemists could discover one."

"I won't do it," I spoke up, taking a step forward. "If I reach out to him, ask him for a favor, who knows what he will force me to agree to."

I didn't speak any of the many ideas racing through my head, but the paling expression of most of the High Faction showed their imaginations were running as wild as my own.

"It's worth a try," my father continued to argue. "You don't have to agree to any bargain, but you never know what he might be willing to give up for you. He has a soft spot for you, it seems." The accusations in his words were strong.

"No." Imogene stood, her fingertips grazing the tabletop. "That is a risk we are unwilling to take. Even if Kasha doesn't agree to a bargain, having her reach out gives power to Elliot. It will make him believe he has more control over her, something we do not have the time or ability to risk."

"Even if she's willing to do it?" Father argued back.

"I'm not!" I yelled, although I didn't think the two High Tribunes even heard me.

"Fine, then let's vote." Imogene stood taller. "Who here votes for Kasha, a dedicated soldier who was kidnapped, tortured, branded and experimented on by Elliot Wells to use the repercussions of said experiment to reach out to him, thus making her even more vulnerable to him?"

No one besides my father raised their hand, everyone avoiding his venomous gaze. My shoulders relaxed a bit, my arm snaking around Nolan's waist to pull him closer to me.

Imogene gave a smug smile to my father. "All opposed?"

Everyone besides my father raised their hands high in the air.

I tried not to cry tears of relief, knowing I wasn't going to be forced to do something I had been actively avoiding for so long.

"Good." Imogene gave my father one last glare before sitting back down and returning to the rest of the group. "Now, I think one of us should also go and oversee the research. We cannot take any chances with this. We need someone there to dispatch updates as much as necessary. Plus, direct involvement will help us get a better idea of how to plan to protect our guard members when the time comes."

When the time comes to face this weapon again. When the time came to attempt to fight against it. When war started.

"I second that," Mitchell nodded to his fellow High Tribune before turning to my father.

He nodded. "I as well."

"Then who shall it be?" Imogene looked around the room, eyeing everyone and looking as if to prepare to force someone to be sent away.

"I'll go," Kyler said, ignoring my father's sideways glare from his left. His tone left no room for questioning. He would be the one to come. He would be the High Faction member who would oversee the team of Alchemists sent to research Taylor.

End of discussion.

Lucas tensed next to me, and I glanced over to make sure he was okay. His blue eyes, unblinking, stared at the screen, his jaw grinding slightly. I nudged him with my elbow, startling him to glance over at me. I gave him a questioning look, but he shrugged before turning back to the discussion.

"The team will be dispatched with Delegate Kyler within a week," Imogene said. "But if anything changes, contact us immediately."

"And make sure you're logging and taking notes on everything Ar Duts," Mitchell instructed Beckett. "We need to make sure we have all the details."

"Yes, High Tribune," Beckett responded.

They clicked off without another word, bathing the screen in black. We stood there in complete silence before people started to slowly leave. Nolan turned to me. "Can I bring you dinner?"

I looked over my shoulder at Lucas, who was already back at Taylor's bedside before looking back at Nolan. "Please."

He nodded, kissing me lovingly on the forehead before departing. I walked right over to Lucas and Taylor, taking the seat across from him. I studied Lucas before asking, "What was that?"

He looked away from his brother, a frown on his face. "What was what?"

"That weird reaction to finding out Kyler was coming. Everything okay there?"

He huffed a breath, shaking his head slightly. "It's fine. I wish no one from the High Faction had to come."

I narrowed my gaze at him. "Anyone from the High Faction?" The reaction seemed too personal.

He glared back at me. "Yes." The harsh tone of his voice let me know this was the end of the discussion.

I didn't push, leaning back and settling in for the next few hours. I couldn't stop myself from replaying the meeting in my mind, my insides trembling at the memory.

Goddess save us because, for the first time during this whole ordeal, the High Faction seemed scared.

CHAPTER 28

Kasha

After two more nights of sleeping in the infirmary with Taylor and Lucas, the rest of the team finally convinced me to sleep in my own bed. They had created a rotating schedule so that at least one additional person would be sitting with Taylor. We knew it was fruitless to attempt to convince Lucas to spend a few hours in his own house.

The only reason I agreed was because of the fearful thought that had started bubbling to the front of my mind the night before. That if I was too exhausted, would I be weakened enough for Elliot to attempt to force another link on me? It was a risk I didn't want to take.

Still, sleep was difficult to come by, even with my cuddly paramour sleeping beside me. My mind kept cycling through memories about the attack on the towns, the experiment on Taylor, and the ongoing research Aggie was doing, which had no updates yet.

I knew it had been less than a week since we dropped her off, but going every day without one only made the days seem to drag on longer, forcing my anxiety to spike constantly. I wanted to reach out, but I promised I would wait for her to contact me for updates. She promised to give me weekly ones, even if there hadn't been any progress, so I was expecting my first one the next morning. A small comfort at least.

I counted down the minutes of the night, trying my best to soothe my constantly worried mind, to settle and find a few hours of peace…

A shrill, deafening ring from our Comms units jolted me out of my overthinking. I grabbed it from under my pillow, the palm-sized screen flashing a bright red, blaring, obnoxious sound with a ten-minute countdown. It was a simple procedure the High Faction would deploy if an emergency meeting needed to be called.

"What in the name of the Goddess?" Nolan grumbled, wiping his hand over his face as he reached to grab his unit and shut it off.

"Nolan…" I had no other words to say as he looked over at me, my stomach sinking even deeper. This wasn't a good sign. It was the middle of the night on a random day. There were few reasons for the High Faction to call such an emergency unless something catastrophic had happened.

The fear and pain reflected in Nolan's eyes said he was thinking the same thing, though neither of us could speak the words out loud.

We made quick work of dressing in warm, comfortable clothes before walking quickly to the conference room. Most of the

Hierarchy was already there, the last few trickling in behind us. Even Lucas stumbled in, showing how important and terrifying receiving this message was. The only one missing before the countdown ended was Emric, who probably wouldn't arrive until after this meeting concluded since he lived off Compound with his husband. We'd have to fill him in after.

We sat in our typical seats, our team wrapped around the table and ready as the screen in front of us clicked on, lighting up to reveal nine small boxes arranged together in a square. The High Faction's space in the center.

Nine. Not ten like there should have been. One territory was missing.

"Brace yourselves," Nolan mumbled, warning all of us, our shifting gazes catching each other before returning to the screen.

Mitchell, seated in the middle, cleared his throat and said, "As of two thirteen this morning, Dalchus has fallen to the illicit militia cult led by Elliot Wells."

The entire room was silent, our faces and body language reflecting the utter terror and shock that rippled through all of us. Nolan gripped my hand under the table, my body going very numb. Beckett pulled Liv's chair closer to him so he could wrap her close. Greyson subtly handed a handkerchief to Eden, who used the thin fabric to wipe away a stray tear that had slipped down her cheek. We all knew what this meant, what our lives were about to spiral into. There was no turning back now.

The war had officially begun.

Dalchus was a random territory to hit first, sitting between Luspan and Xoblar. I would have guessed Elliot's military would start from one coast end or the other, but this put Xoblar in a very weak position. They were now cut off from the rest of the country since the only territory they bordered was Dalchus.

Even with our research and the assignments they had been giving us to prepare for the war, we were still not completely sure what the High Faction's plan was now that war was officially on our land.

A part of me wanted to be smug. When I had warned them that capturing Elliot was only the beginning, not all of them had believed me. Even after they had sent two delegates here to talk to me, take notes, and gather information about my time in Elliot's clutches, they hadn't given me an update on how they were moving forward.

Forever secretive. Forever looking out for what would put them in the best light.

I was only a little jaded by their past treatment.

I shook it away, though because what was most important was the emergency we were now facing. A territory had fallen, and quick enough that no other territory had even noticed. They struck like an assassin and took their first victim before anyone could react.

That thought chilled my veins even further.

"What is happening to their soldiers? Their Faction?" Viktor, Alpha of Adro, spoke up. "And how are they keeping us out of the territory?"

"They have set their own guards around the perimeters, keeping ours back and out. Trying to breach it right now would be a suicide mission, but once we regroup, we will try," Mitchell assured, but his words fell flat, many of the faces on the screen also seeming a bit skeptical. "Some soldiers were able to escape, and they are on their way to the Chateau so we can debrief them and figure out the best plan of attack and learn what their strategy was to win. As for their guard members…"

Before he could finish, a tenth screen popped up, my eyes bugging out at what looked like the Dalchus conference room, but instead of a Faction, there was but a single woman sitting in front of the screen. The table had been removed, so she could sit there like a ruler. Her navy-blue leather armor was smeared in mud and blood, her blond hair braided and her boots scuffed.

She was no friend of ours.

"Oh, please, Mitchell. I think I am the best to finish answering that question." She spoke as though she knew us all personally.

"Who are you?" Imogene nearly growled, half standing from her seat.

"My name is Eva, General of Elliot's Dalchus forces, and the new overseer of his first territory." She smiled, tilting her head. *"Chu Fui na Deithe."*

"How did you get into this feed? It's private," Mitchell said.

"Well, since I am now residing on this lovely Compound with your precious Onyx Guard Faction locked safely in the prison, it was much easier than you would think." She licked her chapped lips, her eyes flashing gold briefly. A Varg Anwyn, then.

"What do you want?" my father asked.

"Now that we have your attention," the lithe woman spoke, her bleak, almost black eyes staring at us all, making my spine shiver. She wasn't even in the same room as me, yet I felt her malicious evil aura seeping through to infect me. "You have two options. Continue to fight and lose countless lives and endanger your people."

"Or?" Mitchell spoke first, his white-knuckled fists sitting on top of the ornate armrests of his High Tribute chair.

"Or you release Elliot and surrender to your future king in peace. No harm will come to anyone who follows the true leader of Kazola."

Imogene scoffed at her words, fearless. "There is no King of Kazola. We are ruled by the people, and it will continue to be that way. Just as the God and Goddess proclaimed at the Unity of Order."

"Are you sure that's your final answer?" She leaned forward in her seat, her long legs crossed at the calf, posture perfect. "Last chance to surrender."

"We will never surrender to a tyrant," my father said, Mitchell and Imogene mumbling their agreement.

"Have it your way, then." She picked up what looked like a white Comms unit and clicked a button before turning back to us with a devious smirk set on her lips. "Good luck." She gave a wave before her square disappeared from the screen.

We all sat in stunned silence, but it was quickly interrupted.

Alarms blared from the speakers, one of the Faction's emitting the noise from their feed. Through screens, we watched as one of the Hierarchies shot from their seats, everyone scrambling to get their Comms out, answering frantic calls from those on the other side of their lines.

Adro Territory. Where Nolan's fathers lived.

My heart sank, my gaze instantly turning to my paramour, whose face was completely drained of color, eyes fixated on the little square that was Adro's team. I squeezed his hand. He had to know I was here.

"Adro!" Mitchell yelled through the connection, the rest of us stumbling to stand as if we could see farther into their small screen by getting closer. "Report! What is going on?"

"We're under attack!" Their Dara, who I did not know, screamed. "Local forces are already in the streets, fighting and evacuating. They are calling for emergency reinforcements, said the attacks have been popping up in multiple towns and cities and they're scrambling to spread the forces properly."

"Have they reached Trevalis yet?" Nolan demanded, but the question was ignored or not heard as the Adro leaders continued to recap. I pulled him closer, my own heart hammering desperately against my chest.

"It's going to be okay," I whispered in his ear, trying to soothe him. He shuddered under my touch, but the tension still pulled tightly in his shoulders.

"They need more soldiers!" the Beta added. "Anyone who can get here as quickly as possible is needed!"

The color drained from Mitchell's face. "We deployed Crelanti's additional forces to Luspan to try and fight our way back into Dalchus. They are too far away to send support and keep our borders secure."

"Call them back!" the Beta screamed.

"We will!" Imogene promised. "But they might not get there in time. Factions, who can prepare emergency support?"

"We can go!" Nolan called out, stepping closer to the screen and pulling me with him. "We'll also call our garrisons as we prepare to leave so they can mobilize as quickly as possible."

"Have them also put up contingencies," Imogene ordered. "Prepare for the worst; to protect Seathra's border."

"We will follow as well. Even if our troops are too minimal, the Guard will be there," Caleb said before Rystin's Ar Duts said they were coming as well.

"We will send you coordinates of the towns you are needed in," Adro's Alpha ordered. "Once you get it secured, call us!"

"We will!" I confirmed before we shut the screen off. "Let's move everyone!"

I briefly turned to Nolan, whose gaze was haunted. "Your fathers are going to be okay," I whispered, my stomach lurching at my words. Neither of us knew if what I said was the truth or a lie.

He nodded, lips in a flat line before pulling me close into a crushing hug. It was but a few seconds before we pulled apart and rushed from the room, following the rest of our team out to begin waking the rest of our Faction up and preparing for battle.

CHAPTER 29

Nolan

My stomach rolled when we crossed into Adro territory, every piece of me on high alert. My mind had spent the majority of the ride filled with worry, my hands shaking on the handles of my lectracyle. I tried desperately to get my head on straight, to remind myself that I was literally riding into battle, but I couldn't stop myself. My fathers were there, in a territory where fighting and killing was occurring. They were in danger. They were in need.

And I was nowhere close to lay my eyes on them and make sure they were all right. There was no way of getting in contact with them.

Even worse, we had been assigned to an area on the opposite side of the territory where my fathers resided. They were on the coast, near the border of Rystin, while we were staying near the border to Seathra. As a soldier, I understood the reasoning behind the maneuvers. As a son, my insides burned with pain, knowing that my family was so close, yet I wouldn't be able to run in and bring them to safety. All I could do was pray to the Goddess that their town had not yet been hit or other military members were protecting them.

I wasn't sure how I would make it through the battle, but I had to. I was an Alpha, and I had a group of soldiers relying on me to protect and lead them. I had to be there for them, and once we won the battle, I could make sure my fathers were okay.

I had to keep telling myself that.

We made it to our assigned town within three hours. I wished it could have been sooner, but mobilizing a majority of our unit besides a few Omegas and Fledglings we left behind to keep an eye on the Compound had been time-consuming and grueling. In my fourteen years in the guard, never had I been called to move a unit of this size. We were typically intended for specialized work, which meant small teams being sent out to different areas.

But this wasn't a typical day at the job. Today, we started a war, and our new way of life was about to settle in.

The sun was rising as we ditched our bikes on the edge of the city, my insides squeezing tightly as all of us raced inside the utter pandemonium that was battle. Civilians ran past us and out of the town lines, children and loved ones in tow, some on foot and others riding horses or carts. Blood-curdling screams filled the air as we moved farther in, all of us pulling our weapons, and me palming an Amalgam blade in each hand.

It took all my self-control not to picture my fathers as the ones fleeing. Bloodied and crying, screaming for help. They were tough; they would make it out. I had to believe in them the way I knew they believed in me.

"You all know the plan." Beckett nodded to the rest of the Keturi, pulling my attention back to the battle at hand. I appreciated him taking the lead as my equal in the Faction, The Ar Duts to my Alpha. I wasn't sure I could speak much right then. "Stay safe."

We all nodded to him. His pale hair was slicked back and ready for fighting. He gave us all a weary smile before turning around with his team. His Treasus, like my Gammas and other assigned fighters, followed him to the west side of the city. They disappeared in mere minutes, Emric and his team setting off in the opposite direction.

We had decided at the Compound that the best way to spread out through the city and actively help as many people as possible meant splitting up. Of course, the only logical way meant that each Keturi member would take a unit and a section of the city to aid the local forces that were currently locked in battle. Which meant Kasha and I were separating. Her heartbroken face had most likely reflected my own crumbling heart when Beckett had suggested the idea.

However, we were both soldiers first, and we knew it was the right call. In battle, in war, we couldn't put our relationship first.

Protect the Peace. We had taken that oath, and right then, we needed to put it first.

Before she turned away, I grabbed her arm, yanking her towards me and planting a feverous, devouring kiss. I memorized every bit of her lips. The movement and feel of them against my own, the delectable flavors of her tongue as we tangled together in the rushed, desperate act, heating my cheeks. I didn't care that our subordinates were most likely watching. Let them see that

Kasha and I were going into this battle with something to fight for.

Let them see how I would let that be a part of my motivation to win.

I pulled away, her hands coming up to grip my face tightly. "Stay safe, sweetness."

"You as well, sweetheart." I kissed her one last time. "I love you."

"I love you too." My heart flipped at her words. I doubted I would ever stop.

She pulled away and gave me a final nod before yelling at her troops to follow, Lucas tight on her heels as they headed north. It was a miracle we were able to convince him to leave, but his devotion to Kasha was obvious, and I had a feeling he knew this was where Taylor would want him to be. Worry spread through my veins as she disappeared into a cloud of smoke from a nearby burning building. I stared after her, biting my lower lip.

I turned to Eden and Greyson, the other Deltas and a few Omegas that were close to finishing their final testing called to battle on an emergent basis staring at the three of us for direction. I cleared my mind, letting my fears and anxieties fall away.

They needed a leader, and that meant pushing aside my worries and issues that were coursing through me. They needed to see that I would fight with all of my focus and dedication, so they would follow and do the same.

My wolf hummed in my chest, surprisingly. I figured he would be angry at getting separated from Kasha and worrying about my fathers, but it seemed my bloodthirsty beast was more interested in getting retribution for those I cared about by taking out some of the Elliot's.

Whatever kept him focused, I really didn't care.

"You know the plan," I surveyed the streets quickly, my team assigned to the south. The sun beat down heavily on us, reflecting on the different buildings. Echoes escaped against the walls, thumping footsteps, and loud, terrified screams. The barrage of people running towards us was an obstacle we would have to force our way through, knowing that beyond them was the enemy we would be forced to finally face. "We stick together as a unit unless I or the Gammas specify. Understood?"

"Yes, Alpha!" they repeated together.

"You've trained for this, and that training will protect you now. Keep your wits about you, and if you see any civilians, get them evacuated as quickly as possible." With that, I turned to an alley off to the right, which I knew led into a populated area that was more residential for this town. I had only been able to study a map of it for about two minutes before we had to head out, but it had been enough.

"*Tsio a Chisan!*" I bellowed.

"Protect the Peace!" they echoed back before we took off, ready to make good on that promise.

It took only seconds before we came upon our first unit of enemy fighters, their dark blue armor already splattered with blood and mud, their weapons dripping it as well. They didn't outnumber us, but they looked frenzied, almost high off the raging battle surrounding them, most of them with shifted red or gold eyes, depending on their species.

They caught sight of us, all of us crouching into defensive positions, engaging immediately, letting no hesitation into our movements as we fought. It was havoc, pandemonium as the ringing of our weapons clashed, tired breaths and grunting pants beating around us as we fought them off. It was the chaos that Elliot was probably relishing in his little cell in prison. He probably knew exactly what was happening. I had no doubt about that.

Was he relishing in it? Was he smiling, knowing that his delusional followers were smearing our country with blood in the streets? Was he eager to join them?

A shiver ran up my spine as I shoved the wooden end of my Amalgam into the belly of a Shrivika enemy, the squishing of skin and muscle conforming around the pointed weapon. Imagining Elliot on the battlefield was enough to make my fear spike once again, which morphed quickly into bloodthirsty revenge.

Elliot needed to die. For all those dying in the street around me. For Cleo and Kasha.

My wolf echoed my thoughts with a deep, throaty growl that turned to a satisfied one when I ripped the wooden blade out of the Shrivika, their body crumbling to the ground ungracefully, deep red blood already leaking out to pool around him.

I couldn't help but notice that the dark coloring of Elliot's navy-blue armor looked very similar to that of the Onyx Guard. Was this on purpose? What would he gain?

I sent a few extra prayers up to the Goddess that she keep an eye on our forces, my friends, so no unnecessary injury came to them. Especially from a comrade's hand that made a mistake in the heat of battle.

After the first half an hour, we had already engaged with three units of soldiers, having to team up with a weakened group of local soldiers who had been outnumbered. Luckily, we were able to save a few of them, but unfortunately, it led to a Delta and an Omega getting injured. So much so that they couldn't continue with us.

I had never been to war, which meant I never had to leave a teammate behind before. It had been almost impossible, but I ripped myself away once I had confirmed with one of the uninjured soldiers from the other unit that they would take care of them while we continued. They said their garrison had an emergency medical tent set up on the outskirts of town and she would transport them with her injured.

It still didn't make me feel good leaving them, but at least I was able to.

We turned a corner, a unit of our local soldiers fighting against a smaller, outnumbered group of rebels. They were holding their own fine, at least four blue-clad rebels laying on the ground, gaping bleeding wounds or missing limbs proof that they were no longer an issue. I let out a shaky breath, a bit of hope blooming in my chest that maybe we could force them out of the city.

"Let's go. They don't need us." I turned to run farther down the street to find anyone who needed our help until someone tugged me back.

"Wait." Greyson pointed to the group of rebels, who were moving into a line formation, retreating from the unit they were engaging with.

What were they doing?

One of the soldiers stepped forward, a rubber mask covering their entire face, the rest of the team following suit and shoving on matching masks. It was just in time for the leader to raise his hand above his head, a silver metal cylinder canister gripped within his fist before he pulled a pin from the edge and threw it at them. My team and I took a few steps back, my arms flinging out to signal for them to retreat. The weapon looked similar to the one Lucas and Kasha had described. The one that had hurt Taylor.

"Duck and cover!" the leader of the soldiers screamed, but it was too late. Instead of sparks flying to blast the soldiers apart, purplish, gray smoke blew out from the can instead, the scent potent from a distance, even though the smoke was nowhere near us.

The burnt floral of Wolfsbane mixed with the bitter dark berry of Blackthorne.

The smoke engulfed the unit in mere seconds, their bodies falling to the ground in a pile when they took their first breath of the noxious fumes. It was instant and it was brutal, made even worse when I saw one of the rebels pull out his dagger and thrust it into the chest of a fallen soldier.

It wasn't the same thing that had hurt Taylor, not specifically meant for the Bridos, but it was as dangerous.

Eden's eyes widened. "Run!" she screamed to everyone, our team retreating.

My gut twisted even deeper at leaving them behind, but there was nothing we could do. We didn't have protection against the smoke like the rebels, and if we were taken out, then there would be fewer people to defend the city.

Nothing we can do. Nothing we can do.

If I kept saying it, I would start to believe it.

We moved as a group, our feet pumping quickly and rounding a corner to a long street of residential houses, my heart cracking a bit at the sight. Windows were broken in, doors ripped off the hinges. About a hundred feet away, we spotted another team of rebels moving in a group down the street, searching the houses.

For survivors and prisoners most likely.

I didn't hesitate before leading my group towards them, the dozen of us attacking.

I fought and slashed and braced. I pushed through as many of them as possible, trying to get the upper hand, but as soon as we made it through half the group, another rebel unit had found us, joining in on the fun.

Where the fuck did they come from?

Yet, with this as a very good distraction to keep my movement occupied, my thoughts kept going to the horrifying, pained look on those soldiers' faces when they went down from the smoke.

Not smoke, poison. A poisoned chemical bomb. How many kinds did Elliot have?

They were using Alchemy to help make up for their lack of numbers, taking out hordes of our soldiers before we could even get close. Only Elliot could come up with something so ingeniously cruel to fight his battles.

And I loathed myself for being slightly impressed. It was smart moves such as this that gave him an upper hand in this war. We were on an even playing field, even with our numbers being larger.

This was exactly what Kasha and I had feared.

I rationalized in my mind that after forty-five minutes of fighting, that had been our first run-in with the bombs, so they couldn't have that many on them. It didn't matter, though. We were vulnerable and I had to let my team know.

I reached out to the entire Hierarchy. *"We've met a dangerous area of enemies. They had another kind of chemical bomb they've been throwing. It's been taking out groups of soldiers."*

"Purple smoke?" Emric asked, and I confirmed quickly. *"We met some of those as well,"* he said. Goddess, no.

"Were you hit?" Lucas asked, frantic concern in his words. *"Kasha wants to know."*

Good, he was telling her what we were saying. I had tried including her when reaching out to the team but noticed her gentle pushback. It still stung my heart that she didn't want me in her mind, but I understood. Her mind no longer felt safe, even if Aggie had said it should be. She needed privacy for a while.

"We got away before the smoke got to us, but it didn't stop us from witnessing almost two dozen soldiers going down." I closed my eyes, biting the inside of my cheek. *"We cannot confirm if they were knocked out or if they have been killed."*

"We are fine as well," Emric said. *"We looped back once the smoke cleared to fight off the hoard that had set it off. They were all knocked out, but that doesn't mean there aren't bombs that are lethal."*

"It smelled like a mix of wolfsbane and Blackthorne," Greyson added.

"Doesn't sound like what hit Taylor. Do you think we can withstand

it?" Beckett asked. *"Will our Brido blood keep us safe?"*

A good question. We were not completely immune to the effects, depending on our species, but we could handle it in higher doses than a typical Shriv or Varg, which meant the bombs might not affect us.

"Kasha wants me to remind everyone that he knows what the Bridos are," Lucas warned us all. *"We can't risk it! If there are chemicals then we have to believe we are all vulnerable. Especially after what happened to my brother."*

"It wouldn't make sense to kill, though," Eden said, her Amalgam slashing out to take out a young Shriv who had tried coming at her with a dagger. The blood spattered across his navy armor that looked brand new. Had he even fought before? *"They risk being affected too. Even with the protective gear they had, it could malfunction."*

"Remember all this for the debriefing," I ordered. *"For now, get back to focusing on the fight."*

The connection was severed quickly, just in time for me to switch around and catch the blade of a Varg who had tried to sneak up on me. I blocked it with my own, the force of it making her stumble and crash into the wall behind her, bits of rocky debris crumbling from the impact. I used her disorientation to my advantage, using a few hits to get her down, knocking her out with the handle of my blade. They were not the best trained, and I had to guess that was why they were on search duty of the rows of townhouses in the area. It was more residential, which meant the typical demographic would probably be easier for them to handle.

My insides twisted with each one I fought, made even worse with each drop of enemy blood that was sprayed across my cheeks or crusted in my hair. I was completely outmatching them. It was like fighting against a new Omega who had barely held a weapon before. I didn't like the feeling, my honor slowly slipping away with each slash and forceful hit of my blade.

I had to ignore the Blackthorne scars I had seen on one of them, the gray-tinged veins snaking up their throat and peeking out from their armor. A past addict, a victim of Elliot brainwashing them.

But I couldn't let that get to me, couldn't let myself falter. They were the enemy, fighting for a man trying to threaten the peace and safety of the people of Kazola. I took an oath to fight against any who threatened that, and they were.

Which is all I could tell myself as we struck them down one by one.

We fought for another hour and came across two more units of barely trained soldiers before a horn blared through the air, making my ears ring and my heart rattle in my chest. It was a signal, and I knew it wasn't one of ours. My team braced ourselves for whatever terror they were about to impose, but instead, the soldiers we were getting ready to engage with ran in the opposite directions towards the edges of town.

They were retreating. We had won.

I looked around at the ravaged houses surrounding me, letting out a breath of relief and checking on every member of my team who had survived the fight. Even though we had won, all of their gazes looked defeated. All of them weary and saddened.

My heart cracked as I led them through the destroyed area, avoiding piles of broken glass splattered with blood and the littering of bodies that lay in all areas of the street, following the post-battle protocol of checking for any injured or trapped soldiers and civilians. The battle was over, and now it was time to pick up the pieces of the destruction Elliot and his people had left behind.

CHAPTER 30

Kasha

Even as a soldier, battle was something I was ill-prepared for.

It became apparent as I fought my way through the town with my team to command, all of us shutting down to horrors that we were participating in. It was difficult to disengage completely, even with years of training to potentially find ourselves here. My wolf had helped fortify me and push me forward, giving me strength with each life I had to hurt or even take. When I had to block out the idea of Nolan and the others getting poisoned by yet another mystery bomb Elliot's teams had.

My wolf had helped me stabilize, but even I could tell fighting in these battles that harming other wolves, Shrivs, and humans disgusted her on a certain level. She didn't relish it, although she and I were both satisfied when we watched the rebels retreat when we succeeded in protecting this town.

These people were still my enemy, following a man who had harmed, tortured, and violated me. I had little sympathy for the ends they would meet one day, and it was an odd dichotomy to rectify within my soul. However, I knew I would have to figure it out if I was to survive this war.

That time wasn't now, though. We needed to focus on the city.

"Search the area," I commanded my team, all of us sweat and blood-soaked from the dozens of enemy rebels we had fought for the past hour. "Find any survivors and get them to a healing tent or help them locate their families. After that, we regroup with the rest of the Faction at the southern entrance we came in from."

Everyone mumbled, "Yes, Beta," before taking an area of the north side of the city, a few of them even pairing off with local soldiers to assist with the post-battle cleanup. I nodded to Lucas before picking a direction. I helped get a few children in the hands of soldiers to escort them around the healer tents to find their families, bound the leg of a soldier who had been stabbed before transporting him, and dug a hiding family out of their home after they had purposefully collapsed the front entrance to keep them safe.

It was grueling and heartbreaking to sift through the remnants of someone's life. But I kept pushing forward. I kept moving to the next person who needed my help.

When I turned a corner towards an area of shops to begin a search, a cloaked person stepped into my path a few feet away. When I took a deep breath to pick up a scent, I got nothing.

Wolfsbane clothing. It was one of Elliot's men.

I rushed him, my blade triggered and ready to slash at the mystery man, but when I got close he didn't raise any weapon. I knew it could be a trap, but I didn't care, using the opportunity to get the upper hand, grasping the front of his shirt and slapping him against the closest wall, the hood falling away to reveal his identity.

"Hello, *Rogthna*." The black-haired man smiled, that angular face easily recognizable.

I shove the metal edge of my Amalgam against his throat. "Nice to see you again, Ezekiel."

My wolf hummed in happiness at such a lucrative catch. After being tied down by him and his men, and having to watch Nolan be tied up by them, it gave me an odd satisfaction to capture the man who had escaped from our clutches, his men sacrificing their freedom to let him get away.

"It took too long to figure out which city in this tiny little territory your team was going to." He rolled his eyes as if I didn't hold a fatal weapon against him.

"Just in time to watch your forces be pulled back." I gave him a smug smirk. I couldn't help it; I was still riding a bit of the adrenaline.

"Yes, well. We may have lost the battle today but not the war." He sagged into my hold on him. "Although, I suppose I will have to learn about it behind a jail cell now."

"That's what happens when you're caught as a prisoner of war."

"Oh, no. You didn't catch me." He tilted his head. "I let myself get caught."

My arms stiffen, but I refuse to let him go. "Excuse me?"

"I needed to get close to you, and I knew I wasn't getting out of here alive or free having to do so." He shrugged. "But it seemed very important to a particular someone that you get your hands on this."

He reached into his pocket, my body stiffening as he pulled out a white Comms unit. An Elliot Comms unit.

"I don't want it," I snarled in his face, dropping my blade back into its holster and replacing it with my hand, wrapping it around his throat so I could feel his pulse beneath my fingers.

"Too bad, because you get it." He smirked. "The person on the other line is eager to talk to you."

This man was even more annoying one on one than he was when he was ranting and raving about how incredible Elliot was during that meeting a few months back. At least back then he had been using his charm to win people over. Now, he was being plain insufferable.

With my free hand, I pulled the Comms unit from his grip, securing it in my pocket along with my blade before reaching up to grip his throat with both hands. He struggled against me, arms flailing and scratching at my arms, desperate for me to let go as I pushed against his windpipe, blocking the airflow to his lungs. I snarled low under my breath as I watched him, mottled red cheeks and bulging eyes desperate for air until, finally, he was dead weight in my grip.

Then, without any care for him, I let his body fall to the ground.

He wasn't dead, just passed out from lack of oxygen. I wiped my hands on my pants, standing guard over his body, and took a quick look around the area to see if I was alone. With an unsteady deep breath, I pulled out the Comms unit, my fingers shaking as I pressed the only contact listed in the unit as anonymous.

A part of me trembled within, terrified that Elliot's face would pop up on the screen like it had in the past. As the waiting for connection screen blinked on, I had to keep reminding myself that he was imprisoned. He could not get me. I was safe from him. And there was no one worse than Elliot who could be on the other end of the connection.

Although, when Ari's face popped up on the screen, sneering at me with those blood-red painted lips of hers, it wasn't much better.

"Wonderful, *you*." I leaned against the wall behind me, a deep frown settling on my lips. Something about Ari really bothered me, even though we had spent little time talking during my stay in Folanoch where I had first met her. Maybe it was her extreme dedication to the cause. Maybe it was her desire to be Elliot's Shrivika consort if he became king. Maybe it was the fact that she constantly had to look perfect. Maybe it was just her. Who knew, but I was too tired to care.

"Yes, *me*," she retorted right away. "You look more tired than usual, Kasha. Like you're having trouble sleeping for some reason. Although, it looks like you got some blood. No more walking around like a starved, feral animal, whining all the time."

I kicked a stray bit of debris that was in front of me to stop myself from kicking Ezekiel's unconscious body. I really wanted to hit something, even with the exhaustion of battle seeping into my bones.

"I just spent the past few hours of my life protecting my country from people like you." I gripped the unit tightly, my knuckles whitening. "The sun has barely risen, yet I'm cleaning up dead bodies and helping injured, terrified people. I am not in a good mood, so get to the point."

"Fair enough. I'll cut right to the chase, then." She leveled her gaze, staring directly into the screen. "Elliot is waiting for you."

I scoffed, my stomach tightening. "Of course he is."

"No, no. Not the way you think." She shook her head. "He's waiting for you to stop ignoring the bond and accept your place. Be the queen you are meant to be."

My wolf stirred in my chest, my eyes sharpening to gold. "I will never be his queen. I will never give in to the bond."

I still had no idea what he was trying to accomplish with this. No idea why me or why he thought I would one day join his side. He was convinced, and this bond he had placed between us was its own brand of torture I was trying my best to live with every day. Reminding myself that Aggie was working on it, that she would find a way, was the only thing keeping my mind even a bit more focused on my day-to-day life.

I needed to calm, my heart racing once again.

Breathe in, breathe out.

My past does not define me. I am stronger than my past.

My old calming phrase was helpful again, becoming a bit of a mantra for me to use when I needed it. Even my wolf settled with each time I repeated it in my mind to get my breathing and the twisting chest under control. Finally, I turned back to the man in front of me.

"Looks like you wasted the freedom of one of your followers for that pathetic message." I angled the camera so she could see Ezekiel's prone form.

"You need Elliot as much as he needs you," Ari argued.

I scoffed again, the only reaction I had to brush off the zip of anxiety working its way through my veins. "I need no one."

"Not even to save that Gamma of yours?"

My blood ran cold. "What do you know about the poison?"

She smirked. "Nothing, but Elliot does. All you have to do is ask."

"I'm not asking him, I'm asking you," I all but growled at her. "You must know something. Tell me."

"Not my place. Besides, I really don't know the technical aspects of it which is what you need to save him. The two of you are destined to rule this country, and putting off forging your bond is only going to make it harder down the line."

I had to suppress a growl at that asinine comment. My whole part of this rebellion was based on some lore that Elliot revolved his whole revolution around. That he and I were prophesied leaders meant to save Kazola one day. A Shrivika king from an original bloodline and a Varg queen who came back from the dead.

Didn't matter that I never actually died or there was no accepted scholarly evidence that this prophecy was nothing more than a conspiracy theory. Elliot believed it and so did his followers.

I swallowed. "What is this bond anyways?" Aggie had given me the technical answers, but maybe Ari would have a better understanding of the motivation behind it.

She smirked at my interest. "It's how the two of you will be the strongest ruling pair you can."

"So, basically, you have no idea."

"I know it is necessary."

I snarled, wishing desperately that I could reach through the screen and smack her across the face. "Taking away someone's choice is never necessary. Which is exactly what he did when he marked me this way."

"You will come to understand one day." Her words were ominous, veiled in darkness. An omen. A warning. "When that final shred of hope for the High Faction to do right by you is ripped away. When that is finally taken from you, you will see that the only way forward is with Elliot. Only then will you be ready to lead. And mark my words, *My Queen*, you will find yourself there."

"You sound so sure." My stomach threatened to revolt, but I pushed through the nausea.

"Because we were all in your shoes once." Her face flitted with fear, ghosts of her past I knew nothing about coming to the surface. "It's when you hit rock bottom that you finally start finding yourself on a better path."

"That path doesn't equal Elliot," I argued.

"Maybe, but in my soul, I have settled that it does." She sounded so sure. No regrets or doubts.

I suppose it wasn't surprising. Elliot did a good job at taking advantage of those in their low points to manipulate them to his side.

"Elliot had a plan—we had a plan—to show you the truth," she continued. "We knew you would never come around with hurt feelings and some sob stories. You needed facts, evidence, and proof. You are an investigator, after all."

"So, you were looking for proof that would sway me?"

"Not looking, collecting. Successfully, I may add." She rolled her eyes at me, the gesture making the fire low in my chest burn a bit brighter.

A spark of memory flitted through my mind, wondering if this was connected. "Does this have anything to do with the empty folders I found in your room?"

She gave a haughty laugh, smiling. "At least our future queen is a quick one. No one will ever be able to call you dense, that's for sure."

"So, that's a yes?" I deadpanned, annoyed with her more and more as the conversation continued.

She nodded. "But your dear Faction found you before we compiled all of it. Don't worry, the project is still ongoing, and very soon you'll have no choice but to stand with us. Not if you want to hold true to those oaths you care so deeply about."

A shiver ran up my spine at her words, but I fortified myself, standing a bit straighter even if she couldn't tell from the small bit of me she saw on the screen.

She did not know the weight those oaths had on my consciences. Nothing she could give me would ever make me consider switching to her side.

Nothing.

"You don't scare me, Ari." I looked to my left and saw Lucas waving to me from down the street. I waved back, beckoning him closer.

"Then be prepared, Kasha." Her voice deepened, eyes flashing to a deep red. "I know my orders, but my patience only goes so far. Forge the bond and step into your role as queen, or you'll soon see a side of me you will one day wish I never let free. Taylor was a warning. You don't want to see what I'm really capable of."

And with those horrid, ominous words, the connection went black.

CHAPTER 31

Kasha

It was about noon when we were finally able to meet up with the rest of the team, and they looked as rundown and dirty as my group felt.

Hours of cleanup had gone by quickly, but the tiring weight of my body seeped deep within me. I needed to sleep for at least the next ten hours to recover. I supposed I wouldn't have trouble falling asleep tonight.

Nolan, Eden, and Greyson led their team back, my spine straightening as I headed right for Nolan. I planned to tell the rest of my team about my call with Ari when we got back to the Compound so we could choose the best way to move forward with the High Faction. However, I wanted to tell Nolan first. The weight of the second Comms unit was heavy against my hip where it was hidden in a pocket. I had to tell him. I had to confide in him first, my heart pulling me to do it as soon as possible.

Yet, when I saw his defeated, worried gaze land on me, all of that fell away. All of my issues were nothing compared to my deep need to make those horrible feelings I knew were brewing within him disappear.

When I was in front of him, I reached up, cupping his cheek. "Sweetness? What is it?"

He nuzzled into my touch, his hands going out to grip my hips and pull me closer to him. "It's my fathers," he whispered. "I tried getting answers from some of the local military, but no one has heard anything about Trevalis and its status."

His fathers' hometown.

I bit my lip, looking up at him. "Do you want to go and check on them?"

"We need to get back home, though." He looked over to the rest of our team, who were gathering up the last of our group and congregating around our lectracycles. We had been dismissed by the Adro Guard team, letting us know that they could handle the rest of the cleanup.

I was exhausted and in desperate need of a bath and a cuddle in bed with Nolan. But that was what I needed, not what he needed.

He needed to go see his fathers. He needed to make sure they, and his hometown, were safe from the war that had fallen on their doorsteps last night.

And at that moment, what Nolan needed was far more important than what I needed.

I gripped his face tighter between my hands. "Take me to meet your fathers, Nolan."

★★★

It wasn't until about halfway through our drive to the northern part of Adro that I realized I was about to meet my paramour's parents for the first time covered in blood, sweat, and dirt, my hair half falling out of its greasy braid, my cheeks a bit sunburned, and my armor a disgraceful mess.

Goddess above, save me now.

Well, at least they couldn't say I was trying too hard to make a good first impression.

Adro wasn't a very large territory, and we got to their house in under two hours. The town was certainly attacked, but it didn't look half as bad as the city we had been fighting in. Since Trevalis resided on the coast, there was a chance that a majority of Elliot's forces didn't make it in time to do any permanent damage. As we weaved our way through the streets, the brick and white stone houses matched well with the briny, salt air that surrounded us. People were already cleaning up the broken windows or damaged exteriors.

I couldn't help but smile at the two-story, gray-green stone cottage-style house we parked in front of. It was quaint and homey. Certainly a place I could picture Nolan growing up. The flowers that had been in front of it were now stomped down and the large bay window that sat to the left of the front door was completely shattered. Someone had painted still dripping red words across the door, that phrase Elliot's people loved to yell.

But, all in all, it could have been worse. We had seen worse already.

Nolan didn't hesitate, basically leaping off his cycle when he parked it, running inside. I quickly turned my own cycle and his off, grabbing the keys he had forgotten before quickly following.

"Dads." I heard Nolan's relieved, exasperated voice before I turned into what looked to be a sitting room, his arms around two men as tall as he was. They gripped their son back even tighter, each one resting a chin on one of Nolan's shoulders.

My heart warmed at the sight, even though we were surrounded by the damage done to their home. I lingered by the door, self-consciousness suddenly thrumming in my veins. I tugged at the collar of my under armor and tried my best to smooth out the hair at the top of my head, which had become even worse from the wind-blown ride.

And it was then that one of his fathers looked up to me, a twinkle of mischief in his bright hazel gaze and a giddy smile spreading across his lips. My stomach twisted even tighter at the sudden attention.

"It seems we aren't alone." He patted Nolan on the back. His husband looked up at me with a more reserved, appraising look in his deep brown eyes, which were partially obstructed by his dark brown hair falling into his face.

"Hello," I said, waving pathetically at the two of them, making their smiles broaden even further.

Nolan turned, making his way over to me in three broad steps before wrapping his arm around my shoulder and pulling me in closer. I relaxed under the touch, nuzzling into his warm embrace. "Dad, Papa, this is Kasha, the incredible woman I've told you all about."

"We assumed, son," the hazel-eyed one said, coming closer to where we stood near the entryway. His warm, tanned skin matched with his short, cleanly kept dirty blond hair. He radiated a similar energy to Nolan; approachable and a little goofy but could switch to a serious mood if necessary. "I'm Leo."

He reached his callused hand out to me, which I happily took. "Kasha, it's very nice to meet you. And you must be Wyatt?" I turned to his husband, his shoulder-length curly brown hair half out of its tether.

"That I am. Welcome to our home, Kasha. Although, this was not how we wished to meet you for the first time." Wyatt shook my hand before turning back to the very damaged furniture. It seemed some of the glass from the broken window had slashed and damaged the couch and chaise chair. Plus, some burn marks scorched the edges of the carpet. "It's going to take me hours to repair all of this."

My heart sank, remembering Nolan had mentioned Wyatt was a furniture designer. He had probably made everything in this room and had to watch his beautiful creations be defiled during the battle. If it had been my piano, where my creative energy flowed from me, I would have been devastated. I could only imagine how Wyatt was processing this.

"Is there anything we can do to help?" I gripped Nolan's waist tightly. I knew there was nothing wrong with what I was asking, yet I couldn't help worrying that I was going to offend them with every word I spoke. Or make them dislike me. Or make them think I wasn't good enough for their amazing son.

Too many whirling thoughts. Too much overthinking.

"You're very sweet," Leo said. "Yet it looks like the two of you need more help than our house does."

My shoulder hunched a bit, my fingers idly trying to brush at my disgusting armor hopelessly. "Yes. I'm so sorry. This really wasn't how I planned to meet you for the first time, but Nolan was worried and I knew it would be best if we came out to check on you right after we were finished with work. We were assigned to a city to help, and battling really isn't the best place to stay clean…"

I rambled on, but my words cut off at the slight pressure of Nolan's lips against my temple. "He's teasing us, sweetheart. He's cruel like that sometimes."

"Oh." My chest squeezed in embarrassment, a fake chuckle leaving my lips. "Of course he was."

"No matter the circumstances, we are happy to meet you." Leo patted my shoulder, his warm smile helping to ease a bit of the tightness in my muscles. "Right, Wyatt?"

Wyatt straightened from where he was mumbling over a particularly nasty gash in the center couch cushion. "Huh? Oh, of course we are. Anyone who makes our son as happy as you do is always welcome in our home."

My heart warmed at their words. "But you've just met me."

"Well, seeing as you are the topic taking up a majority of the weekly letters Nolan sends us, we felt like we met you many weeks ago." Wyatt laughed, Leo gently pulling him closer when he approached us. "So, no need to be nervous. We already like you plenty."

My heart fluttered as I looked up to Nolan. "You talk about me?"

"Of course I do." He winked at me. "Besides, they act like

they want to hear about anything else, but the moment I said we were paramours, their letters seemed to dominate with constant questions and updates about you. So, don't let them believe the discussion of the wonderful subject that is you is a one-sided thing."

"Forgive us for being protective of our child." Leo grasped his chest, looking mock-offended. "How dare we care about our son's life."

I gave a light-hearted chuckle at the dramatics, although a pang of sadness welled in my chest. My own father had never been this way, so invested in my personal life. It was sweet and beautiful. Nolan was lucky to have such wonderful parents in his life.

Nolan's face sobered a bit, a frown settling on his lips. "The two of you should come home with us. You can stay on our Compound during this war."

"We are not leaving our home." Wyatt shook his head, crossing his arms tightly against his chest. "The local authorities haven't said anything about the need to evacuate, plus, the last thing your team needs is guests while you all fight."

"I'm sure there isn't even a place for us," Leo agreed. "The guest houses will have to stay vacant in case of an emergency. You wanted to use it for a personal attachment does not constitute an emergency when we are far from displaced."

I nervously tugged at my fingers. "You could stay in my townhouse. I don't live there anymore."

I hadn't even stepped foot in it since I tried to take my own life within the walls. I could barely look at it from the outside, but if it meant keeping Wyatt and Leo safe, then I would open it back up. I would fight those demons so they would have a place to live without the fear of another attack weighing on them every day.

Wyatt tilted his head in appreciation. "Thank you, darling. That is very sweet of you. But we don't want to leave the home we raised our son in until it's absolutely necessary. And we aren't there yet."

"Dad, please…" Nolan began, but Wyatt put his hand up to stop him.

"Your papa and I discussed this already as we had a feeling you would be showing up sometime today." Wyatt stepped forward to place both hands on Nolan's shoulders, forcing his son's gaze to his. "We stay home for now. We will consider allowing you to move us somewhere safer if it is necessary later down the line, but that is the best we can agree to."

Nolan shook his head slowly, but he sighed in resignation. "Okay, I understand."

Leo gently pulled me towards him, removing me from Nolan's arms, and whispered in my ear. "Now that you know where we live, feel free to send us a message whenever our son is behaving poorly. We'll most likely be on your side."

"I heard that, Papa!" Nolan shook his head, but the joke helped defuse some of the tension that had been stiffening his shoulders and jaw.

The warmth in my chest and the spreading of a smile on my lips showed me how much I was looking forward to getting to know Nolan's incredible fathers even better.

CHAPTER 32

Kasha

Since we knew Nolan's fathers were safe, the pressure building within me to tell him about Ari returned, pressing against me and trying to force its way out.

So, when he had awkwardly brought me upstairs and showed me his old bedroom, I knew I couldn't wait any longer. We sat on the edge of the very narrow bed I couldn't imagine him ever fitting in, and he held on to me tight as I recounted every detail.

It had lightened the weight on my shoulders like talking to him always did, the pressure building rapidly under my skin easing.

I let out a shuddering breath and he pulled me closer, resting my head on his shoulder. "So, what do you want to do?" he asked.

"I don't know," I whispered. "I figured we would tell the team."

"Figured or want to?"

I tilted my head to look up at him. "Is there a difference?"

"Figured means you are resigned to the obligation. Want to means with free will, you choose to." He rubbed his thumb in gentle circles against the pulse point on my neck. "It's okay to say you desire to keep it to yourself."

"But I trust my team." I shook my head. "I've never kept anything like this from them before. Never even considered it."

He nodded in understanding. "Then what about this is making that change?"

I nuzzled into his neck, thinking over the question, letting it stir within my mind. It was a difficult one to answer, as I didn't have a concrete one, just a lot of hard feelings. As an investigator, as someone who thrived on facts and theories, this was not something easily articulated. Yet, I tried my best to explain.

"It's been swirling in my mind since I hung up with her." I stared at the wall, where a painting of this very house hung, a reminder of the home that had been built for him during his childhood. "Her… determination to get this evidence, that something to convince me to betray everyone even exists."

"What about it?"

"I know Elliot and his people thrive on stretching the truth or fabricating it in a way," I explained. "Yet, everything they prey on and talk about is steeped in some truth."

He looked at me, a bit of shock creasing his face. "Do you actually think there is something they could show you that would convince you to betray them?"

My heart lurched at his question. I didn't want to even fathom the possibility that I was capable of betraying the leaders I had spent my entire career following and listening to. For the protection and betterment of Kazola, I had let them lead.

Yet, there was something about Ari's words when she talked

about her own journey of not wanting to believe 'the truth' and how hitting rock bottom forced her to face facts. It was how she spoke about it, with so much personal honesty laced in every word, that shook me to the core.

"My trust in our High Faction is already weakened after my firsthand account of how they treat people in need. I'm not shocked that Elliot and Ari are convinced they could find evidence to convince me that following them is no longer in the best interest of Kazola." My insides heated at the onslaught of memories, but it was becoming easier to push them away, to let them filter through my mind and not dwell on them for too long.

"My gut is telling me there's more to this." I pulled away from him a bit to lean my hands on my knees, bracing myself. "I don't know why, or even what this evidence is, but it scares me. I'm terrified that there's something out there that will finally break me. That I'm closer to switching sides."

Nolan's hand stroked down my spine soothingly. "You know who you are, Kasha. You know what you believe in. Stand strong with that, and not what the High Faction or Elliot is trying to force on you. Be true to what's in here." He pressed his hand against my heart, my own reaching out to place on top of his.

What was in there felt weak and close to breaking some days. What pulsed with each beat of my heart was my dedication not to an entity or leader but to my vows. That I wanted to protect Kazola. That was what was most important to me. And for the first time in my career, I had to consider that the High Faction as it was, was not the best way to protect the people. That maybe they did not have their best interest and safety in mind.

And that thought threatened to bring me to my knees.

"I don't want to tell the High Faction." I finally told the truth I had been keeping bottled up for too long. "If for some reason Ari has evidence of foul play in our government, then we can't trust anyone on that council right now." Even those I had started to find a connection with, like Evette, Kyler, and Imogene. I had respect for them. I had confidence in them as leaders. Yet if this was true, everyone was a suspect. I could not let my personal opinion cloud my reasonable judgment when it came to such a radical accusation.

"I hate that I'm even doubting them. That I've found myself in a place where I'm considering these thoughts." I looked up at him, my heart lurching at the fear I saw him trying desperately to hide in his gaze. "But if there's even one person betraying Kazola, we cannot give them the opportunity to destroy or tamper with evidence and witnesses. They need to be held accountable, even if it's Ari that exposes them."

There was no right side in play, making my heart shatter even further. I found myself in the in-between of belief, knowing my trust lay with no one. Both had to prove to me in a way that they deserved my loyalty. Unfortunately, the red-hot fear thrumming in my veins told me I was in no way sure how that war within my soul would end. I didn't know what side I would find myself on.

That one, simple thought made me dizzy, nausea rippling in my gut.

Was I strong enough to be this person? To reconsider every-thing I had been raised to believe?

I wasn't sure I was, but I might have to force myself to be.

"And the team? Your brothers?" Nolan said, pulling me out of my spiraling fear-filled thoughts. "Are we to tell them?"

I scraped my hands down my face, groaning. "I want to tell them, but is it fair to make them carry this burden? To hold this anxious, paranoid fear while we're in the middle of a war when following the High Faction and having trust in them is imperative? I know their trust in the High Faction is weak right now from witnessing everything I went through, but that doesn't mean it's as fragile as my own. I don't want to…"

I couldn't even finish my thought, looking over at Nolan while my anxious, terrible thoughts raced through my mind at his silence. Did he not agree with me? Did he think my way of thinking was blasphemous and horrible? Was he wondering how I could even consider keeping a secret so big from those I cared about the most? Was he wondering how he had ever fallen in love with someone who could consider doing this?

Then, he finally said, "I think you're right."

I let out a relieved sob. "Really?"

He pulled me closer, pressing my cheek against his chest. "Yes. The two of us may know, and we will work hard to prove or disprove Ari's words, but right now, the fewer people who know about this, the better. We keep it to ourselves and tell them the truth when we know more."

The pressure in my chest eased a bit, knowing he agreed with me. I had never kept something such a secret from them, especially when it came to our work. But there were too many what-ifs, half-truths, and lies brewing in what could be detrimental to the way our country was governed.

To tell them, to force them into this place with me, was not something I was willing to do. Not when a war was beginning and the lives of so many rested on all our shoulders.

"We protect them." I nodded. "Even if they hate us for keeping such a big secret from them if the truth ever has to be set free."

"We may never know if this was the right decision," he soothed. "But we have to stand strong in the choice we've made."

"I'm sorry I burdened you with this," I whispered into his chest.

He held me tighter. "I am your partner in every sense of the word. I'm here to share the burden with you, not to sit back and watch while you carry it alone."

I said nothing else, allowing myself to find a bit of warmth and comfort in his embrace, letting those beautiful words wash over me. This man was something else.

He was mine and I was his, and in that moment, I realized it was a future with him that I was fighting for.

A future that I was starting to believe was mine if I was willing to fight and protect it at all costs.

CHAPTER 33

Kasha

We were back in Seathra and on Compound by that evening, disbelieving that the battle, cleanup, and meeting Nolan's parents all happened within the same day.

I honestly had no idea how I was still standing by the time I parked my cycle in front of Nolan and my house and dismounted. But unfortunately, it wasn't time for bed yet.

In a hazy, half-asleep daze, Nolan and I walked hand in hand to the conference room, sneaking into the back as the High Faction continued to talk about the post-battle statistics and moved up planning phases for the war.

Since everyone else had been back home for hours now, they all looked cleaned up and polished the way we were expected to present ourselves during any kind of meeting with the High Faction. Although we had been able to clean up a bit at Nolan's fathers' house, we were still in our grimy armor and looked like we had rolled around in a puddle of mud.

Typically, in the past, I would have been a bundle of nervous energy, terrified that the High Faction was judging me and considering me incompetent by not only being late but showing up unpresentable. Yet, those thrumming, horrid feelings were nowhere to be felt underneath my skin. I wasn't sure if I was that exhausted or the lack of it was a sign of my slowly fading faith in them. That they were no longer worth the anxious energy I used to give to them in spades.

That latter thought did send a thrill of fear pulsing in my veins.

I shook my head, pressing farther into the corner as Mitchell continued to talk. "Even though we were able to force the enemy out of Adro this morning, this battle and how underprepared we were for it shows that we need to be more vigilant in our preparations to fight Elliot and his people."

I scoffed at that as I continued to listen.

"Your orders still stand to give us ideas on how to boost our numbers to keep fighting off their forces and ultimately win. However, your ideas are now due to us the day after next," Mitchell said. "We need to decide on the best course of action so we can begin recruitment and training. As we have no idea when the next uprising will occur or which territory will be attacked next, we have to be ready for anything as quickly as possible. Understood?"

There were mumbles and nods of understanding. I knew this was part of our orders, and my team had been discussing in circles ideas that no one could agree was a good option to present to the High Faction. Looked like we had to come up with a decision sooner than expected.

"And what is your plan for Elliot?" Luspan's Alpha asked. "Just continue to let him live in that jail cell?"

I froze at that, my stomach twisting. We hadn't told the other Factions about the bond tethered between Elliot and me. All they knew was that I had been taken by him and it was upon my rescue that Elliot had officially been captured.

Mitchell cleared his throat, adjusting the collar of his shirt as if it was too tight. "A group of Alchemists is currently researching and figuring out the best way to move forward with Elliot. As he is the oldest Ibridowyn we have ever encountered, we need to tread lightly on how we remove that from him and ultimately sentence him to death when the time is right."

"To make this man a martyr at the beginning of the war might only fuel his people to fight harder," my father added. "We do not need that as we continue to navigate on how to best protect Kazola and its people."

"Which means executing him at the right time and not making any decision in haste," Imogene concluded. At least they had been prepared for that question.

A half-truth answer, one I was thankful they were keeping. However, that doubt continued to creep deeper into my thoughts. How many half-truths had they told us over the years? When we had gone undercover to the meeting Elliot's people put on, where Ezekiel had ranted about all the things the High Faction was keeping from the people: electricity in their homes, lectracycles, and other technologies available to all, and more advanced treatment facilities for addicts.

For years, I had given the diplomatic answers the High Faction had taught me: we were still building electric mining fields. We would be able to open the purchase of technologies once residential electricity was up and running. Alchemists were constantly working on better treatment options for our state facilities.

Like a parrot, I was able to say them without hesitation.

But did I trust those answers anymore? The pang in my chest let me know I was uncertain.

How many of the answers they had given us over the years had been these half-truths? How many did they already have backup answers to when their original one didn't come to pass? How often were they willing to sacrifice the livelihoods of their people for their own comfort?

Those few questions made the doubt sink in that much deeper.

★★★

"What else can we do besides a draft?" Liv argued. "It's the only way to bolster numbers that can compete with Elliot's."

"Everyone is going to suggest it!" Emric rebutted. "And then we are going to have to deal with trying to wrangle people trying to escape it, undertrain them, and throw them into a war they want no part of."

The team had given Nolan and me a half hour to run to our house, clean up, and change before returning to the conference room so we could decide what we were going to submit as our suggestion to the High Faction. We all agreed we wanted to pick our option by the end of the night so we could put together the proposal tomorrow and send it off by the night. Lucas had asked to be dismissed from the meeting, which we all agreed to, sending him off to be with Taylor.

And in the past hour we had been crowded into this room, it seemed as if we were talking in circles.

"Why don't people want to fight for their freedom?" Eden shook her head.

"Not all of them are trained to," Greyson reminded her. "Not all of them believe in their strength or have the ability to pick up a sword and fight."

"We need to find a better way to get people who are trained to assist us." Beckett followed Greyson's reasoning.

"Maybe a more specialized draft?" Liv said. "Instead of taking everyone who is able to fight, we make those qualified take a test to see their abilities, and if they pass, then they are drafted."

"We don't have time for that," Emric argued again, clearly against the draft.

"It wouldn't be enough even if we did." Beckett shook his head. "People would still try and run or get themselves disqualified. We risk them hurting themselves to get out of it."

"But it might be the best option we have." I sided with Liv on her idea, as it was the only one I thought might be considered a good one. In the end, there weren't many options. "We are a fairly isolated Isle, and we don't have time to send out ships to other continents to broker alliances. Even if we did have the time, our relations with other countries are cordial but nowhere near close enough that they would be willing to risk their people in a war they didn't benefit from. We are limited to the people on the Isle."

A few resigned sighs echoed around me. Beckett was rubbing the bridge of his nose probably attempting to relieve a headache, and Liv was looking up at the ceiling as if trying to will a better idea to pop into her head.

I barely believed in the idea, and even Liv who had come up with it seemed lackluster. But what else could we do except draft?

That question ruminated in my mind, pestering me. My gut was churning, warning me that I was missing something. That I was missing a more obvious answer that could help turn the tides.

What we really needed were people who were already trained, or at least more willing to learn to fight. We needed to feed off their desperation to keep the life they had before the war began.

I knew those people existed, but I wasn't sure if the High Faction was ready to listen to that idea. Goddess above, I wasn't even sure if *I* was willing to think that thought completely through.

As we continued to talk and debate, I looked around the room at my team. I watched them volley back and forth their ideas, teasing and still finding a way to pull laughter from each other after one of the worst days of our careers.

These people were my family. They were the ones who had protected me at all costs, and I was willing to do the same for them every single day of my life. I was keeping a secret from them. I was giving them ignorant bliss during a time some would consider to be the most stressful of their lives.

But was that really fair? Guilt twisted in my veins and made me already second guess the choice Nolan and I had made a few hours before. I wanted to keep them safe, but if I was in their shoes, and I found out that this had been kept from me, the betrayal would stab me to the core.

Yet, I still didn't speak up. I allowed them to talk and be together, knowing it wasn't the right time.

And I was terrified that the right time would never happen.

It settled in quickly that my life was no longer black and white. I was entering the areas of gray that still terrified me.

And as I explored those murky, gray places with blurred moral lines, who would I become when I emerged from them? I was no longer sure.

CHAPTER 34

Kasha

The Alchemists did not waste any time when they arrived three days after the battle in Adro.

They had been delayed due to it, Kyler having to sit in on a few High Faction meetings before leaving. From here on, he would be attending the rest of them via the Comms, which also gave him the opportunity to update everyone on how the research was going on Taylor.

They swarmed around the infirmary, setting up a makeshift lab for them to work in close proximity to Taylor. If there were extensive experiments they had to do, they already had space reserved at the closest Alchemist Lab. They had already been given Lectracycles so they could travel quickly between the locations. They pushed unused beds out of the way to set up portable equipment and Beckett had all but cleared out his desk so they could use the extra table space.

Whatever it took to make Taylor better, that was all that mattered.

Kyler approached us, Lucas and I sitting in our usual spots at Taylor's bedside. I looked over, giving my former Alpha a warm smile, his own full lips pressing up to smile back. Lucas didn't take his gaze from his brother, but I could have sworn his jaw tightened.

"Any changes?" Kyler stood at the edge of Taylor's bed, the many rings on his fingers clanking against the metal of the footboard as he clutched it.

I looked to Lucas, assuming he would answer, but in his silence, I said, "Not to our knowledge, but I suppose the Alchemists and Beckett will figure out if anything has changed."

He nodded. "Is there anything I can do? Do you need food or…"

I was about to suggest some coffee or food, knowing Lucas had barely eaten since we returned from Adro. Instead, Lucas bit out, "No, we're fine."

"Are you sure? You look a bit…"

"I do not need *your* opinion on how I'm handling all of this, and I do not need your help." My mouth gaped at Lucas's harsh, vicious tone, but Kyler just stood there, eyes locked on Lucas. "You are here doing your duty to the High Faction, but you are not needed at Taylor's bedside. You'll get in the way."

"Lucas!" I chastised, giving him a questioning, baffled look but he shook his head at me before returning his attention to Taylor.

A solemn, resigned look overtook Kyler's handsome copper face before nodding. "Is there an office I can use for a bit? I have some work and meetings for the day."

"Take mine," I offered. "You know where it is."

He gave me another nod and one more forlorn look at Lucas before leaving the infirmary. My attention instantly turned to Lucas.

"What was that?" I stared at my Gamma, confusion racing through my mind.

He squeezed his brother's hand tighter. "He isn't a member of this Faction anymore. He isn't my Alpha and I don't care about his High Faction status. I will talk to him with the respect he has earned. Which he all but destroyed."

"What?"

"It wasn't just you he hurt when he voted against you," Lucas whispered, bright blue gaze turning to look at me.

I pulled in a shaky breath. "I didn't realize the two of you had been close when he was here."

Lucas had been a Delta for the whole time Kyler was our Alpha. Although, I tended to favor Lucas and Taylor as my assistants when Kyler sent me on investigations and missions when I was his Gamma. It allowed Kyler to get to know the twins a bit better than the other Deltas and Derchtas at the time. Still, this reaction was…personal.

His eyes flashed gold, warning me. "Let it go, Kasha."

I wanted to question more, but we were interrupted by Beckett coming over with one of the Alchemists, ushering me to move away so she could examine Taylor and take some blood samples. I zoned out, letting them mill around him and ask questions of Lucas and Beckett as she did a work-up on Taylor. My heart ached watching all of it, knowing that this was the last hope for Taylor. If they didn't come up with an antidote, what then?

What would happen to my sweet, incredible Gamma? Would he die or would he be forced to live in a perpetual state of pain, never healing from the toxins that had settled within his body?

I shivered at that thought, praying it was one that would not come to pass.

"When did this start?" The brunette Alchemist asked, the worry creasing her kind face sending a jolt through my spine. I looked down at the vile she had attached to the needle pulling blood samples from Taylor. My heart stilled at what was swirled throughout the glass.

It was blood, but mixed within the rich dark hue were swirled of black liquid. Black blood.

Beckett's eyes widened. "The last time I drew blood from him was yesterday morning, and it all looked normal."

"New development then," she grumbled, frowning deeply as she collected a half a dozen more vials before taping a bandage to the puncture wound. "I'll make note of that with the rest of the team."

"But what does it mean!?" Lucas shot from his chair, turning to the retreating Alchemist. "What's happening to him?"

She stopped, turning to look back at us, a placid, kind look returning to her smooth face. "It could be many things. I don't want to worry you with possibilities before we run tests on the blood to get a better idea of what is happening."

"But…" Lucas took a step towards her, but Beckett reached out to stop him, pushing him back down into the chair. Lucas limply complied, collapsing into it.

"I promise, we will be keeping all of you updated on everything we discover while we're here." She smiled. "Our main focus is to help your brother get better."

Lucas gave a tired nod before dropping his head to the edge of Taylor's bed, his twin not even twitching at the impact.

I took my place back at Taylor's side, reaching out to grasp his cold, paled hand. His russet brown skin had developed a grayish undertone over the past few weeks, his hair now grown past his collarbone defining the curls more. I needed him to wake up and give me that reassuring smile he always had. I needed him to laugh at us for taking all of this so seriously. I needed him to wake up and not be in unimaginable pain.

I needed to know he would be all right.

Tears stung at the edges of my eyes, and I forced myself to stand abruptly, Lucas looking up at me. "I'll be right back. Bathroom."

He nodded before resting his head back down. I walked quickly past the Alchemists, and out of the main infirmary room. Down the hall, I pushed my way into the bathroom, banging the door loudly behind me before I began to let the tears start to fall in earnest. Too many had been shed over the past few weeks. Too many people hurt, including myself.

I finally was able to control my breathing a bit, and I forced my steps forward, going towards the window that sat near the sink. I stared out of it for a few minutes, letting quiet sobs rack through me for a little longer. I didn't snap out of it until the clacking of boots rang down the hallway, slowing close by. A few seconds passed before a gentle knock echoed. When I didn't answer, the slight creaking of the door signaled me that whoever it was let themselves in.

Eden's rich pistachio caramel scent hit me first before she said, "Hey, are you all right?"

I stared out the window, watching the rest of our Faction, all of those not in the Hierarchy, walk around the Compound like it was any other day. Some dressed in training gear on their way to the workout rooms, others in the under armor and chatting in groups. They still clung together and laughed. They still were able to walk day in and day out within the walls of this Compound and live.

I wondered if I ever looked that innocent when I was them.

I hoped they would never lose it, even after we finished this war.

I wiped away the last of my tears, biting at my bottom lip. There was so much about this terrible situation that I could not control. The lives that would be lost, the minds forever changed by the trauma so many people would be forced to endure while fighting for our freedom.

But I couldn't stop myself from thinking that there was one person I could try and help, and he was lying in an infirmary bed in unimaginable pain. With Taylor, there was something I could do to help.

"When you've had to go to your family for help, how long did it take you to decide it was the right choice?" I couldn't bear to look at her, to see the judgment in her gaze, but if anyone would understand the battle of wills echoing within me, it may have been her.

Her footsteps paused. "Why are you asking me this, Kasha?"

"Why do you think?" I whispered, finally turning to face her.

She raced to my side, grasping my forearms and shaking me a bit. "No, you cannot reach out to him."

To Elliot. To use the bond he forced on me to ask him what was happening to Taylor and how to fix it.

"We know he is probably the one who created this poison. No one else would be able to come up with something like this." I shook my head, looking at my best friend. "It doesn't matter that he's been locked up. It probably took years, if not decades to create it. How can we expect to come up with an antidote in mere days."

"Taylor is strong…"

"Taylor is dying!" I shook her right back, being the first to say the terrible words out loud. To say the words we were told would rarely apply to us when we chose to become Bridos. My heart cracked at the admission. "If he doesn't die then he will spend the rest of his living days in utter agony. What kind of life is that? How can I subject him to those horrible options when I could go to the source and find a way to save him?"

"Kasha, Elliot would never give you the answer out of the goodness of his heart," she warned, the slight shake of her head making whisps of blood-red hair fall into her face. "If you ask for the answer, he will expect something in return."

"I know." I nodded, resigned. I did know, my mind having run through the many possibilities over the days I spent sitting by Taylor's side. Watching him get worse, watching his brother deteriorate and slowly fade away as well. There were many things he could ask of me: to break him out of prison, to complete the bond, to stand by him and be his queen. So many horrible, ugly things that I had been actively fighting against for weeks.

And I was very close to giving in. If it meant saving Taylor's life, I would give in.

"We are not there yet," Eden said, sounding so sure it shook me from my far-off thoughts. "The Alchemists just arrived. Give them time to work. There is still hope."

She looked at me with so much pleading in her bright green gaze, begging me to agree, to not give in to the temptation to save Taylor. I shook my head, "But…"

"Kasha, this is exactly what he wants, you'd be playing right into his hands," she reasoned, the logic pulling my gut back in the direction of safety. "Think about why it was your Faction that was targeted for this. Why it was Seathra that had been used as the test field? It was probably to hurt someone you cared about.

"He knows you are willing to sacrifice yourself for innocents, you did it in the woods during the hunt," she pressed on, her grip on my shoulders tightening. "Imagine what would happen if it was someone you cared about that needed saving? He knows that you would give up everything! So please, don't play into his hands. Do not give him what he wants. Taylor would never forgive you if you did."

I choked on the last of her words, more tears starting to fall again. She grasped me, pulling me against her and wrapping me in a hug. "It's going to be okay. We're going to save him."

I wrapped my arms around her, my tears staining her black shirt. I knew she believed in her own words, but that seed of doubt was still in my mind. And it was begging for me to give in.

CHAPTER 35

Kasha

It wasn't my Comms unit that woke us at three a.m. a few days later, or Nolan's. It was the Comms that had been given to me on the battlefield, the one I talked to Ari on. The one that I for some reason kept with me and made sure stayed charged and ready to be answered.

Just in case.

The chirping woke us both, making me throw the covers off quickly and run across our bedroom to grab it from the drawer I had shoved it in. Nolan was sitting up in bed, the moonlight filtering through the bedroom window highlighting the dark black ink that crawled up his chest and arms. He reached his hand out to me, nodding.

With a shaky breath, I answered, and the screen instantly filled with Ari's face.

She looked… different.

She looked as if she hadn't slept in days. Her auburn hair was in a twisted, messy bun on the top of her head, deep purple bruising rimmed her eyes, and her skin was a bit sallow, eyes shifted to the bright Shrivika red.

She looked a mess, and that was what was different. Perfectly primed Ari looked as if she had pulled all-nighters.

"What a pleasant surprise." I tried my best to keep my voice cool, sitting back on the bed and instantly gravitating towards Nolan. He didn't touch me, keeping himself out of the frame of the Comms, but at least I could feel his heat an inch away from me. "What can I do for you?"

I didn't want her to see the fear that was brewing in my gut and the guilt of keeping all of this from most of the people I cared about. She needed to think she was far from affecting me. She needed to believe that I was resolute in my place as a Guard soldier.

"I think it's actually what I can do for you." A half-delirious smile spread across her lips. "Remember that evidence I mentioned the last time we talked?"

My stomach dropped, my jaw ticking. "Yes?"

"It's ready for you." She lifted a cup to her lips, taking a long swig before placing it back down out of frame. By the bright red droplets her tongue reached out to lick off her lower lip, she was drinking blood.

"Sooner than I expected," I mumbled, knocking the back of my head gently against the headboard behind me.

"I decided it was best to expedite the project." She tilted her head at me, making a whisp of hair escape from its tether on the top of her head. "You seemed so intrigued by it before."

I clenched my jaw, Nolan's hand snaking out to rest on my

bare thigh, squeezing gently. I released some of the tension before responding. "Hardly."

Lies. I was intrigued in a way. I wanted to know what they were so convinced would be enough to sway me to their side. She seemed so steady in her belief that I wouldn't be able to ignore it unless I wanted to betray my oaths to Kazola.

But what could these horrible, manipulative people show me? What could possibly be happening that would change my entire perception of this war?

"Those people you allow to lead you aren't who they say they are, Kasha," Ari said.

I snorted. "Already knew that. Try again."

"No, you don't, because you have no idea how deep the corruption goes." She watched me with complete fascination, barely blinking. It was unsettling to say the least. "I have spent the past year researching and looking into every case the High Faction has dismissed or deemed unnecessary. I have seen with my own eyes the faked evidence and horrid lies others have told to push their own agenda. I have collected it all and I have compiled it together so that our future Queen can finally see the light of day. So that she can finally understand why we need her to rise up with her army and fight for us."

Her words were zealous, but her obvious lack of sleep made them sound like the rambles of someone half delusional. Although, with how deep Ari's brainwashing went, she was probably already past that point.

I ignored the passionate words, her beliefs on what my life should be, even though it was the last thing I wanted. I didn't want to be queen. I didn't want to lead an entire army to kill and take over this country. I wanted peace and prosperity. I wanted a life pursuing the job I loved with the Alpha I had fallen head over heels for, my closest friends and beloved family always with me.

I didn't know that was too much to ask for.

I shook it off, focusing on what she was implying. Corruption, faked evidence, cases dismissed for the wrong reasons.

I wished it was anything else, because after what I went through, after finding out that faked evidence had been the reason for my case dismissal…it was enough to sow a seed of doubt in my mind. It was enough for me to wonder: what if she was telling the truth?

My fingers curled into the sheets below me, my claws trying desperately to push out of my nails. "How did you learn all of this? If you have the evidence to back it up, you must have collected it from someone on the inside."

"A contact." She tilted her chin up.

"Who?" I said forcefully, even though I knew it was fruitless.

"Classified." She elongated the word, drawing out each syllable. "Who it is doesn't matter. They are in that Council Chamber constantly and they witness cases being dismissed that should have easily been convicted. Cases like yours."

My chest seized at her claims. I remembered rumors that some of the votes from my trial had been bought or pressured into a no in some way. I wasn't surprised back then, since I was trying to convict the beloved nephew of a High Tribune. Still, I figured Cole was a lone wolf in that way, in how he made sure the cases that involved Logan were dismissed. At least, I had deluded myself into believing that so I could continue following the High Faction like the good soldier I wanted to be.

But if what she was saying had even a sliver of truth, then it wasn't just Cole buying votes and tampering with a case. People who still sat in that room, lording over us, had done the same as him. They had betrayed the vows they had taken when joining the High Faction, choosing their own needs over the needs of the people.

And that sent a fresh wave of fear flooding into my veins.

It was becoming hard to keep my breathing even, to keep my face a cool, collected calm. But I forced myself to, straightening my spine and keeping my gaze solely on the screen.

On the woman right in front of me yet so far away.

"Of all the people to give this responsibility to, why you?" I tilted my head, genuinely curious about the answer. "You hate me, and I don't particularly care for you. So why did Elliot choose to assign you the responsibility of convincing me?"

"He knew I would get the job done," she gritted through her teeth. "He only trusted me to liaise with our contact that helped obtain such information. Plus, why would I make up information to get you to join our cause if I dislike you so much? The last thing I'm gonna do is put in the effort to fabricate this whole thing. I'm impartial in a way."

I snorted at that. She was far from impartial. The only thing that seemed to supersede her hatred of me was her dedication and love for Elliot. If he asked it of her, I was sure she wouldn't deny her 'King'.

"All of the evidence I collected is on its way to you now. Expect it by tomorrow evening." She leaned back, watching me with that smug gaze.

It made my blood boil. "You're not going to tell me about it yourself?"

She shook her head. "I know you well enough to know you'd prefer to hold it all in your hand and read every little detail."

"Then why even call and tell me?" My stomach twisted, fingers numbing. "You could have let it arrive and not go through the hassle of calling me when you should be sleeping. Looks like you need it."

She happily sighed, as if pleased with herself. "I wanted to see you one last time before your entire world came crumbling down around you. I'm looking forward to watching you pick up the pieces. Toodles." She waved her fingers a few times before disconnecting.

When she was gone, I let out an enraged howl, throwing the bright white, pristine unit against the wall across from us, shattering it into many unrepairable pieces. It had been a mistake keeping it, letting her have access to me like that.

I curled my legs up, wrapping my arms around them, starting to rock myself back and forth to calm my racing pulse. I rested my chin on my knees before tilting my head to Nolan, his own terrified, bleak expression probably mirroring mine.

Logic told me not to believe a word she said. Yet it was my gut that was telling me that this time, there were no lies or half-truths. What I would see tomorrow, what I would learn, would be the reality of how our country was truly run.

For once, I prayed my gut was wrong.

CHAPTER 36

Kasha

I needed a distraction from the fact that some big piece of evidence would be with me in a matter of hours. So, I decided to get up early and head to the infirmary to relieve Greyson early from his overnight shift with Lucas. At least sitting by Taylor's bedside, I could focus on him instead of counting down the minutes to whenever this mystery would arrive at my doorstep.

I walked into the building and headed up to the second floor, making my way down the hall with two cups of coffee in my hand for Lucas and me. However, I was intercepted before I could make it to the door, Kyler walking straight towards me.

"Good morning." I gave him a smile.

He looked reminiscent of the Alpha that used to reside here. Gone were the well-matched suits replaced by comfortable-looking black linen pants and a sleeveless shirt that looked like he had ripped the sleeves off a tunic. It showed off the two full sleeves of black tattoos, a patchwork of different art styles. Some new ones had even been added since the last time I had seen them on view. It was nice to see him more relaxed, although the rings still decorated his fingers, and the simple studs were still in his earlobes.

"Can you get Lucas out of here for a bit?" He leaned close, his arms crossed.

"Why, what's wrong? Do they need to do some tests on Taylor and need him out of the way?" I gripped the handles of the cups harder.

He shook his head. "No, nothing like that. He's just…" he let out a deep breath, rubbing his hand across his face, "he hasn't left in days. He's barely eating according to the Omegas I've been having bring him food and he smells like he hasn't showered since you all returned from Adro. He needs real rest and food and to clean himself."

"Did you tell him that?" I asked, a bit curious about his reaction after the other day. "Tell him you're worried about him."

"I tried, but he won't listen to me, telling me to go away with that sharp, grumpy tone of his." His deep russet eyes pleaded with me. "But you all can get him to take care of himself for a few hours."

I narrowed my eyes at him, taking in every inch of his tense, concerned stance. The worry creasing his handsome face and the tight flexing of his fingers by his side.

"What happened between the two of you?" I asked, hoping Kyler would give me an answer.

He swallowed, looking down at his feet, twisting one of the rings on his finger. "You should ask Lucas."

"I'm asking you."

He sighed tiredly, looking back up. "If Lucas wants you to know, he will tell you. Until then, all I can say is he's angry at me and has let me know. Multiple times now."

"Kyler…" I was sick of these non-answers, not sure why I was harping on this little secret detail. Maybe it was because I wanted to know what was causing my Gamma distress. Maybe I was a bit too nosey for my own good. Maybe I needed a distraction from everything.

"Please, get him out of here for a bit. Get him to bathe and eat something. He won't listen to me, but he will to you." He looked over his shoulder towards the entrance to the infirmary room. "He's too exhausted to fight at this point."

I gazed at the worry in his face, the desperate need to protect Lucas, and I couldn't stop myself from comparing it to the way Nolan gazed at me. When I was depressed or overly anxious, how he wanted to do any little thing to help make me feel better. His caring and love shined through his actions.

I don't know what face I made when this realization came to me, but it made Kyler skitter back a few steps, retreating down the hallway towards the exit. "I'll be in the offices if you need me."

I shook off the shock of what I might have pieced together, focusing on his request. That was what was important, not the lingering theory that something had happened between Kyler and Lucas and the many questions that popped rapidly into my mind at the idea.

I pulled out my Comms and dialed Eden. Kyler was right; we had to take care of the second twin too.

***

When five people showed up to watch over Taylor so Lucas could take a step away, he finally agreed. It was more like we bullied and forced him out of the room, but it worked.

I had hauled him from the infirmary and across the way to the townhouses, bringing him to mine and Nolan's instead of his own. I knew the ghosts that could linger in one's house, and I was unsure if Lucas would be able to step foot into the one he shared with his brother for long periods of time. When I walked us through the front door, he let out a shaky breath, his shoulders deflating, signaling that I had made the right call.

I sent him up to take a bath and then ran to his house and rummaged for some clean clothes, keeping it to some worn-in training gear that I knew he was most comfortable in. I left it on the bed of our guest room before heading downstairs and staring at the contents in my kitchen and how I could possibly put a meal together for the two of us.

Where was Nolan when you needed him?

Sitting with Taylor, that was where.

I decided to keep it simple, pulling out some leftover roasted chicken, this cream garlic spread Nolan always kept on hand, some lettuce, tomatoes, and cheese, along with some fresh bread he had baked last night. I started to assemble some sandwiches, proud of what I had been able to pull together.

I brewed some new cups of coffee since I had no idea where

I had abandoned the original cups I had been bringing to the infirmary. It was just about finished, the cups full of the steaming liquid and the sandwiches plated when I heard his bare footsteps padding down the stairs.

He still had that exhausted, terrified look creasing his features, but at least he was clean. At least he looked a bit more comfortable in the fresh clothes and a bit more tension released from his muscles. It was something.

He silently sat at the table as I set down all the food, the two of us sitting side by side at the round table that was set up in the dining room. I didn't want to start talking, as I honestly had no idea what to say. Should I try and distract him? Try and coax him into talking? Maybe try and convince him to sleep now and then in an actual bed and not his brother's bedside?

None of it would have been right, so I let the silence continue, our chewing and slurping the only noises around us.

Halfway through the meal, a sob racked through him, the sandwich falling from his hand and splattering across his plate. His head fell, face covered by his large hands and shoulder shaking with each tear he shed.

Lucas, the forever calm, quiet one in our little trio, broke down. Something I thought I would never see.

I scraped my chair closer, gently grasping his head in my hands and laying it on my shoulder. He clung to me, my arms wrapping around his wide shoulders to hold him close while the tears fell in earnest.

"I can't lose him. He can't leave me." The words were cracking on almost every syllable, the shaking of his body getting worse. "I went into the guard to protect him, to make sure someone always had his back. We promise. We entered the Guard together and we would leave together. And I broke that promise. Goddess, if he doesn't get better… I—I—I…"

"Shh." I hugged him closer, the close cropping of his almost black hair scratching against my cheek. "It's going to be all right. We'll do everything we can to make sure he makes it through."

He sniffled a few times. "How can you be so sure?"

I kissed the top of his head, being there in the way I knew he needed me. "I'll make sure of it."

CHAPTER 37

Kasha

It arrived later that evening, carried by a clueless courier who thought this was nothing more than another delivery being brought to the Faction Compound.

Fear had coursed through me the entire walk to the front gate, refusing to let one of the Deltas or Derchtas on guard bring it to me. I had been twitchy when taking the box from them and had almost started to hyperventilate on my way back to our house.

But I had made it, and now I was here with the supposed evidence that was meant to make me betray my country.

My insides twisted, my fingers going numb as I stared down at the tan-brown cardboard box sitting innocently on our table. It looked exactly like the stacks of boxes that currently littered our conference room, holding the case files from all of the investigations that were related to Elliot when we thought he was nothing more than a serial killer.

My, how the times had changed.

I jolted at the brush of Nolan's hand slipping into mine, his fingers giving me a reassuring squeeze. "Ready?" he asked.

I nodded. "We can't put this off."

With a final deep breath, I pulled the cover off, my eyes widening at the contents of the box. I don't know what I was expecting, but my mind had certainly filtered through the worst: a severed head, an Ogdala Dagger, some disgusting experiment that Elliot had created just for me.

But my mind hadn't gone anywhere nearly as plain and generic as case files.

Because that was what they were: case files. From dozens of trials that were put in front of the High Faction over the past five years.

They were obviously copies, but somehow, someone had gotten their hands on them. I knew they were legitimate, as I recognized a few of the case names from working in the investigation over my years in the Guard. I opened the first one I recognized; a cold case in a town an hour north of us had asked for assistance when new evidence had been discovered. It had taken Eden and me about a week there, but we had tracked down the stalker who had apparently been terrorizing the poor young lady for years. We thought we had gotten enough evidence to get him put away for life, only to find out that it was somehow dismissed due to lack of evidence and expired testing results.

It had been heartbreaking.

The file looked almost exactly the same as when we had sent it in all those years ago. However, there was something different from the typical case file, which was the cover page that now sat pinned to the stack of papers meant to persuade the High Faction to prosecute. It was a chart, listing the results of the High Faction vote that ultimately led to the dismissal of the case. But it didn't just include who voted yes and no.

Next to each vote were notes about why each person chose their vote.

Some of them were listed as bought votes, some as quid pro quo, and others listed as blackmail. Most of the time, it was in favor of dismissal, but in others, it was to get people to vote in favor of prosecuting. Some notes were simple, while others went into detail about who had been lobbying for the vote.

It should have broken my heart when I saw my father's name come up multiple times, both having lobbied for a specific vote or accepted bribes. Yet not a bit of shock coursed through me. Just utter disappointment as usual.

We kept combing through. We drank our coffee and barely spoke as we read every file until the stack was haphazardly strewed across the kitchen table. When I closed my final one, I couldn't stop myself. I let out a deep, guttural crying scream, not caring that most of the Compound had probably heard it.

I was feeling too Goddess-damn much not to let out a scream or two.

"We don't know if any of this is real, sweetheart," Nolan reasoned, still reading through a case file perched on the edge of the table. "These votes and notes could all be faked to make it appear like the High Faction is corrupted."

"I saw your name as principal investigator on some of those files." I looked over at him, resting my neck on the back of my chair. "Was the outcome listed true?"

He nodded solemnly. "Yes."

"And were they cases you were surprised to hear had gone in the direction you were least expecting?"

A grave expression whispered across his face. "Unfortunately, yes. And I even noticed a few things in my old cases that I don't remember adding. Like pieces of evidence that helped strengthen the final voting result."

I scoffed. "Faked evidence?"

"I don't remember every little detail from every case I've worked on, but it became a pattern after I questioned the third one I came across."

"Fucking perfect," I mumbled under my breath, forcing myself not to let out another irritated yell. "You're right, we can't prove if these tallies and notes are real or not. But we need to figure out a way to substantiate or disprove all of this."

"We can reach out to people discreetly. Those we have some kind of relationship with." Nolan finally pushed away the final file, turning his chair to look at me. "We can see if they were surprised by the final outcomes. If they are extra trustworthy to us, we could even show them the files and see if any evidence was added after the investigation was closed."

"We'll tell our Faction about this too." I let out a breath of relief, a bit of weight lifted off me knowing I didn't have to keep this secret anymore. I had seen some of their names on files and we would need their input. "We also need to go through each one and try and find patterns in the voting. See if there were any High Faction members who didn't participate in the doctored voting. Or if there are any major players participating in it."

More relief spread through my veins. This was a plan, and plans at least helped me feel a little better.

"Good idea." Nolan rubbed his eyes with both hands a few times. "How did Elliot even figure out this was going on?"

"We can't be too surprised. He's always twenty steps ahead of us," I said. "It also begs the question, who was this insider Ari worked with to gather all of this?"

I knew the answer already, even though I didn't voice it right away.

"They have to be a High Faction member to have gotten the details of who voted which way." Nolan scratched his chin, frowning at the file he was scanning. "Even if the details on the votes are faked, these case files go on lockdown when they get to the Chateau. The only people allowed to access them or give permission to access them is a High Faction member."

"It's also the only way they would even know about bribery and blackmail." I aggressively tapped my foot against the floor, trying desperately to release some of the buzzing building slowly in my body. "If they were being solicited with them as well."

"Kasha, this means…" His words trailed off, worry creasing his forehead.

"It means we can't talk to any of them. We can't trust any of them until we figure out which one of the High Faction members is on Elliot's side."

"We might be able to narrow it down based on the research," Nolan said. "I'm sure whoever is the double agent isn't involved in any of the tainted votes."

"That's even worse. The traitor hidden among the righteous."

It made my stomach curdle, my ears ringing as my mind began its typical descent into darkened, twisted thoughts I couldn't stop.

All these people, just like me.

They had been promised a fair trial. They had been promised unbiased opinions and a duty to find the truth. They had been promised that their best interest was at the heart of every one of these cases.

Instead, multiple High Faction members used these cases as a way to push their own agendas, protect people they found useful, punish their colleagues they felt deserved it, and leave those who had been through the worst things possible to be let down over and over again.

I dropped my head to the table, willing the tears not to fall.

"I hate them," I whispered, curling my fingers against my knees.

"Who?" Nolan's hand gently smoothed circles along my back. "The High Faction or Elliot's people?"

"All of them," I couldn't stop myself from snarling. "I hate all of them."

I hated Elliot for the tyranny and violence he was pushing in the name of destiny and fate. I hated the High Faction for making us believe they were on our side for all these years.

Ari gave me these files to create doubt. To convince me that the High Faction was the worst choice. That I could 'save' Kazola from their corruption. I was nowhere near the decision to join their side as she had been so convinced I would be. Far from it, as I could never support a side that was so ruthless and determined to bring a dictatorship posing as a monarchy to power.

But it had accomplished the creation of doubt against the High Faction.

It wasn't just these files, but everything that had happened over the past year. Knowing that faked evidence had been used in my trial, that the old High Tribune had used his power to make sure his nephew was released, and how the stain of my coming forward has followed me since that day.

This gave me even more reason to doubt them. When it was just against me, I had convinced myself it was an extenuating circumstance. One bad member in a group of good was abusing his power and it had been taken away from him.

But they were hurting other people. They were destroying other people's peace and closure for their own gains.

And that betrayal stung even deeper.

My descending thoughts were interrupted by my Comms unit ringing, the loud noise muffled from inside my pocket.

I let out a deep groan before sitting up, pulling it from my pocket. My insides squirmed as I answered the call. "Hello, Evette."

"Hello, Kasha." She gave me that warm, inviting smile of hers, instantly making guilt settle in my chest over my doubts. I steeled myself, however, knowing that a kind smile couldn't always be trusted. She may not be worthy of my trust. "I hope this isn't a bad time."

It was the worst, but... "It's fine. How can I help you?"

"Well, hopefully, I come with good news." She pushed a stray piece of black hair out of her face. "We checked in with your grandmother an hour ago. She says she has an update for us."

CHAPTER 38

Kasha

They told me I had to come alone to the meeting.

So, of course, I made sure Nolan was next to me while I pulled the video up on the big screen in the conference room.

There were only three cubes taking up the screen. Mine and Nolan's, Aggie alone in a random office in Folanoch, and the complete High Faction. I knew they were a part of this and that they would be included in all of the updates about the experiments. Still, it didn't stop the snaking of anxiety crawling up my spine, settling at the base of my neck to keep me on high alert. I didn't want them here, learning about the particulars of what was happening to me and how we could stop it.

Especially now that I looked at everyone through a different lens. One that was making me question the loyalty of every single one of them.

"Thank you for coming, Mother." My father was the first to speak, the tables rearranged this time so Mitchell, Imogene, and Alton sat in the center of the frame, their carved High Tribune chairs dwarfing the rest of the High Faction sitting around them. Father was the one in the middle.

She barely cracked a professional smile as she looked right at him. "I am here doing everything I promised to do."

"And being in Folanoch has worked well for you?" His left eyebrow raised in question, his eyes narrowing.

"Absolutely. I know you wouldn't understand completely since you never studied as an Alchemist." She paused, egging him to interrupt her not-so-subtle jab, but he didn't. Although, the tight set of his jaw gave the idea that he was desperately trying to keep himself from speaking. "However, we've been able to match up the equipment and labs that he used to complete this experiment."

"Then please, don't keep us in suspense." Father baited her right back.

I bit my cheek at their petty back and forth, leaning forward. "What is your update, Nana?"

My voice made her tense face soften, the smile spreading to be a bit more genuine. "Well, we started by going through the process that he wrote about being successful in this journal." She held up one of the leather-bound books before lowering it back down off-screen. "We didn't test it on a subject, of course. I would never do that. However, we believe the solution to be the same as what is in Kasha's arm."

"How?" Imogene asked.

"We have been tattooing it on cadavers to check pigmentation, saturation, and to make sure it is reacting to the skin in the same way it did on Kasha." She nodded. "After that, we started working on a solution. It took us a few tries, but we have worked around the clock to try and create a compound that would counteract the effects of the tattoo.

"I won't go into the specifics, as they probably won't make sense and will be a waste of time. However, we have been testing out one of the solutions, which has successfully dissolved the ink from the cadaver's skin. Four times."

I sucked in a shaky breath at her words, my hand instantly reaching over to grasp Nolan's on the table.

"Now, I know there is still plenty that could go wrong, seeing as a cadaver's skin could react very differently from a living patient, however, it is a positive indication that we may have found something that could help."

For once, no one from the High Faction spoke, a mixture of facial expressions littering the group of them, from shocked to grave to impressed. Father was the only one not to give anything away, a stony stare bearing into the screen.

But I didn't care about any of that, my mind dizzy going over the words she was saying. They couldn't have been true. What she said wasn't spoken but a figment of my imagination, making up the best-case scenario in my mind.

But the look on everyone's faces and the tightening of Nolan's fingers around mine told me I wasn't imagining it. She had said those exact words out loud as if they were true.

"Nana, what are you saying?" My voice felt so small. I was shocked it picked up over the connection.

But it did, and Nana's smile widened. "I think I can remove the tattoo, Moonlight."

***

We finished up after an hour of talking through the logistics of doing the first live test of the compound she and her team created.

Nana said it should work to sever the bond by removing it from me, but to play it safe as there were too many unpredictable variables, we would attempt to remove it from both of us at the same time.

Which meant coming face-to-face with Elliot again.

My pulse had sped up, realizing I would have to see him again. But I let out a few deep breaths, reminding myself that this time, he wouldn't be able to hurt me. This time, I would be the one hurting him. We would be removing this terrible bond, and when it was over, I would be rid of him. He wasn't going to win again.

Or he was plotting and planning. Elliot wasn't one to sit still, accepting his fate. He would still be fighting and working with his people even behind jail bars. And now I knew there was a chance that someone on the High Faction was on his side, there was an even bigger chance that the limited guards watching him were aiding not imprisoning.

Everything about this potential revelation shook me to my core. I was raising blessings to the Goddess that this whole meeting wasn't in person, as I would never be able to hide the blasphemous thoughts running through my mind.

Who was the traitor? Who was helping Elliot? Who wanted to destroy all of those they currently called colleagues and maybe even friends? Who was even skilled enough to pull off such a deception?

As always, too many questions and never enough answers.

I couldn't focus on that. What I needed to focus on was getting this Goddess-damn tattoo off my skin so I could once again trust my own thoughts.

Finally, the High Faction hung up, but Aggie stayed on screen with me. We had made a promise before leaving Folanoch, and we would be keeping it no matter what.

"Hold on," I leaned forward, pressing a few buttons on the Comms box in front of us until two new faces popped up. "Hello, brothers. We have good news."

My brothers' faces lit up when Aggie went over all she had said in the High Faction meeting again. It helped lessen a bit of the pressure weighing on my chest.

"How are you feeling?" Nolan asked. He was staring at me directly, and I could feel the weight of all of their gazes on me, waiting for my answer.

"Not to offend, Aggie, but skeptical." My stomach was churning, my mind wandering over all the things that could go wrong.

But I had gotten my hopes up so many times. I had tried my best to survive off it when all hope should have been lost. Yet, I still found myself in situations where I was forced to keep having hope, keep pressing on and trusting the process.

Hope could only go so far. Hope could only last so long before it left you with nothing.

"But," I continued, "if anyone can pull this off, it's Aggie."

"Thank you, darling." She smiled. "We can't synthesize the

new compound until we have your blood samples, and then it will take a week for it to be completed. The team is already packing everything up and then we head to the Alchemist Lab closest to the prison."

"You can stay with me while you're in town, Nana." Caleb smiled, blushing. "At least, if you want to."

"Thank you, dear. That would be great." She gave him a bright smile back. "However, I plan to go home from here for a bit, and because of that I want us all to have a family dinner in the next few days."

Well, that was unexpected. "Excuse me?"

"Nana, don't you need to stay in Crelanti to make sure everything goes okay?"

"Well, someone needs to go and collect the blood from Kasha." She shrugged. "My team is as talented as me, so don't worry. They can handle collecting the blood samples from Elliot."

My insides trembled at the thought of others getting close to him. Even if it was just for the few minutes they needed to extract his blood. I didn't want anyone else around him or getting closer to him, especially Nana. Which was silly, seeing as to complete the experiment to remove the tattoo, she would have to be in the same room as him.

But my churning, nervous stomach wasn't listening to that logic.

Yet, I still asked, "Are you sure? You aren't one to give up control like that. I would understand if you wanted to have Beckett pull the sample so you could handle Elliot."

"The next time I want to see him, Moonlight, is when I am

strapping him down to a chair and undoing the horrendous thing he put into his and your skin." Her eyes gleamed with fury that I had never seen in my grandmother's eyes before. "So, you can come to my house. I can get the sample I need and then we can have a wonderful family dinner. That includes you now, Nolan."

"Really?" His green eyes lit up. "Thank you, Aggie."

"Of course." She beamed. "Anyone who looks at my grand-daughter the way you do deserves to be called family."

Now my stomach was churning even faster, no longer from fear but utter embarrassment.

"You should invite your fathers to come as well." Nana smiled at him, his spine straightening. "That is if they are able to travel from Adro."

Nolan smiled brightly. "I think they would love that. They got to meet Kasha a few weeks ago, but I know they'd love to get to know her more and to meet her family as well."

"Wyatt and Leo? I haven't seen them since they came to help you move to your Delta assignment!" Ollie beamed.

"Wonderful!" Aggie said. "What is their address? I will send them an invitation by Falcon Mail right away."

"I can tell them, Aggie. It's fine."

She leveled one of those grandmother glares at him. "It is impolite to pass on a dinner invitation through another person. I am the host; I will invite them. Address, please."

I bit my lip to hold back a laugh as Nolan rattled off their address, and Aggie scribbled it down.

"And you want me there too, Kasha?" Caleb asked, a somber look on his face.

"Of course I do," I said without hesitation, a surge of shock rising in my veins. "You're my family too."

"Don't tell Father," Ollie teased, yet the strain of his smile let me know it wasn't as much of a joke to him as he was letting on.

We kept talking, making plans, and laughing. It almost made me forget about the war, Taylor's condition, the tattoo, and the experiment that may or may not work on removing it. I had something else to focus on, something that was much more important because of the joy it was lighting in my heart.

This was a big step, introducing families. I had never done this with a paramour before, never feeling as settled as I did when I was with Nolan or thought of our future.

I figured I would be terrified, desperately thinking over every little thing that could go wrong or all the reasons why I should try and stop it.

Yet, only light, fluttering joy pulsed in my chest, counting down the days in excitement instead of fear.

CHAPTER 39

Kasha

They were moving too slowly. Answers were not being discovered fast enough.

I couldn't sleep the night before the dinner with our families, which wasn't that surprising, but the reason behind it was. I should have been too excited to sleep or anxious over my family meeting Nolan's for the first time. I should not be terrified that my Gamma was on the brink of death.

The seizures were getting worse, his blood darkening even deeper. This morning, the Alchemists confirmed that his liver was starting to fail, forcing them to start pumping him with more antibiotics and medicines. He wasn't waking up or getting better.

He was dying, and people believed there was little we could do to help him while the Alchemists tried to find a solution.

Yet, I knew that was a lie. I knew that there was something that I could do. And I could no longer allow myself to sit around and ignore it.

Even if it had been my father who had first suggested it.

Even if it meant potentially giving up my soul to a demon, I would happily do it for the safety of Taylor and any other Brido who could get hit by this poison.

I looked over at Nolan, who was happily snoring next to me. I leaned over, kissing him gently on the temple before quietly getting out of the bed. I slipped on the first clothes I could get my hands on—some flannel pants and one of his sweaters—before tiptoeing out the bedroom door, down the stairs, and out into the cool night air.

★★★

I stared at the door for far too long, my heartbeat banging painfully against my chest as I tried to keep my breathing under control. There weren't many places I could go on the Compound where someone wouldn't look for me. I needed privacy; privacy that not even the dead of night offered me. I needed to hide, so no one could interrupt what I was about to do.

And the only place to do that was to step within the townhouse only a few doors down, abandoned almost a year ago.

My old house.

I didn't have time to waste standing outside. With each minute that passed, Taylor got worse. With shaking fingers, I reached out and unlocked the door with the key I still kept on my keychain. With a slight clack, it unlatched, the door pushing open easily.

I was assaulted immediately with the thick coating of dust on almost every surface, a deep cough escaping me as I moved deeper into the space. My limbs were numb, staring at the preserved place that had been my home for over three years. I had taken only the necessities and sentimental things with me when I moved out, every piece of furniture I had collected over the years to make this space my own still here.

And, I had no idea why, but being here felt like the right place to be when I took this step. When I did the one thing I had promised myself I would never do. In the place where I tried to take my life, that fatal night putting me on the path that had brought me here.

Elliot thought I was his future Queen because I had come back from the dead like the prophecy stated. And although that was anything but true, it was during my last night in this house that gave him the 'evidence' he needed to convince his entire cult I was their future leader.

If that night had never happened, would I still be here tonight? Would I be tied to a psychotic man, determined to get revenge on our country?

An answer I would never get. But there was a different answer I sought. One that I would get tonight. No matter what.

I settled myself on the musty, plum velvet couch, not caring about the dirt clinging to me and itching my nostrils. The gray, wide-knit blanket I used to curl around myself was still slung over the back, and the black metal and glass-top table still sat in front of me. It had been my home for so long, yet it felt like anything but. It would never be my home again.

I sat rigidly straight, fingers curling around my knees as I let out a few deep breaths and closed my eyes. For a few peaceful moments, I allowed myself to live within, in the brief safety of my mind.

And then, I began to reach out.

It came somewhat naturally to me, seeking the exact mind that I wanted to reach, to talk to. Yet, as I continued to search, pushing my abilities to connect with other Bridos to its geographical limit, my eyes began to burn, an aching pulse forming at my temples. I didn't stop, pushing and seeking, searching and reaching out. It was like waving into a dark, bleak void, looking for any escape out of its desolate abyss. I kept pushing through inch by inch…

There, a light. A place I could enter. Yet unlike all of the other minds I had entered in the past, there was no need for knocking. No need for permission. With one final, shaky breath, I did the one thing I never expected myself to be willing to do. I let myself into his mind.

"Hello, Elliot." Slithering, shivering aches crawled up my spine, disgust clogging my throat, making me extra thankful I didn't have to use my voice to speak to him.

"Well, what a lovely surprise so late at night." His words dripped with arrogant glee. *"What can I help you with this evening?"*

Tears slipped down my face, my fingers clutching the hem of my sweater. *"Tell me what your people did to Taylor."*

He said nothing for a beat before asking, *"What did they do to him?"*

I let out a stuttering breath, trying my best not to lash out. I couldn't tell if he was genuinely asking or baiting me for some reason. I couldn't risk it, though. I didn't have the energy for verbal sparring and mind games. So, I told him everything I witnessed, the noxious, black cloud and what Taylor had been enduring slowly for weeks. *"Do you know what they hit him with?"*

A silent beat passed. *"Yes."*

"Is he dying?"

Another silent beat. *"If he doesn't get help soon, then yes."*

My soul shattered at the confirmation, even though we had all known for weeks. He was only deteriorating faster. But to speculate and to have it confirmed brought reality crashing down, pushing me down with its debilitating weight.

"Then tell me how to save him." I let the desperate pleading leak from me, lacing my words. Allowing him that vulnerability, letting him know that I would do anything for his answers. *"Please."*

"Do you think I would give you this information for free?" His voice was so curious, gentle and soft. So very not Elliot.

"I will give you anything. Tell me how to save him." I was no idiot; I knew the consequences. But I didn't care anymore. Taylor had been a part of the group of people who had saved me from myself over the past year. I would not let this be his ending. I would not let this man and his psychotic followers be the reason he fell. Not when there was something I could do about it.

I would do it for any one of them. They saved me, and I would save them. Always.

"I know you think I orchestrated this, and in a way I did," he explained. *"I did indeed create the poison he was hit with, and I instructed my Alchemists to figure out a way to test it. But I never instructed them to target your Faction for practice. I never instructed them to injure one of your Faction mates in an attempt to force your*

hand."

I scoffed. *"I don't believe you."*

"I don't expect you to because it is something I would do, but for once, I did not. Not when I knew it would break you."

He sighed. *"I will not force the bond on you right now, not like this. Not when none of this was a part of my plan."* A spark of hope bloomed until he spoke again. *"But that doesn't mean I will ask for nothing."*

"What do you want?" I rocked back and forth, my breaths shallowing even more.

"All I require is an answer to a question. What did you think of the evidence Ari gave you?"

My heart skipped a beat. Then a second before returning to its erratic pace. *"How did you know about that?"*

"I have my sources, even in this disgusting cell they consider humane enough for someone to live in." He snorted a laugh. *"Does that surprise you, Rogthna?"*

"No," I stated simply. I already knew there was most likely a leak in the High Faction. I had already assumed whoever it was made sure that at least one or two of Elliot's guards in prison were also on their side. He knew too much not to.

"So then? If you want your answer, then I want one in return. What did you think of it, the lies and deceits our esteemed High Faction had traded in over the years?"

I could have lied. I could have told him I believed absolutely none of it. But I knew he would never believe me. He wouldn't believe anything but the truth. At least, I couldn't risk him keeping the answer to Taylor's condition from me. For all I knew,

I had one chance to answer, and I couldn't risk it. Not when it came to my Gamma's life.

I swallowed a lump in my throat. *"It was compelling. It's making me question."*

"Question what?"

I reached up, wiping away the many tears welling from my eyes. *"Everything."*

I swear, I could feel the smile growing widely on his face, even though I couldn't see it. It twisted my gut, rolling it over and over with nausea. *"Have the team of Alchemists working on him test his blood against that of the Removal Serum. They will find the answer there."*

My heart plummeted at that. The Removal Serum unmade the Ibridowyns. It took away what made someone a part of the Onyx Guard. And if that was part of the answer to what was happening to Taylor…

Goddess, I couldn't even complete that thought.

"That's not an answer," I fought back. *"I want the exact way to save him."*

"If I began listing off ingredients and chemical compounds, would you be able to properly communicate that to the Alchemists?" he questioned bluntly. *"Are you willing to risk your Gamma like that? One wrong step in the process and you could make him worse."*

I shook my head slowly, more tears staining my cheeks. He had me there.

"Do not worry, Rogthna," he tried to console me, which made my stomach roll more violently. *"The Alchemists will figure it out quickly. You will save him in time, I promise."*

I hunched over, dropping my head into my hands, letting reality settle into my bones. I hated it. I wanted to reject it, but I didn't have the time. So, instead, I quickly whispered, *"Thank you,"* before escaping as quickly from my mind as I could.

When silence settled back into my mind, I cried in earnest, curling up into a ball and releasing all of the pain and heartache, trying to accept the truth of what Elliot's words probably meant for Taylor.

I couldn't do it. I refused to believe them until the Alchemists told me it was true.

Still, as the sun rose, I wiped the tears from my eyes and dusted off my clothes as best I could. Then, with my head held high, I walked across the Compound to the infirmary, to tell the Alchemists what they had to do next.

CHAPTER 40

Nolan

It was a good sign that Aggie had called me family when she invited me and my fathers to this dinner. It was a wonderful sign that she wanted everyone to get together. It was an incredible sign that even with all of the pain and constant stress we were able to find the time to create happiness.

So, for the love of the Goddess, why was my stomach flipping around like this was the first time Aggie and I were meeting? I had been in the house before; I had met and talked with her on multiple occasions. Yet, my insides were twisted into a bundle of nerves, reminding me of when I was a teenager and scared to meet my first paramour's parents.

I was a touch pathetic back then, and now I felt even more so. Aggie had always been welcoming to me, so I really didn't understand why my mind was working against me at such an important moment.

She had said Kasha and I would make her the most beautiful grandbabies at that first meeting. Good sign, right?

Aggie had insisted that the dinner take place the day before she had to leave for the capital to meet with her team, which all of us happily obliged. I couldn't seem to sit still that night, the whole group of us mingling around the common room and kitchen, sipping on drinks and having a few appetizers that Aggie had already set out when we arrived. Oliver and Caleb were already here and helping their grandmother when Kasha and I showed up, Dad and Papa not far behind us.

Kasha and I stood with my fathers and Caleb talking in front of the large fireplace where a stunning painting of Aggie's three grandchildren in their guard uniforms proudly hung. My fathers and I had been immensely impressed when Kasha mentioned Aggie had painted it herself.

"Next time Nolan brings you home to visit us, you can come and see the school," Papa said to Kasha.

"Hopefully, next time Nolan brings me to your home, I won't be covered in dirt and sweat and blood." She laughed, although there was a tense pitch to it that wasn't normally there, making my pulse speed up a touch. "I'd love to see your school, though. I went to one growing up that really helped me before my Guard career."

"So many of my students would probably love to learn from someone who was still in the Guard, even if it was just for a single class. Nolan has told us in many letters how talented you are with the bow."

"Yes, you're apparently one of the best he's ever seen." Dad winked at her.

Her cheeks pinked, that cute, bashful smile of hers creeping up her face. "Yes, well, I sort of had a need to show off when he first arrived here."

I raised our linked hands, kissing the back of hers. "It certainly made an impression." That made the blush deepen red.

I glanced over at my fathers, who were both looking at me with the goofiest grins. I hadn't seen them this giddy since Cleo and I had told them about our engagement, releasing a bit of pressure from my chest. I knew they had met before, but under the tense, extenuating circumstances, they hadn't seen everything Kasha was to me. An unrealistic part of me had been scared they would compare Cleo and Kasha or would struggle to accept another woman in my life since they had loved Cleo so much.

But the glimmer of hope in their gazes told me I had let that fear get the best of me. They were already besotted with her. It made my heart sing, knowing that she fit in this part of my life too. That she fit in every part of my life so damn perfectly. It was overwhelming in the best way possible.

"If it makes you feel any better," Caleb chimed in, "she has shown off for many years. She's the only one of the three of us who can properly shoot, so she liked to rub it in our faces."

Caleb had been quiet for most of the time, which I wasn't surprised by. He was on edge, muscles tight, but he was trying his best. A part of me was surprised that Kasha was so forgiving of Caleb, especially after the way he treated her at the beginning of our time in Crelanti. I had been ready to rip his throat out or bang his head against a wall until he passed out with the comments he'd made. My blood still boiled with the resurfaced memory of it. What kept me from doing so was the fact it was more satisfying to watch Kasha fight him than my fists hitting him ever would have been. My strong, fierce Beta.

I wasn't sure if I would ever be willing to let that person in again, but to be fair, I was an only child. I would never be able to completely comprehend the special sibling bond the three of them had before the attack.

What mattered was if it was good for Kasha, and I would support her in that however I could, as I knew she would do the same for me.

We continued talking for about another fifteen minutes before I excused myself. Since Kasha seemed comfortable and settled, I knew it was best for me to seek out Aggie. Just as it was important to me for Kasha to get to know my parents better, it was important to her that I formed a connection with the parent figure in her life. Which is why I walked right into the kitchen, where Aggie stood behind the large island working away with Ollie by her side following her every order.

"Can I help at all, Aggie?" I asked her.

She looked up, a spark of delight in her bright gaze as she appraised me. "Of course, dear. You can take over chopping those veggies from Oliver." She cocked her head at one of my oldest friends standing next to her, his brows creased in concentration as if attempting surgery on an onion. And the dices were still incredibly uneven in size. "He's hopeless at this point."

Ollie threw the knife down on the cutting board. "I am trying here, Nana."

"Unsuccessfully, darling," she teased, patting his cheek. "Why don't you go and refresh everyone's drink."

I tensed; she was sending him away. I shouldn't have been surprised. My heart pounded rapidly, knowing there was an interrogation coming my way.

"Sure, Nana," he said, leaning over to kiss her on the cheek.

"And make sure that brother of yours isn't hiding in the corner away from everyone!" She pointed at him.

His smile faltered, but he regained it quickly. "Will do."

He walked past me, clapping me on the shoulder and mumbling under his breath, "Good luck," before walking out of the kitchen.

When he disappeared, Aggie turned to me.

"So, you're in love with my granddaughter?" she asked, without hesitation.

"Very much." I nodded, picking up Ollie's abandoned knife and dicing up the last two onions.

"She also mentioned that you were engaged before, a few years back." There was no malice or disdain in her voice, mere gentle curiosity. Like investigators, Alchemists were wired to search for the truth, and that was exactly what Aggie was doing.

"I was." I nodded, working on some orange wedges for a salad. "Her name was Cleo, and she died in the line of duty about four years ago."

"I am very sorry for your loss." She gave me one of those motherly smiles full of nurturing comfort.

My gaze fell, forcing myself not to do my usual habit of gently tracing the diamond ring that hung on a necklace under my forest-green button-up shirt. My hands were too sticky from cutting the oranges and I would not stain this shirt in front of

Aggie. "Thank you."

"You and my granddaughter have been through quite a lot between the two of you." She pointed out, pulling the pork roast out of the oven, the deliciously salty aroma settling my twisting stomach a bit. "Some might not be able to handle it."

"True, but I think it's what helps Kasha and me," I explained, trying to keep my voice as even as possible. "We see the struggles, and although we don't completely understand what the other went through, we understand pain, hurt, loss, and the trauma that comes with it. We support each other through that, in the way that we need, and in a way, it strengthens us individually and together."

I had never explained it out loud before. It had become so instinctual between us, to protect and comfort the other in the specific ways we needed. A flash of memory came to me, of the night I first shared a bed with her. How she was patient and loving, giving me control and letting me make the choice. It made it so much easier to slide into that bed with her, to hold her for the first time. My heart fluttered at the memory, an unbidden smile pushing my lips upward. I hoped that I was able to do the same for her.

"I agree." She nodded, walking to the sink and rinsing her hands off. "All of this needs to rest for a bit. Could you come upstairs with me? There's something I want to grab, and I could use your help."

My hackles rose a bit, knowing by the vague wording that she was up to something. With a bit of a wicked glint in her eye, she was excited, so it couldn't be bad per se, but it still made me nervous.

Still, I kept my smile plastered on my face as I walked over to wash my hands and said, "Sure."

We quietly snuck upstairs, the lithe woman leading me into a small office, painted a lovely sage green with a simple walnut desk, a bookshelf made of the same material, and a white stone fireplace, the embers still dancing brightly as we entered.

She went right to her desk, rummaging around. My muscles tightened as I stood on the other side, watching her every move. What in the name of the Goddess was she looking for? And why did she need me here of all people?

My eyes widened as her hand emerged from the drawer, a palm-sized black velvet box clutched in it.

That… was the last thing I expected.

I had to force myself not to let my jaw drop as my gaze zeroed in on it, my mind blanking of all coherent thought, breath caught in my chest.

"I want you to have this." She walked around the desk, standing in front of me, hand outstretched.

My gaze finally lowered to it, my lips parting but no sound came out. I didn't have to open it up to know what was nestled inside.

"Aggie…" I tried to push the box away, but she insisted, grabbing my wrist and forcing it into my hand. "Kasha and I haven't talked about Mating yet. I can't spring it on her. She… I… we aren't…"

"I know," she said gently. "And that's okay. I'm not expecting you to waltz down there and get on a knee in front of everyone."

"Then why…"

"With the way the world is developing, I want you to have it now." Aggie took a step forward, grasping my free hand in hers. "You love each other, and from one widow to another, let me tell you a secret. One thing we learn from the loss of a loved one is that life is shorter than we think, even with possibly hundreds of years ahead of us. Don't let life get in the way of spending it with those you love and care for the most."

She was right. Cleo and I had done that, and I lost her before our Mating Ceremony. I didn't want history to potentially repeat itself, even if I wasn't completely ready to give this to Kasha yet. Although, maybe that was more out of fear she wasn't ready.

"You are a very observant person, Aggie." I chuckled.

"Of course I am." She laughed. "But I wasn't just watching how you looked at her. I noticed how she looked at you. All love and adoration in that gaze, as if you are the stability in her life that she craves. And don't think I haven't seen the difference in her mood and self ever since you walked into her life."

"That was all her," I insisted.

"Oh, I know," she said without any doubt. "But to make it through such trauma, one must have the correct support to stand by while a person fights for themself. You were the missing piece she was waiting for."

My heart fluttered at that.

She nodded down to the still-closed box in my hand. "Well, take a look, will you?"

With a deep breath, I finally opened the box, my eyes widening at the stunning engagement ring inside. Four oval black opals nestled together in a diamond pattern, the stones glinting in the light, casting veins of midnight blue and flecks of silver shimmering across the smooth surface. They were set in a platinum band, with a barely-there diamond chip nestled right in the center, bringing the four large stones together as one.

It was stunning and mysterious and perfect for Kasha.

"Kasha's grandfather had that ring custom-made for me sixty-five years ago," she explained. "And it was her mother's after that. Alton had given it back to me after Allona's passing, asking me to keep it safe for whichever grandchild I chose. Honestly, I think it pained him too much to have it around the house."

"May I ask…" My voice trailed off, not wanting this question to come off as insensitive, but I was curious.

Her eyebrows raised. "Yes?"

"Why Kasha? Shouldn't her brothers get the option first? They are older."

"If I was a traditional person, sure." She shrugged, her long, silver braid falling down her side at the movement. "However, those boys got the most years with their mother, when Moonlight lost her at such a young age. If anyone deserves to carry a piece of her around for the rest of her life, it's Kasha."

I looked back down at the beautiful ring one last time, my heart hammering in my chest. This was the last thing we should have been thinking about. With war looming on the horizon and everything Kasha was going through with Elliot, I couldn't imagine proposing to her.

And it wasn't just that. The fear coursing through my veins was palpable, making my pulse push aggressively against my throat.

My relationship with Kasha had always been natural. Even when I let my fear and anxiety get the best of me, she proved that what we had together balanced me in a way I hadn't realized I needed. But something about this step, asking her to be my Mate, made me question my strength. Would I survive if I lost her to Elliot? Would I be able to make it through the days and fight if he took her from me again?

I knew in my heart that she was my future, but making it official, putting this ring on her finger, would bring me to a place of vulnerability that in my darkest moments after Cleo's passing, I promised myself I would never let happen again.

And although I knew that the mourner's promise was a stupid one, to take this step in the midst of a war where the mastermind behind it had fixated on her, I couldn't stop myself from letting the fear take hold of me once again.

Yet, Aggie's words rang true. I had let work and life get in the way of mating with Cleo and, although I loved Kasha and the future we were building together, it would always be a regret of mine. Would I be willing to risk making the same mistake twice?

I closed the box, wrapping it delicately in my fist and holding it to my heart. "Thank you, Aggie. You have no idea what this means to me, and to Kasha."

She leaned forward, tilting her head up to press a motherly kiss to my cheek. "You give it to her when both of you are ready."

"I will." I nodded, putting it safely in my pocket. But as we walked back downstairs, the weight of it pressed against my thigh, it made me realize I was more ready for that step than I originally thought.

CHAPTER 41

Kasha

The dinner was going well. Thank the Goddess.

They thought I didn't notice, but I saw out of the corner of my eye when Nana had led Nolan upstairs, presumably to her office. My stomach had flipped when they'd disappeared from sight, and it took a lot of control to keep myself rooted in my place, continuing the pleasant conversation with Leo and Wyatt. Still, I knew my grandmother was probably interrogating my paramour up there; she was a hard lady to please sometimes.

I breathed a sigh of relief when they emerged again and Nolan rejoined our conversation and seemed calm, happy almost. The conversation must have gone well. I had pulled him aside when Aggie had called dinner ready and asked him what had happened. He had said she asked about his intentions and showed him a family painting she did of me, my siblings, and my parents when I was a baby. I almost choked on my sparkling water when he told me that.

When dinner started, the conversation fell into happy memories to embarrass Nolan and me while amusing the other. Discussions on everyone's lives so we could all get to know each other, and even talk of the future.

I tried not to dwell on the potential that the future might be completely different than we were all hoping for.

It was difficult, though.

I saw where Nolan got his outgoing, slightly goofy personality. His parents had the same sense of humor and they had passed it in full force to their son. The way they looked at Nolan, with so much love and respect and happiness, was bittersweet. Nana looked at me like that, and so did my brothers, but it wasn't the same as your own parents. I had faint memories of Mama's encouragement, and even Father's before her death, but they seemed almost dream-like: far away and doubting reality.

It was gut-wrenching to know Mama would never meet Nolan, or Leo and Wyatt. Father, even if asked, would probably have had little desire to be here. To pretend like he approved of me and the way I had chosen to lead my life as a Guard member.

At least Wyatt and Leo had been warm and welcoming, already treating me as part of their family. That alone had brought me so much warmth and happiness, yet another reason to fight for my future. If this was the family I could potentially Mate into, it was quite the bonus perk of falling in love and spending my life with Nolan.

After we all polished off our frozen custard desserts, Nana suggested Nolan take his fathers into the living room for after-dinner drinks so she could pull the blood samples she needed from me. It wasn't the most pleasant thing to watch vials of blood be drawn on the same table we had just eaten at.

"Do you really think this will work?" My gut twisted, finally asking the question that had been humming in my mind for the past week since Aggie told us about this idea. My brothers sat across the table, their eyes wide and intent on our grandmother. waiting for an answer.

She corked the last vial, gently placing it in the rack of four before reaching forward and removing the tourniquet strapped above my elbow. The tiny pinprick where the needle had been had already healed over.

Once she removed her gloves, she looked at me. "I have hope that it will."

My shoulders deflated a bit. I wasn't sure why, but it wasn't the answer I was looking for.

She squeezed my shoulder gently. "Don't worry, I have enough hope for the both of us right now."

"Thank you." I rolled the sleeve of my long black sweater back down, beginning to nibble on the biscuit Aggie had made Ollie grab from the pantry so I could have a snack afterwards. Didn't matter that I had just eaten a three-course meal.

"I am going to get these all stored and ready for transport tomorrow." She pulled the vials closer. "I'll be back down soon."

She walked away, heading towards the stairs. A week from today, I would be in Crelanti, in an Alchemist lab, waiting to be the first live person this cure was tested on. And I prayed to the Goddess that not only did it work, but that it would never be needed again. What Elliot had created with this bond, with this invasion of another person, was vile. It was repulsive and had to be destroyed.

I would burn the journals myself to make sure his horrible experiments died with him.

I didn't wish for battle or war. I didn't wish for innocent lives to be caught in the crossfire that Elliot's people were causing with their rebellious ways. Yet a part of me craved it for the distraction it would allow me over the next week. Keeping myself moving, my mind focused.

That way, I wouldn't spend all my time focusing on the finger-numbing, mind-spinning anxiety that was already trying to claw its way up my throat. I wouldn't exert all of my energy trying to prepare myself to see Elliot once again, face to face.

Having him in my mind had been torture, even when it had been myself reaching out to him willingly. Seeing him with my own eyes was a moment I wish never needed to happen.

But I was too much of a realistic person to think that was ever a possibility.

My head turned towards the doorway that led to the living room, muffled talks and bright laughter echoing towards us. My heart fluttered at Nolan's, which I had come to know so well, wiping away the horrid thoughts that were trying to consume me.

I fell back in my chair, taking a long sip of water. "Do you think the night is going well?" I turned to look at Ollie and Caleb.

Ollie's smile finally appeared. "Yes, they love you."

"You're not just saying that?"

He laughed. "No. I met them many times when Nolan and I were stationed together. Leo does a pretty good job at hiding his opinions, but Wyatt is a horrible liar. If he didn't like you, it would be written all over his face."

Ollie's words helped to settle a bit of the anxiety pressing against my spine.

"Are you sure you don't want to come back with Nolan and me, Caleb?" I tapped my finger against the table. "The drive back to Crelanti is going to be a bitch this late at night."

He chuckled at that, his gaze lowering to the table. "No need. I'm going back to Vapalles with Ollie."

Ollie's smile fell, dipping low into a frown. I tilted my head to them. "You're not going home?"

"No." Caleb shook his head. "Ollie and I have a few things we need to work on before I return home." His jaw tensed, fingers twitching at his side. I opened my mouth, ready to ask him to elaborate when he abruptly stood from the table. "A drink sounds nice."

He was gone quickly, disappearing through the door. I turned back to my older brother, my eyebrows pinched downward. "Want to explain that to me?"

Ollie scraped his hand down his face, loosening a few strands of hair onto his forehead. "He reached out to me before the dinner, saying we needed to talk to repair what broke between us as well."

Shock shot through my veins. "Really?"

"I was just as surprised." He gave a haughty laugh. "I expected him to use his actions towards you as a good enough reason for me to forgive him as well, but…he didn't. He said we need to do it just the two of us."

"Good for him." I watched my brother, confusion setting in.

This was a good thing, Caleb taking responsibility. Yet, he still looked disappointed. "What's wrong?"

Silence fell, Ollie's face twisting in that way that meant he was pondering something that sat a bit too close to his heart for his comfort.

"A lot happened between us, Little Shadow, that even you don't know about," he whispered. "I am not sure if my soul is as forgiving as yours is."

"What happened?" I asked, many, many ideas popping into my head at once.

But he shook his head. "That's between Caleb and me. It mostly happened when you were staying and being treated at the clinic, and I never wanted to burden you with it."

"Ollie…" I leaned forward, trying to catch his hand.

He pulled away. "I still don't want to. You and he are repairing things, and Goddess, Kasha, I want to repair it as well. I want my brother back too."

My heart cracked at his words, the hurt laced within them.

"But you know me, I hold grudges. It's easier for me to keep them tightly in my grasp than let them go." He shook his head, his blue eyes, Mama's eyes, reflecting the anguish he so rarely showed to the world. "Him coming home with me is our last idea, and chance, for me to get past my grudge and him to apologize the way I need him to."

I understood exactly what he meant. The betrayal and hurt Caleb caused the two of us, although tangled together, were completely different. Caleb was doing what I needed him to do to fix our relationship, but that didn't mean it was the right way to fix his relationship with Ollie.

And although Ollie was in pain, and could indeed hold a grudge, I knew him well enough to know that if he didn't want to fix this, he would not be allowing Caleb to come back home with him.

They could do this. My brothers were strong, and they would make it through.

I had to pray that they didn't kill each other in the process.

CHAPTER 42

Kasha

I had not been in an Alchemist Lab since the day I was made an Ibridowyn.

It was colder than I remembered. When I was newly eighteen, only two months after my first transition into my wolf form, I was officially cleared to join the Guard, to take that step I had been so eager for most of my life. I remembered parts of it: being escorted to the room where they would inject me, the deep red hair of the Alchemist who would be doing it, and the warmth of the lights that hung from the ceiling.

Then, this place had brought me hope and excitement for my future. To finally put my plans into action, to make a difference and take the oaths that my parents and brothers had all taken before me. This place had been almost magical, the bridge that brought me from my childhood dreams into living them.

But now, I saw it for what it really was. A lab. A place to experiment. A place that could either change the world for the better or potentially divide it.

Everything was so white. Had it been this white when I joined? I had been transitioned in this very lab, as it was where all my family members had been treated. White walls, white ceiling, white floors; even the bright lights shining down had a white undertone instead of a typical softer yellow. Which made the metal tables, instruments, and cabinets look even harsher, reflecting everything.

The only thing that looked remotely comfortable was the cushioned reclining chair that I would be sitting in when she injected me. It was shoved to the far back wall so that they could keep Elliot near the entrance in case they needed to remove him quickly and efficiently.

Goddess, did minutes always take so damn long to pass by? This was nightmare-inducing.

Although, it was highly entertaining to see Aggie in her element in a lab. I had never been allowed inside when I was younger. By the time I was cleared, she was retired. But I could certainly see why this was her life for so long. She fit here, moved about as she did in the kitchen of her home. She would be the only Alchemist in the room, Elliot's guards the only others allowed within. We had all agreed the fewer people exposed to Elliot, the better.

My foot tapped against the floor, my boots making an obnoxious noise, echoing off the walls. This had to work. It had to.

Nolan, who was standing right next to me, hand in mine, straightened his spine, looking off to the door. Someone was talking to him. "What is it?"

"They're here." His voice strained over those two simple words.

"They're coming down the hall now."

"It's going to be all right, Kasha." Aggie came up to my left, smoothing my hair back from my face. "He didn't break you before, and he won't this time, because you are my strong, beautiful girl who has always proven those who tried to take you down how wrong they were to go up against you."

She leaned forward, kissing me on the forehead in that special way only a grandmother could. She pulled away, giving me a wink before walking back to the table where all of her supplies were. I repeated her words a few times in my head, letting them remind me that I have not broken, and I would never break. Not for anyone.

It calmed me down until the door opened up and a face that had terrorized me for far too long entered my space once again.

They pushed him in, strapped to a wheelchair. He was chained up as much as possible, a thick iron collar around his neck, connected to chains running down his front to secure his arms and hands to his chest. A different set of chains wrapped around his hips, extending down to the manacles securing his feet together.

And with all that, they had shoved a thick gag into his mouth so that even his muffled noises escaping sounded like whimpers.

Still, in such a submissive, chained-up position, wearing the simple gray linen prison outfit, he looked exactly the same. Not in looks, as his hair and stubble had grown out and were completely unkempt, his face smeared in dirt. It was the gleam in his eyes that looked so utterly familiar. Confidence. Certainty. Arrogance.

He was a prisoner, our prisoner, yet he still did not believe it. There was no fear, no worry. There was nothing about him that even remotely gave a clue that he was about to crack under the pressure of being in solitary confinement for months. Most would have gone crazy under those conditions.

And maybe that was why he found solitary confinement not so bad; he was already psychotic.

Every inch of me was begging to run, my wolf deep within clawing at my mind and heart, wanting me to fight the threat now present in the room. Take him down. Make him bleed. Make him hurt like he made me hurt.

The cacophony of emotions was debilitating: fear and anxiety, anger and vengeance. All of it was flourishing, fighting for dominance, trying to control my movements and actions.

I refused to give in to myself, to let him see everything within that was trying to overtake me. My fingers wanted to shake, sweat forming along my brow bone and dripping underneath my tunic and down my spine. And when he saw me and smiled at me through the gag, my heart picked up its pace to what would be considered a dangerous level to most.

But no, he would not get my fear or my anxiety. My anger or vengeance. He would not take even more from me.

He tried to make me small. He was trying to make me his puppet, but never would I let someone control me again. Never would I sit by and watch myself perform for the whims of others.

"Hello, Rogthna." He stared into my eyes as he spoke right into my mind, making it almost impossible to conceal the shiver running up my spine.

I didn't answer, just stared him down. The gleam in his eye brightened even more.

"Secure his chair over there," Aggie instructed, turning her back on him. I saw the ghost of her past flicker in her gaze. She was seeing her old colleague for the first time in decades. So much had changed since then. "Kasha, you can sit down now. Nolan, you can stand next to her if you'd like, on the opposite side of the tattoo."

We took our orders, Nolan helping me down into the chair before standing to my right. I settled down, rolling up my sleeve to expose the tattoo that was forced upon me. I had been avoiding looking at it for a long time and hadn't noticed it had already started to fade, now more of a brownish-red instead of a rusty red. To see that symbol etched onto my skin, the snake wrapped around the moon surrounded by thorns, made me want to be violently ill.

Hopefully, after today, it would be destroyed. No longer marring my skin as a constant reminder of what Elliot tried to make me. I already had the scar from what Logan pushed me to, I did not need a physical reminder of this as well.

After today, I could focus on more important things. The war. Helping Taylor, who was still waiting for the Alchemists to figure out what was wrong. Although they seemed confident that they were close when I checked in with them before leaving for the Capital.

"Here is how this is going to work." She pulled out a vial of murky red liquid, turning it upside down and gently prodding a needle into it, removing the serum and pulling it into the syringe. She watched it with the utmost attention but spoke to the two of us. "I will be injecting this into the tattoo itself, dividing the dose into the four outer points of it. With the cadaver, it took about ninety seconds to start showing signs of dissolving, with the whole thing dissipating within four minutes. I will be timing this to see how it's different in a living person."

"And once this tattoo is gone…" I couldn't finish the question, my words cutting themselves off.

She looked over to me, the syringe full of my last hope clutched in her fingers. "Then the bond should be broken as well. Without the tattoo in place to keep the tether stable, it will disappear along with it."

I nodded to her, but I couldn't help but see Elliot roll his eyes from behind her.

What did that mean? Was he convinced he was too smart to be outdone or did he know something we didn't? This was his experiment, and there was a chance he had kept facts out of the journals to be safe. Aggie always talked about how when working on a theory, you must write everything down; the wins, the failures, and the theories. You never knew what you needed to go back to in the middle of an experiment.

Still, if anyone was arrogant enough to keep some facts in their head instead of on paper, it was Elliot.

I shook it off, removing my gaze from him and turning to watch Aggie approach me. She took an antiseptic-soaked cloth and wiped down the injection site, threw it in a small pale, and then poised the needle by the top point of the tattoo, the snake's head.

"Ready?" Aggie looked down at me, that gentle smile of a grandmother and not an Alchemist on her lips.

I nodded, balling my left hand into a fist as I watched the needle press into my skin, stinging as all needles do, before she slowly started to press the plunge downward, forcing a quarter of the liquid into me. She did exactly as she said, repeating the movement four times at different points of the marking.

When the syringe was empty, she nodded and stepped back, grabbing the second dose and heading across the room. I stared up at the ceiling, beginning to count in my mind.

Three, four, five, six…

A moment of nothing. Then blinding, uncontrollable fire consumed me inch by inch in a matter of seconds, ripping me apart from within, tugging at my skin, wishing to tear it off me bone by bone. I gave up on counting, not able to focus on anything but the flames licking across me, disintegrating me into ash.

Make it stop, make it stop, make it stop!

I screamed, I pleaded, I cried.

Hands pressed down on my shoulders, trying to keep me in my seat, but it made it worse, concentrating the pain in one place, making me thrash even harder.

"Keep her steady." The voice was firm, the hands not enough to keep me down. "Damn, we should have tied her down."

"No." A growl erupted from next to me, the only voice I could recognize in the painful chaos surrounding me. Nolan. "She can do this."

Could I, though?

I knew I was saying words, I knew I was yelling at them, but I could not understand what was coming out of my mouth, so I doubted they could. It was too much, and how much longer would it last?

It had been going on for far too long. It had to have been longer than four minutes, right? I was too locked in a hurricane of pain that even time made absolutely no sense. Nothing made sense except the agony.

"You said ninety seconds," Nolan's voice said, frustration in it. I finally opened my eyes to look up at him, wild concern creasing his face. "Why isn't it fading?"

"I also said it could be different in live people. Give it time." That was Aggie. What were they talking about? Was it not working?

No, no, no. It had to work.

If I was going through this much damn pain, I better get something out of it!

I banged my head against the chair, willing it to stop, to work, to do something besides torture me.

Too much, too much, too much…

I looked over to the other screaming figure in the room, Elliot's painful sounds muffled by the gag, his chains keeping him from flailing wildly, although I did notice they had removed his tattooed arm from its original bindings against his chest and had strapped it to the arm of the wheelchair.

He was fighting as much as I was to escape the pain. Finally, for the first time since I knew him, he looked pathetic too.

And then, all of my vision shifted abruptly, Elliot no longer in my line of sight but myself. Sweaty and bright red, clutching the chair like my life depended on it. My mouth opened in agonizing screams that were echoing around me, my eyes wild and shifting rapidly from gold to blue. Nolan stood beside me, hands braced on my shoulders while Aggie held my tattooed arm down and watched it like a hawk eyeing its prey.

How? How was this happening? Was I dying? Had my soul left my body and now I was witnessing my final moments of life?

No, I was fighting too hard, and I could still feel every bit of fiery pain that consumed me.

Then, what was…

Then it clicked. Then I realized all too soon what was happening to me and it was even more painful than what my body was trying to endure.

I wasn't seeing through my own eyes, but Elliot's.

The second link, the sensory link, was trying to form.

CHAPTER 43

Kasha

I had no idea how I did it, how I was able to pull away, but I did, ripping my consciousness from his. My eyes took time to get back into focus, but once again I was seeing through my own gaze, Nolan above me to my right and Nana to my left.

I had to keep him out, I had to do everything possible to not allow myself to form that second link in the weakened state.

I did the only thing that came to mind and started to repeat the names of those who had supported me throughout it all. Those who constantly reminded me that I was stronger than the storm I had weathered, stronger than the trials I was constantly forced to face. It was because of them I had found the strength to survive and I would use their memories to make it through now.

Nolan. Ollie. Aggie. Beckett. Liv. Eden. Greyson. Lucas. Taylor. Emric. Lea. Caleb.

Nolan. Ollie. Aggie. Beckett. Liv. Eden. Greyson. Lucas. Taylor. Emric. Lea. Caleb.

Nolan. Ollie. Aggie. Beckett. Liv. Eden. Greyson. Lucas. Taylor.

Emric. Lea. Caleb.

Again and again, I kept repeating them in my mind, letting the image of their smiling, happy faces bring warmth to my heart and strength to my mind. Finally, the pain began to decrease, the pressure that had been sitting on my chest lightening, the fire in my veins slowly dying out until it was completely gone, a cool brush of air finally grazing against my cheeks.

I could still hear Elliot's muffled cries from the other side of the room, his body still reacting from getting the serum second. I blocked it out though, focused on the one question that mattered most to me.

My voice was hoarse, my throat in scratchy pain, but I forced myself to ask, "Is it gone?"

When I looked up into their grave, saddened faces, I knew the answer before I even looked down onto my arm to see the branding tattoo as bright and pigmented as ever.

"No!" I wailed, the word blending into the angry, violent sobs that raced through me.

This wasn't over. I wasn't free of him. I was not only stuck with him in my mind, ready to pounce into it whenever he pleased, but I had nearly linked with him in yet another weakened state.

Never again. That could never happen again.

"We'll keep trying." Aggie soothed me, using a damp cloth to wipe the sweat from my face, the gentle movement soothing. "Maybe the serum wasn't potent enough. If I adjusted some of the components to be more fitting for a living person than…"

Her words were cut off by the bone-chilling noise drifting from the other side of the room.

His crying had stopped, replaced by maniacal, evil laughter.

And that was enough to break me free of my sorrow, my rage now taking over.

I ripped myself from my chair, Aggie and Nolan stumbling back as I raced towards the horrible man in front of me. The guards tried to block me, but I was too far deep, determined to get to him. I threw them to the side, grabbing Elliot first by the throat before ripping the gag from his mouth. His laughter only intensified.

"What is so funny?" I snarled at him, my vision hazing over with gold, the extra pressure of my sharpening teeth pressing against my bottom lip.

"The fact that you believed removing this was possible. With a simple serum no less. It's quite comical."

"It worked on the cadavers. It should have been more success-ful than this." Aggie was shaking her head, frantically looking through a journal that had been sitting on the table of supplies. "Why didn't it partially work?"

"Because there was no link to break," Elliot said, so matter of factly that it didn't matter that I still held his throat in a vice-grip. "The bond we have between us is a formidable opponent. Really, Agatha, I thought you were cleverer than that."

With my free hand, I slapped him, letting all the pent-up rage, pain, and anger that he had put there over the past few weeks out. "Don't talk to her."

"Fine then, I'll talk to you, *Rogthna*." He looked up at me, face smoothing to a serious, business-like look. Didn't matter that he was chained up, that it was taking the last shred of my self-control to not let my claws out so I could tear the delicate flesh that was pulsing against my palm. "I created the bond, so you better believe I made sure that, once tethered, it would be unbreakable."

"What was created can be unmade," I said, my tensed arm starting to shake. "Ibridowyns. Even life. Whatever you did to us, whatever you made, we can find a way to unmake it."

"True, but with a bond like this, it will take your ultimate sacrifice to get rid of it." He looked up at me. "Only that can break something blessed by the God and Goddess themselves."

And that last shred of control disappeared completely.

My claws sprung completely out, the slightly curved nails pressed tightly against his tender throat, drawing blood to drip down towards the collar of his prison shirt.

"For someone who claims to be so dedicated to our deities, I have never heard such blasphemous words spoken in my life." My grip tightened, his blood staining my skin down to the second knuckle.

"So, you believe we've had peace for the last few decades?" he asked. "Is that what the High Faction is doing, then?"

My mind stuttered before recomposing myself enough to say, "As a member of the Onyx Guard, I took an oath to protect the peace that the people and the High Faction want to uphold."

"That's why you take orders from them?" He raised his eyebrow, my hackles rising, sensing a trap being set for me.

I gulped. "Yes."

"Because you trust the High Faction implicitly, right?" He struggled to speak each word, but it didn't make the impact any less painful.

I froze, my breath caught in my throat. The weight of everyone's stares burrowed into my back, all of them waiting for me to reply. But with each second that passed, I damned myself even more.

Because I could not deny it. I did not trust the High Faction. I was not sure I would ever be able to trust them again.

So how could I follow them, fight for them, if I was questioning my trust and belief in them?

I stumbled away, looking at the two soldiers who stared at me with wide eyes. "I am so sorry. Did I hurt you?"

One of them shook their head while the other looked at me and said, "No, Beta, we were more caught off guard than anything else."

"All right." I turned my back on Elliot, walking to Nolan, who opened his arms to me. When I was safely in his grasp, I turned back to the soldiers and Elliot. "Take him away."

They rushed to order, starting to prepare him to leave, my mind spiraling until that now familiar presence snuck right in.

"You are on the path to truth, Rogthna." He spoke right into my mind, eyes never leaving me while they re-secured his arm to his chest and replaced the gag. *"You can either stand with the people who want true freedom and make a difference in this county or fight for the people who make decisions and vote based on what they gain from it, not the people."*

"I don't even know if this evidence is true."

"I would never have Ari fabricate evidence. I have more honor than that." I stopped myself short of scoffing, as that was debatable. *"What I know is as the queen you are meant to be, you would never*

let those innocent lives suffer for your selfishness. You would protect them. You would bring forward justice. You would make sure that advancement and healthcare were available to all not the select. That is what I want, Kasha. Are you trying to tell me that you disagree with me on that stance?"

Once again, I could not deny his words.

"You want to see change in the world, Kasha? I am giving you a place of power, with people ready to stand behind you and fight with you. Be the change. Be the leader I know you to be."

And with that, they wheeled him away, his presence disappearing from the room and my mind.

***

Aggie had moved us to another exam room, this one with a similar comfortable chair for me to rest in. I stared up at the ceiling, somehow my mind completely blank of any thoughts. I just sat there, barely blinking with one question repeating over and over in my mind.

"Because you trust the High Faction implicitly, right?"

He was trying to make me burrow that question deeper and deeper into my mind until I came to a place where I could no longer in good conscience follow them.

And it was working.

I shook my head, trying to force rational thoughts into my mind. Even if it did work, even if I found myself incapable of trusting them completely, it did not mean that I was going to find myself on his side of the war. It did not mean that I would betray all the people I love or try and convince them to join Elliot.

It didn't mean any of that.

Then why was my gut still twisting around in knots with those rational thoughts swimming through my mind?

"You need to drink some water, sweetheart." Nolan handed me a cup with a straw, the pleading in his gaze easily getting me to relent and take a few long sips.

"This isn't over, Moonlight." Aggie settled into a chair on my other side, looking a bit more like my grandmother since she removed her lab coat. "My team is already packing everything up to head back to the lab in Folanoch. We are going to keep trying, researching, and coming up with ways to get rid of it. We'll have a new idea as soon as possible for us to test…"

I flinched at her words, the fresh memory of seeing myself through Elliot's eyes, through the almost-formed second link, allowing a fresh wave of fear through my veins.

"No." I shook my head, tears beginning to press against my eyes. "I can't go through that, not again."

"Kasha…" Nolan reached for my hand, but I pulled away.

"It almost happened again." I leaned back in the chair, staring up at the ceiling once again to tell them the truth. "In that weakened state, I almost accepted the second link. He almost got another part of me. I will not put myself back in a weakened state. I will not do it."

"Moonlight, please…" She didn't have time to finish before the door was banging open, a scent I had known since childhood flooding the room.

"The High Faction wants an update."

"Hello, Father." My eyes did not leave the ceiling, refusing to look at him.

"Unsuccessful then?" I could hear the disappointment oozing from his words.

"Add it to the list of reasons why I'm such a failure of a daughter," I mumbled, not really caring.

"Goddess, can't you be a bit respectful to your father?" I could hear the eye roll in his words; I didn't even have to look up to witness it.

"Respect is earned," Nolan mumbled under his breath.

By the sharp inhale, I knew Father was about to say something, but I didn't care what he had to say.

"Where is Caleb?" I sat up. "He said he was coming home today and would stop by to check in on me after the experiment was finished."

I didn't want my father. I wanted my brother, and that one thought warmed my heart. To be back in a place where Caleb felt a bit like comfort. It was a place I never expected to find myself again.

Father's spine straightened, jaw tensing. "We had to detour him. He had been away from his Compound for too long and ordered him to report right there. He had work to do."

A sense of doubt slithered up my spine, however Father's words did make sense. He had stayed in Vapalles for a full week. When I checked in with him last night, he seemed hopeful that those extra days were productive with Ollie, and he said he believed they were back on the right path together.

But being away for so long, especially in a time of war, meant that he had a lot of catching up to do. The High Faction could have exerted their power to send him right back to duty. And although he was no longer under our father's influence, he was still a soldier who knew how to follow orders when necessary.

Still, something seemed off.

"Well, you have your update, Anton." Aggie stood to her full height, almost the same as my father. "You can leave now."

He eyed his mother skeptically. "You don't have the authority to kick me out."

She scoffed at him. "As the Alchemist currently using this lab, with a patient of mine, and as your mother and grandmother to your children, I have all the authority I need."

Yeah, I loved my grandmother.

My father's jaw set tensely, staring down his mother like his life depended on it. Still, Aggie didn't back down under the scrutiny, straightening her spine even more and raising one questioning eyebrow at Father as if daring him to say anything more.

Finally, he took a step back, letting out a short puff of air before turning on his heels. However, it didn't stop all three of us from hearing, "Father would be rolling in his grave knowing how this family turned out." Before slamming the door behind him.

"What a brat," Aggie mumbled before turning back to me. Her face softened, my stomach rolling. "Do not listen to him, Moonlight. The one your grandfather would be most disappointed in is his own son, not you. He may have dedicated his life to the Guard and the High Faction, but in the end, the love of his family came first. Your father lost that a long time ago."

I nodded at her words, finally letting Nolan grasp my hand next to me. She was right, Father had lost that part of himself many years ago.

The day my mother died, a part of my father died along with her.

CHAPTER 44

Kasha

"What do you mean there is nothing you can do?" I balked at the Alchemist, Delany, who had been leading the research on what had poisoned Taylor.

"That is not what I said." She gave me a disapproving look, narrowing her gaze at me. "I can't do anything to bring him back to full health as an Ibridowyn. Your tip to research into the Removal Serum was a good suggestion, Beta."

My gaze lowered, heavy under the stares of all my Faction teammates. I had been honest with them once word got around that I had given the suggestion to the Alchemists, that I had reached out to Elliot. Although some of them chided me for it, even told me it had been a stupid mistake, they couldn't hide the relief in their eyes that the Alchemists seemed to be getting somewhere in their research to save Taylor.

"What we are witnessing is an Ibridowyn who has only been given a partial dose of the removal serum. It seems Elliot and his Alchemists figured out a way to create a gas form of it and compress it into a smoke bomb." Her face paled, but she continued. "However, the gas isn't as potent as the injection, forcing him into the stasis of clinging to his Ibridowyn abilities and finishing the removal to his Varg Anwyn self. It's slowly poisoning him, and as his body tries to heal, it weakens everything in his system. As of this morning, his liver, kidneys, and heart have started going into failure."

"He's dying?" Eden's voice cracked, Greyson shifting closer to her as she stared down at her fellow Gamma.

"If we do nothing, then yes."

"Does that mean you have a way to save him?" Lucas's voice cracked. He was the only one sitting, clutching his unconscious twin's hand tightly in his grip.

"We believe that if we give him a diluted dose of the Removal Serum, it will save him." She pulled out a vial, the murky gray liquid swirling within.

"Believe? Not a guarantee?" Beckett asked.

"It's not like we've had past subjects to test it on. He would be our first."

"Goddess." Lucas lolled his head forward, bringing his and Taylor's clasped hands to his forehead.

"If you do nothing, he will most likely die," she explained. "If we give him the serum, he has a better chance of surviving."

"What about giving him the Ibridowyn serum instead?" I suggested, not sure if it made any sense. "Restrengthen that part of himself."

She shook her head. "The serum has never been able to create a Brido post removal that we have tried. He's already going through the process. I don't think it will do anything."

"But you've never tested it on anyone who was only given a half dose of the removal serum, right?" I pushed. This couldn't be the only option, we had to find another one.

"Well, no, but I don't believe he is strong enough to handle it at this point." She looked down at Taylor's prone form. "Maybe if we had given it to him when he had been poisoned, his body still would have been able to handle it, but not now. You've all been through the process. You know how painful it is and the physical requirements necessary to get the injection. You know you never would have survived if you were in Taylor's current state."

I closed my eyes, leaning into Nolan's tight hold around my waist, willing the tears not to fall. She was right, though.

"There is really nothing else you can do?" Liv asked desperately. "He's… he's one of us. We can't lose him."

She let out a deep breath, sadness reflecting in her gaze. "If we had the time to do proper research, we may be able to create a cure to this, but we don't. It's up to his next of kin to decide what treatment you would like us to do. Give him the removal, which is my professional suggestion, give him the Brido serum and hope it works, or do nothing and pray that his body is strong enough to fight for itself."

Lucas sat there, eyes closed and shaking his head, not caring that all of us were staring at him, waiting for his answer. Finally, after a few minutes of silence, Kyler cleared his throat, stepping forward. "Maybe you could give Lucas time alone with his team. He needs time to think."

"Of course," Delany said, giving us one more somber look before leaving the infirmary room, her clicking heels echoing away.

"He should be allowed to make this decision for himself," I whispered, memories of Nolan explaining to me the agony it had caused him and my brothers when they had to decide if giving me the Removal Serum was the right choice. It was an eerily similar situation, and all because of the same man and his disgusting ways.

"Yes, he should, but he can't." Lucas shook his head, rubbing a hand down his face. "He can't because he is too hurt and dying and I have to be the one to make the decision for him."

He finally stood up, fingers tapping against his leg as he looked over at Beckett. "What would you do? As a medical professional."

Beckett looked at Taylor. "Delany is right. We have no idea how any of this is going to help or harm Taylor. However, she's done her research, and I would trust in her suggestion. Even if it's not the one we wanted, even if it takes Taylor away from our team, he would be alive. He would still be in our lives."

"He struggled to find a place in the world for so long, but he found one in the Guard. It was his life." Lucas shook his head. "How can I take that away from him, even if it's his best chance of survival?"

"You know him better than anyone," Kyler encouraged him. "You of all people know what he would have wanted. Believe in that and you'll make the right decision."

Lucas looked over at him, eyes glassy but unable to look away from him. Kyler reached over, wrapping his arm around Lucas and grasping his shoulder tightly. To my surprise, Lucas didn't pull away this time but leaned into it for a few seconds. He then stiffened, almost realizing what he did before disentangling himself from his old Alpha.

"Maybe you should…" Liv stepped forward, hand reaching out to comfort him as well.

"Just let me think!" Lucas screamed, all of us backing away for a few steps. He paced back and forth, all of us standing around, suffocating in the room as we watched him, waiting, being there for him however he needed. I looked around, all of our faces slowly morphing into a resigned, knowing look. We all knew what was the best path, even if we all hated it.

When Nolan had pushed for Ollie to not give me the Serum, it was because there was still a chance I could fight myself back to who I was. I could defeat the blood lust. But this was different. Taylor was being poisoned, killed slowly and torturously. He didn't have the same options as I did. He didn't have the ability to fight for himself when the chemicals swirling in his system were forcing him to shut down.

He had to survive, we had to save his life. Even if it meant losing my Gamma, at least he would be alive. That, at this point, was all that mattered.

I wasn't sure how long had passed, but eventually, Delany came back, a weak, professional smile on her face. "Have you made a decision?"

Finally, Lucas looked up, a resigned look in his gaze as he said to the Alchemist, "Give him the serum."

And then my heart broke in two.

I collapsed on the ground, kneeling in front of Taylor, his

breaths so shallow, his skin so green and pale. Nolan kneeled next to me, wrapping his arm around me as I watched Lucas take his place back on Taylor's other side, kneeling as well and brushing back his brother's hair. "You're going to be alright, Taylor. I pray you'll forgive me for this choice."

Delany didn't hesitate, grabbing a clean syringe and needle from a nearby cabinet and a rubber tourniquet, securing it around Taylor's arm above his elbow. Then, she slowly started to prepare the syringe.

The crowd pushed in tighter, closer to the bed as each member of the Hierarchy began to kneel, surrounding Taylor with the family we had all created and cherished over the years. Hands reached out, placing them gently anywhere each person could rest a touch to him. No matter what, even in unconsciousness, we wanted him to know that we were all here. That he was not alone as he was forced into this step.

"Are you ready?" Delany asked Lucas.

He nodded. "Save him."

"We're all here, Taylor," I whispered to him, leaning in close to his ear as if it would make him hear me in his coma. My tears fell rapidly down my cheeks, staining the white sheets he was wrapped in, my fingers so cool against his overheated, feverish skin. "We are all here."

I looked around the room, all of us crying and puffy-eyed, most whispering some kind of beautiful, encouraging words as Delany disinfected his arm and moved to inject him. Greyson and Eden were next to Nolan and me, while Liv, Beckett, and Emric were on the other side with Lucas. Even Millie and Colton, Emric and

Beckett's other Treasus, kneeled by Taylor's feet.

And as Delany pushed the serum into his veins, his breathing rapidly increasing and body starting to shake, I knew it didn't matter if he was no longer an Ibridowyn. He was a part of this team, always. He would never be anything less, even if he would eventually have to leave and join the standard military or do something else. He had forever left a mark on this team, particularly my heart.

He would always be my Gamma. No matter what.

CHAPTER 45

Kasha

Almost a week had gone by since Caleb had returned home, and I had heard nothing from him. I had called him every day, and in the past two days multiple times a day. Always, his Comms unit never connected to mine. I hadn't seen his face since the dinner at Nana's.

And after all that had happened with Taylor, who was still unconscious but recovering according to the Alchemists, my instincts were extra sensitive. My wolf stirred knowing that someone I cared for might be in danger. I had to figure out where he was.

Finally, I had called his Beta and then his Ar Duts partner. Both had told me that Caleb had been sent out on a special mission for the High Faction and was barely reachable because of it. When I had pressed for details about it, they gave the excuse that is usually only true half of the time: classified.

Was it probably classified? Yes. But was it classified for the reasons they were telling me? I had a deep gut feeling that was untrue.

"It could just be a coincidence." Nolan tried to reason with me, watching me from the couch as I paced in front of the large bay window in our common area. I paused, giving him the most skeptical stare I could muster. "Yeah, those words sounded a lot more pathetic when I spoke them out loud."

"Goddess, I need answers." I looked up to the ceiling, knowing what I could do to get them. It made my skin crawl knowing I was resorting to it. Still, it was my last hope.

First, though, I had to make sure I wasn't the only one getting denied an update. I plopped myself on the couch next to Nolan, who pulled me tight against his side as I took out my Comms unit and called my other brother. I nuzzled deeper into Nolan's embrace, taking my free hand to grasp his.

In a few seconds, Ollie's face lit up my screen. "Hey Little Shadow, how's it going?"

"Have you talked to Caleb since he left?" I asked without an opening greeting.

Ollie's brow creased. "No, I've been trying, though. When I asked some of his teammates, they said…"

"Classified." I knew he was probably in the same boat as me. He nodded. "Let's get answers then."

I fumbled a bit with my Comms, pushing the few buttons that would add someone to the call. Nolan pulled away so he was no longer seen on the screen, but kept our fingers linked in our laps as we waited. It took calling the connection three times before my father's familiar face appeared on a third of the screen. "It is the middle of the day, Kasha. I'm working."

"Where is our brother?"

"What?" He tried his best to sound completely unbothered, as if I was a nuisance, but one thing Father couldn't hide from me was the fear in his eyes. Not about Caleb. That he had been caught.

"You heard me, now answer the question."

"Well, if you had done any research before pointlessly calling me you would know that the answer is classified."

"And we know when that word is being used to cover something up that you don't want us to know," I said, my hand squeezing Nolan's tighter. He squeezed right back. "So, tell us the damned truth before I start going to other High Faction members that might be a little more willing to talk."

"Please, you wouldn't dare."

I raised my eyebrow at him. "Wouldn't I? So, tell me, Father, do you want to be the one to tell us like a respectable High Tribune and father, or would you like us to hear it from someone else?"

My threat wasn't empty, and by the seething, annoyed look twisting on his face, he knew I had him. He had colleagues, people forced to work with and respect him. I, however, had made alliances in that High Faction. Even though I was still doubting every single one of them since starting to learn how deep the corruption went, they didn't know that. If I needed to call in a favor to get answers, I would do it.

And my father, though many horrid things, was no idiot. Which is why he was grinding his jaw in a way I knew meant he was probably going to have a migraine after this.

He knew my threat wasn't empty and was still debating on what to do.

"Tell us where our brother is, father." Ollie's voice went low, his eyes gleaming bright gold. "Now."

A faint click echoed from father's connection before he settled, sitting in a chair I recognized from his office. "Fine. However, this is classified, and you will keep it that way."

"Fine." Ollie and I said together.

"Alpha Carrigen," my father called to Nolan. "No matter what my children have told you, I am no idiot and know you're there. I need to hear your confirmation as well."

I rolled my eyes but adjusted the camera so Nolan and I were both on screen. "I agree as well."

Father nodded before a somber frown settled on his face. "A week ago, when he was scheduled to return to his Compound, he never arrived. At first, his team thought he must have been delayed or stopped for lunch on the way, but soon too much time had passed for an excuse to be made. They called it in to us and said they were sending out search parties. That was why I gave you an excuse when I saw you at the lab. The parties were just leaving to try and find him."

"No…" Icy chills sped through my veins, my heart pumping uncontrollably.

"His lectracycle was found about two miles over the border into Crelanti, all of his belongings ransacked and strewn about." Father's jaw ticked again. The only sign that this was bothering him. That maybe there was still a bit of a soul left in his body. "Blood was found that they identified as his based on the scent of it. They tried to follow the trail, but it disappeared about three miles into a heavily wooded area."

"Father." Ollie's tone was laced with a threat. "What does this mean?"

Father took a deep breath. "It means that Caleb has been labeled missing in action for the past six days."

No. No, this was not happening. My brother was not missing.

My heart and stomach sank as it all settled in, my torso going a bit limp, Nolan bearing the weight for me. He pulled me closer, although the grip on my Comms never loosened.

No, he wasn't gone.

But…he was.

"Our brother is missing and you kept it from us?" I seethed, that rage I was feeling for too many people in my life bubbling to the surface again.

"We did not want to cause mass panic."

"Fuck that!" Ollie said.

"It was Elliot's people, wasn't it?" I knew the answer, because who else would kidnap the brother of the supposed queen that wasn't committing? They had taken a hostage. To pressure me or punish me, I did not know. Although, maybe it would end up being both.

"Someone had drawn a crude version of the tattoo on your arm onto the side of his bike. In his blood." Bile rose in my throat at that. "As we have kept the details of your tattoo classified, it is more than likely that it is someone on Elliot's side."

"I have a second brother, you idiot. I have friends. All of which are potential targets for being snatched. You didn't think that telling me and others who are potential targets would be the reasonable thing to do?"

"Most of which are in the guard and trained," my father tried to reason.

"Lea isn't!" Ollie challenged back. "She's your daughter's best friend."

"And someone Elliot had targeted before." It was taking every bit of me not to start pacing again. But to be fair, I wasn't sure my legs were strong enough. "You're lucky I moved her onto the Compound weeks ago. She probably would have been the first target if not for that and then you would be dealing with a civilian kidnapping."

Disgust rose in my belly, venomous and hot. He had taken vows to protect people, to give them the best life through policy and politics. But that was the last thing he was doing with these decisions.

Yet another reason to have doubts. Which were settling deeper and deeper the longer this went on.

"We have had undercover teams searching for him non-stop. We haven't just left him to fend for himself." He shook his head. "We figured the fewer people who knew, the better it would be."

"Of course you did." I shook my head. "Because if one Guard member can be taken by these people then others can. And none of you wanted to show weakness so you kept it quiet. Right?"

His silence was all the answer I needed.

"We need…" I was all but ready to hear whatever excuse he had, but he was cut off yet again, but it wasn't from Ollie or me this time.

It was from the blaring alarms ringing out from Ollie's office.

Screams erupted from Ollie's connection, and then warning

bells rang loudly to get the attention of everyone on that Compound.

Danger.

"Oliver?" I shot from the couch, Nolan standing too, steadying me by grabbing my hips. "What's going on?"

Noises from too far away filtered through the unit, my brother's face morphing from shock to terror to Alpha. He turned back to us. "Vapalles is under attack. Elliot's forces are rising."

"We'll get backup forces to you right away," Father said, his own unit shaking around as if fumbling to keep it in his grasp while running. "I'll get the other members together now so we can rally soldiers from other units to your aid."

"We're on our way too!" I moved too, Nolan right behind me as I rushed for the door. "No need to reach out to my team, Father, but there are plenty of our bases close enough to Vapalles to help."

He nodded. "Be safe, my children," he said before cutting off the connection.

"The team is already starting to prepare," Nolan said, tapping the side of his head. Thank the Goddess I had him, especially when I didn't feel safe using my own mental connection. "We have to get into our gear and get out of here."

"Good." I nodded, allowing Nolan to take my hand and drag me to the front door so we could rush to our offices where we kept everything. "We'll be there soon, Ollie. Don't worry."

"Little Shadow?" Ollie's voice quieted, my steps stopping as I looked at him. "I love you. Be safe, please."

"You too, big bro. I love you too."

He gave me a grim nod before the connection went black.

CHAPTER 46

Nolan

This battle was nothing like Adro.

No, this was a bloodbath.

We lost so much precious time traveling to Vapalles, going straight to the capital to assist Ollie and his team. Even with it being right over the border, we had arrived to bodies lying in the street, half alive soldiers fighting for their lives. We followed the same plan as Adro, though, splitting into four teams, each led by a Keturi member. My team went west this time, Kasha going north to follow her brother's scent.

After what happened the last time we separated in a battle, my instinct to follow her had been even more intense. It was like ripping away a piece of my soul and letting it wander away from me into danger.

It had been torturous, but I had kissed her goodbye and trusted her to protect herself and her Faction members.

I shook off that particular worry and focused on what was around me, what I was needed for. Instead of stalking the street to take down groups of betrayers, they came directly to us, attacking with everything they had. We barely made it two steps into a dank, narrow alleyway before they were on us, slashing and trying to puncture any of our vital organs, all of them carrying a mix of wooden and silver blades to cover their bases. They were quick and precise, moving with fluid grace and determined agility.

It was a minefield to keep up with. Adro's was a test, this was a true battle. This was what war looked like.

My skin prickled with constant awareness, keeping myself on high alert each time we took down a group. For weeks, we had been wondering why Elliot's people hadn't attacked other territories. Why, after Adro, things went quiet.

This was why. They had been training. They had found their weakness and fixed it.

While our High Faction continued to fight in circles. It burned my chest to think about it.

They were going harder here, no more half-trained soldiers like we found in Adro. These were their best. These were those who did not hesitate to kill, stab, and let blood drip down their blades and onto their hands. They were ruthless, heartless killers, doing what they thought was right for their futures.

What about Vapalles was different?

As I stabbed through the heart of a half-wild Varg, his body crumbling into the mud speckled along the street, my heart pounded loudly in my ears as I wondered if this had to do with Kasha. Ollie lived here. Since Caleb was taken, was this a way to draw out a second weakness of hers?

Or really, to force out most of her weaknesses? We were all here, besides Lea and Aggie. Fighting on this battlefield, trying our hardest to protect the people we took oaths to fight for. Vulnerable, weakened, and thrown into a chaos that one could very easily get lost in.

Shit, I needed to remember to breathe.

Slashing at a Shriv coming right at me, I parried his weapon and struck, slashing upwards to his very exposed neck, blood spraying across my chest and face. He screeched, grasping at the deep wound I was able to inflict, falling to his knees before I smashed the end of my Amalgam into his delicate temple, making him crumble into unconsciousness.

My own Faction could be on the receiving ends of these blades. They could be bleeding and screaming in pain. They could be caught in a trap meant to take them prisoner. They could be overwhelmed and scared, and that could make them falter.

Kasha could be taken from me. Again.

That horrid thought almost made me lose my footing, falling face first into the next opponent that was running towards me, his silver, blood-speckled weapon pointed right at me.

Focus! There is a literal war going on around me!

Shaking off yet another wave of debilitating fear, I refocused my mind and dedicated everything I could to those around me.

We all fought, the clashing of weapons and bodies falling around us. My team had to split up to keep up with the assistance needed by the local guard as they tried to take down the enemies, Eden at my back as we found ourselves in what was once the town center. It was all but destroyed, abandoned food and ware carts turned over or ransacked, and what was once a marble-crafted fountain half blown to bits. The crunching of its debris under my boots made my feet ache even deeper as I fought every soldier coming for me.

I had to look away from all of the dead soldiers scattered around what used to be a welcoming, lively place. I had to put on blinders and fight the enemies that were in front of me, or else all these soldiers who had sacrificed their lives for a free Kazola would die in vain.

I fought for them and the freedom they wanted to keep for those of Kazola. They may not have been part of the Onyx Guard, but they were still my brothers and sisters in arms. They still carried out the same motto as me.

They had been protecting the peace, and I would not let their deaths go to waste.

When this was over, I would mourn every single one. For now, I kept fighting.

It took only a moment, my back turned as I took down another enemy. The scream that erupted from behind, the piercing cries of pain before the thumping of a body onto the ground, my heart clenching, my veins chilling with ice as I turned to look at my Gamma bleeding out on the dirty ground in front of me.

"Eden!" I screamed, rushing to stab the Shriv standing over her with his weapon drawn. The squelching of his heart through my blade was quick before he slid off, collapsing next to her. I shoved him away, kneeling on the ground next to her.

"Keep us protected," I ordered the group of Deltas with me, all of them surrounding us to fight off any of the attackers that would use this as an opportunity to take me down. Once the perimeter was set, I turned back to my Gamma.

She was choking, blood spilling from her lips, the wound having gone right through the gap in her leather armor, most likely puncturing a kidney or her stomach. Panic clawed its way up my throat, pressing against me from the inside out, desperate to escape. I wanted to scream and rage, but I had to stay calm, for Eden. I pressed my hand against her wound on instinct, although I knew the only way to make this better was to feed her and then move her out of the battle. She needed a physician to patch her up.

She looked up at me, her face paled and sweaty, her bottle-green eyes reflecting the pain she was trying so desperately to hide. "No... Nolan..."

"Shh, don't talk." I shook my head, her body starting to convulse, eyes beginning to shift to gold, fangs and claws starting to extend. I held her tight against me, trying to keep her as still as possible, her blood smearing across my chest plate. Her scent enveloped me quickly, a wave of dizziness sweeping through me. "We're gonna get you out of here, all right?"

She nodded, her body starting to calm the convulsing, but her body trying to shift back and forth from human to wolf was rapidly picking up, making her howl in pain.

"EDEN!" A roar came from our right, Greyson on her other side in a flash. He had been a few paces behind, helping some of the Delta's dispatch a group of rebels.

No surprise to me, he was feral, eyes glowing gold, canines extended and lips curled upwards in a low, angry growl. He reached for her, basically ripping her from my grasp and gathering her limp, half-alive body in his arms. "Rascal, what happened?"

Eden just laughed, blood coating her teeth. "You weren't there to watch my back, Rebel. You owe me one now."

My eyes widened at their words. Rascal? Rebel? They had never called each other those names before. At least, not in front of others.

"This is not a joking matter!" He growled at her, smoothing back pieces of hair from her face, the red tip of her braid splattered with mud. "We need to get you to a physician. You need to drink my blood so we can get you to safety."

"No! You need your strength!" She struggled to get the words out but still found enough to bat his wrist away from her face. "Give me to a Delta, they can take me."

"No!" He hugged her tighter to him, and I could not look away from the exchange, even though I should have been getting back to fighting the battle around us. "Let me take you."

"I—I—can't…." Her words trailed off, her hand reaching out to grasp her throat as she struggled to breathe, the gasping, wheezing puffs too shallow. Her eyes bulged out, looking between Greyson and me with a pleading, helpless gaze.

"Eden, what is it?" I reached out, loosening the upper part of her armor to check her airways, though nothing seemed to be clogging it. Still, she could not get a full breath of air in.

And then, black inky vines started crawling up her hands, neck, and face, her veins tinted in an unmistakable sign of one thing. Blackthorne.

"The blade that hit her must have been poisoned." I shook my head, looking around at the dead body I had pushed away only minutes before, grabbing his discarded blade. Sure enough, an oily, almost iridescent substance was mixed with the blood still coating it. "Futecha."

"Blackthorne doesn't affect Bridos, though," Greyson tried to reason, holding Eden close as she began to seize again.

My blood ran cold as I looked up at my Gamma. "It does if Elliot figured out a way to alter it." I stared down at Eden, going over every symptom she had shown since getting hit. "She's been struggling to hold a form too, shifting back and forth between wolf and human. Which is a sign of…"

"Wolfsbane," Greyson finished for me. "Goddess, he figured out how to combine them."

"Possibly, but right now, we have to get her to safety." I looked up, but Greyson's pained gaze was completely stuck on the woman in his arms.

My heart cracked deeper, watching him lose it over his best friend's injuries. If I was crumbling under this, he had already shattered. His breathing turned ragged, claws starting to extend, and his skin started to thin, readying for his fur to burst free. His wolf was taking over, ready to go wild on anyone who had hurt his best friend.

My blood ran cold. No, he needed to keep his head, if not for the battle, then for Eden.

I grabbed him by the front of his armor, shaking him a bit. "Greyson! Focus!"

When a wolf was poised to take over, you needed to reason with their logical, human side. Facts helped, even if they were ones a person would typically know.

His golden eyes shot to me, a low growl still echoing from his lips, but I continued, "It was not a killing blow or with a weapon that could hurt her. Even with the drugs affecting her, the dose shouldn't be enough to cause lasting damage." I was unsure if that was true, but I had to believe it. His breathing started to steady a bit, his skin plumping back up slowly. It was working. "She is going to be finehe needs to get to a medic tent. We will send a Delta…"

"No!" He barked at me, the rough, domineering command something you usually only heard from Alphas. "I will take her."

I balked at him, my mouth gaping open. What in the name of the Goddess?

"Greyson!" I all but screamed at him, my patience wearing thin. This was not the time for him to be insolent. "I need you on this field. I can't lose both of my Gammas. Let a Delta take her."

"Would you let a Delta take her if it was Kasha?" He lashed back, pressing her even closer to his chest.

My eyes widened, cheeks heating. "That's different, and you know it."

"No." His voice lowered, his gaze catching mine with unspoken emotions. "It's not different. Believe me."

Well, I couldn't say I was too surprised at that admission, but I sure wasn't expecting him to utter it as war raged around us.

His shoulders slumped, gaze lowering. Submission to his Alpha. "Please, Nolan. I won't be of any use to you if I'm worrying about her. Let me do it."

My insides rumbled, my soul settling because I knew he was

right. If it was Kasha, I would be no use until I knew she was safe. Goddess, thinking about it being Kasha threatened to make my wolf spiral. He was doing far better at controlling himself than I probably could. My resolve cracked before I finally let out a slow breath.

"Get her to a medic tent and then get your ass back into the fight," I ordered. I grabbed the sheath from the dead body and shoved the poisoned blade into it. "Take this with you and give it to the physicians. Make sure they know what we think it's coated in."

He nodded quickly, shoving the sheath into his belt and picking her up. "Yes, Alpha." He confirmed before turning and running with her in his arms.

I shook my head one last time before standing and jumping right back into the fray. My group was significantly smaller now, but we kept pushing forward. We did not falter or give up. We fought and slashed and took down any enemy we came across. Yet with every one that fell, it was like three more came to replace them. How?

As always, there were too many questions about Elliot and what he was planning. It set me on edge, but I used that anger, that pulsing vengeful need I had against him, to keep fighting. To keep going. To do everything in my power to stop him.

He would not win. He would not conquer. I would rather die before that happened.

Yet it seemed that would have to happen another day as a howl erupted into the air. I knew right away it was from one of our own. It was pained and upset, but we all knew what it meant:

retreat. Get to safety.

"Retreat!" I ordered my team, all of us running to get out of the city limits and to our caravan of cycles we had ditched near one of the healer tents. I prayed to the Goddess that was the one Greyson sent Eden to.

Cheers erupted around us as we fled, not from those of my comrades, but of the enemy, leering and mocking us as they watched us run. My stomach twisted and soured, my wolf unhappy with the cowardly command I had given, but there was no other choice. We had lost and if we didn't get out of the city limits and over the Vapalles border, we could become prisoners of war. Better to fight another day than be stuck in a cell or worse, killed.

My team and I had to regroup, and we also had to get as many of Ollie's team to our Compound before they were lost to the enemy as well.

But, in all of the chaos unfolding around me, only one question repeated over and over in my mind...

Did Kasha get to Ollie in time?

CHAPTER 47

Kasha

My heart basically stopped when the howls to retreat rang through the air, my team and I halting in our tracks to listen.

The warning was urgent and clear. We had lost this battle and had to get back over to Seathra before we became prisoners of war.

No, not now. I needed more time.

We were only four miles from Ollie's Compound. I had tried hunting him down in the fray that was the battle in their capital city. I knew his scent as if it were my own, having been surrounded by it most of my life. I knew within the first fifteen minutes of fighting that he hadn't made it to the battle.

It had set my instincts off to find him, protect him, get him to safety. My wolf was humming within, itching and pleading for me to lay eyes on Ollie. My gut was telling me that if I didn't get a visual on him, I would never be able to focus on the battle around me. So, I split my team by having my assigned Deltas stay and fight in the battle while I took Lucas as backup, racing out of the city and towards Ollie's Compound. I knew I should have left Lucas in the fighting, but I needed him by my side.

If Ollie wasn't in the battle, then he must have been kept behind to defend the Compound. It was policy to keep a team there and hold the gates for as long as possible.

He had to have taken the lead there.

All I had to do was find him and know he was safe.

But with this howling call, our orders were clear: get to our lectracycles and get back to Seathra. We would need to be there to help with any displaced citizens and soldiers. Our territory was about to be overrun with them and I needed to be the good soldier I was expected to be and get back home to safety, where I was most useful.

Unfortunately, I hadn't been known for my ability to follow orders recently. Which worked to my benefit.

I moved to take a step forward, not towards Seathra but the path to Ollie.

"We have to get out of here, now," Lucas said, yanking me back. "You know we do."

I nodded. He was right, everyone needed to get safe. "Find our team in the fray and take them back to where the cycles are, mount them, and get out of here to safety."

"Kasha..." He narrowed his eyes at me, grip tightening. "Please, don't do this."

"I have to." I yanked away from his grasp. "You would do the same if it was Taylor."

He swallowed, the pulse on his neck quivering. He couldn't

deny my words. Still, he said, "But unlike you, Taylor and I aren't targets of the people we are trying to fight. We have to keep you saf—"

I knew he had more to say, but I ran before he could finish. I knew I was being a terrible leader. I was getting my subordinates out, but I was not going with them.

Because I wasn't a soldier or a Beta or a leader. I was, first and foremost, a sister. A baby sister who found out one of her older brothers had been taken, and the snaking, sinking pit in my stomach was warning me it was about to happen again to Oliver.

To sweet, carefree, funny Ollie. The brother who, no matter what, could always bring a smile to my face. He snuck me my favorite food when I was in the clinic and was sick of the disgusting bland stuff there. He came to visit me every week, so I knew I still had family standing behind me.

And because of me, he was being targeted. He was being hunted.

I could have been wrong. I prayed to Lunestia I was. But I could not leave without having Ollie with me. If I was getting to safety, then it would be with my brother by my side. Then, we could work together to find Caleb and bring him home.

Born by Blood. Bound by Loyalty.

I had meant every word when we took that vow. And if I had to choose between my loyalty to my brothers and the loyalty to the Onyx Guard and High Faction, then I would choose my family every single time.

I picked up the pace, running and keeping my focus on trying to pick up his scent. It didn't matter that my under armor was sticking to me uncomfortably, making my skin itch, or that my breath was starting to labor, my chest tightening. I kept pushing myself forward, running, running, running…

I had to find him. He had to be here.

Three miles to go…

Another howl rang out in the air, urging everyone to get out. Get to safety. Time was running out.

I was being an idiot. If I got stuck in Vapelles by the time Elliot's forces closed down the borders, I was screwed. There would be no hiding for long: they would find me. They would have their Queen captured once again.

I couldn't let that happen.

But I couldn't leave without Ollie either.

I would get to the Compound. If I didn't pick up his scent by the time I got to the gate, I would turn back and get to safety.

Two miles to go...

He was protecting his Faction. He was protecting his Compound. Or he had already escaped to the border and was at Seathra. There was no reason why he wasn't okay. He was a strong, capable soldier. He was one of the best in my opinion. No one could hurt him.

But I would have said the same thing about Caleb.

One mile to go…

There. There it was, the bright tangerine and sweet vanilla scent that was Ollie. It was here. He was here.

I halted, closing my eyes and focusing on the familiar, pulling in a deep breath to find the direction it was coming from. My heart steadied and I focused, opening my eyes as I turned to the left. That was where it was coming from; a thicket of trees.

My heart sank even lower into my belly.

Why was he in the woods?

I took off once again, pumping my legs as fast as I could without losing the scent trail. It grew stronger and stronger, beckoning me forward to find him. Get to him. Protect him. Finally, a glint of metal caught the light filtering through the trees, leading me to where his scent was most potent. Where his lectracycle stood alone in the forest.

"No!" I screamed, not caring that the branches began to whip at me, one scratching me deeply across the face. I had to get to it. I had to see it up close.

I cried out again, my throat aching at my high-pitched wails. When I was next to the cycle, the scent trail halted completely.

And I knew both of my brothers had been taken.

It was exactly how Father had described Caleb's cycle on the side of the road. His abandoned lectracycle, pools of Ollie's blood surrounding it. Blood that had been used to draw a clumsy version of the branding forced into my skin. My throat burned with bile, my stomach threatening to retch up all its contents right in front of me.

It was exactly the same. Both attacked and taken.

However, there was one difference.

Sitting on top of the cycle, pristinely perfect amidst the chaos surrounding it, was a palm-sized box wrapped perfectly in brown paper. And written on the top was one single word: Kasha.

CHAPTER 48

Kasha

The only reason I made it out of Vapalles alive was because I took Ollie's cycle to make it faster to mine. I transferred and raced my way back through to Seathra before the border closed. Or maybe they were instructed to let me through. I didn't think too hard about it. Not when my entire focus was on the package I had shoved into my pocket that was burning into my thigh.

I didn't have to guess. I knew what it was and who had left it. I knew I was being beckoned and called once again by these people. Treated as a pawn. As a puppet to force around and play their little games.

I was over it.

I was no one's toy. I was no one's to control. I was my own person, and I made my own choices. Not the High Faction, not the rebels, not Elliot. Me.

And right then, all I cared about was getting my brothers back. All I cared about was seeing their faces and bringing them home. They had been taken, because of me. They were in danger because of me. This was all my fault.

I had no idea how I stayed on the roaring lectracycle the whole way home, my emotions bouncing around inside me, oscillating from one intense reaction to the next. I almost crashed into a tree when my wolf tried desperately to transition, then once I got myself under control, I bawled my eyes out like a whaling child. That was my entire ride back: trying to control my vicious anger and letting the painful tears fall.

By the time I rolled up to the Compound, the place frenzied with people I recognized and didn't recognize packed into the heavily guarded place, I bypassed the townhouses where I usually parked and rode right to the office building. I had barely pulled the keys from the cycle before I was racing off of it, up the stairs, and bursting into the conference room.

My entire team was there, once again covered in the dirt, grime, and fluids of a battle. Kyler was there too, the only one clean and dressed in civilian clothing from having stayed on Compound. He wasn't allowed to fight as a High Faction Delegate.

Everyone looked all right except Eden. She was extremely pale, a gray tint across her skin, deep purple bruising around her eyes, and holding her side, barely able to stay seated in her chair. Greyson was right next to her, the arms of their chairs pressed together as she leaned into him, his arm wrapped tightly around her. He was also holding a cup of blood as she sipped it dutifully through a straw. If my focus wasn't solely on one thing, I would have rushed to her side.

"Kasha…" Nolan came to approach me, but I pushed him out

of the way as gently as my half-feral self could, marching to the end of the conference table and pulling the package from my pocket. I ripped into it, snarling as I threw the paper over my shoulder like a greedy child on their birthday and removed the shining white Comms unit from its perfectly nestled place in the box.

I knew they were all staring at me, the weight of their gazes suffocating me from every angle, but I didn't care. I pushed a few buttons on the screen before clicking a number to dial. The only one programmed into the new unit. As it rang, I quickly hooked it up to the larger unit that projected onto the wall, the image of the screen transferring there in time for Ari to pop up.

I didn't even give her a chance to say anything. "Where are my brothers?"

There was nothing else to focus on except the raging anger, pain, and fear lancing through every bit of me. It thrummed through my veins, pumping straight from my heart and bleeding into me like a poison slowly making its way into every crevice of my body. I wanted to get my brothers back and then punish her for everything she had ever done to me. I wanted to watch her bleed, slowly and painfully. I wanted to watch the light leave her eyes. I wanted to feel the last of her heartbeats under my palm.

That darkness I had been so scared of, the one Elliot had been convinced existed inside of me, was starting to take over, and I really didn't care to try and force it away. Instead, I wanted to use its strength to my advantage.

"Oh, you mean these brothers?" A villainous smile crept across her still red-painted lips as she maneuvered around a bit. The camera shook until two new faces came into the frame. Faces that I recognized, but barely.

I wanted to rage and scream, but the shock must have stunned me into silence, tears escaping down my chapped, wind-blown cheeks as I took in the agonizing sight.

Ollie was tied to a chair, ropes crawling up his arms to tether them behind his back. His left eye was already swollen shut, and cuts and bruises from some well-aimed punches littered his cheeks and jaw. His nose was crooked, most likely dislocated, and his reddish-brown hair had blood caked at the tips. He moaned loudly, whispering to Ari, "Get that fucking thing out of my face."

She laughed maniacally at his words.

But that was nothing, not compared to my oldest brother tied up right next to him.

Caleb… I barely recognized him through the swelling. Both eyes were black and puffed up to the point where I couldn't even see his silver irises through the connection. One cheek had a deep gash from eyebrow to lip, which must have been carved into him from a dagger of some kind. His shirt had been ripped off, more intentioned cuts carved along his chest and collarbone and disappearing from the camera. He was caked in dry, crusting blood and was barely conscious, but I heard the moaning whisper of "Kasha," mumbled through his barely moving lips.

They had been torturing him. All while I had been here, safe and ignorant about where he was.

The anger came back in full, tidal wave force. I slammed my fists down on the desk, the whole thing shaking, hairline fractures webbing from where I hit.

"Give them back," I growled, my vision tinting gold. "Now."

She pursed her lips, eyes looking up as if in contemplation before turning back to the camera, the brattiest, smug smile creasing her face. "No."

"Ari," I snarled again, my chest shaking. "What do you want?"

"You've always liked playing Elliot's games." She lowered herself so all three of them were now in the frame, her crouching between their two chairs. "Now it's time to play one of mine."

"Why are you doing this?" I demanded, not caring that my long claws were scratching into the table, marking it forever. I was not in a place to force control on the wolf within me. I needed her to feed into the frenzy, to give me the power I had been missing for so long. I would not force her away, not when she was desperate to get to my brothers. To bring them home to safety.

It was all I wanted too.

"Because you ruined everything."

"What are you babbling about?"

"You were supposed to turn yourself over to us." The screen went unsteady as if her hand was shaking. Her eyes widened, gleaming with frantic energy. It was the most uncomposed I had ever seen her. "Once you got all the data and evidence we collected, you were supposed to join us. Lead us as the queen Elliot made you. Bring our king home. Bring our country back to glory!" She scoffed, her nose scrunching up in disgust. "Instead, you stayed there. With that Faction of yours, fighting for the government that does nothing but hurt people and put their own power before the safety of our people! You have betrayed all of those who believed in you and you had to answer for it!"

"You kidnapped and tortured my brothers out of spite?" I balked at her.

"Partially for punishment," she said. "But mostly so you can show all of those who are ready to follow you how far you're willing to go for those you love. How, when you choose to protect certain people, you are willing to lay down your own life for them."

"That doesn't even make any sense, you fucking psychopath!" I screamed, picking up an abandoned mug sitting idly on the table and throwing it clear across the room, people ducking to get out of the way.

I was so lost within myself and this conversation, I forgot my entire team was witnessing my meltdown. The pulsing, painful energy within me was buzzing, aching under the skin, desperate to release itself from me. I had to get it out, let it free.

The shattering of the glass barely let enough escape.

I was losing it when I couldn't afford to. I had to rein it in.

But maybe I was too far gone.

"I'd be careful not to insult the woman who holds your brothers' lives in her hand." Her gaze narrowed at me, lips pressing down into a frown. "And you can earn their freedom back by solving one little riddle and coming to get them. No backup, no love-struck paramour by your side. Just you. Break that rule and both your brothers die."

No.

"Don't do it, Little Shadow." Ollie's voice was shaking, hoarse and dry but strong. "She can hurt us, but she can't kill us."

A glimmer of hope shimmered in my chest, but her frenzied laughter washed it away quickly. She tilted her head at him. "You may think we have no way of killing you, but your Little Shadow knows we have the very weapon that can take you glorified science experiments down."

My veins ran cold. "You're lying."

"You know Elliot created one." She shrugged so innocently. "You know he killed one of your own with it."

My gaze flicked up to my paramour, who stood across from me at the table, eyes glowing bright gold, arms tensely crossed over his chest that all his muscles were working overtime. My heart ached for him, desperation ramming into me, wanting to run to him and comfort him. I shook it off quickly, focusing on the more urgent matter at hand.

"Doesn't mean you have it."

"You're right. But are you really willing to play that gamble with your brothers' lives?" She tilted her head. "Especially since you are well aware there are other methods we could use to torture them. Your Gamma certainly learned that a few weeks ago. Oh, and that pretty red-haired Gamma friend of yours. I heard she got a taste of our newest poison today."

My eyes widened as I looked up at Eden, a single tear slipping down her face at the mention. A new poison? She nodded in confirmation, wiping away at her cheek. I looked back at Ari, contemplating my options.

She may not have had Elliot's contraband Ogdala dagger. I could try calling her bluff.

But I knew for a fact they had never found one during their sweep of Folanoch, I'd triple-checked. Which meant it was still out there. And I knew if Elliot was going to trust the only weapon that could kill him and me to anyone, it would be the most loyal of his followers.

Ari was many things, but the one thing you couldn't question was her loyalty to Elliot.

Which meant, she most likely did have the dagger that could kill both of my brothers. Their lives were at risk. And even if she didn't have the blade, she had too many poisons at her disposal now that could harm them, torture them, and kill them eventually.

If I didn't play her game, I was condemning them both.

I would never take that chance.

Goddess, I really hated this bitch.

"Fine." I forced the single word through my grinding teeth. "Give me the riddle then."

"Come to the last place the three of you were truly happy and together." She stood, making my brothers disappear. "To the place you had to hide and run, where the water flowed freely and the memories surrounded every inch. Find us at the castle your brothers built for you."

My heart stopped, my body quivering as more hot, angry tears fell down my face. "How do you know about that place?"

"We've studied everything about you, Kasha." She shook her head in mock disappointment. "Elliot wanted to know everything. Don't you remember telling him about this?"

No, I didn't, but if he knew about that special place, then I must have. Focus seemed almost impossible, but I pushed through all the thoughts rampaging in my mind. I had to think through the pain and the bloodthirsty anger. My spine straightened, my breath stuttering from my lips.

I had never told Elliot about that place. But I had told Benji. Elliot's bartender alter ego.

It had been no big deal. I had been sitting at the bar one random evening, waiting for Caleb and Ollie to show up so the three of us could head to dinner at Nana's. It had been a month before Logan attacked me and our entire relationship crumbled to pieces. We decided to meet at the Blood Moon. I went in for an ale and I casually talked to Benji, who was still new at the time, about my brothers.

Even back then, even before I had almost died and he chose me as his fate-brought Queen, he was listening. He was observing.

He remembered it all.

Her evil smile grew wider as realization must have dawned in my facial expression. "Hurry, My Queen. Wait too long and they both die."

And the line went dead.

CHAPTER 49

Kasha

I tried running from the room, desperation coursing through my veins to get to them. Save them. Help them.

Kill her.

But I was yanked back as Lucas and Kyler blocked the door. I turned, a snarl already on my lips to tell whoever was holding me back to let go, but it evaporated from my throat when my eyes locked with Nolan.

"Breathe, Kasha."

"I have to get to them." I tried pulling away in earnest, but he held tight, yanking me closer to him. My voice cracked. "I have to save them."

"And you will." He leaned forward, placing a firm kiss on my forehead. "But you need to breathe first and figure out a plan."

"I don't have time..."

"Make it," Beckett said from across the room. "You are not stupid; you know there is a trap waiting for you. You need to make a plan before rushing in there."

I clutched onto Nolan, letting the words of my team flow through me, to break through the utter panic that was trying to consume every inch of me.

Plan. I needed a plan. It was the only way I would save my brothers.

But the longer I took to plan, the more chance that they could be killed. She hadn't given me a time limit, but I had seen it in her eyes. She wasn't used to things not going her way, and when I didn't turn myself over to their cause immediately after she had given me the evidence, something had cracked within her.

She had failed Elliot. She had failed the cause. She needed to get it back on track to make it up to him.

So, she was resorting to threats and Goddess knew what else when I arrived there.

I would kill her for it.

My emotions were everywhere, running haywire in a way that I had no idea how to control. It was too much, all-consuming and suffocating.

"Start with what you know. Where are they?" Nolan asked, giving me something to tether my thoughts to.

"They're in Seathra." My breath was coming out labored, my mind spinning. I still couldn't believe he remembered that story. "They're at our old property from when I was growing up and my parents were stationed here. It's not far."

"Good, which means you can get to them quickly," Nolan encouraged. His eyes were still gold, but the creasing on his face had smoothed out. He was trying so hard to stay calm, even though one of his oldest friends had his life in the balance and his paramour had to go in and save them.

"I'll be there within the hour," I said. My parents had wanted property for us, so had decided to commute to work so we could have an enjoyable childhood playing in the woods and yard.

"Do we tell the High Faction?" Eden said from her seat, the words shaky.

My immediate, jumping instinct told me to yell no, but I pushed through that thought and instead said, "Give me a twenty-minute head start." My gaze looked over to Kyler, who nodded agreement to my request.

I didn't know what would come out of this, but blood would be spilled today. They would need to send out a team, most likely mine, to make the rescue official. But I wanted Ari nice and preoccupied, if not already taken down, by the time backup arrived.

Even with that, it was still a risk. She said I had to go alone, or else they died.

"What else can we do to help?" Liv asked from beside Beckett.

I laughed mirthlessly. "Nothing. We don't have time to plan or the resources to do anything immediately. I have to go, and I have to go alone."

"We've been here before," Nolan said. "It didn't end well last time."

"And it probably won't end well this time either," I said honestly. There was no use in denying it. "That's what happens when we face these people. We always lose something in the process. But I can't just leave them there."

A low snarl released from his lips before he crashed them

against my own, devouring me. I melted into it, letting myself get lost in the one glimmer of happiness that I had been viciously clinging to for the past few weeks. Through the torture of this fake bond Elliot created and the war that was starting to rage, he had been the one thing keeping me afloat. He had been the stabilizing presence I had always needed to flourish under the harshest of circumstances.

And once again, I had to leave it behind. Once again, I had to let him sit by and watch as I willingly walked into danger.

I did not deserve this man. Yet I knew I would spend the rest of my life, no matter how short or long it may be, proving to him that I would try and be all that he deserved.

I only prayed I got the opportunity to do so.

Finally, after he had debauched me thoroughly, he pulled away. I rested my forehead against his. "You have to let me go."

"Never," he whispered back, but his hands released their possessive grip, his eyes never leaving me as I backed up from him and towards the door.

***

This was completely against regulation and protocol, but as I pushed my way into the house Lea was staying at, I really didn't care.

She was sitting on the couch, legs curled up under her and a book in hand. She looked up, and when we locked eyes, it slipped from her fingers, clattering to the floor. "What happened?"

"They took my brothers."

Four simple words was all it took for me to collapse, crumpling to the ground. My knees ached from the hard impact against the wooden floor, but it was inconsequential compared to the ravaging of pain surging within my heart and soul.

Everything was falling apart. Everything was collapsing around me.

My eyesight blurred a bit, my body swaying. but soon it was stabilized by a gentle embrace holding me up. Lea steadied me, a hand reaching up to cup my cheek. "Who's they?"

"Elliot's people." The words tasted like poison on my tongue.

"Oh, Goddess." She choked on the words, her hand releasing my cheek to cover her mouth, muffling the dry sobs starting to rack through her own body.

She had known them almost as long as I had. She, an only child, spent so many days with me and ultimately my brothers. She had been a part of our family for a long time, and she deserved to know that they were in danger as any other family member would be.

My heart was aching, cracking and breaking. How had I ended up here, crumbled on the floor, willing myself to get my head on straight so I could save the two people who had been my protectors since I was a child? How was I now the one forced to protect them?

"You'll find them…"

"I know where they are." I shook my head, trying to clear it as best as I could. Beckett was right. I could not go off and fight these horrendous people with such a broken, fragile mindset. I would lose. To what capacity I was unsure, but it would be a hefty price.

With my brothers' lives in the balance, it was a risk I was

unwilling to take. I had to pull myself together. For them.

"I'm going to get them." If it was any other enemy, I would have had so much more confidence in myself. Yet, even with Elliot behind bars, the people I was about to face were within his inner circle, those he had trusted the most. They were almost as dangerous as he was.

If not worse, as they were desperate to please their king.

And by the fearful look reflecting in Lea's gaze that she was trying so desperately to hide, she could hear the lack of confidence I had in myself.

I grabbed her shoulders, shaking her a bit to get her attention. "Promise me, if I don't come back, you will not leave this Compound."

"Kasha…"

"Promise me." I shook her a bit more. "They targeted my brothers, and they tried to target you once before. If I can't be here to protect you, then you have to stay put, in the one place I know you'll be safe. Please, I can't lose you too."

She reached out grabbing my upper arms, steading my shaking body as best she could. Her deep brown eyes softened, brown cheeks blushing deeply as she said strongly, "I promise. I'll let your team continue to keep me safe."

A deep, aching shiver ran through me at her words, rushing a bit of comfort through my system. My shoulder sagged, and I was helpless to fight as she pulled me closer to her, wrapping me in a warm, sisterly embrace I had been used to for many, many years. Through the loss of my mother and her many broken hearts, we had cried together.

I really hoped that this would not be the last time. I hoped we returned home from what was about to be the most dangerous fight I would ever encounter.

Even if I survived, I was unsure if I would be coming back completely intact.

She kissed my cheek, pulling me from my dizzying thoughts, her curly hair tickling my nose as I wept into her neck. Before I pulled away, she whispered fiercely into my ear, "Bring them home."

CHAPTER 50

Kasha

Driving up to my old house for the first time in too many years should have been a nostalgic experience, happy memories assaulting me, too many to choose from.

Instead, I raced right past it through the backyard, not even caring that the tires of my cycle were digging into the moist grass and pulling it up by the roots. I rushed to the opening in the tree line down the dirt path I had run up and down countless times as a child and made my way to the waterfall pond Caleb had taught me to swim in.

Before I could break into the clearing, I skirted to a stop, my cycle throwing dirt around me at the sudden halt. Two rebel soldiers I did not recognize stood in front of the entrance, but they were in similar armor to those I had been fighting on the battlefield. They each held daggers, approaching me.

I put my cycle in park, dismounting quickly. "Are you the welcoming committee?"

"We've been instructed to have you remove all of your

weapons before letting you inside."

"These?" I pulled out the two Amalgam daggers on my hips, triggering one to release a silver blade and the other a wooden one. I couldn't get a good sniff of their scent to know if they were Varg, Human, or Shriv, so one or the other just in case.

Then I launched myself at them.

I went for the shorter one first, parrying his lunging, weak attacks. It took only a few swift moves to disarm his dagger before slamming my own into his thigh, making him fall to the ground with a cry of agony escaping his lips. That gave me enough time to focus on the other, grabbing him by the wrist and twisting it to a completely unnatural angle so he was forced to let it go. As they both wailed in agony on their knees, I punched them with all my strength, knocking them out for a good long while.

Nothing would stand in the way of me getting to my brothers.

I wiped my daggers off, keeping them firmly gripped in my hand as I stepped over the bodies and into the clearing, where the moonlight sparkled off the lake and illuminated the small structure to the left of it. The last place the three of us had been truly happy together.

My castle.

It wasn't a real castle, but that was what Caleb and Ollie named it when they built it for me as a birthday present when I turned eleven, right before Caleb was set to go into the Guard.

It was a simple structure, like a treehouse but built on the ground instead of the treetops. The wood was painted black, and it had been big enough for the three of us to fit in there and camp out inside the night before I was set to leave for my first day in the

Guard. It had been full of laughter and joking, unhealthy food, and midnight swimming.

And then I joined the guard. The last of the siblings to grow up and become an adult.

I was shocked it was still standing, although I knew father had people come to the property and maintain it. I guess they were making sure all of the land was properly tended to.

I gave the castle a quick glance, but my attention went right to the group that was gathered in front of it. Instantly, I found my brothers, tied with their arms to their side and hands behind their backs, ankles tied together and kneeling in the dew-touched grass. A vicious-looking soldier stood behind each, a hand gripping their ropes to keep them upright.

"Kas." Caleb's worried, familiar voice called to me. His face looked even worse in person. Although, his eyes seemed less swollen so I could see his silver irises and the crusted blood on his chest had been cleaned up a bit. Although, it twisted my gut to see that the vicious, deep cuts criss-crossed all over his abdomen. Ollie, still not as bad as Caleb, was unconscious, his head hanging and the guard behind him the only thing keeping his body upright.

I jerked to lunge forward but was unsurprisingly stopped when someone grabbed me from behind, garroting me with a rope around my throat. My heart pounded in my chest, my hand shaking as I released the silver dagger from my hand and reached up to alleviate some of the pressure on my windpipe, desperate to escape.

"Glad you could finally make it," a voice slithered into my ear, laughter echoing in each word.

"Ari." I somehow croaked out through the pressure, jerking my body to no avail, using all of my energy to keep a grip on the last dagger in my hand.

"Took you long enough." She loosened her grip and passed the rope keeping me contained to someone else. She moved in front of me, a lamp in her hand to illuminate the space between us. She wasn't in her usual business dresses and clothes, but armor. She moved towards my brothers, flicking Ollie on the nose. "Too bad your favorite brother isn't awake to greet you."

Both Caleb and I snarled. "Get away from him."

"Touchy, touchy!" She put her hands up, turning back to me. "Doesn't matter, you're the only one that I care about anyways. They're just props."

"I'm here like you asked. Now give me back my brothers before I kill everyone here." I watched her every move, noticing out of the corner of my eye two other men prowling forward to take up places standing behind each of my brothers as if we were about to escape. Six enemies in total. Six bodies standing between me and getting my brothers to safety.

"Yes, you came and protected the innocent, as any great Queen would do. Well done." She smiled, relishing having me at her mercy. I knew she resented me, hated that Elliot wanted me to be his queen even though she was a Shrivika and not eligible in Elliot's screwed-up monarchy plans. She had told me she was in line to be his consort, although I was curious if she knew his real age. Maybe the fact that he was in his seventies would turn her stomach from that idea.

She prowled towards me until we were mere inches apart, her breath grazing over my cheek, sending a shiver of disgust up my spine. "You know what else a queen has to be willing to do, Kasha?"

I didn't respond, just spat in her face instead. It was answer enough.

She gave a humorless laugh, wiping it off with a cloth she pulled from her pocket. "They need to be good at making the hard decisions. The impossible ones."

I gripped my fingers tighter around my blade before raising it to press against her throat, making her still quickly but not back away. "Let my brothers go."

"Oh, I will, once you choose which one gets to go free and which one dies here on the ground." She said the words so steadily, like giving a command to clean one's room or do a simple chore.

Yet, within my heart, everything gave way, shocking me, forcing me to face and process the words she was saying and what she was about to force me to do.

"You wouldn't dare," I said, my voice low and threatening.

She withdrew a dagger from a sheath at her side, Caleb and I freezing at the Ogdala Dagger in her grip. "Wouldn't I?"

Elliot had told me that he had illegally created one years back. It was nothing like the military-grade ones we had but a weapon to make a statement. The Iona silver had been oxidized, making it look black as it twisted with the carved fuili wood to form a perfectly pointed tip. It was secured in a polished silver handle, a snake carved into the hilt, the head resting below the pommel where a large cut ruby sat nestled in the center surrounded by the moon phases.

She moved over to Caleb, gently swiping the flat side of the blade against his cheek, making him wince. "Not so fearless now, are you?"

He snarled at her, trying to lurch forward, but his captor kept him secured on his knees. A groan escaped Ollie, giving us a clue that his consciousness was imminent. She pulled the dagger away before handing it to the guy securing Caleb. "Hold this for me, will you, Mick?"

He smiled widely at her, taking the long dagger and resting it against Caleb's throat, making him somehow turn even paler through the countless bruises on his face.

"As I said, queens have to be willing to make the most difficult choices, so now you will prove to us that you can do it. By picking which of your brothers die and which one walks out of here with you alive."

My pulse pounded against my neck, my palms sweating. This couldn't be happening. After everything I had been through, I never expected this. It was a nightmare come to life, pulled from the darkest parts of my soul and exploited. Making a choice between loved ones. Damn one to save the other. The impossible choice.

My mind moved quickly, searching through any loophole to get us out of here. I could easily get out of this hold and take down the man behind me, but if I did, the two only a few paces to my right would attack and I'd have to take them on and then Ari before I even made it to my brothers. I could do it. I had taken down that many opponents before, but it would take time.

It wasn't enough. Especially with the Ogdala in play. They could kill one or both of my brothers before I could even make it to them. They would, I had no doubt. Ari had been in Elliot's cult for years. He had taught her everything he knew. Particularly how to trap someone within their own worst nightmare. How to exploit every fear. He would be proud of his little prodigy.

But that wouldn't get us to safety, and it wouldn't get my brothers to safety. So, I gave her something I knew would throw her off a bit. Something she probably would relish in. I begged.

"I will not make that choice." I shook my head. "Give me any other test. Give me any other options, but please, do not make me choose between my brothers. Anything else. Please, Ari."

"You were supposed to show us that you could make the hard decisions when you renounced your place in Guard and joined our side." She spread her arms wide, gesturing to all of the Elliot followers around her. "Which, really, after all of that evidence I gave you, shouldn't have been that hard, but alas, you need a second chance, I suppose."

"How did you even get all of that information?" I wanted to stall, so I could figure out how to get out without having to make that horrible, terrible choice, but I also wanted answers. "You had to have someone on the inside. It's the only way you could have gotten concrete evidence for those numbers. Someone who was in the voting room."

"No shocker you figured out that one of the High Faction is on our side." She smiled at me. "Lucky for you, he's here tonight. Why don't you come out and join us, hm?"

Him. My mind raced through who it could be, my heart dropping at the idea that it could be Kyler, betraying me once again. Or even Mitchell, who had played his part so well, seeming to be on my side sometimes.

What I did not expect was to see quiet, unremarkable Terrence walk out from my castle, dressed in the military uniform that matched all those traitors around us.

He wasn't someone I knew well. He was a Shivika, had been in the High Faction for about five years now, and I had crossed paths with him more professionally than anything else. He had come to our Compound with Violet and my father only a few months ago to check in on us when we thought this whole thing was nothing more than a serial killer case.

I had never really had an opinion of him. He always seemed to fly under anyone's notice. Realization prickled at my throat; that was exactly what he wanted.

"Of all the people." I shook my head, the scratchy rope rubbing uncomfortably against my throat. "And now you're going to abandon your place?"

"My eyes were opened within the first year of joining the High Faction," he said. "The only reason I stayed was to be Elliot's eyes and ears while we planned to take over the country. Then it was to get the evidence needed to bring our queen to his side. Now I have done my duty, it is time for me to return to my rightful place."

I scoffed, hot pinpricks simmering against my skin, eyes narrowing at him. "Glad to see our leadership is so dedicated to the people of Kazola."

He didn't even look a bit fazed, his gaze focused and blank.

"Why don't you take over watching Oliver." Ari gestured to Terrence, who took hold of my middle brother and pulled out a weapon to lay against his throat, making my stomach drop even further.

In Terrence's hand was one of the military-issued Ogdala Daggers. So, now they had two. One pointed at each brother.

"Now that we have that out of the way, back to the matter at hand." Ari clapped her hands. "Make your choice."

I shook my head, heat flushing every inch of me. "No."

She walked forward, putting herself in between me and my family. "Make the choice, or I will. Either way, you're walking out of here today with one less sibling."

My mind ran at a million miles trying desperately to come up with anything, any idea on how to get them out. How to bring us all to safety. Nothing came to mind, and I wanted to scream. I did, the anger-filled howl echoing off the treetops, making birds scatter into the night air.

"Take me." Caleb's voice was unwavering.

"Caleb, don't!" I shouted, reaching my free hand out to him, but the soldier holding me yanked me back by the rope, causing me to choke.

She turned slowly to him. "You want me to kill you and set them free?"

He nodded. "If that is what it takes to keep her from having to make this choice, I will gladly do it."

"Intriguing." She walked over to him, crouching down to stare right into his eyes. "You would truly die for her?"

His gaze never wavered from hers. "Yes."

A massive groan broke their staring contest, everyone turning to Ollie lifting his head up.

"What is happening?" Ollie finally started to look around.

"Tell our idiot older brother he cannot sacrifice himself for us!" I snarled, Ollie's eyes widening.

"What?" That brought him to alertness, his body squirming in the ropes as he turned to look at Caleb, Terrence tightening his grip. "You can't!"

"It's either I sacrifice myself or she has to choose which one of us lives. I won't let that happen."

Ollie turned to Ari. "Take me then!"

"No!" Caleb and I bellowed together.

"What loyal brothers you have." Ari laughed at me, shaking her head. "But I'm afraid it isn't your decision to make. It's hers. Time is running out, My Queen. It's your last chance to choose."

My whole body shook, my fingers screaming in pain at how hard I gripped my dagger. I wanted to fight and get to them, I wanted to set them free. There was so much I wanted to do and yet no feasible way to do it. I wasn't one to delude myself into believing that I could win in this situation. That I could save us all. Only two of us would be walking out with our freedom.

I was stuck. I was trapped. I was more desperate than I had ever been before.

I slumped, my mind blanking, unable to pick a name. I silently shook my head, unable to say the word no once again. Not when I had to form a new idea, a more enticing way to get Ari to let them go.

I might have one, but it would be a sacrifice I knew my brothers would hate me for.

But I really didn't care.

"Times up," Ari whispered, turning her back on me. "Kill the middle one."

"No!" I screamed, fighting in earnest now, ready to tear myself from the garrote, but the two soldiers who had been watching from the left leapt into action, each one taking one of my arms, removing my final weapon from my grip. The three of them held on tight, keeping me pinned, the garrote keeping my face in place and forcing me to watch what was about to unfold in front of me.

Terrence removed the dagger from Ollie's throat, twisting it in his grip and readying to pull back and smash it through his chest.

"Don't do this, please!" I continued to fight, the three soldiers' grips painful and one now pressing a dagger against my abdomen, but it didn't slow me down. I kicked and snarled, Caleb's voice echoing loud, angry shouts at everyone to stop, to take him instead.

I had to get to them. I had to save them, no matter the cost.

Terrence lifted the dagger overhead, signaling only seconds to save Ollie's life.

So, I screamed the only thing I could think of, the only loophole I could come up within my desperate, angry, and anxious mind.

"What if I give my life instead?"

CHAPTER 51

Kasha

Everything seemed to stop the moment the words left my lips. Silence fell, and all shocked gazes turned slowly to me. Terrence lowered his weapon, and I was able to take my first full breath at the sight.

Ari stepped forward, arms crossing against her chest. "We cannot kill you. You are our queen."

"No, not to kill." I shook my head. "This whole thing is because I didn't join your side quick enough, right? Well, now I will."

She narrowed her eyes, obviously not believing me, trying to figure out what deception I was trying to pass her. Unfortunately, there was none. I had run out of options. "That isn't enough. We don't want a prisoner, we want a leader."

"And you'll have one," I urged, pressing against the tight holds the three soldiers hadn't let up on. "I will come with you willingly. I will join your forces and help you get Elliot out of prison. I will help you take over all of the territories and put us on the thrones." She still looked at me skeptically, eyes narrow.

I swallowed, everything inside of me crumbling as I said, "I will complete the bond with Elliot."

That made her perk up. "You will do it now."

Bile rose in my throat, but I nodded. "The moment my brothers are safe, I will."

"Sacrificing yourself for them. I see." She tilted her head. "I shouldn't be surprised."

I would never let my loved ones die or suffer if there was a way I could help them. She knew I would give up my freedom if it meant saving them. It was how Elliot got me the first time, and she was upping the stakes by taking my brothers and risking their lives.

And it made me wonder if this was her plan all along. If this entire threat was to get me to go with them willingly. To get the bond forged no matter what.

Even if it was all a big game, my answer wouldn't change. I would still give myself for them. Every time.

"As you said, being a queen is about making the hard choices. Ones that protect those I care about and the people I vow my life to." I took another tentative step forward. "Well, if you know me as well as you claim, then you are aware that this, me agreeing to it, is the hardest choice I have ever had to make. But for them, I will do it. Just let me brothers go."

"That is very true. Although, after everything he put you through, I am surprised that you didn't give Caleb's name." She smiled venomously at me. "But I suppose you are more forgiving than I'd ever be. Must be why Elliot sees you as a wonderful queen. You'll help control those pesky killer impulses of his."

But she didn't know how deep our bonds went. Even after the past year, after everything we went through, it was not enough to cleave us apart. We had found our way back, and although we had been healing over time, that bond was always there. It would not break, even under the tightest of pressure.

"You cannot take her from us!" Caleb shouted, his blond hair falling into his eyes.

"And yet, she offers herself willingly. I'd be grateful if I were you." She shrugged.

"Even if she goes with you, she will never be on your side," Caleb tried to reason, to poke holes in Ari's devious plans. "She will be as much of a prisoner as she once was."

"Ah, but that's not true." Ari shook her finger at him. "Because this time she will be bound to Elliot. Eventually, she will understand and be the queen we need, even if he has to force her into it."

My pulse was the only thing I could hear, blood rushing in my ears as I processed the words. He would use the bond to make me do what he pleased. He would force my hand and make me his puppet if necessary.

"So then, do we have a deal?" Ari stepped forward, hand outstretched.

There was only one choice, and if it meant keeping my brothers safe, I would make it.

I took in a deep breath, ready to agree, to give myself over to them once again and forge this bond they were so desperate for.

"No!" Ollie's screams were feral, eyes glowing gold and fur beginning to morph from his skin. Another vicious howl rang from him, the ropes starting to rip away from the pressure of his half-transformed body.

His focus was completely on Ari, sharp teeth growing longer, lips curled away to reveal his imposing bite. Murder reflected in his gaze, his clawed fingers tearing away at the remnants of the ropes now falling away from him.

"Ollie, don't!" My heart pounded viciously, eyes wide, knowing instantly that this was a horrible idea.

I went to reach for him, but it was too late. He was lost to the frenzy of his wolf, and the tight hold of the soldiers lifted me from the ground, forcing me to watch from afar as Ari turned slowly to the half-person, half-wolf threat now clawing to get at her. She sighed dramatically, as if he was a pesky nuisance, before she turned her gaze to Terrence.

That was all it took, one flick of her gaze. One dart from Terrence to Ollie for everything to descend into true madness.

Terrence lunged for Ollie, ready to stab him through the back and into his heart.

I screamed his name, my voice grating and painful in my throat.

He turned, ready to face the man wielding the one weapon that could kill him.

I screamed his name again, sheer terror coursing through my veins.

And then, Caleb was there, pushing him out of the way just in time.

Just in time for the dagger to pierce his chest instead of his younger brother's.

My screams morphed into howling cries, Ollie's protests mixing with mine as one of the soldiers came up and restrained him so he couldn't get to Caleb. Caleb, whose wails of agony rose above all of our own.

Terrence's eyes grew wide in shock, holding the blade in place, watching my brother suffer around the only weapon that could kill us. The heart had been pierced, but not enough for an instant kill. Caleb was still breathing, struggling to escape what was unimaginable pain that was most likely lancing through his body.

Still, I was no optimist. I knew there was no coming back from this. Even if we could get a medic here, there was nothing they could do. He would succumb to the poison of the elements used to create the blade before we could even stitch him back together. He had minutes, and I was forced to watch from afar.

No, I couldn't, my mind now focused on one thing. *Get to him.*

I followed Ollie's lead, turning myself over to my wolf and transitioning partially. The popping of my joints was enough to loosen my captor's grip, my claws reaching up to rip away the rope around my throat, forcing them to all stumble back.

I turned to them, popping my arms back into place so I could fight on two legs, all of them starting to pull out their weapons and push their feet into defensive positions.

Funny, they thought that would protect them.

I grabbed the closest one to me, dragging him towards me and sinking my sharp teeth into his delicate throat, his blood instantly flooding my mouth. His pained screams fueled me, thrumming through me as I gripped him even tighter before ripping his throat clean out.

He crumbled to the ground at my feet before I spit his disgusting flesh onto his now-dead body.

It wasn't enough; they had all hurt Caleb. They had all been a part of his pain.

I wanted to make them bleed too.

I picked up my abandoned weapon from the ground, turning to the two soldiers who had restrained my arms. My golden-hued gaze focused only on them. Kill, hurt, bleed.

I lunged and didn't hold back, combining my skills with the Amalgam blade with the wild instincts my wolf granted me. I slashed with my blade followed by my claws. I kicked and swiped, until I had the second one in my clutches, close enough for me to strike his weapon out of his hand and land a clean stab through his chest.

Two down. One to go.

"We have to get out of here." Terrence's voice broke through my frenzied haze, but I didn't stop fighting my final opponent. His heart was still beating, but not for long.

"But we had her!" Ari's shrill voice sliced into me, making my rage boil even fuller.

"It doesn't matter. She'll kill us if we try to take her now. Let's go!" Terrence screamed to her as my dagger punctured the final soldier, his eyes widening as he fell limply from my blade.

She would not get away.

Turning to face them, Terrence trying desperately to drag Ari out of the clearing, I charged. Terrence barely had time to register my approach before I grabbed hold of Ari, ripping her from him and pointing the tip of my wooden blade against her chest.

"A life for a life," I growled, pulling my arm back, ready to strike true, her terrified screams echoing around us.

"I wouldn't do that if I were you, My Queen," Terrence called from behind, a bow with a notched arrow now held confidently in his grasp. It was aimed at Ollie, who was surrounded by the bodies of his own vengeful carnage.

Ollie's chest was heaving heavily, but he stood as still as possible, his gaze connected to the sharp silver point of the arrow. An arrow that was dripping with some kind of liquid. A poison. But which one was the question.

"That can't kill him." I snarled.

"You don't know that. Even if it can't, it could torture him." Terrence shrugged. "You've already been introduced to two poisons that can weaken you. Who's to say there aren't more?"

My arms started to shake, my insides trembling.

"So, Kasha, what will it be? ill Ari and lose a second brother tonight, or let her go and have the opportunity to say goodbye to the one already dying?" His gaze flicked over to me, my grip on the front of Ari's armor tightening. "By the sound of his wet breathing, I would say Caleb doesn't have long."

Tears pricked the edge of my eyes, as I saw Caleb's squirming body on the ground, my heart shattering. I needed to get to him. I had to help him.

I had to say goodbye.

My grip loosened from Ari, and she stumbled away, running to Terrence, who quickly disarmed his weapon and followed Ari out of the clearing.

When they disappeared, pain lanced through me, the grip on my blade barely keeping it in my hand as I transitioned back fully into my human self.

I had to face the truth, my heaving breath impossible to control, my body shaking. I wanted this to all be a dream, to be another nightmare my traumatized subconscious had created.

Yet I knew it was real. The pain surrounding my body and soul was real life and there was nothing left to do but face it.

I turned to the horror I knew was behind me, the one thing I had been desperate to avoid when I stepped into the woods tonight. Slowly, I shifted around, locking eyes with a raggedly breathing Ollie before we both lunged towards our brother's side.

I rushed to kneel beside him, sawing through the ropes on Caleb chest as Ollie did the same on the other side. Caleb's body convulsed, skin graying quickly. He coughed through ragged breaths, roaring thunders of engines surrounding us. I knew Ari and Terrence had gotten away, but I didn't care. The ropes finally slipped away.

"Caleb." I gathered him up, his head cradled in the crook of my arm. I shook him a bit. "Caleb, please."

His eyes fluttered open, those silver irises so tired, weak, and barely able to keep the light within. He reached up, bloody hand cupping my cheek. "I love you, Kasha. Even when it seemed like I didn't, you were always my baby sister. I can't wait to see you again in the After. I'll say hi to Mama for you."

My tears fell in earnest, a sob escaping my lips.

Ollie was on his knees in front of me, Caleb lying in between us, who looked over to his younger brother.

"Thank you for taking care of her, Oliver." Caleb looked at our brother, blood trickling down his chin. "I failed to do so, but you never did. You were always there for her, and I know you always will be."

"Don't you dare do this!" Ollie cried. "Don't you dare abandon us again!"

"I will never abandon you. I'll still be around." He smiled, so resigned to fate waiting for him. So accepting of his sacrifice.

He looked at both of us, hand barely gripping Ollie's. "Don't make my mistakes. Live outside this stupid job. Fall in love and live."

"You could have had that too." Ollie squeezed his hand tighter, lifting it to his bare chest. "You idiot. You could have had that too."

Caleb gave a wet, tired laugh. "Too late now."

"Caleb…" I sobbed, my hot tears rolling down my cheek and landing on his neck. He couldn't do this. He may have been ready, but I wasn't. He couldn't do this. He couldn't die.

He couldn't leave me.

"Don't give up." He looked back up at me. "Don't give in to him, ever. You can fight him and win. If anyone can do it, it's you."

"Caleb…" It was the only word I knew. The only one that could leave my lips.

"I…" He coughed, and blood and saliva spewed from his mouth. My heart fractured, breaking slowly with each labored breath he took, with each drop of blood that slipped from his chest and through my fingers pressing down on it. "I'm sorry for everything, little sister. I'm sorry I couldn't be the biggest brother you deserved."

"I forgive you." I held him tighter, leaning down to make sure he heard me. I would not let him die without knowing this, without hearing these words. "Do you hear me, Caleb? I forgive you, for all of it. You saved us, and I forgive you."

He smiled at me, his silver eyes lighting up one more time, pure unadulterated happiness glistening within them for a whispering moment before it dimmed completely. His body went limp in my arms, the last beat of his heart pressing against my palm before stopping entirely. I shook him a few times, refusing to believe this was it, that he was gone. Ollie let out a coughing cry, dropping to rest his forehead against Caleb's stomach, wrapping his arm around his body.

And with that final breath, my heart shattered, a tornado of pain and agony whipping through my core and decimating my body and soul.

My brother was gone, and there was nothing I could do. He was forever lost to me.

So, I did the only thing I could do. I let the tears fall free and howled my anguish to the moon.

CHAPTER 52

Kasha

Time moved around me, and I barely noticed as the sun and moon rose, days passing.

I refused to leave Caleb's side, as we waited for his Last Rites to come. In the Varg culture, we said goodbye to our loved ones under a New Moon, burning their bodies so their souls could return to Lunestia. Until then, we protected the bodies, holding them in a Temple of Tranquility where an Acolyte prepared the body and loved ones watched over it in a special chamber that was adjacent to the main temple area.

We moved the body to Crelanti. My team arrived soon after Ari and her crew escaped, finding me and Ollie kneeling on the ground covered in our brother's blood and clutching his lifeless body between us. We didn't shower or go back to the Compound. We wanted to go right to the Temple where we had held Mama before her Last Rites. We had to get him here, and we did.

Ahren had been waiting for us when we arrived, ready to clean and prepare the body for the day we would say goodbye. That had been six… oh, seven, days ago.

Numbness and nothingness, hatred and pain, sorrow and emptiness. My emotions couldn't decide what they wanted. One moment, I needed to cry every last drop of tears my body had, while others, I wanted to punch one of the pristine, dark blue tiled walls that made up the chamber. It was decorated the same as the main temple, but instead of the mosaic design describing the Unity of Order, it was merely decorated as the night sky, the moon phases running across the ceiling. It was meant to bring peace, to remind us where our loved ones were about to return.

But it did not bring me peace. It brought nothing.

I had been ready to accept the bond, even though it was the last thing I had wanted. I didn't want to give Elliot that power over me, but for my brothers, I would have. The past with Caleb, what had transpired over the past year, didn't matter anymore. All that mattered was that he would be able to live, to finally learn the man he was destined to be, without my father's influence and grooming directing him. Yet, just as he was starting that journey, he had given his life, for me and Ollie.

My twisting gut and aching, half-alive heart were the first signs that I felt unworthy of that gift.

"I forgive you."

"Don't give in to him, ever. You can fight him and win. If anyone can do it, it's you."

I had no regrets over my last words to him, I had forgiven him, even before that night, I knew. That didn't mean I deserved life more than he did. Thirty-five and taken away from this world before he could have ever truly lived. He should have had centuries before we were here. He should have been allowed to live.

What had he missed out on because of me? He said he had no regrets, but had he meant it?

"Oliver?" I looked over to the other side of the altar, my last surviving brother sitting there, our shifts with Caleb crossing.

Ollie looked over at me, his eyes devoid of anything. No frown or smile on his lips. It was the most neutral expression I had ever seen Ollie give, which unsettled me even more. I always knew what he was feeling and thinking, I could read him like a book most days. Yet, in grief, I barely recognized him.

"Yes, Little Shadow?"

"Did Caleb ever… date anyone?" I had told Caleb that although he had always been my brother, we had never been friends. Which had been true, but I still had never heard him talk about dating or falling in love, even when both Ollie and I had dated during our tenure in the Guard.

Ollie took a deep breath, his unshaved cheek twitching a bit before his gaze went to Caleb resting in between us. "No. I had asked him about it a few years back after I teased him one too many times about never dating. He said he'd fall in love and date after he left the Guard. He never outright said it, but I think he wanted to wait until after, because of Mama. He saw what happened when Father lost his Mate, and I think he wanted to see if he would be putting someone in danger because of his career."

A few fresh tears slipped from my eyes, my lower lip wobbling, a fresh lance of pain shooting through my chest.

Another hour passed before the wooden door to the chamber opened, the click of expensive, well-polished shoes echoing off the wall getting closer and closer. I smelled that fresh ocean and balsam scent before Father even turned the corner into our alcove. I knew I must have looked almost as bad as Ollie, both of us unkempt, faces blotchy and red from crying, and deep bruising under our eyes from lack of sleep. Yet Father looked exactly the same, perfectly polished in a black and gray suit, hair freshly washed and slicked back, and no signs of tears or restless nights marring his face.

Why wasn't I even a little bit surprised?

"Come to take a shift, Father?" My voice was hoarse, barely used and scratchy from the bouts of crying that plagued me at random times of the day.

Ollie and I had mostly been taking the shifts to watch over the body, as per tradition until we moved him behind the Temple to burn his body and place his memorial headstone next to Mama's in our family plot. A few of his Faction partners had come to sit with us, but Ollie and I refused to leave him alone. This was the first time Father had even appeared in the Temple.

"I came to see the two of you, actually." He kept himself straight, standing a few paces away, eyes looking anywhere except the body that lay next to me.

"About?" Ollie glared up at him.

"The High Faction has talked through the next steps in our strategy." He cleared his throat. "After the Last Rites of Caleb, you will return to your Compound to continue supporting your local military to keep hold of Seathra. Oliver, you will stay here and assist Crelanti as interim Alpha of our Faction. There, the two of you will wait for further instructions on where we will send your teams for battle."

Ollie gaped at Father, most likely thinking exactly what I was. Was Caleb so easily replaceable?

"I want to go and hunt them down, though." I had mentioned to the members of the High Faction that had debriefed me that I wanted to be sent out on a mission to find Ari, Terrence, and her team and bring them in for questioning. Part of it was driven by my emotions, a desperate need to see my brother's murders taken down. But I had learned enough in Elliot's captivity to know that Ari was a strong leader in his cult. The longer she stayed on the streets, the more danger she would cause.

I knew her scent and her patterns. With Lucas's help, who I had requested join me on the mission, I could easily take her down.

He stood up a bit straighter. "That mission has been denied."

"What?" I leaned forward. "We need to catch these people. Not just because of what they did to Caleb, but Terrence knows everything about our current plans and military statistics."

Their military leadership was strong, united much more than ours. So, even though a good portion of their soldiers were under-trained, they still were beating us in battles, which meant we needed to start cutting down where they were strong.

"You will stay with your Faction and continue to fight in the war where we, your leaders, see fit."

"He was your son!" I sneered at Father. "Don't you want to see his murderers put behind bars?"

"They will be when we win this war and bring them to justice."

Father nodded, his stony face irking me.

I stood slowly. "Father, we have already lost two territories to this war and almost lost a third. We never know when they're going to strike until it's too late if history has anything to say about it."

"They took us by surprise, and we are preparing to make sure that doesn't happen again. But to do that, we need both of you where we believe you will be most useful. And that is not chasing around a handful of people to who knows where."

"Don't any of you understand?" I shook my head, shocked and confused. "All of this is a giant game to Elliot, even behind bars he is influencing everything. We need to start treating it like a game to be won and not a war to be fought. Typical, dated war tactics are only going to make us lose this battle quicker."

"That is not your decision to make, but the High Faction's." He leveled his gaze at me, his jaw tightening. "As a member of the Guard, you are to obey what we decide and that is it."

I narrowed my eyes at him. "Did you agree with these terms? To keep fighting this way?"

"I did." Father nodded. "It was the right decision for Kazola."

I took a step back, blankness enveloping me while my world shattered around me to truths I had refused to see before.

My father was but a shadow of the man I remembered from childhood. He was nothing more than a power-hungry member of the High Faction, caring more about his status and reputation than that of his family and the lives of Kazola's people. He was nothing more than one of the statistics that Ari and Terrence had collected for me.

I should have noticed it sooner. It had been there all along.

How was this type of man worthy of leading Kazola? How was he better than the tyrant we were trying to defeat?

I couldn't come up with an answer, which only made the hatred inside me worsen.

My hands balled into fists, my insides quaking, I charged towards him, reading to scream or throw a punch, I wasn't exactly sure. I didn't care that there were other mourning families around us that could hear what we were saying. I didn't care that we were in a temple. I needed to get this out of me, or it would consume all of me.

I charged, but Ollie was faster, cutting me off before I could make it to Father, his arms wrapping around my waist. I tried to fight out of the grip, squirming, but all I could do was twist in his hold so we were chest to chest, my gaze going over his shoulder to stare at my father. "You heartless, worthless man. Do you have any loyalty to your family? Even the one who gave up everything for your approval? Your perfect little soldier?"

"He knew what he was doing when he took those oaths." Father crossed his arms. "He knew the risks, and yet he still made the stupid choice to sacrifice himself at the end. Tell me why I should now be proud of him?"

"Because he did everything for you!" I defended Caleb. "He wanted to protect his younger siblings, which is admirable. Something I can't say he got from you. I can't even believe you are my father most days!"

"Oh, stop making a spectacle of yourself, Kasha. You've done that enough over the years." Father shook his head, glaring over at me. "Once you calm down, I want you to stop being a brat and follow the rules like I taught you. There's nothing you could say that would surprise me anyway."

I growled, Oliver's hold on me the only thing keeping my wolf from taking over and attacking my father.

He thought he knew me so well, did he? Well, he was about to find out exactly who I had become over the last year, because of him.

"Nothing, huh?" I screamed over Ollie's shoulder, his grip on my waist tightening, his chin resting on my shoulder as he held me back. "Well, how about this? I have very few regrets in life, especially the choices I made about telling the truth about Logan. But one regret is that you weren't there with us the other day. Because if you had been, I would have felt nothing giving them your name."

"You don't mean that." Father's voice rumbled from his chest, his eyes darkening into their wild honey hue.

"I have never been more honest in my life." My fingers flexed at my sides, the nails growing into my sharp, vicious claws. Everything was tearing inside, the anger and hurt over Caleb's sacrifice still a fresh wound gaping in my chest, oozing and festering. I was letting it infect me. I was letting it drive me, and I didn't care, my grief getting the best of me. "I may be alive because of you, but I have only started to live again in spite of you. You deserve no credit for the woman, and leader, I have become."

His lips curled up in disgust, hatred contorting his features. "You are a Guard member because of me. You are strong because of me! You are who you are because. Of. Me!"

He startled back a bit, as if shocked by his own outburst, my insides rumbling. He blinked rapidly a few times before straightening his tie and brushing his hands down the front of his jacket. "Now, I came here to give you that update, but I must get back to work. I will see you both looking presentable for the Last Rites. That means pull yourself together. Understood?"

All of the hatred, pain, and anger my father had caused me over the past year was finally at a breaking point. I had spent so long pushing it down, repressing it and pretending that it didn't exist, but I could not ignore it any longer. He was only a weak, power-hungry man. He had lost himself, maybe in the grief of losing his Mate or the pressure of being on the High Faction. Or maybe he had always been this man, and I was just too hopeful when I was younger that he would be better, for his family and kids.

But you can only hold out hope for so long and let yourself get hurt for so long before you have to let it go. For your own safety and peace, it was the only way sometimes.

My chest squeezed at that, my throat closing, but I pushed through. I untangled myself from Ollie's grip, his gaze narrowing at me before letting me go. I cleared my throat.

I schooled my features, looking my father straight in the eye, "Understood. We will see you at the Last Rites then."

Ollie stiffened next to me, the first glimpse of emotions flashing across his features at my acceptance of Father's words, but he stayed silent. Father nodded, giving us no more of his words before he turned his back on us and towards the exit.

He walked away without a second look back, and the void in my chest confirmed that I didn't care in the least.

If he wanted to be a part of the problem, then he made his choice. Didn't mean I had to agree with him, not anymore.

But it wasn't just my father that was the problem. He may personally have been the worst to me, but that was because he had raised me. But there were so many other High Faction members who wanted nothing more than to watch Kazola never change, just keep the status quo while others were too scared to speak up. And sometimes, we saw those in power use it to their benefit, like Cole had to keep Logan protected, even when he was guilty of raping women.

I knew a few were working hard to make a change. Evette and Kyler, maybe even Imogene and Mitchell. But they didn't even make up a third of the High Faction, let alone the majority that was needed to make most laws and changes pass based on our country's current laws. There was no way to remove a member of the High Faction unless they committed a crime and there was no limit to how long they could hold term. Humans tended to overturn the quickest since their lifespans were shorter than the Vargs and Shrivs, but even then, they would last decades if they wanted to hold onto power.

That dark, inky part of myself swirled within my stomach, pressing within me, begging to be released. Those terrible thoughts that I always tried to ignore came to the forefront, whispering terrible, traitorous things to me once again.

They do not protect. They do not save, care for, or serve the people of Kazola. All they care about is themselves and their power.

They could not protect you. They have let you down again and again and again, and you are a member of their beloved Guard. How do you expect them to protect a typical citizen?

This is how Elliot has achieved so many followers. This is why people follow him.

They want someone who cares about them.

Maybe this had been Elliot's plan all along. The death of my loved one could have been my final breaking point. He had been pushing me to accept my darkness for so long, and I had survived countless times before.

I was spiraling, my thoughts darkening and deepening, going from doubt to pure rage and hatred. It was festering and consuming, dangerous to who I had spent so many years building myself to be. I should push it aside, remind myself of why I do this, why I continue to fight against this terrible part of myself. Yet I couldn't find the strength, not when I finally admitted to myself that I understood.

They say it is with light we extinguish darkness. But sometimes, it is within the darkness that we find our true selves lying within.

And maybe it was time for me to find out exactly who that was.

CHAPTER 53

Kasha

No moon hung in the air as we descended the steps from the back entrance to the Temple of Tranquility into the open courtyard beyond. It was in this courtyard that we were to say goodbye for the final time, where I would have to let go of my oldest brother for the rest of my life.

Nothing could have prepared me for this day, and no matter how hard I shut my eyes or pinched myself, I didn't wake up from the nightmare I wished I was in.

The slightly chilled air welcomed me and my family, who were the last to arrive, torches of fire collected from the Sanctuary of Lunestia's Temple gripped in our hands. The crowd was bigger than most Last Rites I had ever been to, so many people attended to not only say goodbye to Caleb but to support our family as well. Caleb's Faction stood off to the left, with members from Ollie's unit there as well. Our extended family was to the right, mostly from our mother's side, and even some members of the High Faction attended.

The entirety of my Faction, besides Taylor who had woken up but was still too weak to get out of bed, along with Lea and Nolan's fathers were situated by his feet, right where I told them to be. My family and I circled the body, the four of us located at the four points, for when we would have to step forward and complete our part of this ritual. I walked right to my friends, Nolan and Lea waiting for me at the front, the rest of them crowding around me.

Both of my hands were clutching the torch, their shaking so apparent that I was too scared I would drop it if I tried to only use one, so Nolan wrapped his arm around my shoulder, gripping it tightly with his hand, Lea linking our arms and nestling close. And even though none of the others were touching me, I felt their presence and relished the strength they were pushing to me, helping me through this.

Although, even with it all, the gutting, twisting pain racking my body from head to toe was impossible to ignore.

Just as in the sanctuary, Caleb looked peaceful. He had been prepared and dressed in simple black linen pants and shirt, his hands resting gently on his stomach, his familiar silver eyes shut to the world never to open again. Sticks and leaves were crowded around him, with small bouquets of poppy flowers nestled throughout. The wood and leaves were for kindling, the flowers were for us. Mother had been sent off the same way, and I had insisted he be surrounded by them as she had.

When we had all settled into our positions, Father at the head, Ollie to the left and Nana to the right, Cheathra Ahren, our cousin on our mother's side, stepped forward. Another request from me and Ollie, that Ahren be the one to perform the ceremony. Although, this time there was very little pushback now that he had been an acolyte for over a decade.

"To Lunestia we pray, as we say goodbye to Caleb Mallanis, son, grandson, older brother, dedicated Alpha of the Onyx Guard, and packmate." Ahren stood at the top of the wooden palette, by Caleb's head, a step in front of Father. His white robes glistened under the starlight, his hood placed on the top of his head so we could still see his face. His eyes were full of sadness, and I watched his throat bob as he continued to speak the opening prayers, all of us repeating or responding where necessary. The struggle to keep his composure was written on his face, but not a tear shed as he continued his duty to his Goddess and his family.

I, however, could not say the same. My tears began to flow when he began to speak, my sobs shaking my shoulder, and I didn't care that I was surrounded by too many people. I leaned into Nolan's hold, his chest rising and falling deeper than normal. My eyes wandered to the rest of my family, Nana crying just as blubbering as myself, Ollie trying his best to hide it, but silent tears slid down his cheeks, and my father still looking the picture of the professional High Faction man he was.

This was his precious son's Last Rites. Could he show some Goddess-damned respect and give an inkling that he had a heart?

No, apparently that was too much.

And in the past, that would have brought so much anger to me, but not in this moment, when I was so pitifully deep in my sorrow. It made me sink even deeper into the suffocating pain.

I turned away from my father and returned my attention to

Caleb, reminding myself that this was the last time I would ever see his handsome face in person, that this was our last goodbye, our final farewell.

That thought brought a fresh wave of pain lancing into my chest, warm tears running down my cheek and staining the black collar of my blouse.

All too soon, Ahren chanted the last of the goodbye hymns and took a step to the right, looking at the four of us holding our torches.

It was time.

"I ask the loved ones of Caleb to step forward and release his soul from his body, so he can forever run free with our Goddess in the After." Ahren gestured for us to step forward.

My fingers white-knuckled around the wooden handle of the torch. I couldn't do this. I didn't want to watch him burn, to disappear from my life forever. No longer would I see his smiling face back from a run or his coarse laughter when Nana chided him for cutting a tomato wrong like she did almost weekly at family brunch. No longer would he be there to listen to me when I needed to talk through a problem or particularly hard case. I went to Ollie when I needed to vent and have sympathy, but I had gone to Caleb when I needed a different perspective to look at a case in a new light.

He had written to me every week when he had left for Omega training in the Guard and had bumped it up to three times a week when Mama died and he wanted to constantly check in on me even though he couldn't leave. He would run with me in the woods when he was a teenager and I was his annoying little sister who always wanted to spend time with him. He had indulged me, snuck me sweets when Mama and Father told me I'd had enough, and taught me to swim.

Past year aside, I always knew he was looking out for me, my biggest brother.

And now, he was taken from the world, at the hands of evil that decided his life was expendable. That he was an easy target to manipulate me to their ways.

I shouldn't have let them take him.

I should have forged the bond and let them use me. At least Caleb would be alive.

"You can do this, sweetheart," Nolan whispered in my ear, squeezing my shoulder tightly before releasing me. Lea gave me a watery smile as well, before nudging me forward, Ollie, Father, and Nana already in their spots.

With one final deep breath, I walked forward, all four of our gazes catching before we slowly lowered our blazing torches to the kindling underneath, all of us whispering. *"Marsin Lat."*

Goodbye.

Goodbye to my oldest brother.

Goodbye to one of the best Alphas I knew.

Goodbye to a dedicated soldier.

Goodbye to a man taken from this world too soon.

"Nat sperta thasinn oiliac sinn." Ahren chanted as the first flames caught, the rest of the crowd repeating it over and over.

To the skies we release you.

The fire spread along the circle of kindling, rising up and up, the smoke filling the air around Caleb, beginning to obstruct the body from our sight. I couldn't do it anymore, throwing the torch onto the palette, Ollie and Nana following soon after as I stumbled back into Nolan's waiting arms, my heart finally cleaving in two, breaking me down from the inside out. He hugged me close, my cheek resting against his chest as he stroked my hair, even though my gaze refused to look away from the flames now reaching for Caleb's body.

I should have said yes.

But still, even with that bit of guilt eating at my conscience, I didn't blame myself for his death. I blamed the brainwashed cult members who thought it would be entertaining to play with the lives of my family. They had taken from me. They had forced the three of us to make the impossible choice.

They did this. They killed him, and so many others.

He didn't deserve to die, but Ari and her goons certainly did.

And I wanted to be there when her heart stopped beating. I wanted to be the one to ram the blade through her chest and watch the light disappear from her eyes.

I wanted to kill her. I wanted revenge.

There had been so much darkness blooming within me for far too long. Darkness I refused to accept, to believe I was capable of, and Elliot had been trying to manipulate me into tapping into it from the beginning. He wanted to relish in it, capitalize on my pain and hurt and sorrow for his own selfish desires.

But it clicked within my mind as I watched the flames lick over Caleb's body, rising higher and higher to consume him, that I realized Elliot wasn't the one to create this darkness in me, to force me to put a leash on it. It was others. Those who pretended to be my allies.

But it was the High Faction who chose to do nothing. It was them who had betrayed me. It was them and Logan and Cole and Father who had cast the first shadow, who had created this essence within me.

It was because of all of them that I had to pretend like there wasn't a part of me that wished for vengeance. As the last of the flames took my brother from me, the smoke too thick to see him anymore, I felt the shift within, the darkness coming forward and tempting me to a place I never thought I would find myself. But today, I was hurt, beaten down, and… angry. I was so angry at all those who had hurt me, who had abused and used me.

It festered and slithered into my veins, called to me in a way I had refused to listen to before. Yet it tempted me to no end now that my heart and soul were weakened by this loss, ready to give in for the first time.

Ahren closed out the ceremony and the flames were doused out. As I stepped forward and picked up the waiting basket to collect a few scoops of Caleb's ashes to spread in our family plot, where his memorial would be waiting for us to put up next to Mother's, I realized I was left with only two options.

I could sit by, continue to fight for a leadership I no longer believed had the best interest in Kazola's protection.

Or I could do something about it. I could lead. I could hold true to the vows I took seriously and protect this country.

And maybe that meant unleashing the darkness I had been so scared of.

Maybe it was the only way.

CHAPTER 54

Nolan

Before we could leave for home the next day, the High Faction called a meeting for all Guard members currently at the Chateau.

With so many having attended Caleb's Last Rites, we were unable to fit in the council chamber. So instead, we gathered in the domed entryway, all of us standing at attention on the floor facing the grand staircase that led up to the different levels of the building. All Keturi members stood in the front line, with the descending lines behind us going by rank. The High Faction towered over us on the staircase. Mitchell, Imogene, and Alton stood on the landing while the other Delegates stood below them on the stairs.

I dared to quickly reach over to Kasha, grabbing her hand and giving it a quick squeeze, her hand squeezing back. She looked over, giving me a weak smile, her eyes still reflecting the sadness and anguish that had been there for days. She had cried herself to sleep and I had held her the entire time, taking advice from my fathers to be there for whatever she needed. It still didn't feel like enough, my heart weary and my mind running through any ideas I had to help her through the pain that had almost taken me years ago. Yet nothing ever seemed like enough.

The only thing that would was if I could bring her brother back. And that was the only thing not in my power to give her.

My heart cracked even more.

A shout took my attention back, making me release her hand and turn to the High Faction as Mitchell stepped forward, clearing his throat.

"Thank you, everyone, for taking the time to attend before you head back home." His voice boomed off the high ceilings. "We wanted to give you all the important update that the High Faction has come to a decision on the sentencing of Elliot Wells."

Murmurs rose within the crowd, my breath intaking sharply as I waited for the news.

"It has been decided that Elliot will be sentenced to life on Challaire Island, where he will spend the rest of his existence in solitary confinement in the prison."

Even though it was out of turn as we stood at attention, the murmurs grew louder, my own eyes widening at the announcement, my palms sweating. Challaire Island was a glorified rock off the coast of Rystin. It lay about five miles away from Kazola and held but one building, the highest security prison under the High Faction's control. Those who were considered some of the most dangerous, worst criminals imaginable were sent there, to live out their final years, sometimes decades depending on the species, alone. Rumor had it that most of the prisoners went mad within the first year, as no one was socialized or let out to see the sun.

To some, it would be a punishment worse than death, to be trapped there. Maybe it was for the best for Elliot, but my heart hammered in my chest. It wasn't enough, it would never be enough. As long as he lived, as long as he was somewhere, his followers would always have hope that they could set him free. It didn't matter that no one in the history of the Isle had escaped Challaire. It didn't matter that even if they did get to him, he could be half-mad and unable to properly speak anymore.

As long as they had hope, they were dangerous. I did not like this outcome.

"I promise you, this was not an easy decision," Kasha's father continued. It took all the effort of my training to keep my face neutral, even though my lip wanted to curl up in a sneer at the atrocious man. "But we have reason to believe that Elliot's people are somehow able to get communications to him. We need to cut that off, and the only way to do that is to send him to the most secluded prison that we have."

"That might not be enough," Beckett whispered to all of us. *"I'm not sure his people will ever stop."*

"At least this will make it harder for them," Liv commented. Some of us muttered agreement in our mind-speak, my heart still aching at the absence of Kasha within our group. It didn't matter that it had been weeks since the last time I heard her voice in my mind, I would never get used to being cut off from her.

Especially at a time like this, when I wanted nothing more than to comfort her with words. When I wanted to talk to her and understand how she was feeling, knowing that Elliot would continue to live. Knowing that the bond she was forced to share with him would soon be tied to a man who would start slowly going mad.

Would he use their connection to keep himself sane? Constantly trying to talk to her and pressure her? She told me he had been silent for a while. He hadn't reached out to her since she begged him for the cure for Taylor. Probably because of the plan he set in motion with Ari. But now that it was over, now that Kasha was still on our side, would he go back to constantly trying to break her down from the inside out?

My stomach ached at the thought. My heart squeezed when I realized if he did try to do those things, there was nothing I could do to stop him. There was nothing Kasha could do.

Powerless.

"The rest of his generals will be transferred to the high-security prison in Rystin as well, however, they will not be going to Challaire," Imogene explained. "We plan to keep them on the Isle in case we need them for further... questioning as the war continues."

As in torture.

"It will take some time to get everything in order and arrange proper transport to take such a dangerous criminal to the prison," Imogene said. "So, the transfer will occur in twenty days. If you are needed for assistance, we will call on the Factions' members individually to arrange the assignments."

They were really doing this. Allowing him to *live.*

I dared to steal a glance at Kasha standing next to me, my heart hammering, wondering what she was feeling. Instead, all she did was stand there, still tall and at attention, her face covered in an eerie sense of calm that washed over her expression. My veins cooled at the easy, non-reactive look. She was finding out that the man who tortured her was basically being sentenced to life in prison. It was called Challaire Island because it was the old Kazalonian word for "lost".

He deserved so much worse than a life sentence in prison. I understood wanting to get him as far away from his followers as possible, but it didn't stop the hot churning of my gut, the rising anger that Cleo's murderer and Kasha's torturer was getting off too easy.

Yet, Kasha didn't even seem a bit phased. Her gaze was calmly settled on Imogene as she spoke about a few other specifics having to do with some new war plans. Plans that Terrence wouldn't have passed on to Elliot's Generals.

"We know this war is daunting, and it's easy to lose hope in our ability to fight back now that we discovered a mole in our government." Imogene scanned the crowd, so many soldiers tightening their stance at her dower words. "But trust that we will change the tide soon, that we are strong enough to defeat the evil that is trying to harm all that Kazola is. Trust that a plan will soon arise to take back our country once and for all."

Now that got a reaction out of her, just a flicker, something very few would notice unless they knew her well. And I knew her like my own soul, and that flicker…

That was a dangerous look.

For the first time since meeting my paramour, I feared she

was about to go too far. I wondered if her grief had gotten the best of her, and if she was about to make a rash, potentially life-threatening choice. I wasn't sure why that was where my mind first went, maybe anxiety from almost losing her. Maybe it was my memory of being bloodthirsty after Cleo's passing. Or maybe it was nothing more than a flicker of pain that I was misreading.

Still, my muscles tightened, and I couldn't seem to look away from her.

She had promised me that we would always fight together, that she would not leave me behind again.

I had to hold onto my trust in her to never break a promise.

CHAPTER 55

Kasha

I walked down the hall, my bags already packed, and changed out of my formal uniform from the unsurprising announcement the High Faction gave us. Of course, their answer was to throw the problem in a secluded area, so they never had to see him again.

It was the cowardly thing to do.

I made it to a door only a few away from mine, knocking lightly. It opened, my brother's tired, slightly gaunt face welcoming me with a weary smile.

My only brother now.

I swallowed back the terrible pain that ached in my chest at the thought, the one that seemed to follow me everywhere. We moved farther into the one-room suite he had been taking up for the past few weeks, his own, half-packed bags laid on the bed, clothes half folded as if I had interrupted him.

"Are you leaving too?" I looked back at him.

His shoulders deflated. "Yes, I was told before the group meeting that it was time for me to transfer to Caleb's Compound now that he…" His gaze lowered, his head shaking.

Now that he had been laid to rest.

"Heartless," I mumbled under my breath, moving to the table set up in front of the fireplace. Ollie slumped into the chair across from me. "Are you moving into his penthouse?"

He shook his head. "His team was nice enough to set up the guest room for me instead. Brielle and I talked this morning over coffee about it."

"How is she doing?" I hadn't seen her since before the Last Rite when she had come to sit with us for a bit in the Temple. She had been Caleb's Beta for almost five years, and they had even done Omega training together.

"I don't know. She won't talk to me about him, just work." He rubbed his hands over his face. "I even apologized for having to start so soon. She ended up crying."

"You didn't choose to be transferred there," I whispered, my fingers shaking in my lap.

"I know," he sighed, rubbing at his weary face. "It feels so wrong. He was not replaceable like that, none of us are."

Silence fell, my gaze roaming around the room unable to focus on anything. The past two weeks since his death had been a whirlwind. The war continued, fights popping up in different towns and territories, but no more full territory attacks had arisen since Vapalles. I wasn't sure if they were regrouping, trying to figure out a way to release Elliot, or if having long periods of time between uprisings was all a part of their plan.

Yet, I had barely focused on any of it, too lost in my grief.

The only reason I remembered the war and the battle for power was because it had taken my brother from me and was trying to suck me into the darkness that had been building within my heart and soul ever since I held my dying brother in my arms. It had been consuming me, my thoughts and my dreams, since that very night.

I couldn't seem to stop it, and I knew there was a part of me that didn't want to stop it but feed it.

I looked up at Ollie. "How are we supposed to go back to life?"

Ollie looked over at me, letting out a deep breath. "Because life keeps going, even when one person's does not. We must keep fighting in the war. It's what Caleb would have done and wanted for us."

"Don't you want revenge?" I leaned forward, my insides rumbling at this realization.

I suppose all people grieve differently, want different things to help them get past the hurt. But all I could see was the rage and the pain that Ari and those horrid people had caused me. It was because of them my chest felt hollow. It was because of them that I could barely sleep or felt on the verge of tears randomly throughout the day. They had caused all of this, and they deserved to be punished.

I wanted to punish them.

He shrugged. "What good would it even do? More bloodshed? Nah, I want to…. I don't know, try and process this all and then move on. The best revenge I can get is stopping them from gaining the power they desire so badly, I suppose."

I shook my head, understanding his words yet not agreeing

with him.

"I want them dead, Oliver." I curled my fingers against the arm of the chair. "I want them to bleed as they made Caleb bleed."

"A life for a life isn't always the answer, Little Shadow," he whispered.

I frowned. "Yet sometimes it is."

His gaze snapped back to me, his head tilting. "Kasha, what…"

A knock on the door jolted me from my bloodlust. Ollie shook his head but kept a concerned gaze on me as he stood up to answer it. "Oh!" A light, feminine voice said.

I turned to see my best friend standing at the door. "Lea?" I stood up, walking a few steps toward them.

"Sorry, I just…uh…" Lea looked back and forth down the hallway, her light brown cheeks heating with rosy color. "I didn't mean to interrupt."

Ollie gave her a kind smile. "Is everything okay, little Lea?"

She rolled her eyes at the nickname before holding out a small paper bag from a local bakery in the city. "It's your favorite, roast beef and provolone cheese."

I tilted my head, watching the interaction. He frowned at the bag. "You didn't…"

"You haven't been eating. So, yes I did." She peeked around Ollie to me. "I left two for you and Nolan at your room so you could eat before heading home."

"Thank you." I walked up to her, giving her a tight hug. "Are you sure you're okay staying here?" After the Last Rites, Ollie and I agreed that it would be best if we could find a place for Lea here, so we sat her down together to suggest the idea. She was a target now because of me, and how close we were. I wanted her to be as protected as possible, even if it wasn't by my side. But the Chateau would be heavily guarded during the war, and Ollie and I had used connections to lobby for a place for her to stay here.

And although a part of her hated it, she had understood and agreed to move here.

She nodded. "I know it's the safest place for me. Keep your fingers crossed I have a forge to go back to when I go home."

I gave her a tight smile at the joke.

"I'll take care of her, don't worry, Little Shadow." Ollie patted my shoulder. It did help to alleviate some of the anxiety around being so far away from her.

"Eat the sandwich," She pointed to the bag now in Ollie's hand and then turned to me. "I'll come by in a little bit to say goodbye before you leave." And with that, she walked away, Ollie closing the door before turning back to me, my eyes still glued to the door as if Lea was still standing there.

"You promise to take care of her right? Check in on her while she's here?" I looked over at him, his forehead creasing at my question as if he hadn't just promised to. "Not just now, but in case… in case…"

I couldn't get the words out, my throat clogging with pain.

Ollie's eyes went wide before pulling me to him, crashing me into a hug. "Hey, nothing's going to happen to you. It's going to be all right."

I hugged him back, not completely believing his words. Elliot and his people may not want me dead, but that didn't mean I was safe.

CHAPTER 56

Kasha

I tried my best to enjoy myself, to forget what was going to happen in a mere four days.

This was the full moon, and we were able to come together as a Faction and spend it camped in the woods like we normally would. If you tried to forget about the war that was currently ongoing outside of these clusters of trees, it could be peaceful.

I did try my best not to think about it, to constantly remind myself that this war had already taken my brother and forced me to constantly be worried for the safety of myself and those I loved. I didn't think about the fact that the darkness that had been festering in me since the Last Rites was gaining strength by the day. That my final meeting with the High Faction, and all I learned there, reminded me that their treatment had turned people so desperate for change that they put their faith in Elliot. I tried not to think about my own dwindling faith in those I was supposed to be loyal to.

Running under the power of the full moon helped calm the

thoughts at least.

My paws pounded against the cool forest floor, pushing myself harder and harder to run faster. Although spring was fast approaching, nights still carried the cool sting of winter in the chilled air, whipping my fur around my four-legged body, my wolf humming inside of me about finally being let free. I hadn't had as much time for runs over the weeks. She had become utterly restless within me and was relishing her freedom.

She was also preening a bit since her favorite wolf was hot on her heels chasing us through the woods.

A nip on the edge of my tail made me yelp before pushing even harder, wanting to beat him back to the clearing we had started our race in. We were a few miles away from the rest of the camp by this point, which was not uncommon, especially when couples wanted to use the wild freedom of the full moon to their full advantage.

Even with the pain and torture of loss aching my insides, what settled me was being around Nolan. His presence was a balm on my pained heart and tired soul, helping to calm a few of the thoughts that I wished desperately to forget. He had obviously noticed my recent attachment to wherever he went. If he was working out, I was there. If he needed to do paperwork, I brought my own into his office. I sat with him while he cooked, and we curled up on the couch and read our own books in peaceful silence.

It was making each day a bit easier, and I needed to soak it up.

Even so, I couldn't let him win, which gave me the last bit of energy to rush ahead and break the clearing to mark me the winner. I collapsed, my lungs burning as my paws scraped against the dirt, my belly shifting the dead leaves below to get a stick out from poking me. A hum of satisfaction echoed in my veins as I evened out my breathing, my sweat-matted fur starting to itch as dirt caked into my underbelly. Oh, well. I was used to it after so many years shifting.

Weight fell onto my back, an oomph rushing from my lungs at the impact of a giant black wolf finally catching up to me. He climbed up my back, resting his muzzle below my shoulder, his hips nuzzled quite close to my own.

I snorted, rolling to my side so he went crashing down, his breath whooshing out of him. He playfully knocked our snouts together, and I nudged him right back before reaching out my tongue and giving him a nice long lick across the face. Even in wolf form, he tried to look disgusted, but it came across as a smiling wolf instead. I flipped onto my back, four legs in the air, and basked in the moonlight for a few more deep breaths before closing my eyes and focusing on shifting back to human. Unlike a few months ago, it came naturally, my arms and legs sprawled to the side and my skin sweat-soaked in place of fur.

"Were you trying to mount me?" I laughed as I heard the telltale rustle of him shifting back as well.

A warm arm snaked around my waist, pulling me against a hard chest. "Why? Interested?" He nipped at my ear, a shiver running up my spine.

I looked up at him, kissing his chest. "You're tempting, that's for sure."

He shook his head at my coy response before giving me one

last peck on the cheek and sitting up. I propped my head up in one of my hands, watching him survey the clearing before he picked me up gently and moved us towards one of the towering trees. He leaned his back against the tree but settled me between his legs lying down, his arms wrapped gently around my upper body. We were both still completely naked, and the skin-to-skin contact enhanced the thrill skimming up my spine even more.

I rested my head on his thigh, his fingers going to comb the tangles from my breast-length locks. I hummed in approval, nuzzling closer to him and pulling in deep breaths of his citrus cinnamon scent mixed with the saltiness of his sweat and the woodsy undertone that made him Varg and was even more potent with a full moon.

For the briefest of moments, I forgot about the world outside of this bubble and found peace in his arms. It was what made him special to me. It was one of the many things that made our bond exactly what I needed to make my life complete.

And that thought brought my heart lurching back to what was happening outside this copse of trees, and what would have to happen once we departed.

In four days, Elliot was to be transferred to Challaire Island, and the High Faction was preparing to pretend he no longer existed. They hoped that shoving him away would make this war seem like an inconvenience when it was only getting started.

And yet, even in that chaos, I was forever grateful to Lunestia that she had brought me this man, this special, goofy, incredible Alpha, into my life.

"Thank you," I whispered against his skin, calm washing over me with each pass of his hand.

"For what, sweetheart? I didn't let you win. You did that all on your own."

I swatted at his knee. "No, you fool. I'm trying to be sentimental here."

"Ah, well then, don't let me stop you."

I shook my head but shifted upward so I could look up into his beautiful face, his eyes still glowing gold. "Thank you, for not letting me go or giving up on me, even when I made it difficult. Even when I was being bratty and acting out when you first got here. For not giving up the fight to get me back all those months ago and for advocating and believing that I was strong enough to come back from the bloodlust. For standing by my side during this heartbreaking time. For still believing I am strong enough, even when I doubt myself. I know you believe in me enough for both of us."

"Kasha," he whispered, a tear welling in his eye. I reached up to brush it away. He leaned down, cupping my face in his hands and kissing me.

I wasn't always the best at bearing my heart and soul to someone; I had never done that with past paramours, but it showed how different Nolan was. Past lovers were never bad, but Nolan and I were connected in a way that brought me safety and understanding. It was calm when I needed peace from my raging thoughts, playful when I needed a laugh, and passionate when I needed to feel consumed.

And that made my heart sing and ache at the same time, fear rippling down my spine, with the winds of change shifting in the air with the war. The future was never definite, and my gut knew this wasn't the end of the struggles we faced.

I needed him, wholly, to remind me that no matter what happened, he was mine and I his. We were joined and shared every piece of ourselves, and I was not afraid to give my heart to another.

I broke the kiss before crawling up his body, desperate not only for his lips but his chest pressed against mine, and the heat of his now hardening cock nestled against my core. His hands went under my arms to slowly slide up my spine, fingertips tickling along my skin as I leaned forward and pressed our lips back together. I didn't hesitate to plunge my tongue into his pliable mouth, thrusting it in a few times to tangle with his own, his fingers curling inward on my back to scrape his nails down it, which only spurred me on more.

I rocked back and forth, teasing my entrance and his readying cock nestled underneath me. It wasn't enough though, and maybe another day I would enjoy drawing out the teasing and listening to the desperate whimpers he made against my lips, but not today. Today, I was frantic for him, to show him how I trusted him with every part of me.

"I need you," I growled against his lips, shifting my hips up so I could grasp his now rigid length firmly in my hands. He shivered as I stroked it a few times, his head falling back against the tree. "I need to feel you inside me right now."

"Goddess, yes!" He lunged forward, his lips latching onto my shoulder and sucking at the sensitive flesh that bridged up to my throat. I shivered, notching him against my entrance before slowly lowering myself down his length, low groans escaping both of us as I reveled in the incredible feel of him filling me completely.

"I fit so perfectly inside you," he whispered in between peppering kisses along the arch of my breasts, his hips beginning to ungulate upward to rock deeper inside me. "Perfectly mine."

"Yours, only yours," I said breathlessly, beginning to match his pace with my rocking hips, my head thrown back at the hard brush of my clit against his pelvis and the sparkling shocks running through my core at each stroke of him against my inner walls. He really did fit perfectly, gripped tightly within, filling me up with pleasure and love and heady desire.

I needed him deeper, my fingers scrambling to grip his shoulder so I could lift myself slightly before slamming as hard as I could back down, a scream erupting from my lips and blissful tingles spreading along my core and up my spine. I kept going, riding him, his hands gripping my waist in a bruising hold to encourage me, helping to lift me up and down on him, the slickness of our combined arousal making the pleasure rise faster and faster, brighter, and fuller, and perfect.

It was fevered and desperate, fueled by a passion that was burning me from the inside out and I indulged in every searing lick of heat coursing through my veins as I rode him harder, faster, chasing the high that I was desperate for, wanting him to climb higher and higher with me. To fall over the edge and delight in what was completely us.

"I need… I need…" My words felt impossible to get out.

"I know, sweetheart. I know." His hips moved to meet mine,

his lips pressed against my cheek, whispering huskily in my ear. "Come for me while I'm nestled deep within your tight pussy. Come on my cock like the good little Beta you are."

His dirty, filthy words were wholly unexpected but sent rippling pleasure, enhancing everything that was already on the precipice of exploding. It was enough to push me over the edge, my inner walls fluttering, my body consumed by the Earth-shattering pleasure we had created together. I kept riding, my movements haphazard and erratic, but I didn't stop, not until the heat of his release pulsed within me, his desperate groans whispered against my skin as his rocking within me slowed, our movements gradually stopping as we came down from our releases.

I collapsed against him, arms securely around his neck, crushing him against me, refusing to pull off him. He held me tight, rocking us back and forth, peppering kisses along my neck and shoulders. I knew he was relishing in the post-orgasm bliss that was only heightened by the full moon. I suppose he thought I was doing the same, but I was clutching at him for dear life.

I didn't want to let go ever. I never wanted to be separated from these protective arms.

Yet even I knew that was only a beautiful dream.

CHAPTER 57

Kasha

One last chance. I would give them one last chance.

I had called an emergency meeting to see the High Faction, Nolan and I driving overnight to make it as soon as possible. They had approved it for very early, and I was ready to see them when their session opened.

I had enough time to clean up in a guest room and get a good luck kiss from Nolan before heading downstairs to the Council Chamber. Nolan had offered to come with me, but I told him to stay behind.

This I had to do alone.

I didn't dress in my uniform, staying in a pair of black pants, black boots, and a sleeveless black shirt. I strode into the Council Chamber, my bag slung over my shoulder. Instead, I walked right up to the dais where they all sat and began to walk slowly back and forth in front of it. Their gazes were hot and heavy on me, my own trained on them, slowly roaming over to watch them all, to see how they reacted to me. It was mostly a mix of shocked and horrified faces. My father looked downright pissed with how red his face was turning.

I was going to get answers.

"This is highly unprofessional, Beta." Mitchell glared down at me from his place at the human table, eyes trailing as I paced in front of them.

I stopped in the center, two steps below where their tables sat on the dais. "My father told me that you all denied my request to hunt down Ari and Terrence."

He tilted his chin up. "We feel it is best to keep you with your team while we are in battle."

"One of your own betrayed us." My gaze flicked over to the empty seat on the Shrivika's side, to the left of Evette. "He had been working for Elliot almost the entire time he worked with all of you. You would think, with all of the insider information he has most likely passed on, you would want to apprehend him and punish him as soon as possible."

Father leaned forward. "And we will. We plan to send a team out…"

"Just one that doesn't include me?" I tilted my head. "When I am an obvious choice. I know both Ari and Terrence's scents. I am an excellent tracker and I was enmeshed in this cult's inner circle during my time in captivity. I know how they think, how they plot. I could have them tracked down quickly along with making a statement to all of the people who believe me to be their Queen where my true loyalty lies. Yet, you want to keep me tucked away."

Father's lips pursed, but no words came out. Wow, I had caused him to go speechless.

"Tell me the real reason." I spread my stance, widening it so I had a more secure placement. A fighting stance, ready for any attack, verbal or physical that I knew was about to be thrown at me.

"We believed you would be safer staying with your Faction," Mitchell spoke first, his cheeks blotching red.

I tilted my head, fingers gripping the strap of my bag tighter. "Safer?"

"You do have an entire cult interested in getting you to their side," he reasoned. A good reasoning to be sure.

I looked at the few people I trusted in this room, particularly Kyler and Evette, who had been eerily quiet this whole time. They both avoided my gaze expertly, my heart beating faster. A resigned, submissive look.

They had been instructed not to talk. So, only the High Tribunes would be talking to me today.

"This cult has been after me long before we even knew it," I said. "And that didn't stop you from ordering me undercover or to take a challenge that resulted in me getting kidnapped for a month."

Their negligence had caused me to be tortured for weeks, starved to the point of hallucination, and branded with an artificial bond against my will. But back then, I had been an asset. Now, with all that was happening, how this war had evolved and how the state of our country was tenuous, I was a liability to them. No, I was more than that.

I was a threat.

Yet, they didn't even know how deep of a threat I could be.

"We learned from our mistakes." Mitchell clenched his jaw. They were hiding something.

"You're lucky we didn't lock you up." Imogene's gaze drifted over to stare at my father. "That particular suggestion had been taken a bit too seriously during our conversation about what to do with you."

"What to do with me?" I raised an eyebrow at her. The wording cut me too deeply, like I was a child in need of punishment, when all I had done was try and be the best soldier I could, to follow the law and oaths I took.

"Poor wording on my part." Imogene watched my every move. "But you need to be kept safe. We can't risk them getting their hands on you again."

A fair point, although I knew it was not all of it. If I ended up with Elliot's people, against my will or on my own accord, it would look bad to those still following them. First, a High Faction member had abandoned us to join the enemy. and to then lose an Onyx Guard member who came from a legacy family would force people to start asking questions.

Questions I bet most of the High Faction didn't want people finding out. The answers to which I had tucked neatly in the bag on my shoulder.

"You know, half of the reason I came here was to know the real reason why you had denied my request." I unzipped my bag slowly as I walked up the two stairs. "However, there was one more thing I felt needed to be brought to your attention."

I ascended the stairs, the aids that typically passed around evidence standing like shocked statues behind their assigned delegates. I approached the Shrivs first, the table on the right, and yanked out a handful of the folders that I had brought all the way from Seathra. With a loud thump, I dropped them in the middle of the table, every single one of the delegates staring at the mystery pile.

I moved, going to drop a similar stack on the other two tables. "Terrence is accusing most of you of buying and blackmailing votes for past cases." Mitchell flinched as I slammed the stack in front of him. "He spent most of his time sitting in this very room, gaining your trust, so he could smuggle out information about why voting went a certain way. Once he figured out the reason for everyone's vote, he recorded them. Once he had enough cases to show how corrupt a good chunk of the people sitting in this room are, he passed them along to me."

"And why would he give them to you?" Father questioned, our gazes locked as I approached his table, moving to stand directly in front of him. I pulled out the largest and final stack from my bag, gripping it in both hands before slamming it right in front of him.

Watching him flinch at the loud, echoing impact made my belly roll in a satisfied way.

"To show me why I should betray all of you." I took a few steps back, staying on the dais near the edge. "To show me why Kazola needs a queen to save them all."

"Well, since Terrence has been a traitor all along, you can't seriously trust that the information in those files is true." Mitchell tried to laugh it off, although, by the way his fingers were obsessively tugging at one another, I had a feeling he wasn't as secure in his words as he wanted me to believe.

"Well, that's why I'm bringing them to you." I shrugged, keeping the burning anger simmering in my chest as restrained as possible. "So, you can explain it to me."

I tried to look innocent, like the perfect little soldier they all expected me to be. Bringing the incriminating evidence right to them so they could talk their way out of it. And maybe they could. Maybe they had a way to prove everything in those folders wrong. But I wasn't naïve, and I had looked into it. Between the cases I recognized and the ones Nolan had, the voting corrupting was a way of explaining it all. They didn't know how long I had these, though. For all they knew, I had just gotten them. I wasn't stupid enough to think they all believed that.

However, it was my father who called me out first. "You did no research into these, then?"

I smirked at him. "Maybe a little. There were a few cases of my own that had interesting outcomes. One that the evidence we collected for you didn't completely support. Can't help but wonder why that is."

Imogene was the first to reach for the stack, Mitchell following and then my father before the rest of the Delegates picked up a few to take a look at. Imogene's glare went from me, down to the first folder she opened, her angular face staying in a stony expression that was unreadable.

I let the minutes pass. I let them read and look through them all and not a word was said, but plenty of expressions told me everything I needed to know. It confirmed all I needed to know.

I had tallied up the numbers from every folder. I had figured out who was the most corrupt and who was somewhat close to innocent. One or two had even been completely free of taking any bribes or voting against what they believed to be right.

Thank the Goddess Evette had been one of them, her jaw grinding tightly as she looked over her second folder. And by the wide-eyed, shocked expression on Kyler's face, it showed me he really didn't understand how deep the corruption went. He had been listed one or two times, including with my case. However, I knew this was due to blackmail or pressure from when Cole led the Varg branch. He may have made a mistake, but I knew he could learn from it. He could redeem himself.

And some of the others that sat in front of me could too. But not all. Some were completely lost to the power-hungry way this High Faction had become. There was no redeeming them.

"They say silence can be even more deafening than outage." I scanned over them all, taking in who looked horrified and who looked shocked. "You are all saying so very much in your silence, that's for sure."

"This is completely pointless." Father threw the one folder he had looked at. The one I had made sure was purposefully on the top of his stack so he would be forced to look at it. The one that had torn our family to shreds.

"How so?"

"You are not a part of the High Faction. You do not understand what it takes to sit up here and make the right decisions to keep the people of Kazola safe." The snide tone of his voice made that slithering darkness within me deepen, and the hatred for him burned a bit brighter. "We do what needs to be done, and the oaths you took included following what we as you High Faction deem necessary. That is your job, not listening to traitors and the fake, doctored evidence he is trying desperately to pass on as truth."

"I could have kept it a secret. I brought it to you because I wanted to hear that it was a lie."

"It is," my father leveled a hardened gaze at me. "We all took our place in this government to make sure that Kazola continued to be the place of peace our God and Goddess intended it to be. We vote and we rule in a way befitting them and we will not be insulted by these lies. Do you understand, Beta?"

I nodded, even though they had done nothing to prove themselves innocent. They were relying on my loyalty to them as a member of the Onyx Guard, but how easily they forgot they betrayed that trust already many months ago and had yet to rebuild it with me.

But I didn't want them to know that. Instead, I lowered my gaze to the floor, slumping my shoulders into a submissive stance. "I am sorry for any insult. It was not my intention. But I knew you had to be made aware of the lies Terrence was trying to spread."

"We thank you for giving us more evidence to use against Terrence when we capture him." Imogene pulled the stack of papers to her, signaling that I would not be taking them with me. "This will be very helpful when we convict him."

"We ask you now to head back to your Faction by tomorrow morning," Mitchell said dismissively, also gathering the folders to himself. "We will need you and Alpha Carrigan to be at your Compound ready to fight when we call on you. Any more requests to come to the Chateau will be denied until further notice. You are needed in Seathra, and that is where you will stay until we say so. Are we clear, Beta?"

I tilted my chin up, squaring my shoulders. "Yes, High Tribune. Thank you all for your time today."

I saluted like the follower they wanted me to be, clicking my feet together and tapping my closed right fist before tapping it against my chest. It was a sign of respect that I was very used to giving to the group of people in front of me.

I looked around the room, and all of those who sat within it, one last time before turning my back on them and walking out the door.

I had gotten the answers I needed, and I knew what I had to do.

CHAPTER 58

Kasha

The family clearing was empty, save for the two headstones now sitting within. The smoke and ashes had all since blown away, Caleb's body now scattered to the earth and soul safely with Mama in the After with Lunestia.

The wash of grief that had consumed me as a teenager was back again, tears already starting to well in my eyes at the new sight of Caleb's headstone. I never thought about what this day would be like, even with three of us being in the military. I wasn't prepared to say goodbye to yet another person who had been there for me through most of my life.

"I love you both so much." Was the first thing I was able to whisper, the first thing I knew I had to tell them both. I turned to face Caleb's stone. "You should be here right now. I will forever be grateful for the sacrifice you made, and I hope you will understand that it is because of that sacrifice that I must make some of the hardest decisions I ever had in my life." I turned to Mama's stone. "I hope you are proud of me. I hope you have watched me for the past many years and known that my life in the Guard, my dedication to this life, was not just because of the family legacy but to keep a part of you close to me."

I always loved the stories she told me about her time in the Guard, and when I lost her, it solidified my decision to go into it as well. I wanted to create my own stories, I wanted to make her proud.

My fingertips pressed into my knees, my ankles going numb at my sitting position, but I didn't dare move. "Everything is changing, and I don't know what's going to happen. What I do know is that I can't sit by and watch as the Isle we all dedicated our lives to protect is condemned to ruin because of egos and a hunger for power. I didn't take my oaths to follow people who only cared about themselves," I continued, a warm breeze kissing my cheeks in response. "I can't live in that world, I can't…"

I looked up through the treetops, the sun setting beyond the horizon, the dusty pink sky already reflecting the stars within.

"It has taken me a long time to re-learn, but I must follow my gut on this. I have to believe that my instincts on how to best protect and serve this country are correct." I looked back at the stones. "I'm not sure if it will work, but at least I will fight for what I believe to be right. At least I will go down knowing that I did everything I could to protect the peace I vowed to. That we all vowed too."

I could have kept talking for hours, but I didn't have that kind of time. I needed to return soon. In the peace of the forest, with the whispering of the wind through the trees and the soft chirping of the birds beginning to return, I knew they were both with me.

I knew they understood all of the terrible choices that I would have to make, the dangerous games I had been forced to play. They understood, and somehow, deep in my heart, I felt their promise to protect me through it all branded within.

With their strength guiding me, I would do what must be done.

I stood up, looking down at the memory of them both, and took a step toward them. I pressed my lips to each stone, tears sliding down my face to stain the cool, polished surface. I patted them each one last time. "Goodbye, Mama. Goodbye, biggest brother."

I turned and walked out of the clearing, heading back to the Temple of Tranquility, where a certain green-eyed Alpha waited for me.

★★★

I soaked up the last of Nolan's warmth as I snuggled close to his naked body, our legs entangled together. We didn't stay at the Chateau, instead choosing to rent a room at a beautiful inn located near the Temple. The fire was half-alive in the hearth, our dinner plates still stacked on the dining table that sat in front of it. We had spent the last hours together, locked within this room, a protective bubble around ourselves as we pretended that everything outside of that door was fine. The world, the people we loved, and the future were safe and protected.

And now, as he slept soundly next to me, his arms firmly

wrapped around my waist, his breath tickling my forehead as it blew across it, I committed to memory every inch of his body. The details of his scent, and the soft caresses of his fingertips against my skin. I wanted to remember every detail. I never wanted to forget that I was wholly his and he completely mine.

When I was around him, I once again felt alive, invincible.

He had become the most important person in my world, consuming my heart and showering me with the love I never thought I would earn or deserve.

And it was because of him, and this love and how pure and precious it was to me, that I knew what I had to do. I was at a crossroads, and once I made this choice, there was no going back. It was a risk, and for many, might not be worth taking. But if I wanted to be a part of a country that truly protected its citizens, then I knew what I must do, even if it meant losing everything. Even if it meant making a choice I never thought I would have to.

That was the world I wanted to live in. That was the world where Nolan and I could not just exist, but live. Together, not apart.

His breath was steady, his mind already deep within sleep and dreams as I gingerly grasped his face between my palms and gently kissed his lips. They did not reciprocate, but it didn't stop me from darting my tongue out to gently caress them, wanting to remember his delectable taste. All too soon, I knew I had to pull away, taking my time to remove myself from his protective grip. Once I was free, I slowly untucked myself from the heavy covers, a chill running up my spine at the late-night air caressing my naked flesh.

I tiptoed around the room, dressing quickly. I secured my final dagger to my hip before walking back to the bed, Nolan having turned over in his sleep to lie on his back. I reached out one last time, caressing his cheek with my thumb.

"I love you, sweetness." I leaned down, pressing a kiss to his forehead. He let out a deep sigh, as if even in sleep he was trying to say, *"I love you too, sweetheart."*

I refused to cry as I placed a small envelope on my abandoned pillow and took a step back. Then another. And another, until I was at the door. With one final look and a final lurch of my heart starting to break in two, I disappeared into the night.

CHAPTER 59

Kasha

It was ominously dark, nothing but the fading full moon and sparkling stars illuminating the long stretch of abandoned countryside road I was staking out.

This was the perfect spot for me, where I could hide within the thick trees that lined the path, but there was enough visibility up the road, and it was illuminated enough by the moonlight for my advanced eyesight to be comfortable with. Now, all I had to do was wait. I knew I had timed this perfectly. They would be coming by this way soon, as long as they had left the capital at the right time. I was far enough away that we shouldn't catch anyone else at this late hour.

It was time. I could do this.

I had been planning this for far too long, ever since my final days in Ilfra after Caleb's Last Rites. Weeks of planning and anxiously waiting for the day to finally come. All of it came down to this moment, and depending on how this went, my life could change drastically.

I knew, when the sun rose, my life would never be the same.

It took another twenty minutes before the distant sound of clomping hooves against packed earth crept towards me. It took another thirty seconds before they were finally visible. They were not moving fast, but at a quick enough pace that they could run anyone over in their path if they were not careful. I had only a few seconds to take stock of what I was facing, quickly counting eight soldiers surrounding a heavily constructed iron prison cart. It was completely covered, no bars or windows to let light into the space, only a few air holes drilled in from the bottom so they wouldn't suffocate. Whoever was in there was in a void of darkness, most likely suffering from multiple senses now being cut off.

The soldiers were split in half, four Onyx Guard members and four military. Four of them were shifted into wolf form, trotting to the left and right of the cart, and two soldiers sat in the coach seat of the cart, leading the four horses pulling it. The final two guards took up the rear. All of them were heavily armed with weapons, ready to strike if attacked.

I snapped a few twigs and made a crashing noise with a broken branch, catching the attention of all the guards, exactly how I had planned it. The lead soldier raised his arm, halting the caravan. Everyone looked around, every single one on high alert trying to see if they could sense anyone wishing to cause them harm.

It was now or never.

Securing the rubber mask across my whole face before pulling the looped pin from the metal cartridge I had gotten from the Chateau vaults. I launched it without hesitation into the center of the group, a mere second passing before the gas within erupted around them, covering them in the ominous gray cloud I had seen for the first time on a bloody battlefield, the whispering scents of Blackthorne and Wolfsbane lingering. I couldn't see a damn thing, but their coughs and wails of pain certainly echoed into the air. Too bad there was no one else but me to help them.

It took another minute before the thumps started to sound and silence fell, my heart picking up rapid speed and my palms sweating as I counted all eight. After three more minutes for the gas to dissipate, I let out a ragged breath as I pulled the mask off and emerged from the trees; their bodies were scattered around the road. Even the Vargs were still in their wolf forms, however, the horses were subdued, but it seemed the gas made them more docile without knocking them out completely. Good. I didn't need to worry about them getting spooked.

Now, there was nothing standing in my way of the iron cart, which sat like a void in the middle of the road, waiting to be approached. Waiting to be breached.

I ducked down, grabbing the keys from one of the knocked-out Guards, not wasting any time as I rounded the cart to the back door. My fingers shook as I unlocked the thick padlock, the door swinging open with a creak to reveal the one man sitting inside.

"Hello, Elliot," I said in greeting.

He was heavily secured with chains, some around his ankles, tethered to the floor of the cart, another set around his wrists, secured to a chain around his waist, and a final iron collar around his throat, also secured to the waist chains. His clothes were plain, all gray of a prisoner, his hair barely washed and the start of a salt and pepper beard growing along his jaw. It was the most unkempt I had ever seen him, and yet he still held that air of power around him, even in captivity.

"Hello, Kasha." He tilted his head, eyes appraising me. "To what do I owe the pleasure?"

"I thought you would be happy to see me."

"Always." That made a smile begin to bloom on his face. My stomach curdled at the sight. "However, I can't say I expected to see you in the middle of the night, on an abandoned road on the way to a high-security prison. And, if I'm not mistaken, you knocked out the many soldiers that have been escorting me so far. So, you're either here for one of two things. To kill me or to save me. Which is it?"

I reached out to grab the sides of the carriage, steadying my shaking legs. I didn't take my eyes off him. "I haven't decided yet."

He raised one eyebrow at me. "Color me intrigued."

"I've learned a lot over the past few weeks, from both sides of this war." My insides were shaking, my mind going back and forth between trying to convince myself to run and pretend this never happened or to keep going, to get the answers I wanted. "And yet, I still have one question that only you can answer."

"And what is that?"

"Why me?" A question I had wondered for so long. A question I had always been too scared to get the answer to. Until now. It was the only answer I needed before I made a choice.

He smiled genuinely at my question. "I was wondering when

you would finally get around to asking me that."

"Then you must have a comprehensive answer prepared. So, by all means, tell me."

"Even before your near-death experience," he paused when I scoffed at his polite wording, "I liked you. You were dedicated and passionate about what you did. You loved your job and all it stood for. Yet the more we talked and the more you opened up across that bar from me, I saw the real reason that job fit you so well. You purely believed in your vows of protecting the innocent. You wanted nothing more than to make sure every person on this Isle felt that protection, believed in it. It was awe-inspiring to the point where I was already planning a way to bring you to my side. I wanted you as one of my Generals at first."

My gaze lowered to the ground, my stomach tightening. I had to force myself to breathe through the onslaught of information, to process and understand it. I had to be informed if I was going to make the right decision. If I was going to change my life, I would do it with all the facts in place.

"But once I heard from one of my people that you had died and come back to life, well, I knew it was a sign from our Gods that the time was finally upon us." He smiled viciously at me. "That I had finally found my queen."

I looked back up to him. "But you of all people know I didn't actually die. You know what kept me alive."

"Your heart may not have stopped beating, but you brought yourself back to life when you decided to fight against all of those who tried to force you to yield to them. I need a queen like that.

Kazola deserves a queen like that." He looked down at my left arm, to where the tattoo he had forced on me was hidden beneath my armor. "Do you know why I created that and made sure you and I were the only ones to have one?"

"You wanted to create a binding so you could parade us around as some Gods-blessed united pairing."

"It tethers our fates as one, *Rogthna*," he said. "We are the chosen king and queen of the God and Goddess. We are meant to save Kazola. That's what our followers want. A better country. A safer one."

I tried not to squirm at his use of 'our' as if I was already a part of this. As if I had accepted this bond.

"Do you just keep repeating these things in hopes I or you will believe them?"

"I do believe them." His voice was so calm, so normal. There was no flirtation or teasing like he used to be like with me. It was more… professional. "Let's say this is nothing, we aren't chosen. There are still hundreds of people in this country who feel unheard by the High Faction. Who have been hurt or lost something because of their government's mistreatment. They want change, so I am giving them a reason to fight for it. If you had the ability to change how the High Faction works, after everything they've done to you, would you just sit back?"

I couldn't deny that. They had hurt me with their lack of empathy for my case, for half of them being able to be manipulated and bought for votes, and now with the war, handling it in a way that was nothing more than denial. They refused to believe we could lose this war or that so many people disliked their current regime. Their pride might have been their downfall, yet they still refused to admit they were defeated.

It was almost physically painful, burrowing deep within me, but it was a fact that I could no longer deny. I wanted to be a part of that change. I want to watch the High Faction fall and new leadership rise.

It was time.

"Does that answer your question?"

I nodded slowly, my lip quivering as the truth of what I was about to do washed over me. "It does."

"Then I'll ask you my question again. Are you here to kill me or to save me?"

I swallowed a heavy lump in my throat. This was it, the moment I could never turn back from. I could lose everything, everyone that I ever cared for, with a few words spoken on an abandoned road in the middle of a random night. There would be no turning back.

And for once, I was all right with that. There was no fear in my veins or anxiety in my mind. I knew what I had to do, and I would not be afraid to follow through.

"I'm here to make a deal."

CHAPTER 60

Nolan

My Comms was blaring in my ear too early in the morning, my body slow to rise as if I had barely gotten any sleep. I flipped over, eyes still blurry as I noticed the immediate summons to the High Faction Chamber flashing across my screen. By the looks of it outside, dawn hadn't even broken through the horizon yet, which meant it had to be serious.

I flipped over, my chest squeezing at the cool touch of sheets instead of the warmth of Kasha's body next to me. She must have been gone for hours, a palm-sized envelope now sitting where her head should have rested. I grabbed it as I shot out of bed and hurried to the bags sitting in the corner to begin dressing for whatever meeting they were calling us for.

Something was wrong. Very, very wrong. But I kept pushing forward, pretending it was completely normal that she wasn't here. Pretending that she must have run out to get coffee or pastries to surprise me and would meet me at the Chateau. Yeah, that was it.

I dressed quickly in my own set of leathers, forgoing the usual formal uniform that was expected in the Chamber. I didn't feel like stuffing myself into the uptight outfit, so they would have to be okay with this.

I should have tried to pick at some of the leftovers still sitting on the table from dinner, get something in my system, but my churning, sinking stomach was not in the mood. I wasn't even sure I would be able to keep it down if I tried. So, instead, I put the last of my daggers in their sheathes, shoved Kasha's letter in my pocket, and headed out the door.

The trip to the Chateau was impossibly long even though it was only a couple of miles away. I stopped my cycle out front, not even bothering to park it somewhere proper, running inside and straight to the Chamber. The entire High Faction was already there and sitting in their respective seats, grave, stoned faces staring back at me as they gestured for me to stand to the side, one of their assistants setting up the group Comms screen for the Factions to call into.

The connection came through, only eight Faction squares now on the screen instead of the typical ten. I saw my team in one of them, all of their faces confused. I wanted to wave, but I knew from this vantage point, they wouldn't be able to see me.

Imogene stepped forward, placing herself in front of the screen, somehow still put together in a navy blue pantsuit, her short blonde hair swept back from her face. Her sharp cheekbones seemed more pronounced, the frown on her lips deep as she took a deep breath and faced the remaining Factions of the Onyx Guard.

"As of three forty-two this morning, as we were transporting Elliot to the coast to be transferred to Challaire Island for imprisonment, his convoy was attacked and ransacked. The guards on duty had been knocked out with an anesthetic bomb before the culprit responsible for this escape was able to rid Elliot of all his chains and transport him away from the High Faction's custody."

Imogene took another shaky breath before facing us all again. "After questioning the guards after waking up and doing a thorough sweep of the area, we found two abandoned Amalgam blades in the cart along with a letter for us to find, that simply read, 'Your King and Queen are coming for you'. Because of this, we are without any doubt sure of who is responsible for Elliot's escape.

"Kasha Mallanis of the Onyx Guard, Beta of the Seathra Faction, has committed treason to Kazola by organizing and successfully executing the release of Elliot Wells."

Kasha Mallanis was a traitor to Kazola.

My Kasha was now being labeled a traitor.

Stay calm. Stay calm. Stay calm.

I heard my entire team through the connection scream and rant, telling the High Faction they must be wrong. Ollie's voice was mixed in there as well, yet her father, sitting in his gilded High Tribune chair, sat without a lick of emotion gracing his cold face. He had nothing to say for the daughter now officially lost to him.

It didn't stop anyone who loved Kasha from screaming and fighting back against what Imogene claimed.

But the High Faction wasn't wrong. She wasn't here, next to

me like she should have been. I kept my back straight and my eyes on the High Faction, even though my insides were roaring, desperate to run out of there and find her, save her, protect her.

Imogene ignored the uproar and continued. "We have reason to believe that she is still with him, having changed to his side and joined the revolution."

I kept reminding myself to stay calm, and my currently vicious wolf within. I wanted to react, to rage and scream and fight, but I kept my face stoic. If I showed the wrong emotion, the ones I was actually feeling, I would say the wrong things and then The High Faction would have my head. They would use it as an excuse to get me out of the way, to deem me as a traitor as well.

It didn't matter that my heart was splintering in my chest, that I felt cleaved in two now she had run. A part of me had gone with her, and I wasn't sure when or if it would ever return.

Safer to keep my reaction to myself.

So, I kept my face calm. I tried to be as natural as possible as they continued to say vile things about her. How she was to be captured on sight. How they were going to put out a reward for anyone who found her and Elliot. How no one from my Faction was allowed to touch any of her things, as they would all be confiscated to be researched and see if there was any evidence of her betrayal. A representative of the High Faction was already on their way to our room at the inn to collect her bag of things.

My wolf growled within, not wanting them to touch anything that belonged to her.

I tapped out the anger as best I could, forcing my eyes to stay green and my claws not to peek out. But with each second that passed and each word they spoke against her, my internal chant morphed into something else entirely:

Liars. Liars. Liars.

★★★

It was many hours later when I was finally able to make it back to the room to collect my stuff, my heart and soul weary from the questioning they put me through after the announcement was over. Did I know what she had planned? Did I suspect that she was about to change sides? Was I worried at all? Was there any suspicious activity I should have reported?

It had been a long string of no, of course nots and lots of cursing by the end. I had a feeling most of them were sick of me or thought I was lying, but since they had no proof that I was somehow a part of Kasha's betrayal, they sent me on my way to collect my things from the inn and back to my Faction where I was needed.

I collapsed on the still unmade bed, the housekeepers having not arrived yet since it was barely even ten in the morning. I raked my hands through my hair, dragging them down my face to try and rub a bit of warmth into my cheeks. What was to happen? What were we supposed to do?

I knew the High Faction expected the entire team and me to play pretend and act like Kasha's choices were nothing to us, as if she meant nothing to us. They didn't know us well enough if they thought that was how we would react. I dreaded going back home. To face our friends and partners, and to once again be surrounded by all of her things, in the home we were starting to build together. It would be tortuous having to continue as if the love of my life wasn't in the hands of our enemy.

I let out a shaky breath, sitting up enough to pull the note from my pocket, now a bit crinkled from sitting in there for hours. I gingerly pulled out the piece of parchment, but instead of some kind of goodbye like I expected, one simple line was scrawled across in her familiar handwriting:

The enemy of my enemy is my friend.

What in the name of the Goddess was that supposed to mean? Her parting words to me were a riddle?

"Seriously?" I mumbled, throwing it down on the bed next to my Comms. My heart was pounding rapidly now, trying to figure out what that was supposed to even mean. My enemy was Elliot and all of those who followed him. I supposed that meant Kasha now as well. I wanted to vomit at that notion, but I pushed through.

Was she trying to explain why she was doing this? Was she trying to warn me about something? Did she really have to speak in riddles *now*? Of all times?

My fingers instinctually went to the chain around my neck, lacing through it to pull it out from under my shirt. I was going to have to be much more diligent in making sure I kept it well hidden under my clothes. I shouldn't even have been wearing it in the first place, but I refused to take it off, even if it was a danger to me and her.

Because Cleo's ring was no longer alone on the platinum chain, a familiar black opal Mating Ring now hanging there as well.

A ring fit for the woman I loved. A ring she had loved when I showed it to her but a few days ago. When I had slipped it onto her finger and took beautiful vows under a temple's roof.

I gripped it gently, lifting it to my lips and kissing the diamond pattern of stones before whispering against it as if she could hear me, "You better know what you're doing, Mate."

End of Book Three.

THE STORY CONTINUES...

Kasha and Nolan's story concludes in...

RUINED BY VENGEANCE

Coming 2025

Acknowledgements

First off, I must thank you and all of the readers who just took the time to read the second part of Kasha and Nolan's story. Were you surprised and excited to see Nolan starting to throw his two cents in? Trust me, so was I! I hope you enjoyed every moment of the book and the characters journeys. I cannot wait to continue on in the final book!

To my family and friends, who stand by me during the crazy times and listen to me rant about my bookish habits. My husband, Nathaniel, my sister, Dr. Liz, my parents, Ellen and Mark, and my besties Meaghan, Chelsea, and Alyson. You all bring a special light to my life every day and your encouragement to follow these dreams of mine will be something I forever cherish.

To my amazing writer friends Brianne, Leah, and Renee. This book would not be the same without you. Thank you for reading my books when I needed advice, hyping me up when I needed motivation, and letting me bounce dozens of ideas off of you as I figured out exactly how Kasha and Nolan's journey was supposed to go. I could not do it without you all!

To my incredible editors, Cassidy and Karen. It is because of both of you that I discovered new sides of myself as a writer. You challenged me and pushed me to be better, and I will forever be grateful for all of your hard work and collaboration on these books. Can't wait for you to see what I have planned for you next. And of course, a huge shoutout to my Beta reader team who helped me complete that final developmental polish. I hope you all loved the final product!

To my cover artist, Jupiter. Your artwork is impeccable and working with you and watching you create such perfect covers for this series has been one of the highlights of publishing these books. Thank you and can't wait to start showing off book three's cover!

To all of you, thank you for making this adventure of mine a bit extra special. Until next time, happy reading!

About the Author

Kathryn Marie is the indie author of the fantasy series, the Kazola Chronicles and the Midnight Duology. She began writing at the young age of thirteen, when she was stuck in bed recovering from spinal surgery. Ever since then, she's loved creating stories and characters for others to enjoy. When she is not at work or busy writing in her home office, Kathryn can be found spending time with her wonderful husband or friends, experimenting with new makeup techniques, or watching reruns of her many beloved TV shows.

Follow Kathryn on social media for updates!

Website Newsletter: www.authorkathrynmarie.com
Instagram: @author_kathrynmarie
TikTok: @author_kathrynmarie
Facebook: @authorkathrynmarie

www.ingramcontent.com/pod-product-compliance
Lightning Source LLC
Chambersburg PA
CBHW061537190726
48289CB00004B/1071